VIA CRUCIS

"SO GILBERT FIRST MET THE QUEEN"

VIA CRUCIS

A ROMANCE OF THE SECOND CRUSADE

BY

FRANCIS MARION CRAWFORD

AUTHOR OF "SARACINESCA," "AVE ROMA IMMORTALIS,"
"CORLEONE," ETC.

ILLUSTRATED BY LOUIS LOEB

WILDSIDE PRESS

Published by
Wildside Press, LLC
P.O. Box 301
Holicong, PA 18928-0301 USA
www.wildsidepress.com

Wildside Press Edition: MMIII

LIST OF ILLUSTRATIONS

v

VIA CRUCIS

CHAPTER I

THE sun was setting on the fifth day of May, in the year of our Lord's grace eleven hundred and forty-five. In the little garden between the outer wall of the manor and the moat of Stoke Regis Manor, a lady slowly walked along the narrow path between high rose bushes trained upon the masonry, and a low flower-bed, divided into many little squares, planted alternately with flowers and sweet herbs on one side, and bordered with budding violets on the other. From the line where the flowers ended, spiked rushes grew in sharp disorder to the edge of the deep green water in the moat. Beyond the water stretched the close-cropped sward ; then came great oak trees, shadowy still in their spring foliage ; and then, corn-land and meadow-land, in long, green waves of rising tilth and pasture, as far as a man could see.

The sun was setting, and the level rays reddened the lady's golden hair, and fired the softness of her clear blue eyes. She walked with a certain easy undulation, in which there were both strength and grace; and though she could barely have been called young, none would have dared to say that she was

1

past maturity. Features which had been coldly perfect and hard in early youth, and which might grow sharp in old age, were smoothed and rounded in the full fruit-time of life's summer. As the gold deepened in the mellow air, and tinged the lady's hair and eyes, it wrought in her face changes of which she knew nothing. The beauty of a white marble statue suddenly changed to burnished gold might be beauty still, but of different expression and meaning. There is always something devilish in the too great profusion of precious metal — something that suggests greed, spoil, gain, and all that he lives for who strives for wealth; and sometimes, by the mere absence of gold or silver, there is dignity, simplicity, even solemnity.

Above the setting sun, tens of thousands of little clouds, as light and fleecy as swan's-down, some dazzling bright, some rosy-coloured, some, far to eastward, already purple, streamed across the pale sky in the mystic figure of a vast wing, as if some great archangel hovered below the horizon, pointing one jewelled pinion to the firmament, the other down and unseen in his low flight. Just above the feathery oak trees, behind which the sun had dipped, long streamers of red and yellow and more imperial purple shot out to right and left. Above the moat's broad water, the quick dark May-flies chased one another, in dashes of straight lines, through the rosy haze, and as the sinking sun shot a last farewell glance between the oak trees on the knoll, the lady stood still and turned her smooth features to the light. There was curiosity in her look, expectation,

and some anxiety, but there was no longing. A
month had passed since Raymond Warde had ridden
away with his half-dozen squires and servants to do
homage to the Empress Maud. Her court was, indeed,
little more than a show, and Stephen ruled in wrong-
ful possession of the land; but here and there a sturdy
and honest knight was still to be found, who might,
perhaps, be brought to do homage for his lands to
King Stephen, but who would have felt that he was
a traitor, and no true man, had he not rendered the
homage of fealty to the unhappy lady who was his
rightful sovereign. And one of these was Raymond
Warde, whose great-grandfather had ridden with
Robert the Devil to Jerusalem, and had been with him
when he died in Nicæa; and his grandsire had been
in the thick of the press at Hastings, with William
of Normandy, wherefore he had received the lands
and lordship of Stoke Regis in Hertfordshire; and
his name is on Battle Abbey Roll to this day.

During ten years Stephen of Blois had reigned
over England with varying fortune, alternately victor and vanquished, now holding his great enemy,
Robert of Gloucester, a prisoner and hostage, now
himself in the Empress's power, loaded with chains
and languishing in the keep of Bristol Castle.
Yet of late the tide had turned in his favour; and
though Gloucester still kept up the show of warfare
for his half-sister's sake, — as indeed he fought for her
so long as he had breath, — the worst of the civil war
was over; the partisans of the Empress had lost faith
in her sovereignty, and her cause was but lingering
in the shadow of death. The nobles of England had

judged Stephen's character from the hour in which
King Henry died, and they knew him to be a brave
soldier, a desperate fighter, an indulgent man, and
a weak ruler.

Finding themselves confronted by a usurper who
had no great talent to recommend him, nor much
political strength behind his brilliant personal courage, their first instinct was to refuse submission
to his authority, and to drive him out as an impos-
tor. It was not until they had been chilled and disappointed by the scornful coldness of the Empress
Queen's imperious bearing that they saw how much
pleasanter it would be to rule Stephen than to serve
Maud. Yet Gloucester was powerful, and with his
feudal retainers and devoted followers and a handful of loyal independent knights, he was still able
to hold Oxford, Gloucester, and the northernmost
part of Berkshire for his sister.

Now, in the early spring of this present year, the
great earl had gone forth, with his followers and
a host of masons and labouring men, to build a new
castle on the height by Faringdon, where good King
Alfred had carved the great white horse by tearing the turf from the gravel hill, for an everlasting
record of victory. Broadly and boldly Gloucester
had traced the outer wall and bastions, the second
wall within that, and the vast fortress which was to
be thus trebly protected. The building was to be
the work of weeks, not months, and, if it were possible, of days rather than of weeks. The whole
was to be a strong outpost for a fresh advance, and
neither gold nor labour was to be spared in the

execution of the plan. Gloucester pitched his sister's camp and his own tent upon the grassy eminence that faced the castle. Thence he himself directed and commanded, and thence the Empress Maud, sitting beneath the lifted awning of her imperial tent, could see the grey stones rising, course upon course, string upon string, block upon block, at a rate that reminded her of that Eastern trick which she had seen at the Emperor's court, performed by a turbaned juggler from the East, who made a tree grow from the seed to the leafy branch and full ripe fruit while the dazed courtiers who looked on could count fivescore.

Thither, as to a general trysting-place, the few loyal knights and barons went up to do homage to their sovereign lady, and to grasp the hand of the bravest and gentlest man who trod English ground; and thither, with the rest, Raymond Warde was gone, with his only son, Gilbert, then but eighteen years of age, whom this chronicle chiefly concerns; and Raymond's wife, the Lady Goda, was left in the Manor house of Stoke Regis under the guard of a dozen men-at-arms, mostly stiff-jointed veterans of King Henry's wars, and under the more effectual protection of several hundred sturdy bondsmen and yeomen, devoted, body and soul, to their master and ready to die for his blood or kin. For throughout Hertfordshire and Essex and Kent there dwelt no Norman baron nor any earl who was beloved of his Saxon people as was the Lord of Stoke; wherefore his lady felt herself safe in his absence, though she knew well enough that only a small part of that devotion was for herself.

There are people who seem able to go through life, with profit to themselves, if not to others, by a sort of vicarious grace arising out of the devotion wasted on them by their nearest and dearest, and dependent upon the success, the honour, and the reputation of those who cherish them. The Lady Goda set down to her own full credit the faithful attachment which her husband's Saxon swains not only felt for him, but owed him in return for his unchanging kindness and impartial justice ; and she took the desert to herself, as such people will, with a whole-souled determination to believe that it was all her due though she knew that she deserved none of it.

She had married Raymond Warde without loving him, being ambitious of his name and honours, when his future had seemed brilliant in the days of good King Henry. She had borne him an only son, who worshipped her with a chivalric devotion that was almost childlike in its blindness ; but the most that she could feel, in return, was a sort of motherly vanity in his outward being ; and this he accepted as love, though it was as far from that as devotion to self is from devotion to another — as greed is far from generosity. She had not been more than sixteen years of age when she had married, being the youngest of many sisters, left almost dowerless when their father had departed on a pilgrimage to the Holy Land, from which he had never returned. Raymond Warde had loved her for her beauty, which was real, and for her character, which was entirely the creation of his own imagination ; and with the calm, unconscious fatuity which so often underlies the characters

of honest and simple men, he had continued throughout his married life to believe that his wife's affection, if neither very deep nor very high, was centred
upon himself and upon Gilbert. Any man a whit less
true and straightforward would have found out the
utter emptiness of such belief within a year. Goda
had been bitterly disappointed by the result of her
marriage, so far as her real tastes and ambitions were
concerned. She had dreamt of a court; she was condemned to the country. She loved gayety; she was
relegated to dulness. Moreover the Lord of Stoke
was strong rather than attractive, imposing rather
than seductive, and he had never dreamed of that
small coin of flattery which greedy and dissatisfied
natures require at all costs when their real longings
are unfed. It is their nature to give little; it is
their nature and their delight to ask much, and to
take all that is within their reach. So it came to
pass that Goda took her husband's loving generosity
and her son's devotion as matters foregone and of
course, which were her due, and which might stay
hunger, though they could not satisfy her vanity's
large appetite; and she took, besides, such other
things, both good and bad, as she found in her path,
especially and notably the heart of Arnold de Curboil, a widowed knight, cousin to that Archbishop of
Canterbury who had crowned Stephen king, after
swearing allegiance to Maud. This Arnold, who
had followed his great cousin in supporting King
Stephen's cause, had received for his service broad
lands, both farm and forest, in Hertfordshire, border-
ing upon the hereditary estates of the Wardes; and

in the turmoil and chaos of the long civil war, his
word, at first without Raymond's knowledge, had
more than once saved the latter's little castle from
siege and probable destruction. Warde, in his loyalty
to the rightful sovereign, had, indeed, rather drawn
back from the newcomer's friendship than made
advances to win it; but Raymond had yielded in the
end to his wife's sarcasms and to his own sense of
obligation, as he began to find out how, again and
again, in the turning tides of civil strife, his neighbour, though of opposite conviction, served him by
protecting his bondsmen, his neat cattle, and his
growing crops from pillage and destruction. Raymond did not trace such acts of neighbourly kindness to the day when, hawking with his lady and
little Gilbert, then hardly big enough to sit upon a
horse, they had been overtaken by a winter storm
not far from Arnold's lands, and when Arnold himself, returning from a journey, had bidden them
take shelter in a small outlying manor house, where
he was to spend the night, and whither his servants
had brought his little daughter Beatrix to meet her
father. Raymond had accepted the offer for his
wife's sake, and the two families had made acquaintance on that evening, by the blazing fire in the
little hall.

Before supper, the men had talked together with
that sort of cheery confidence which exists almost
before the first meeting between men who are neighbours and of the same rank, and the Lady Goda had
put in a word now and then, as she sat in the high-
backed chair, drying the bright blue cloth skirt of her

gown before the crackling logs ; and meanwhile, too, young Gilbert, who had his mother's hair and his father's deep-set eyes, walked round and round the solemn little dark-faced girl, who sat upon a settle by herself, clad in a green cloth dress which was cut in the fashion for grown-up women, and having two short stiff plaits of black hair hanging down behind the small coverchief that was tied under her fat chin. And as the boy in his scarlet doublet and green cloth hose walked backward and forward, stopping, moving away, then standing still to show off his small hunting-knife, drawing it half out of its sheath, and driving it home again with a smart push of the palm of his hand, the little girl's round black eyes followed all his movements with silent and grave curiosity. She was brotherless, he had no sisters, and both had been brought up without companions, so that each was an absolute novelty to the other ; and when Gilbert threw his round cap, spinning on itself, up to the brown rafters of the dim fire-lit chamber and caught it upon one finger as it came down again, the little Beatrix laughed aloud. This seemed to him nothing less than an invitation, and he immediately sat down beside her on the settle, holding his cap in his hand, and began to ask her how she was called, and whether she lived in that place all the year round ; and before long they were good friends, and were talking of plovers' eggs and king fishers' nests, and of the time when they should each have a hawk of their own, and a horse, and each a hound and a footman.

When supper was over and a serving-woman

had taken the little Beatrix away to sleep in the
women's upper chamber, and when the steward of
the manor farm, and his wife and the retainers and
servants, who had eaten and drunk their fill at the
lower end of the hall, were all gone to their quarters
in the outbuildings, — and when a bed had been made
for Gilbert, in a corner near the great chimney-
piece, by filling with fresh straw a large linen sack
which was laid upon the chest in which the bag was
kept during the daytime, and was then covered with
a fine Holland sheet and two thick woollen blankets,
under which the boy was asleep in five minutes, —
then the two knights and the lady were left to themselves in their great carved chairs before the fire.
But the Lord of Stoke, who was a strong man and
heavy, and had eaten well and had drunk both ale
and Gascony wine at supper, stretched out his feet
to the fire-dogs, and rested his elbows upon the arms
of his chair, and matched his hands together by
the thumbs and by the forefingers, and by the other
fingers, one by one; and little by little the musical,
false voice of his lady, and the singularly gentle
and unctuous tones of his host, Arnold de Curboil,
blended together and lost themselves, just as the
gates of dreamland softly closed behind him.

The Lady Goda, who had been far too tired to
think of riding home that night, was not in the least
sleepy, and, moreover, she was profoundly interested
in what Sir Arnold had to say, while he was much too
witty to say anything which should not interest her.
He talked of the court, and of the fashions, and of
great people whom he knew intimately and whom

the Lady Goda longed to know; and from time to
time he managed to convey to her the idea that the
beauties of King Stephen's court would stand in a
poor comparison with her, if her husband could be
induced to give up his old-fashioned prejudices and
his allegiance to the Empress Maud. Lady Goda
had once been presented to the Empress, who had
paid very little attention to her, compared with the
interest she showed in Sir Raymond himself. At the
feast which had followed the formal audience, she
had been placed between a stout German widow lady
and an Italian abbot from Normandy, who had talked
to each other across her, in dog-Latin, in a way
which had seemed to her very unmannerly; and the
German lady had eaten pieces of game-pie with her
knife, instead of using her fingers, as a lady should,
before forks were invented. On the following morning the Lady Goda had been taken away again by
her husband, and her experiences of court life had
been brought to an abrupt close. If the great Earl
Robert of Gloucester had deigned to bestow a word
upon her, instead of looking through her with his
beautiful calm blue eyes at an imaginary land-
scape beyond, her impressions of life at the Empress's court might have been very different, and she
might ever afterwards have approved her husband's
loyalty. But although she had bestowed unusual
pains upon the arrangement of her splendid golden
hair, and had boxed the ears of a clumsy tirewoman
with so much vivacity that her own hand ached perceptibly three hours afterwards, yet the great earl
paid no more attention to her than if she had been

a Saxon dairy-maid.   These things, combined with
the fact that she unexpectedly found the ladies of
the Empress's court wearing pocket sleeves, shaped
like overgrown mandolins, and almost dragging on
the rushes as they walked, whereas her own were of
the old-fashioned open cut, had filled her soul with
bitterness against the legitimate heir to King Henry's
throne and had made the one-sided barrier between
herself and her husband — which she could see so
plainly, but which was quite invisible to him — finally
and utterly impassable.   He not only bored her himself, but he had given her over to be bored by others,
and from that day no such thing as even the mildest
affection for him was to be thought of on her side.

It was no wonder that she listened with breathless interest to all Sir Arnold told her, and watched
with delight the changing expression of his smooth
face, contrasted at every point with the bold, grave
features of the Lord of Stoke, solemnly asleep beside
her.   And Curboil, on his side, was not only flattered,
as every man is when a beautiful woman listens to
him long and intently, but he saw also that her
beauty was of an unusual and very striking kind.
Too straight, too cold, too much like marble, yet
with hair almost too golden and a mouth like a
small red wound ; too much of every quality to
be natural, and yet without fault or flaw, and too
vivid not to delight the tired taste of the man of
pleasure of that day, who had seen the world from
London to Rome and from Rome to the imperial
court of Henry the Fifth.

And she, on her side, saw in him the type to which

she would naturally have been attracted had she been perfectly free to make her choice of a husband. Contrasted with the man of action, of few words, of few feelings and strong ones, she saw the many-sided man of the world, whose mere versatility was a charm, and the thought of whose manifold experiences had in it a sort of mysterious fascination. Arnold de Curboil was above all a man of tact and light touch, accustomed to the society of women and skilled in the art of appealing to that unsatisfied vanity which is the basis of most imperfect feminine characters. There was nothing weak about him, and he was at least as brave as most men, besides being more skilful than the majority in the use of weapons. His small, well-shaped, olive-tinted hand could drive a sword with a quicker thrust than Raymond Warde's, and with as sure an aim, though there might not be the same massive strength behind it. In the saddle he had not the terrible grip of the knee which could make a strong horse shrink and quiver and groan aloud; but few riders of his day were more profoundly skilled in the art of showing a poor mount to good advantage, and of teaching a good one to use his own powers to the utmost. When Warde had ridden a horse six months, the beast was generally gone in the fore quarters, and broken-winded, if not dead outright; but in the same time Curboil would have ridden the same horse twice as far, and would have doubled his value. And so in many other ways, with equal chances, the one seemed to squander where the other turned everything to his own advantage. Standing,

Sir Arnold was scarcely of medium height, but
seated, he was not noticeably small; and, like many
men of short stature, he bestowed a constant and
thoughtful care upon his person and appearance,
which resulted in a sort of permanent compensation.
His dark beard was cut to a point, and so carefully
trimmed as to remind one of those smoothly clipped
trees representing peacocks and dragons, which have
been the delight of the Italian gardener ever since
the days of Pliny. He wore his hair neither long
nor short, but the silky locks were carefully parted
in the middle and smoothed back in rich dark waves.
There was something almost irritating in their
unnatural smoothness, in the perfect transparency of
the man's healthy olive complexion, in the mouse-
like sleekness of his long arching eyebrows, and in
the perfect self-satisfaction and confidence of his
rather insolent reddish-brown eyes. His straight
round throat, well proportioned, well set upon his
shoulders, and transparently smooth as his own
forehead, was thrown into relief by the exquisite
gold embroidery that edged the shirt of finest
Flemish linen. He wore a close-fitting tunic of
fine scarlet cloth, with tight sleeves slightly turned
back to display his shapely wrists; it was gathered
to his waist by a splendid sword-belt, made of
linked and enamelled plates of silver, the work
of a skilled Byzantine artist, each plate representing
in rich colours a little scene from the life and passion
of Christ. The straight cross-hilted sword stood
leaning against the wall near the great chimney-
piece, but the dagger was still at the belt, a marvel

of workmanship, a wonder of temper, a triumph of
Eastern art, when almost all art was Eastern. The
hilt of solid gold, eight-sided and notched, was cross-
chiselled in a delicate but deep design, picked out with
rough gems, set with cunning irregularity ; the guard,
a hollowed disk of steel, graven and inlaid in gold
with Kufic characters ; the blade, as long as a man's
arm from the elbow to the wrist-joint, forged of
steel and silver by a smith of Damascus, well
balanced, slender, with deep blood-channels scored
on each side to within four fingers of the thrice-
hardened point, that could prick as delicately as a
needle or pierce fine mail like a spike driven by a
sledge-hammer. The tunic fell in folds to the knee,
and the close-fitted cloth hose were of a rich dark
brown. Sir Arnold wore short riding-boots of dark
purple leather, having the tops worked round with a
fine scarlet lacing ; but the spur-leathers were of the
same colour as the boot and the spurs themselves of
steel, small, sharp, unornamented, and workmanlike.

Six years had passed since that evening, and still,
when the Lady Goda closed her eyes and thought of
Sir Arnold, she saw him as she had seen him then,
with every line of his expression, every detail of his
dress, sitting beside her in the warm firelight, leaning forward a little in his chair, and talking to her
in a tone of voice that was meant to be monotonous
to the sleeper's ear, but not by any means to her
own. Between Warde and Curboil the acquaintance had matured — had been in a measure forced in
its growth by circumstances and mutual obligations ;
but it had never ripened into the confidence of

friendship on Warde's side, while on Sir Arnold's it had been but a well-played comedy to hide his rising hatred for the Lady Goda's husband. And she, on her side, played her part as well. An alliance in which ambition had held the place of heart could not remain an alliance at all when ambition had been altogether disappointed. She hated her husband for having disappointed her; she despised him for having made nothing of his many gifts and chances, for clinging to an old cause, for being old-fashioned, for having seen much and taken nothing — which makes 'rich eyes and poor hands' — for being slow, good-natured, kind-hearted, and a prey to all who wished to get anything from him. She reflected with bitterness that for a matter of seven or eight years of waiting, and a turn of chance which would have meant happiness instead of misery, she might have had the widowed Sir Arnold for a husband and have been the Archbishop of Canterbury's cousin, high in favour with the winning side in the civil war and united to a man who would have known how to flatter her cold nature into a fiction of feeling, instead of wasting on her the almost exaggerated respect with which a noble passion envelops its object, but which, to most women, becomes in the end unspeakably wearisome.

Many a time during those six years had she and Sir Arnold met and talked as on the first night. Once, when the Empress Maud had taken King Stephen prisoner, and things looked ill for his followers, Warde had insisted that his neighbour should come over to Stoke Regis, as being a safer place

than his own castle ; and once again, when Stephen
had the upper hand, and Sir Raymond was fighting
desperately under Gloucester, his wife had taken
her son, and the priest, and some of her women, and
had ridden over to ask protection of Sir Arnold,
leaving the manor to take care of itself.

At first Curboil had constantly professed admiration for Warde's mental and physical gifts ; but little
by little, tactfully feeling his distance, he had made
the lady meet his real intention half way by con-
fiding to him all that she suffered, or fancied that
she suffered — which with some women is the same
thing — in being bound for life to a man who had
failed to give her what her ambition craved. Then,
one day, the key-word had been spoken. After that,
they never ceased to hope that Raymond Warde might
come to an untimely end.

During these years Gilbert had grown from a boy
to a man, unsuspicious, worshipping his mother as a
kind of superior being, but loving his father with
all that profound instinct of mutual understanding
which makes both love and hatred terrible within
the closer degrees of consanguinity. As time went
by and the little Beatrix grew tall and straight and
pale, Gilbert loved her quite naturally, as she loved
him — two young people of one class, without other
companions, and very often brought together for
days at a time in the isolated existence of mediæval
castles. Perhaps Gilbert never realized just how
much of his affection for his mother was the result
of her willingness to let him fall in love with Beatrix. But the possibility of discussing the marriage

was another excuse for those long conversations with
Sir Arnold, which had now become a necessary part
of Goda's life, and it made the frequent visits and
meetings in the hawking season seem quite natural
to the unsuspecting Sir Raymond.   In hunting with
Sir Arnold, he had more than one narrow escape.
Once, when almost at close quarters with an old
boar, he was stooping down to meet the tusker with
a low thrust.   His wife and Sir Arnold were some
twenty paces behind him, and all three had become
separated from the huntsmen.   Seeing the position
and the solitude, the Lady Goda turned her meaning
eyes to her companion.   An instant later Sir Arnold's
boar-spear flew like a cloth-yard arrow, straight at
Sir Raymond's back.   But in that very instant, too,
as the boar rushed upon him, Warde sprang to one
side, and, almost dropping to his knee, ran the wild
beast through with his hunting sword.   The spear
flew harmless over his head, unseen and unheard, and
lost itself in the dead leaves twenty yards beyond
him.   On another day, Raymond, riding along, hawk
on wrist, ten lengths before the others, as was his
wont, did not notice that they gradually fell behind,
until he halted in a narrow path of the forest, looked
round, and found himself alone.   He turned his
horse's head and rode back a few yards, when suddenly three masked men, whom he took for robbers,
sprang up in his path and fell upon him with
long knives.   But they had misreckoned their distance by a single yard, and their time by one second,
and when they were near enough to strike, his sword
was already in his hand.   The first man fell dead;

the second turned and fled, with a deep flesh wound
in his shoulder; the third followed without striking a blow; and Sir Raymond rode on unhurt, meditating upon the uncertainty of the times. When he
rejoined his wife and friend, he found them dismounted and sitting side by side on a fallen tree,
talking low and earnestly, while the footmen and
falconers were gathered together in a little knot at
some distance. As they heard his voice, Goda
started with a little cry, and Arnold's dark face
turned white; but by the time he was beside them,
they were calm again, and smiled, and they asked him
whether he had lost his way. Raymond said nothing
of what had happened to him, fearing to startle the
delicate nerves of his lady; but late on the following night, when Sir Arnold was alone in his bed-
chamber, a man ghastly white from loss of blood
lifted the heavy curtain and told his story in a low
voice.

CHAPTER II

Now Raymond and his son had gone over into Berkshire, to the building of the great castle at Faringdon, as has been said; and for a while Sir Arnold remained in his hold, and very often he rode over alone to Stoke, and spent many hours with the Lady Goda, both in the hall and in the small garden by the moat. The priest, and the steward, and the men-at-arms, and the porter, were all used to see him there often enough, when Sir Raymond was at home, and they thought no evil because he came now to bear the lonely lady company; for the manners of those days were simple.

But on a morning at the end of April, there came a messenger from King Stephen, bidding all earls, barons, bannerets, and knights, upon their oath of fealty, join him with their fighting men in Oxford. For form's sake, the messenger came to Stoke Regis, as not admitting that any Norman knight should not be on the king's side; and the drawbridge being down, he rode under the gateway, and when the trumpeter who was with him had blown three blasts, he delivered his message. Then the steward, bowing deeply, answered that his lord was absent on a journey; and the messenger turned and rode away, without bite or sup. But, riding on to Stortford Castle, he found Sir Arnold, and delivered the king's bidding with more effect, and was hospitably treated with meat and drink. Sir Arnold armed himself slowly in full mail, saving his head, for the weather was strangely warm, and he would ride in his hat rather than wear the heavy steel cap with the broad nose-guard. Before an hour had passed he was mounted, with his men, and his footmen were marching before and behind him on the broad Hertford road. But he had sent a messenger secretly to the Lady Goda, to tell her that he was gone; and after that she heard nothing for many days.

In the morning, and after dinner, and before sunset, she came every day to the little garden under the west wall of the manor, and looked long toward the road — not that she wished Sir Raymond back, nor that she cared when Gilbert came, but she well knew that the return of either would mean that the fighting was over, and that Sir Arnold, too, would be at leisure to go home.

On that fifth of May, as the sun was going down, she stood still and looked out toward the road for the tenth time since Curboil had gone to join the king. The sun sank lower, and still she saw nothing; and she felt the chill of the damp evening air, and would have turned to go in, but something held her. Far up the road, on the brow of the rising ground, she saw a tiny spark, a little dancing flame like the corpse-candles that run along the graves on a summer's night — first one, then all at once three, then, as it seemed to her, a score at least, swaying a little above a compact dark mass against the red sky. The lights were like little stars rising and falling on the horizon, and always just above a low, black cloud. A moment more, and the evening breeze out of the west brought a long-drawn harmony of chanting to the Lady Goda's ear, the high sweet notes of youthful voices sustained by the rich counterpoint of many grown men's tones. She started, and held her breath, shivered a little, and snatched at the rose bush beside her, so that the thorns struck through the soft green gauntlet and pricked her, though she felt nothing. There was death in the air; there was death in the moving lights; there was death in the minor wail of the monks' voices. In the first moment of imperfect understanding, it was Arnold whom they were bringing home to her, slain in battle by her lawful husband, or by Gilbert, her son; it was Arnold whom they were bringing back to her who loved him, that she might wash his wounds with her tears, and dry his damp brow with her glorious hair. Wide-eyed and silent, as the train came near, she moved along by the moat to meet the procession at the drawbridge, not understanding yet, but not letting one movement of the men, one flicker of the lights, one quaver of the deep chant, escape her reeling senses. Then all at once she was aware that Gilbert walked bareheaded before the bier, half wrapped in a long black cloak that swept the greensward behind him. As she turned the last bastion before reaching the drawbridge, the funeral was moving along by the outer edge of the moat, and between the procession and her there was only the broad water, reflecting the lights of the moving tapers, the dark cowls of the monks, the white surplices of the song-boys. They moved slowly, and she, as in a dream, followed them on the other side with little steps, wondering, fearing, starting now with a wild thrill of liberty at last, now struggling with a half conventional, half hysterical sob that rose in her throat at the thought of death so near. She had lived with him, she had played the long comedy of love with him, she had loathed him in her heart, she had smiled at him with well-trained eyes; and now she was free to choose, free to love, free to be Arnold's wife. And yet she had lived with the dead man; and in the far-off past there were little tender lights of happiness, half real, half played, but never forgotten, upon which she had once taught her thoughts to dwell tenderly and sadly. She had loved the dead man in the first days of marriage, as well as her cold and unawakened nature could love at all — if not for himself, at least for the hopes of vanity built on his name. She had hated him in secret, but she could not have hated him so heartily had there not once been a little love to turn so fiercely sour. She could not have trained her eyes to smile at him so gently had she not once smiled for his own sake. And so, when they brought him dead to the gate of his own house, his wife had still some shreds of memories for weeds to eke out a show of sorrow.

She passed through the postern in the small round tower beside the gateway, knowing that when she came out under the portcullis, the funeral train would be just reaching the other end of the bridge. The little vaulted room in the lower story of the

tower was not four steps in width across, from door
to door; but it was almost dark, and there the Lady
Goda stopped one moment before she went out to
meet the mourners. Standing still in the dimness,
she pressed her gloved hands to her eyes with all
her might, as though to concentrate her thoughts
and her strength. Then she threw back her arms,
and looked up through the gloom, and almost
laughed; and she felt something just below her
heart that stifled her like a great joy. Then all
at once she was calm, and touched her eyes again
with her gloved hands, but gently now, as though
smoothing them and preparing them to look upon
what they must see presently. She opened the
little door, and was suddenly standing in the midst
of the frightened herd of retainers and servants,
while the last strains of the dirge came echoing
under the deep archway. At that instant another
sound startled the air — the deep bell-note of the great
bloodhounds, chained in the courtyard from sunrise
to sunset; and it sank to a wail, and the wail broke
to a howl, dismal, ear-rending, wild. Before it had
died away, one of the Saxon bondwomen shrieked
aloud, and the next took up the cry, and then another, as a likewake dirge, till every stone in the
shadowy manor seemed to have a voice, and every
voice was weeping for the dead lord. And many of
the women fell upon their knees, and some of the
men, too, while others drew up their hoods, and
stood with bent heads and folded hands against the
rough walls.

Slowly and solemnly they bore him in and set the

"SHE . . . FELL UPON THE BODY IN A STORM OF TEARS"

bier down under the mid-arch. Then Gilbert Warde
looked up and faced his mother; but he stood aside,
that she might see her husband; and the monks and
song-boys stood back also, with their wax torches,
which cast a dancing glare through the dim twilight.
Gilbert's face was white and stern; but the Lady Goda
was pale, too, and her heart fluttered, for she had to
play the last act of her married life before many
who would watch her narrowly. For one moment
she hesitated whether to scream or to faint in honour
of her dead husband. Then, with the instinct of the
born and perfect actress, she looked wildly from her
son's face to the straight, still length that lay beneath the pall. She raised one hand to her forehead,
pressing back her golden hair with a gesture half
mad, half dazed, then seemed to stagger forward
two steps, and fell upon the body, in a storm of
tears.

Gilbert went to the bier, and lifted one of his
mother's gloved hands from the covered face, and it
dropped from his fingers as if lifeless. He lifted the
black cloth pall, and turned it back as far as he could
without disturbing the woman's prostrate figure; and
there lay the Lord of Stoke, in his mail, as he had
fallen in fight, in his peaked steel helmet, the
straight, fine, ring-mail close-drawn round his face
and chin, the silky brown hair looking terribly
alive against the dead face. But across the eyes
and the forehead below the helmet there was laid a
straight black band, and upon his breast the great
mailed hands clasped the cross-hilted sword that lay
lengthwise with his body. Gilbert, bareheaded and

unarmed, gazed down into his father's face for a
while, then suddenly looked up and spoke to all
the people who thronged the gateway.

"Men of Stoke," he said, "here lies the body of
Sir Raymond Warde, your liege lord, my father.
He fell in the fight before Faringdon Castle, and
this is the third day since he was slain; for the way
was long, and we were not suffered to pass unmo-
lested. The castle was but half built, and we were
encamped about it with the Earl of Gloucester, when
the king came suddenly from Oxford with a great
host; and they fell upon us unawares at early morning, when we had but just heard the mass and most
of us were but half armed, or not at all. So we
fought as we could, and many fell, and not a few
we killed with our hands. And I, with a helmet on
my head and a gambison but half buckled upon my
body, and my hands bare, was fighting with a full-
armed Frenchman and was hard pressed. But I
smote him in the neck, so that he fell upon one knee
and reeled. And even in that moment I saw this
sight. A score of paces from me, my father and
Sir Arnold de Curboil met face to face, suddenly and
without warning, their swords lifted in the act to
strike; but when my father saw his friend before
him, he dropped his sword-arm and smiled, and
would have turned away to fight another; but Sir
Arnold smiled also, and lowered not his hand, but
smote my father by the point, unguarded, and thrust
his sword through head and hood of mail at one
stroke, treacherously. And so my father, your liege
lord, fell dead unshriven, by his friend's hand; and

may the curse of man and the damnation of
Almighty God be upon his murderer's head, now
and after I shall have killed him. For, as I would
have sprung forward, the Frenchman, who was but
stunned, sprang to his feet and grappled with me;
and by the time he had no breath left, and the light
broke in his eyes, Sir Arnold was gone, and our
fight was lost. So we made a truce to bury our
dead, and brought them away, each his own."

When he had spoken there was silence for many
moments, broken only by the Lady Goda's unceasing
sobs. In the court within, and on the bridge without, the air grew purple, and dark, and misty; for
the sun had long gone down, and the light from the
wax torches, leaping, flaming and flickering in the
evening breeze, grew stronger and yellower under
the gateway than the twilight without. The dark-
robed monks looked gravely on, waiting till they
should be told to pass into the chapel — men of all
ages and looks, red and pale, thin and stout, dark and
fair, but all having that something in their faces that
marks the churchman from century to century. Between them and the dead knight, Gilbert stood still
with bent head and downcast eyes, with pale face
and set lips, looking at his mother's bright hair, and
at her clutching hands, and listening to the painfully
drawn breath, broken continually by her agonized
weeping. Suddenly the bloodhounds' bay broke out
again, fierce and deep; and on the instant a high young
voice rang from the court through the deep arch.

"Burn the murderer! To Stortford, and burn
him out!"

Gilbert looked up quickly, peering into the gloom
whence the voice had spoken. He did not see how,
at the words, his mother started back from the corpse,
steadied herself with one hand, and fixed her eyes
in the same direction ; but before he could answer,
the cry was taken up by a hundred throats.

" Burn the traitor ! burn the murderer ! To Stortford ! Fagots ! Fagots and pitch ! "

High, low, hoarse, clear, the words followed one
another in savage yells ; and here and there among
the rough men there were eyes that gleamed in the
dark like a dog's.

Then through the din came a rattling of bolts and
a creaking of hinges, as the groom store open the
stable doors to bring out the horses and saddle them
for the raid ; and one called for a light and another
warned men from his horse's heels. The Lady Goda
was on her feet, her hands stretched out imploringly
to her son, turning to him instinctively and for the
first time, as to the head of the house. She spoke to
him, too ; but he neither heard nor saw, for in his
own heart a new horror had possession, beside which
what had gone before was as nothing. He thought
of Beatrix.

" Hold ! " he cried. " Let no man stir, for no
man shall pass out who would burn Stortford. Sir
Arnold de Curboil is the king's man, and the king
has the power in England ; so that if we should burn
down Stortford Castle to-night, he would burn Stoke
Manor to-morrow over my mother's head. Between
Arnold de Curboil and me there is death. To-morrow I shall ride out to find him, and kill him in fair

fight. But let there be no raiding, no harrying, and no burning, as if we were Stephen's French robbers, or King David's red-haired Scots. Take up the bier; and you," he said, turning to the monks and song-men, "take up your chant, that we may lay him in the chapel and say prayers for his unshriven soul."

The Lady Goda's left hand had been pressed to her heart as though she were in fear and pain; but as her son spoke, it fell by her side, and her face grew calm before she remembered that it should grow sad. Until to-day her son had been in her eyes but a child, subject to his father, subject to herself, subject to the old manor-priest who had taught him the little he knew. Now, on a sudden, he was full-grown and strong; more than that, he was master in his father's place, and at a word from him, men-at-arms and bondsmen would have gone forth on the instant to slay the man she loved, and to burn and to harry all that was his. She was grateful to him for not having spoken that word; and since Gilbert meant to meet Curboil in a single combat, she felt no fear for her lover, the most skilled man at fence in all Essex and Hertfordshire, and she felt sure, likewise, that for his reputation as a knight he would not kill a youth but half his age.

While she was thinking of these things, the monks had begun to chant again ; the confusion was ended in the courtyard ; the squires took up the bier, and the procession moved slowly across the broad paved space to the chapel opposite the main gate.

An hour later Sir Raymond's dead body lay before the altar, whereon burned many waxen tapers. Alone, upon the lowest step, Gilbert was kneeling, with joined hands and uplifted eyes, motionless as a statue. He had taken the long sword from the dead man's breast, and had set it up against the altar, straight and bare. It was hacked at the edges, and there were dark stains upon it from its master's last day's work. In the simple faith of a bloody age, Gilbert Warde was vowing, by all that he and his held sacred, before God's altar, upon God's Sacred Body, upon his father's unburied corpse, that before the blade should be polished again, it should be black with the blood of his father's murderer.

And as he knelt there, his lady mother, now clad all in black, entered the chapel and moved slowly towards the altar-steps. She meant to kneel beside her son; but when she was yet three paces from him, a great terror at her own falseness descended into her heart, and she sank upon her knees in the aisle.

CHAPTER III

VERY early in the morning, Gilbert Warde was riding along the straight road between Sheering Abbey and Stortford Castle. He rode in his tunic and hose and russet boots, with his father's sword by his side; for he meant not to do murder, but to fight his enemy to death, in all the honour of even chance. He judged that Sir Arnold must have returned from Faringdon; and if Gilbert met him now, riding over his own lands in the May morning, he would be unmailed and unsuspecting of attack. And should they not meet, Gilbert meant to ride up to the castle gate, and ask for the baron, and courteously propose to him that they should ride together into the wood. And, indeed, Gilbert hoped that it might turn out so ; for, once under the gateway, he might hope to see Beatrix for a moment ; and two weeks had passed, and terrible things had happened, since he had last set eyes upon her face.

He met no one in the road ; but in the meadow before the castle half a dozen Saxon grooms, in loose hose and short homespun tunics, were exer· cising some of Curboil's great Normandy horses. The baron himself was not in sight, and the grooms told Gilbert that he was within. The drawbridge was down, and Gilbert halted just before entering the gate, calling loudly for the porter. But instead

31

of the latter, Sir Arnold himself appeared at that moment within the courtyard, feeding a brace of huge mastiffs with gobbets of red raw meat from a wooden bowl, carried by a bare-legged stable-boy with a shock of almost colourless flaxen hair, and a round, red face, pierced by two little round blue eyes. Gilbert called again, and the knight instantly turned and came towards him, beating down with his hands the huge dogs that sprang up at him in play and seemed trying to drive him back. Sir Arnold was smooth, spotless and carefully dressed as ever, and came forward with a well-composed smile in which hospitality was skilfully blended with sympathy and concern. Gilbert, who was as thorough a Norman in every instinct and thought as any whose fathers had held lands from the Conqueror, did his best to be suave and courteous on his side. Dismounting, he said quietly that he desired to speak with Sir Arnold alone upon a matter of weight, and as the day was fair, he proposed that they should ride together for a little way into the greenwood. Sir Arnold barely showed a slight surprise, and readily assented. Gilbert, intent upon his purpose, noticed that the knight had no weapon.

"It were as well that you took your sword with you, Sir Arnold," he said, somewhat emphatically. "No one is safe from highwaymen in these times."

The knight met Gilbert's eyes, and the two looked at each other steadily for a moment; then Curboil sent the stable-boy to fetch his sword from the hall, and himself went out upon the drawbridge and called to one of the grooms to bring in a horse. In

less than half an hour from the time when Gilbert
had reached the castle, he and his enemy were riding
quietly side by side in a little glade in Stortford wood.
Gilbert drew rein and walked his horse, and Sir
Arnold instantly did the same. Then Gilbert spoke.

"Sir Arnold de Curboil, it is now full three days
since I saw you treacherously kill my father."

Sir Arnold started and turned half round in the
saddle, his olive skin suddenly white with anger; but
the soft fresh colour in Gilbert's cheek never changed.

"Treacherously!" cried the knight, with indignation and with a questioning tone.

"Foully," answered Gilbert, with perfect calm.
"I was not twenty paces from you when you met,
and had I not been hampered by a Frenchman of
your side, who was unreasonably slow in dying, I
should have either saved my father's life or ended
yours, as I mean to now."

Thereupon Gilbert brought his horse to a stand
and prepared to dismount, for the sward was smooth
and hard and there was room enough to fight. Sir
Arnold laughed aloud as he sat still in the saddle,
watching the younger man.

"So you have brought me here to kill me!" he
said as his mirth subsided.

Gilbert's foot was already on the ground, but he
paused in the act of dismounting.

"If you do not like the spot," he answered coolly,
"we can ride farther."

"No, I am satisfied," answered the knight; but
before he had spoken the last word he broke into a
laugh again.

They tied up their horses to trees at a little distance, out of reach of one another, and Gilbert was the first to return to the ring of open ground. As he walked, he drew his father's sword from its sheath, slipped the scabbard from the belt, and threw it to the edge of the grass. Sir Arnold was before him a moment later; but his left hand only rested on the pommel of his sheathed weapon, and he was still smiling as he stopped before his young adversary.

"I should by no means object to fighting you," he said, "if I had killed your father in treachery. But I did not. I saw you as well as you saw me. Your Frenchman, as you call him, hindered your sight. Your father was either beside himself with rage, or did not know me in my mail. He dropped his point one instant, and then flew at me like a bloodhound, so that I barely saved myself by slaying him against my will. I will not fight you unless you force me to it; and you had better not, for if you do, I shall lay you by the heels in two passes."

"Bragging and lying are well coupled," answered Gilbert, falling into guard. "Draw before I shall have counted three, or I will skewer you like a trussed fowl. One — two —"

Before the next word could pass his lips, Sir Arnold's sword was out, keen and bright as if it had just left the armourer's hands, clashing upon Gilbert's hacked and blood-rusted blade.

Sir Arnold was a brave man, but he was also cautious. He expected to find in Gilbert a beginner of small skill and reckless bravery, who would expose himself for the sake of bringing in a sweeping blow in carte, or attempting a desperate thrust. Consequently he did not attempt to put his bragging threat into practice, for Gilbert was taller than he, stronger, and more than twenty years younger. Unmailed, as he stood in his tunic and . hose, one vigorous sword-stroke of the furious boy might break down his guard and cut him half in two. But in one respect Curboil was mistaken. Gilbert, though young, was one of those naturally gifted fencers in whom the movements of wrist and arm are absolutely simultaneous with the perception of the eye, and not divided by any act of reasoning or thought. In less than half a minute Sir Arnold knew that he was fighting for his life ; the full minute had not passed before he felt Gilbert's jagged blade deep in the big muscles of his sword arm, and his own weapon, running past his adversary, fell from his powerless hand.

In those days it was no shame to strike a disarmed foe, in a duel to the death. As Sir Arnold felt the rough steel wrenched from the flesh-wound, he knew that the next stroke would kill him. Quick as light, his left hand snatched the long dagger from its sheath at his left side, and Gilbert, raising his blade to strike, felt as if an icicle had pierced his breast ; his arm trembled in the air, and lost its hold upon the hilt ; a scarlet veil descended before his eyes, and the bright blood gushed from his mouth as he fell straight backward upon the green turf.

Sir Arnold stepped back and stood looking at the fallen figure curiously, drawing his lids down, as some short-sighted men do. Then, as the sobbing breast ceased to heave and the white hands lay quite still upon the sward, he shrugged his shoulders, and began to take care of his own wound by twisting a leathern thong from Gilbert's saddle very tight upon his upper arm, using a stout oak twig for a lever. Then he plucked a handful of grass with his left hand and tried to hold his dagger in his right in order to clean the reddened steel. But his right hand was useless ; so he knelt on one knee beside the body, and ran the poniard two or three times through the skirt of Gilbert's dark tunic, and returned it to its sheath. He picked up his sword, too, and succeeded in sheathing it. He mounted his horse, leaving Gilbert's tethered to the tree, cast one more glance at the motionless figure on the grass, and rode away towards Stortford Castle.

CHAPTER IV

Two months after Sir Arnold de Curboil had left Gilbert Warde in the forest, believing him to be dead, the ghostly figure of a tall, wafer-thin youth, leaning on the shoulders of two grey brothers, was led out into the warm shadows of the cloister in Sheering Abbey. One of the friars carried a brown leathern cushion, the other a piece of stiff parchment for a fan, and when they reached the first stone seat, they installed the sick man as comfortably as they could.

Three travelling monks, tramping homeward by the short forest path from Harlow to Sheering, had found Gilbert lying in his blood, not ten minutes after the knight had ridden away. Not knowing who he was, they had brought him to the abbey, where he was at once recognized by the monks who had formed the funeral procession on the previous evening, and by others who had seen him. The brother whose duty it was to tend the sick, an old soldier with the scars of a dozen deep wounds in him, and by no means a despicable surgeon, pronounced Gilbert's condition almost hopeless, and assured the abbot that it would be certain death to the young Lord of Stoke to send him back to his home. He was therefore laid upon a new bed in an upper chamber that had fair arched windows to the west, and there the brothers expected that

Gilbert Warde would before long breathe his last
and end his race and name. The abbot sent a messenger to Stoke Regis to inform the Lady Goda of
her son's condition, and on the following day she
came to see him, but he did not know her, for he
was in a fever; and three days passed, and she came
again, but he was asleep, and the nursing brother
would not disturb him. After that she sent messengers to inquire about his state, but she herself
did not come again, whereat the abbot and many
of the monks marvelled for a while, but afterwards
they understood.

Gilbert lived, and the desperate wound slowly
healed, for he was strong and young, and his blood
was untainted; but when at last he was allowed to
stand upon his feet, he seemed to be little more than
a fine-drawn shadow. They dressed him first in a
novice's frock, because it was easier for him to wear,
and at last he was well enough to be carried down
from his room, and to sit for an hour upon the stone
bench in the cloister. One of the brothers sat down
beside him and slowly fanned his face with a stiff
sheet of yellow parchment, such as the monks used
for binding their books; the other went away to his
work. Gilbert leaned back and closed his eyes,
drinking in the sun-sweetened air and the scent of
the flowers that grew in the cloister garden; and
the indescribable sense of peace descended upon his
body and soul which comes to men wrested from
death, when danger is passed and their strength is
slowly growing again within them.

It is impossible for any young man of sensitive

and believing mind to spend two months in a great
religious institution of his own faith without feeling
himself drawn to the religious life. Lying in his
room, alone for many hours of the day, alone in
waking watches of the night, though a brother was
always within call, Gilbert had followed with a sick
man's second sight the lives of the two hundred
monks who dwelt in Sheering Abbey. By asking
questions, he knew how they rose at dawn, and
trooped into the dim abbey church to early mass, and
went to their daily work, the lay-brethren and
novices in the field, the learned fathers in the library
and the writing-room. He could follow their daily
round of prayer and work, and his heart was with
them in both. Bloodless and emaciated as he lay
there, the life of love and war which had once
seemed to him the only one worth living, faded
away into the dimness of an undesired impossibility.
He had failed, too, in his first great deed of arms;
his father's murderer was alive, and he himself had
most narrowly escaped death. It seemed to him
that his thin white hands, which could hardly pull
the blanket to his chin when he felt cold, could
never again have strength to grasp sword-hilt or
hold bridle, and in the blank collapse of his physical
existence the image of himself as a monk, young,
ascetic and holy in his life, presented itself with a
marvellous and luring attraction. He made the
nursing brother teach him prayers from the offices
of the night and day, and he repeated them at the
right hours, feeling that he was taking a real part
in the monastic existence. Gradually, too, as he

caught the spirit of the place, the gospel of forgiveness, ever the stumbling-block of fighting men, appeared to him as something that could be practised
without dishonour, and the determination to kill
Sir Arnold gave way to a sort of attempt at repentance for having even wished to be revenged upon
him.

One thing troubled him constantly and was altogether beyond his comprehension. His mother
seemed to have forgotten his very existence, and
he had not consciously seen her since he had been
wounded. He asked questions every day, and
begged the abbot himself to send word to the Lady
Goda asking her to ride over to the abbey. The
abbot smiled, nodded, and seemed to promise; but
if the message was ever sent, it elicited no answer,
and after a time, as Gilbert grew steadily better,
not even a messenger came from Stoke Regis to ask
about him. Now Gilbert had worshipped his mother
as a sort of superior being, and, like his father,
had deceived himself with the belief that she was
devoted to him; so that, as time went on, and he
was utterly neglected by her, the conviction was
forced upon him that something terrible and unfore-
seen had happened. Yet the abbot would tell him
nothing, nor the brothers who tended him ; to the
best of their knowledge, they said, the Lady of Stoke
was well.

"Before long," Gilbert would answer, "I shall be
able to go home and see for myself."

And at this the abbot smiled and nodded, and
began to talk of the weather, which was hot.

But to-day, since he had been allowed to leave his room, Gilbert was determined to force an explanation. It lacked yet an hour of midday and dinner-time when the abbot came sauntering along the cloister, followed at a respectful distance by a couple of monks, who walked side by side with downcast eyes and hands hidden in their sleeves, their cord girdles bobbing and swinging rhythmically as they walked. As he came up to Gilbert, the nursing brother rose and hid his hands in his grey woollen sleeves.

Gilbert opened his eyes at the sound of the abbot's footsteps, and made a movement as though he would have risen to greet the lordly churchman, who had so often visited him in his room, and for whom he felt a natural sympathy, as for a man of his own race and breeding ; for Lambert, Abbot of Sheering, came of the great Norman house of Clare, which had taken Stephen's side in the Civil War, a fact which did not prevent the aristocratic abbot from talking with gentle satire and occasional bitter sarcasm about the emptiness of Stephen's claims.

He laid his hand on Gilbert's sleeve to make him keep his seat, and sat down beside him on the bench. He waved the monks away, and they retired to the other end of the cloister, where they all three sat down together in silence. The abbot, a delicately made man, with high Norman features, a colourless beard, once fair, and very bright blue eyes, laid one of his beautiful hands kindly upon Gilbert's.

" You are saved," he said cheerfully. " We have done our part ; youth and sunshine will do the rest; you will grow strong very quickly, now, and in a week you will be asking for your horse. They found him beside you, and he has been well cared for."

"Next week, then," said Gilbert, "I will ride over to Stoke and see my mother. But I think I shall come back and stay with you again — if you will have me."

Gilbert smiled as he spoke the last words; but the abbot's face was grave and his brows were drawn together, as though he were in some trouble.

"Better stay with us altogether," he said, shaking his head and looking away.

Gilbert sat motionless for a few seconds, as if the remark had made no impression upon him; then, realizing that the words contained some special meaning, he started slightly and turned his hollow eyes to the speaker's face.

"And not go to see my mother?" His voice expressed the utmost surprise.

"Not — not at present," answered the abbot, taken off his guard by the directness of the question.

Weak as he was, Gilbert half rose from his seat, and his thin fingers nervously grasped his companion's arm. He would have spoken, but a sort of confusion came over him, as if he could not decide which of many questions to ask first, and before words could form themselves, the abbot was speaking to him with gentle authority.

"Listen to me," he said; "sit quietly beside me and hear what I have to say, for you are a man, now, and it is better that you should know it all at once, and from me, than get it distorted, in miserable morsels, from the gossip of the brothers within the next day or two."

He paused a moment, holding the young man's hand soothingly while keeping him in his seat and making him feel that he must stay there.

"What is it?" asked Gilbert, nervously, with half closed eyes. "Tell me quickly."

"An evil thing," answered the churchman, "— a sad thing, and one of those that change men's lives."

Again Gilbert started in his seat, more violently this time than before, and there was the broken ring of genuine fear in his voice.

"My mother is dead!" he cried.

"No, not that. She is in no danger. She is well. She is more than well; she is happy."

Gilbert was staring almost stupidly at his companion, not in the least understanding that there could be any evil news about his mother if all these things were true.

And yet it seemed strange that the abbot should lay stress upon the Lady Goda's happiness, when Gilbert had been at death's door for many weeks, and when, as he well knew, she was without news of him.

"Happy!" he echoed, half dazed.

"Too happy," answered the prelate. "Your mother was married when you had been scarcely a month here with us."

Gilbert stared into the older man's face for one moment after he had ceased speaking, and then sank back against the wall behind him with something between a groan and a sigh. One word had struck the ground from under his feet; the next was to pierce his soul.

"Who is her husband?" he asked under his breath.

Before the abbot answered, his grasp tightened upon Gilbert's hands with a friendly grip that was meant to inspire courage.

"Your mother has married Sir Arnold de Curboil."

Gilbert sprang to his feet, as though he had been struck in the face by an enemy. A moment earlier he could not have risen without help; a moment later he fell backward into the abbot's arms.

Nothing that he had felt in his whole short life — not all the joys and fears of childhood, which, after all, contains the greatest joys and fears in life, compounded with the clash of his first fighting day and the shock of seeing his father killed before his eyes — not all these together could be compared with what he felt at that plain statement of the dishonour done upon his house and upon his father's memory. Yet he was not unconscious.

"Now, by the Sacred Blood — "

Before he could pronounce the solemn vow of revenge that was on his lips, the abbot's delicate hand was almost crushing his mouth with open palm to stop the words.

"Arnold de Curboil, perjured to God, false to his king, the murderer of his friend, the seducer of his friend's wife, is fit for my prayers," said the abbot, "not for your steel. Swear no great oaths that you will kill him; still less swear that you will be avenged upon your mother; but if you must needs swear something, vow rather that you will leave them to their fate and never willingly cross their path again. And indeed, whether you promise that or not, you must needs keep away from them until you can claim your own with the chance of getting it back."

"My own!" exclaimed Gilbert. "Is Stoke not mine? Am I not my father's son?"

"Curboil has got Stoke Regis by treachery, as he got your mother. As soon as he had married her he took her with him to London, and they two did homage to King Stephen, and the Lady Goda made apology before the king's court because her former husband had been faithful to the Empress Maud; and she besought the king to bestow the lordship of Stoke Regis, with the manor house and all things thereto appertaining, upon their present lord, Sir Arnold de Curboil, disinheriting you, her son, both because you are true to the Empress, and because, as she did swear, you tried to slay Sir Arnold by stealth in Stortford woods. So you have neither kith nor kin, nor lands nor goods, beyond your horse and your sword; wherefore I say, it were as well for you to stay with us altogether."

Gilbert was silent for some time after the abbot had ceased speaking. He seemed to be utterly overcome by the news that he was disinherited, and his hands lay upon his knees, loosely weak and expressive of utter hopelessness. Very slowly he raised his face at last and turned his eyes upon the only friend that seemed left to him in his destitution.

"So I am an outcast," he said, "an exile, a beggar — "

"Or a monk," suggested the churchman, with a smile.

"Or an adventurer," said Gilbert, smiling also, but more bitterly.

"Most of our ancestors were that," retorted the abbot, "and they have picked up a fair living by it," he added. "Let me see: Normandy, Maine, Aquitaine, Gascony — and England. Not a bad inheritance for a handful of pirates matched against the world."

"Yes, but the handful of pirates were Normans," said Gilbert, as if that statement alone should have explained the conquest of the universe. "But the world is half won," he concluded, with a rather hopeless sigh.

"There is enough to fight for yet," answered the abbot, gravely. "The Holy Land is not half conquered, and until all Palestine and Syria shall be one Christian kingdom under one Christian king, there is earth for Norman feet to tread, and flesh for Norman swords to hack."

Gilbert's expression changed a little, and a light came into his eyes.

"The Holy Land — Jerusalem!" The words came slowly, each with its dream. "But the times are too old. Who should preach another crusade in our day?"

"The man whose word is a lash, a sword, and a crown — the man who rules the world to-day."

"And who is that?" asked Gilbert.

"A Frenchman," answered the abbot — "Bernard of Clairvaux, the greatest man, the greatest thinker, the greatest preacher, and the greatest saint of these late days."

"I have heard of him," Gilbert answered, with a sick man's disappointment at not learning anything new. Then he smiled faintly. "If he is a miracle-worker, he might find me a good subject."

"You have a home here, Gilbert Warde, and friends," said the abbot, gravely. "Stay while you will, and when you are ready for the world again you shall not lack for a coat of mail, a spare mount, and a purse of gold with which to begin your life."

"I thank you," said Gilbert, feebly, but very gratefully. "I feel as if my life were not beginning, but ending. I have lost my inheritance, my home, and my mother in one hour. It is enough, for it is all, and with it is taken love also."

"Love?" The abbot seemed surprised.

"Can a man marry his mother's husband's child?" asked Gilbert bitterly, almost contemptuously.

"No," answered the abbot; "that would be within the forbidden degrees of affinity."

For a long time Gilbert sat still in mournful silence. Then, seeing that he was very tired, the abbot beckoned to the brothers, who came and led him back to the stairs, and carried him up to his room. But, when he was gone, the Abbot of Sheering walked thoughtfully up and down the cloister for a long time, even until the refectory bell began to ring for dinner, and he could hear the shuffling steps of the two hundred hungry monks hurrying to their food, through the distant staircases and corridors.

CHAPTER V

An autumn morning at dawn, the beach at Dover, the tide at flood, and a hundred half naked sailors launching a long, black Norman sea-boat bows on, over chocks through the low surf to the grey swell beyond. The little vessel had been beached by the stern, with a slack chain hooked to her sides at the water-line, and a long hawser rove through a rough fiddle-block of enormous size, and leading to a capstan set far above high-water mark and made fast by the bight of a chain to an anchor buried in the sand up to the heavy wooden stock. And now a big old man with streaming grey beard, and a skin like a salted ox-hide, was slacking the turns of the hawser from the capstan-drum as the boat moved slowly down over the well-greased chocks, stopping short now and then of her own accord, and refusing to move on till twenty stout sailors on each side, their legs half buried in the sand, their broad shoulders flattened under the planking, their thick brown hands planted upon their thighs, like so many Atlases, each bearing a world, had succeeded, by alternately straining and yielding, in making the little vessel rock on her keel, and start again toward the water's edge. On board, the master stood at the stern, ready to ship the long rudder as soon as she had taken the water. Two men in the bows took in

48

the slack of the cable, by which the anchor had been dropped some fifty yards out, so as to keep her head straight when she should leave the temporary ways. By the mast, for the vessel had but one, stood Gilbert Warde, watching all that was done, with the profoundly ignorant interest which landsmen always show in nautical matters. It seemed very slow to him, and he wondered why the man with the long beard, far up the beach, did not let go, so that the boat might launch herself. And while he was trying to solve the problem, something happened which he could not understand : a chorus of wild yells went up from the sailors under the sides, the master in the stern threw up one hand and shouted, the old man let go and yelled back an answer, Gilbert heard a rattling of chains, and then all at once the boat gathered way, and shot like an arrow through the low curling surf, far out upon the heaving grey water beyond, while the two men in the bows got in the slack of the cable, hand over hand, like madmen, panting audibly, till at last the vessel swung off by her head and rode quietly at her anchor. An hour later, with twenty sweeps swinging rhythmically in the tholes, and a fair southwesterly breeze, the sharp-cut boat was far out in the English Channel, and before night, the wind holding fair and freshening, the master dropped anchor almost under the shadow of the Count of Flanders' castle at Calais.

So Gilbert Warde left England, a wanderer, disinherited of all that should have been his, owing all that he had to Lambert de Clare, Abbot of Sheering, in the shape of mail and other armour, with such fine clothes as a young nobleman should have with him on a journey, two horses, and a purse of which the contents should last him several months on his travels. For attendants he had with him a fair-haired Saxon lad who had run away from Stoke to Sheering, and had refused to leave Gilbert, whom he looked upon as his lawful master; and there was with him, too, a dark-skinned youth of his own age, a foundling, christened Dunstan by the monks after a saint of their order, brought up and taught at the abbey, who seemed to know neither whose child he was nor whence he came, but could by no means be induced to enter the novitiate so long as the world had room for wanderers and adventurers. He was a gifted fellow, quick to learn and tenacious to remember, speaking Latin and Norman French and English Saxon as well as any monk in the abbey, quick of hand and light of foot, with daring black eyes in which the pupils could hardly be found, while the whites were of a cold, blue grey and often bloodshot; and he had short, straight black hair, and a face that made one think of a young falcon. He had begged so hard to be allowed to go with Gilbert, and it was so evident that he was not born to wear out a church pavement with his knees, that the abbot had given his consent. During the last weeks before Gilbert's departure, when he was hourly gaining strength and could no longer bear to be shut up within the walls of the convent, he had made a companion of Dunstan, walking and riding with him, for the fellow could ride, and sometimes entering into long arguments with him about matters of belief and conscience and honour, and the two had become attached to each other by their unlikeness; not precisely as friends and equals, yet by no means as master and man; it was rather the sort of relation which often existed between knight and squire, though the two were of the same age, and though Gilbert had no immediate prospect of winning knightly spurs.

It would have been hard, however, to admit that Dunstan could ever develop into a knight himself. There were strange little blanks in his ideas of chivalry, curious, unfeeling spots in his moral organization, which indicated another race, another inheritance of thought, the traditions of a world older and less simple than the one in which Gilbert had been brought up.

For Gilbert was the type of noble youth in the days when the light of chivalry had dawned upon an age of violence, but was not yet fully risen. God, honour, woman — these made up the simple trinity of a knight's belief and reverence, from the moment when the Church began to make an order of fighting men, with ceremonies and obligations of their own, thereby forever binding together the great conceptions of true Christianity and true nobility.

In the absence of anything like real learning among the laymen of those days, education in its simplest and most original sense played a very large part in life, and Gilbert had acquired that sort of culture in its highest and best form. The object of mere instruction is to impart learning for some distinct purpose, but most chiefly, perhaps, in order that it may be a means of earning a livelihood. The object

of education is to make men, to produce the character of the man of honour, to give men the inward
grace of the gentleman, which cannot manifest itself
outwardly save in good manners, modesty of bearing,
and fearlessness; and such things in earlier days were
profoundly associated in the minds of men with the
inward principles and the outward rites of Christianity. It was the perfect simplicity, and in a measure
the ample harmony, of beliefs, principles, and rules of
action that made life possible at all at a time when
the modern art of government was in its earliest
infancy, when the idea of a constitution had been lost
in the chaos of the dark ages, and when the direction
of kingdoms, principalities, and societies was a purely
personal matter, wholly dependent upon individual
talent or caprice, virtue or vice, charity or greed.
Without some such foundation in the character of
the times, society, the world, and the Church must
have fallen a prey to the devouring ambitions of that
most horrible of human monsters, the princely unbeliever of the middle ages, who flourished again
and again, sporadically, from England to Constantinople, from Paris to Rome, but who almost
invariably ended in disastrous failure, overcome and
trodden down by the steadily advancing morality
of mankind. Such men were John the Twelfth, of
the evil race of Theodora in Rome, and the Jewish
Pierleone who lived a hundred years later, and King
John of England, and last and greatest of all, perhaps,
as he was most certainly the worst, Cæsar Borgia.

To be a gentleman when Henry Plantagenet was
a boy of twelve, and Gilbert Warde was going to the

Duke of Normandy's court, implied not many gifts,
few principles, and two or three accomplishments
at most; but it meant the possession of those
simple requirements in their very best accepted
form, and that species of thoroughness in a few
matters which has been at the root of social superi-
ority in all ages. We have heard of amateur artists,
amateur soldiers, amateur statesmen ; but no one
has ever heard of an amateur gentleman. Gilbert
Warde knew little Latin beyond the few prayers
taught him by the manor priest at Stoke ; but in the
efficacy of those prayers he believed with all his
heart and soul. The Norman French language of
the nobles in England was no longer that of their
more refined cousins over the water ; but though his
tongue betrayed him for an Englishman, Gilbert had
the something which was of more worth among his
equals than a French accent — the grace, the un-
affected ease, the straightforward courtesy, which
are bred in bone and blood, like talent or genius,
but which reach perfection only in the atmosphere
to which they belong, and among men and women
who have them in the same degree. Possessing
belief and good manners, the third essential was
skill in arms, and, as has been seen, Gilbert was a
match for a swordsman of considerable reputation.
The only absolutely necessary accomplishment for
a gentleman in his day was a thorough knowledge
of the chase as a fine art in all its branches, from
falconry to boar-hunting, and in this respect Gilbert
was at least the equal of the average young noble.
In spite of his youth, he was therefore thoroughly

equipped for the world ; and besides the advantages
here set forth, he had the very great one of feeling
that, although he might be going among strangers,
he was going to meet men all brought up to act and
think like himself, in the belief that their ways of
acting and thinking were very much better than
those of other people.

But as he rode along the dunes, he was not
reflecting upon his own gifts or prospects. His life
was strange to him by its sudden and complete
change, from an existence of more or less peaceful
enjoyment, in which the certainty of fortune, local
dignity, and unthwarted love made the idea of
ambition look empty and foolish, to the state of possessing only a pair of good horses, good weapons, and
a little ready money, with which to lay siege to the
universe. Yet even that wide difference of conditions
was insignificant beside the deeper and sadder misfortunes upon which the young man brooded as he
rode, and which had already embittered his young
existence by the destruction of his highest and most
beautiful illusion and of his dearest and happiest hope.

In the fall of his mother's image from the altar
upon which he had set it, there was the absolute
destruction of his own past childhood as it had
always appeared to him. In the fearful illumination
of her true nature, in the broad glare of evil, the
little good there might have been had faded to
nothing. It was not possible that she who had
married her husband's murderer within the month
could ever have felt one sincere impulse of love for
Raymond Warde, nor that she could ever have

known the slightest real affection for the son whom she had first left to his fate, and then treacherously cheated of his birthright. The temple where she had been was still in his heart and mourned her in emptiness. For nothing else had taken the place of her there; she was not transformed, she was gone, and had taken with her a lifetime of tender and gentle memories. When his inward eyes sought her they found nothing, and their light was quenched in her darkness. She was not as his father was, dead in fact, but dead in honour. There he lay, as Gilbert had last looked upon his white face and stiff, mailed form, himself still, himself as he had been in life and as he was thereafter, in that place of peace and refreshment where brave men rest. In the quiet features was reflected forever the truth whereby his life had been lived; in the crossed hands upon the breast was the last outward symbol and sign of the simple faith that had been life's guide; in the strong, straight outlines of a strength splendid in death was the record of strong deeds well done. Alive, he had been to his son the man of all others; dead, he was still the man of men, without peer and without like. It mattered not that he was silent, for he had spoken the truth; that he was as motionless as a stone, for the cold hand had been swift to thrust and smite, and had dealt unforgotten blows in a good cause; that he was deaf, for he had heard the cry of the weak, and had forborne; that he was blind, for his eyes had seen the light of victory and had looked unflinching upon an honourable death. Loyal, true, brave, strong, he lay in his son's heart, still at all points himself. And Gilbert turned his mind's eyes to the darkness on the other side, and many a time, as the unwept tears burned in his brain, he wished that his mother were lying there too, beside his father, dead in the body but alive forever to him in that which is undying in woman ; to be cherished still, still honoured ; to be loved, and still obeyed in the memory of precept and teaching ; to be his mother always, and he to be in thought her child, even until the grey years should be upon him, and the Bridge of Fear in sight.

Instead, as his thoughts went back to his home, the woman herself faced him, not as he had always seen her, but as she had been sometimes seen by others. The deed she had done — the greatest, the worst, the most irrevocable — was in her face, and Gilbert's unconscious memory brought back the details his love of her had once rejected. The cold face was as hard as flint, the deep blue eyes were untrue and unbelieving, the small red lips were scornfully parted to show the cruel little teeth, and there were dashes of flame in the russet hair. Better she had been dead, better a thousand times that she had come to the sharp end before her time, than that such a face should be her son's only memory of his mother.

The lines of the image had been etched in the weak places of his heart with the keen point of his first grief, and the biting acid of a new and unnatural hate was eating them deeper day by day. And when, in spite of himself, his mind dwelt upon her and understood that he was cursing her who had borne him, he turned back in sheer despair to the thought of a religious life.

But though it drew him and appealed to all in his nature which had been uppermost when death had almost tripped him into his grave, it spoke but half a language now, and was less than half convincing. He could understand well enough that the monastery might hold the only life for men who had fought through many failures, from light to darkness, from happiness to sorrow — men who loved nothing, hoped nothing, hated nothing any longer, in the great democracy of despair. They sought peace as the only earthly good they might enjoy, and there was peace in the cloister. Hope being dead in life, they tasted refreshment in the hope of a life to come. The convent was good enough for the bankrupt of love and war. But there must be another rule for those in whom youth was wounded but not dead, whose hearts were offended but not slain, whose blood was still strong and hot for good and evil, for men whose battles were before them still. There must be a remedy against fate which should not be an offence to God, a struggle against God's will which should not be a revolt, a life in which virtue should not mean a prison for soul and body, nor the hope of salvation a friar's cell.

Like many enthusiasts, knowing nothing of the world save by guesswork, and full of an inborn belief in the existence of perfection, Gilbert dreamed of realizing the harmony of two opposites — the religious life and the life of the world. Such dreams seemed not so wild in those days, when the very

idea of knighthood was based upon them, and when
many brave and true men came near to making
them seem anything but fanciful, and practised virtue in a rough-and-ready fashion which would not
pass muster in modern society, though it might in
heaven.   The religious idea had taken hold of Gilbert strongly, and before he had left the abbey he
had fallen into the habit of attending most of the
offices in the choir, still wearing the novice's frock
which had been at first but an invalid's robe.   And
now that he was out in the world to seek his fortunes,
tunic and hose, spur and glove, seemed strange to
him, and he would have felt more at home in a
friar's hood.   So he felt that in his life he should
never again quite lose the monastic instinct, and
that it was well for him that he could not.   He
stood on that perilous thin ridge between past and
future to which almost every man of heart is sooner
or later led by fate, where every step may mean a
fall, and where to fall is almost to be lost.   The
things he had lived for, the things he had hoped,
the things he had loved, had been taken from him
violently, and all at once.   There was neither clue,
nor guide, nor hope, and on each side of him yawned
the hideous attraction of despair.   Even the recollections of a first love were veiled by what he
understood to be the irrevocable interdiction of the
Church, and, in his strongly spiritual mood, to think
of Beatrix appeared to him like a temptation to
mortal sin.

In leaving England, without any definite aim, but
with a vague intention of making his way to Jeru-

salem, he had obeyed the Abbot of Sheering rather
than followed friendly advice, and his obedience
had savoured strongly of the monastic rule. Lambert de Clare, a man of the world before he had become a churchman, and a man of heart before he was
a ruler of monks, had understood Gilbert's state well
enough, and had forced the best remedy upon him.
The cure for a broken heart, if there be any, is not in
solitude and prayer, but in facing the wounds and stings
of the world's life ; and the abbot had almost forcibly
thrust his young friend out to live like other men of-
his order, while suggesting a pilgrimage to the Holy
Land as a means of satisfying his religious cravings.

As for the material help which Gilbert had received, it was no shame, in an age not sordid, for a
penniless gentleman to accept both gifts and money
from a rich and powerful person like the Abbot of
Sheering, in the certainty of carving out such fortune
with his own hands as should enable him amply to
repay the loan. So far as his immediate destination
was concerned, the abbot, who considered his house
to be vastly superior to political dissension, and
secretly laughed at his cousins for supporting King
Stephen's upstart cause, had advised Gilbert to make
his way directly to the court of Geoffrey Plantagenet,
Duke of Normandy, and Grand Seneschal of France,
the husband of the Empress Maud, rightful Queen of
England. Thither he was riding, therefore, with
Dunstan on his left hand, mounted upon his second
horse, while Alric, the sturdy little Saxon groom and
archer, rode behind them on a stout mule laden with
Gilbert's possessions.

CHAPTER VI

THOSE were the early days of Geoffrey's lordship in Normandy. Twice and three times he came up from Anjou with his men-at-arms and his footmen to take possession of his wife's lawful inheritance. Again and again he was repulsed and driven back to his own dominions, but at the last he prevailed, and the iron will of the man whose royal race was to give England fourteen kings, forced Normandy to submission, and thereafter he ruled in peace. Yet he was not so strongly established but that he desired sound friendships and strong alliances to support him, and at the same time he was anxious to obtain help for his wife in her prolonged struggle for the English crown. In his office of Grand Seneschal of France he generally caused himself to be represented by a deputy; but he had lately determined to make a journey to Paris, in the hope of winning over the young King Louis, and perhaps the beautiful Queen Eleanor, who was feudal sovereign, in her own right, of Guienne, Poitou and Aquitaine, and in reality a more powerful personage than the King himself.

So it fell out that before Gilbert reached his destination he met a great and splendid train riding toward him on the highroad, two hundred horse, at the very least, and as many footmen, followed by a long line of sumpter mules. The road was narrow at

that place, so that Gilbert, with his two men, saw that
it would be impossible to pass, and though it was not
natural to him to cede the right of way to any one,
he understood that, in the face of what was a little
army, it would be the part of wisdom to draw aside.
A thick growth of thorn bushes made a natural
hedge at that part of the road, and Gilbert and his
companions were obliged almost to back into the
briers, as four handsomely dressed outriders trotted
past abreast, not without a glance of rather super-
cilious inquiry, for they did not fail to see that
Gilbert was a stranger in their country ; and, for
a traveller, his retinue was anything but imposing. He, however, barely glanced at them as they
passed him, for his eyes were fixed upon the advancing cavalcade, a river of rich and splendid colour
flowing toward him between soft green banks. They
were men who rode in peace ; for though a standard
rose in the middle rank, it was furled and cased in
leather, and the horsemen who surrounded it were
dressed in tunic and hose — crimson, green, rich dark
brown, with the glint of gold, the sheen of silver,
the lightning of steel, relieving the deep hues of
dark cloth and velvet here and there.

A length behind the furled flag rode a man and a
boy, side by side, and the next riders followed two
or three lengths behind them. The man, mounted
on a huge white Norman weight-carrier, kept the
off side of the road, his great beast trotting leisurely
with a long pounding step, and an occasional lazy
shake of the big white head with the iron-grey fore-
lock and the well-combed mane. The rider sat

square and upright in the saddle, the plain leathern bridle neither too short nor too long in the light strong hand, that just moved perceptibly with the horse's step. He was a man evidently of good height, but not over tall, of surpassing beauty of form, young in figure, but past middle age if one judged by his hard features and already furrowed brow; his deep grey eyes looked steadily ahead from beneath black eyebrows which contrasted oddly with hair that was already iron-grey. There was something immovable and fateful about the clean-shaven jaw, the broad flat chin, the wide strong mouth — something strangely durable that contrasted with the rich softness of his splendid dress, as though the man, and what the man meant, were to outlive the fashions of the world.

The boy who rode by his near side, a lad of little more than twelve years, was both like him and unlike. Sturdy, broad, short-legged, square beyond his age, any one could see that he was never to inherit his father's beauty of proportion and grace of bearing; but there was something in his face that promised all his father's strength and an even greater independence. The grey eyes were the same, but nearer together, and almost sinister in their gaze, even at that age; the nose was already long and rather flat than sharp, and the large straight lips, even and close set, would have seemed strong even in a grown man's face. The boy sat upon his small grey Andalusian horse as if he had lived a lifetime in the saddle, but his twelve-year-old hand was heavier on the bridle than ever his father's had been.

There was something in the bearing of the two,

father and son, so kingly and high that Gilbert, who had been brought up in Norman courtesy, involuntarily rose in the saddle as much as his long stirrups would allow, and lifted his cap from his head, supposing, as was natural, that he was saluting the lord of the lands through which he was travelling. The other returned the salutation with a wave of the hand, looked sharply at Gilbert, and then, to the latter's surprise, drew rein, the lad beside him ranging back half a length so as not to be in the way between the other two. For a few seconds neither said a word. Then the elder man, as though expecting something of which the younger was not aware, smiled kindly and spoke. His voice was strong and manly, but clear and sweet.

"You are strange here, sir," he said, with something more like an assertion than a question in his turn.

"From England, sir," answered Gilbert, bowing slightly in the saddle.

The elder man looked hard at him and knit his brows. Few English gentlemen had refused allegiance to King Stephen.

"From England? And what may you be doing in Normandy, young sir? Stephen's friends find little friendship here."

"I am not of them, sir," answered Gilbert, drawing himself up somewhat haughtily. "I am rather of those who would shorten Stephen's reign by the length of his life, and his body by a head."

The broad, handsome face of the man with whom he was speaking relaxed into a smile, and his son, who had at first eyed Gilbert with distrust, threw back his head and laughed.

"Then I suppose that you are for the Empress," said the man. "But if you are, why are you not in Gloucester?"

"Sir," answered Gilbert, "being made homeless and landless by Stephen, I chose rather to cut a fortune out of the world than to beg one of the Queen, who has none left to give."

"You could fight for her," suggested the other.

"Ay, sir; and I have, and will again, if such gentlemen of Normandy as you will cross the water and fight also. But as the matter stands to-day, whosoever shall break the truce shall break his own neck, without serving the Empress. And meanwhile I ride to the Duke of Normandy's court, and if I may serve him, I will, but if not, I shall go farther."

"And who are you, sir, that seek the Duke?"

"I am Gilbert Warde, and my fathers held Stoke Regis in Hertfordshire from Duke William. But Stephen took it when I was lying ill of a wound in Sheering Abbey and bestowed it upon another. And you, sir? I crave your name."

"Geoffrey Plantagenet," answered the Duke, quietly. "And this is my son Henry, who by the grace of God shall yet be King of England."

Gilbert started at the name, and then noticed for the first time that both father and son wore in their velvet caps a short dry sprig of the broom-plant. He sprang to the ground and came forward on foot, bareheaded, and stood beside the Duke's near stirrup.

"Your pardon, my lord," he said; "I should have known you."

"That might have been hard," answered Geoffrey, "since you had never seen me. But as you were on your way to find me and wished to serve me, mount again and ride with us to Paris, whither we go."

So Gilbert mounted, and would have fallen back in the train among the young squires, behind the five ranks of knights who rode after the Duke. But Geoffrey would not let him take his place at once, for he was glad to have news of the long struggle in England, the end of which was to set a Plantagenet upon the throne; and he asked many questions which the young man answered as well as he could, though some of them were not easy; and the boy Henry listened with grave face and unwinking eyes to all that was said.

"If I had been in my mother's place," he said at last, in a pause, "I would have cut off Stephen's head in Bristol Castle."

"And let your uncle Gloucester be put to death by Stephen's wife?" Geoffrey looked at his son curiously.

"She would not have done it," answered Henry. "There could have been no more war, with Stephen dead. But if she had killed my uncle, well, what of that? The crown of England is worth one life, at least!"

Gilbert heard and wondered at the boy's hardness, but held his peace. He was surprised also that the Duke should say nothing, and the speech of the one and the silence of the other clearly foreshadowed the

kingdom for one or both. But the boy's words
seemed heartless and not altogether knightly to
Warde, who was himself before all things a man of
heart ; and the first impression made on him by the
precocious lad was more or less a wrong one, since
Henry afterwards turned out a just and kind man,
though often stern and unforgetful of offence. And
Gilbert was very far from guessing that the young
prince was suddenly attracted to him in the strongest
possible way, and that in the first meeting he had
unconsciously laid the foundations of a real friendship.

After a time, as the Duke asked no more questions,
Gilbert took it for granted that he was no longer
wanted, and fell back to his proper place among the
riders. The young squires received him with cordiality and not without a certain respect for one
who, though not even a knight, had been so much
honoured by their sovereign. And Gilbert himself,
though he felt at home amongst them at first, as a man
feels with his own kind, yet felt that he was divided
from them by the depth of his own misfortunes.
One of them spoke of his home at Bayeux, and of his
father, and Gilbert's face grew grave ; another told
how his mother had herself embroidered in gold the
fine linen collar that showed above his low-cut tunic.
Gilbert bit his lips, and looked away at the rolling
green country. And one, again, asked Gilbert where
his home might be.

" Here," answered Warde, striking the pommel of
his saddle with his right hand and laughing rather
harshly.

He was older than most of them, for they ranged
from fourteen to eighteen years, and were chiefly
beardless boys who had never seen fight, whose
fathers had fought Geoffrey Plantagenet until they
had recognized that he was the master, as the great
Duke William had been in his day, and then, being
beaten, had submitted whole-heartedly and all at
once, as brave men do, and had forthwith sent their
sons to learn arms and manners at Geoffrey's court.
So none of these youths had slain a man with his
own hand, as Gilbert had at Faringdon, nor had
any of them faced an enemy with plain steel in a
quarrel, as Gilbert had faced Sir Arnold de Curboil. Though Gilbert told little of his story and
less of his deeds, they saw that he was older than
they, they felt that he had seen more than they had,
and they guessed that his hand was harder and
heavier than theirs.

As the day wore, and they rode, and halted, and
dined together in the vast outer hall of a monastery
which they reached soon after midday, the young
men who sat beside Gilbert noticed that he could
repeat the Latin words of the long grace as well
as any monk, and one laughed and asked where he
had got so much scholarship.

"I lay two months in an abbey," answered Gilbert,
"healing of a wound, and the nursing brother taught
me the monks' ways."

"And how came you by such a wound?" asked
the young squire.

"By steel," answered Gilbert, and smiled, but he
would say no more.

And after that, two or three asked questions of Gilbert's man Dunstan, and he, being proud of his master, told all he knew, so that his hearers marvelled that such a fighter had not yet obtained knighthood, and they foretold that if Long Gilbert, as they named him for his height, would stay in the Duke's service, he should not be a squire many weeks.

And on the next day and the days following it was clear to them all that Gilbert was in the way of fortune by the hand of favour; for as the company rode along in the early morning by dewy lanes, where Michaelmas daisies were blooming, a groom came riding back to say that the young Henry — the Count, as they began to call him about that time — wished the company of Master Warde, to tell him more of England. So Gilbert cantered forward and took his place beside the young prince, and for more than an hour answered questions of all sorts about English men, English trees, English cattle, and English dogs.

"It will all be mine before long," said the boy, laughing, "but as I have never seen it, I want your eyes."

And every day thereafter, in the morning and afternoon, Gilbert was sent for to tell the lad stories about England; and he talked as if he were speaking to a grown man and said many things about his own country which had long been in his heart, in the strong, good language of a man in earnest. Henry listened, and asked questions, and listened again, and remembered what he heard, not for a day only, nor

a week, but for a lifetime, and in the boy the king
was growing hour by hour.

Sometimes, while they talked, the Duke listened
and said a few words himself, but more often he
rode on out of the train alone, in deep thought, or
called one of the older knights to his side ; and when
Gilbert's quick ear caught fragments of their conversation, they were generally talking of country matters — crops, horse-breeding, or the price of grain.

So they rode, and in due time they came to fields
of mud left by a subsiding river, and here and there
green hillocks rose out of the dreary expanse, and
on them were built castles of grey stone. But
in the flats there were mud hovels of brickmakers
and of people living miserably by the river ; and
then all at once the ground rose a little to the
bank, with a street, and houses of brick and stone ;
and between these, upon an island, Gilbert, rising
in his stirrups to see over the heads of his companions, descried the castle of the King of France,
with its towers and battlements, its great drawbridge, and its solid grey walls, in those days one
of the strongest holds in all the world.

Then they all halted, and the Duke's herald rode
forward to the gate, and the King's herald was seen
within, and there was a great blowing of horns and
a sound of loud, high voices reciting formal speeches
in a monotone. After that there was a silence, and
horns again, and more recitation, and a final blast,
after which the Duke's herald came back, and the
King's herald came out upon the drawbridge, followed
by men in rich clothes of white cloth, embroidered

with gold lilies that shone in the autumn sun, like little tongues of flame; and the Duke's standard was unfurled to the river breeze, and the goodly train rode slowly over the drawbridge at the end of the solid wooden causeway which spanned the main width of the stream, and so, by the main gate, into the great court of honour. And Gilbert rode close behind young Henry, who called him his chancellor in jest, and would not let him ride out of his sight.

Within the court were great buildings reared against the outer walls; but in the midst was the King's hall and dwelling, and in the porch at the head of the steps which led to the main door, the King and Queen were waiting in state, in their robes of ceremony, with all their household about them, to receive their Grand Seneschal and brother sovereign, Geoffrey Plantagenet. But Gilbert, looking boldly before him, saw that the King of France was a fair, pale man with a yellow beard, strong and knightly, but with dull and lifeless blue eyes; and Gilbert looked at the lady who sat beside him, and he saw that the Queen of France was the most beautiful woman in the world; and when his eyes had seen her it was long before he looked away.

He saw a being so unlike all he had known before, that his idea of woman changed from that hour for his whole life — a most perfect triplicity of beauty, grace and elastic strength. Some have doubtless possessed each separate perfection, but the names of those who had all three are as unforgotten as those of conquerors and supreme poets. Gilbert's eyes fixed themselves, and for a moment he was in a sort of waking trance, during which he could not for his life have described one feature of the Queen's face; but when she spoke to him, his heart leapt and his eyelids quivered, and her image was fixed upon his memory forever. Young though he was, it would have been contrary to his grave and rather melancholy disposition to lose his heart at first sight to any woman, and it was neither love, nor love's forerunner, that overcame him as he gazed at the Queen. It was a purely visual impression, like that of being dazzled by a bright light, or made giddy by sudden motion.

She was as tall as the King, but whereas he was heavily and awkwardly built, her faultless proportion made an ungraceful movement an impossibility, and the rhythmic ease of her slightest gesture expressed an unfaltering bodily energy which no sudden fatigue nor stress of long weariness could bring down. When she moved, Gilbert wished that he might never see her in repose, yet as soon as the motion ceased, it seemed a crime upon beauty to disturb her rest.

Her face and her throat, uncovered to the strong morning light, were of a texture as richly clear as the tinted leaves of young orange-blossoms in May; and like the flowers themselves, it seemed to rejoice in air and sun, in dew and rain, perfected, not marred, by the touch of heat and cold. The straight white throat rose like a column from the neck to the delicate lobe of the faultless ear, and a generously modelled line sprang in a clean curve of beauty to the sudden rounding of the ivory chin, cleft in the midst by nature's supreme touch. Low on her forehead the heavy waves of her hair were drawn back to each side under the apple-green silk coverchief that was kept in place by the crown of state. But she wore no wimple, and the broad waves flowed down upon her shoulders and hung behind her like a heavy mantle. And they were of that marvellous living hue, that the westering sun casts through oak leaves upon an ancient wall in autumn. All in her face was of light, from her hair to her white forehead; from her forehead to her radiant eyes, deeper than sapphires, brighter than mountain springs; from the peach-blossom bloom of her cheeks to the living coral of her lips.

She wore a close-fitting upper garment of fine green cloth, embroidered with a small design in silver thread, in which the heraldic cross of Aquitaine alternated with a conventional flower. The girdle of fine green leather, richly embroidered in gold, followed exactly the lower line of this close garment round the hips, and the long end fell straight from the knot almost to the ground. The silken skirt in many folds was of the same colour as the rest, but without embroidery. The mantle of state, of a figured cloth of gold lined with straw-coloured silk, hung in wide folds from her shoulders, her hair falling over it, and it was loosely held in place by a twisted cord of gold thread across her breast. Contrary to the fashion of the day, her sleeves were tight and closed at the wrists, and green gloves encased her hands, and were embroidered on the back with the cross of Aquitaine.

Gilbert was standing two steps behind young Henry, who was on his father's left, and was consequently directly opposite to the Queen, as the boy bent one knee, and taking her gloved hand, touched the embroidery with his lips. Gilbert was hardly aware that she was looking into his eyes, while his own were riveted on her face, and when she spoke, he started in surprise.

"And who is this?" she asked, smiling, as she saw what an effect her beauty produced upon the young man.

Henry turned half round, with a step backward, and took Gilbert's hand.

"This is my friend," he said, dragging him forward; "and if you like me, you shall please to like him, too, and tell the King to knight him at once."

"You have a strong recommendation to grace, sir," said the Queen.

She looked down at the imperious boy's square face and laughed; but looking up and meeting Gilbert's eyes again, the ring of her laugh changed oddly and died away in a short silence. It was long since she had looked upon so goodly a man; she was weary of her monkish husband, and she was the grand-daughter of William of Aquitaine, giant, troubadour, and lover. It was no wonder that there was light in her eyes, and life in every fibre of her beautiful body.

"I think I shall like your friend," she said, speaking to Henry, but still looking at the man.

And so Gilbert first met the Queen; and as she held out her hand to him and he took it, kneeling on one knee, she unconsciously drew young Henry close to her, and her arm was round his neck, and her hand pressed his shoulder in a very gentle way, so that he looked up into her face. But if any one had told her then that she should love the man in vain, that she should be divided from the fair-haired King beside her and become the wife of the broad-faced, rough-fisted little boy whose curly head barely reached her shoulder, the prophet might have fared ill, as readers of the future often do.

But meanwhile the King stood talking quietly with Duke Geoffrey, who presently crossed to salute the Queen, not dreaming what strange spirits had taken possession of the hearts of three persons in one moment. For the third was Henry himself. When the Queen gave her right hand to his father her other was still on the boy's shoulder, and when she would have withdrawn it he caught it with both his own and held it there; and suddenly the blood sprang up in his cheeks even to the roots of his hair, and for the first and last time in his life Henry Plantagenet was almost ridiculous, and wished that he might hide his head. Yet he would not loose his hold on the Queen's hand.

CHAPTER VII

WHILE Duke Geoffrey tarried in Paris, receiving much honour at the King's court, but obtaining very little encouragement in his hope of help against Stephen, the time was heavy on the hands of some of his followers; but others of them, seeing that they had little service and much leisure, made up their minds to do not only what was good in their own eyes, but sometimes also that which was evil, as a certain chronicler once said of the English knights. For the wine of Gascony was good, but some said that the vintage of Burgundy was better, and a matter of such weight was evidently not to be left undecided; yet the more often it came to judgment, the more evidence and testimony were required in the case, so that the court sat night and day without agreeing upon a verdict.

But Gilbert had never learned to sit for hours over a cup, slowly addling his wits and marking the hour when the room should begin to swing upon the pivot of his head; and Henry kept him constantly by his side, saying that he was the only sober man in his father's court, knight or squire; nor would the boy let him go, excepting when he himself could pass his time with the Queen, and then he was more than anxious that Gilbert should disappear. At first Eleanor was amused by the lad's childish pas-

sion, but as she herself greatly preferred Gilbert's
society to that of Henry, she soon grew weary of
the rather tame sport which consisted in making
a boy of twelve years fall desperately in love with
her.

Moreover, Henry was precocious and keen-sighted
beyond his years, and was not long in discovering
his idol's predilection for his friend. His chief consolation was that Gilbert himself seemed indifferent,
and came and went at the Queen's bidding as though
he were obeying an order rather than an impulse.

One lazy autumn afternoon, when the air was as
hot as summer, and the flies were swarming about the
open doors of the great stables, and before the deep
archway that led into the main kitchen, and about
the open windows of the knights' and squires' quarters, — when the air was still and lazy, and not a
sound was heard in the vast enclosure of the castle-
yard, — Henry and Gilbert came out to play at tennis
in a shady corner behind the church, where there
was a penthouse that would serve.

In half a dozen strokes Henry had scored high to
Gilbert's nothing, and the boy dropped the ball at his
feet to tighten the network he had made on his hand
by winding a bowstring in and out between his fingers and across the palm, as men did before rackets
were thought of. Suddenly he turned half round
and faced Gilbert, planting himself with his sturdy
legs apart and crossing his arms, which were bare to
the elbow ; for he had taken off his cloth tunic, and
his embroidered shirt, girdled at the waist by a
leathern belt, hung over his scarlet hose, and was

wide at the neck and turned back above his elbows. He was hatless, ruddy, and hot.

"Will you answer a fair question fairly, Master Gilbert?" he asked, looking his friend in the eyes.

Gilbert had fallen into the habit of treating him like a man, as most people did, excepting the Queen, and gravely nodded an answer.

"Do you not think that the Queen of France is the most beautiful woman in the world?"

"Yes," answered Gilbert, without a smile, and without the slightest hesitation.

The boy's eyes, that were so near together, gleamed and fixed themselves in rising anger, while a dark red flush mounted from his bare throat to his cheeks, and from his cheeks to his forehead.

"Then you love her?" he asked fiercely, and the words were thick on his lips.

Gilbert was not easily surprised, but the conclusion was so sudden and unexpected that he stared for a moment in blank amazement before he smiled.

"I?" he exclaimed. "I love the Queen? I should as soon think of coveting the King's crown!"

Henry looked into Gilbert's face a moment longer, and the blood slowly subsided from his own.

"I can see that you are in earnest," he said, picking up the ball at his feet, "though I cannot see why a man should not covet a king's crown as well as a king's wife." He struck the ball.

"You are young," said Gilbert, "to ride atilt through all the Ten Commandments at once."

"Young!" exclaimed the boy, keeping the ball up. "So was David when he killed the giant! So was

Hercules when he strangled the serpents, as you told me the other day. Young!" he cried a second time, with forcibly concentrated contempt. "You should know, Master Gilbert, that a Plantagenet of thirteen years is the match of any other man of twenty. As I can beat you at tennis, though you are six years older than I, so I can beat you in other matters, and with the Queen herself, even though she is half in love with you already, as all the court is saying ; and she shall belong to me some day, though I have to slay that dish-faced prayer-master of a king to get her."

Gilbert was no more morally timid than he was physically a coward, but he looked round with some anxiety as the boy uttered his outrageous boast.

The place they had chosen for their game was the deep and shady corner where the church made a right angle with the royal palace. The grass was cropped during several hours every morning by a dozen sheep and lambs kept in a stable at the other end of the castle-yard during the rest of the day. The springing turf was kept fresh even in summer's drought by the deep shadows. The church wall, built of well-hewn blocks of stone, was flat and smooth, and was strengthened at regular intervals by buttresses springing straight up from the sloping penthouse of masonry, some two yards high. The interval between the last buttress and the wall of the palace made an admirable court, and, indeed, the tennis-courts of later days all seem to have been modelled upon just such corners of old church architecture. The wall of the palace was also smooth and almost

without windows on that side. There was one on
the lower floor, at a considerable distance from the
corner, but the other was at least four or five yards
from the ground, just above the point where Gilbert
and Henry were playing, and was made in Norman
fashion of two round arches springing from the
rough-hewn capital of a small stone column between
them. Gilbert had often noticed this window,
though it was above an ordinary side glance, as he
played the ball at the other wall; and even as he
turned now, he looked instinctively behind him and
towards the distant lower window.

A sweet low laugh rang out into the summer air
just above his head. He looked up to meet the
sound, and young Henry missed the ball and turned
his eyes in the same direction. His bluff, boyish
face blushed scarlet, but Gilbert turned slowly pale,
stepped back, and took his round pointed cap from
his fair hair in acknowledgment of the Queen's
presence.

"You were listening, Madam," cried the boy, red
in his anger. "But I am glad you did, since you
have heard the truth."

The Queen laughed again, and drew back her head
as if to see whether there were any one in the room
behind her, her white hand lying over the stone sill,
meanwhile, as if to show that she was not going
away. Gilbert even thought that the slender fingers
tapped the stone ledge in a reassuring way. Then
she looked out again. A few late flowers and sweet
herbs grew in an earthenware trough in one division
of the window. There was sweet basil and rosemary,

and a bit of ivy that tried to find a hold upon the
slender column, and, partly missing it, hung down
over the window-ledge. A single monthly rose made
a point of colour among the sweet green things.

The Queen was still smiling as she rested her
elbows upon the sill and her chin on her folded
hands. She was near enough to the tennis-players
to be heard by them if she spoke in a low tone.

"Are you angry because Master Gilbert is frightened?" she asked, looking at Henry. "Or are you
frightened because his lordship, the Count of Anjou,
is angry?" she inquired, turning her eyes to Gilbert.

He smiled at her way of opening the conversation,
but Henry thought that she was laughing at him and
grew redder than ever. Not deigning to answer, he
picked up the ball and served it over the penthouse
to himself, striking it back cleverly enough. The
Queen laughed again as he kept his face resolutely
turned from her.

"Will you teach me to play, if I come down to
you?" she asked, looking at the back of his head.

"It is no game for women," answered the boy,
rudely, and still keeping the ball up.

"Will you give me a lesson, Master Gilbert?"

The laughing eyes were suddenly grave as they
turned to the young Englishman, the smiling lips
grew tender, and the voice was gentle. Without
turning round, Henry felt the change and knew that
she was looking at his friend; he served the ball
with a vicious stroke that brought it back too high
for him. Without turning his head to see where it
had rolled, the angry boy walked off, picked up his

tunic, which lay on the turf at a little distance,
threw it over his arm, jammed his pointed cap upon
his head with his other hand, and departed in offended
dignity.

The Queen smiled as she looked after him, but
did not laugh again.

"Will you teach me to play tennis?" she asked
of Gilbert, who was hesitating as to what he should
do. "You have not answered me yet."

"I shall at all times do your Grace's bidding,"
answered Gilbert, inclining his head a little and
making a gesture with the hand that held his cap as
if to put himself at her disposal.

"At all times?" she asked quietly.

Gilbert looked up quickly, fearing lest he might
be tricked into a promise he did not understand, and
he did not answer at once. But she would not repeat
the question.

"Wait," she said, before he spoke. "I am coming
down."

With an almost imperceptible gesture, like a
greeting, she disappeared. Gilbert began to walk
up and down, his hands behind him, his eyes on the
ground, and he did not see the tennis-ball which
Henry had lost until he almost stumbled over it.
The boy's words had roused an entirely new train of
ideas in his mind. Perhaps no man could be so free
from vanity as not to be pleased, even against his
will, with the thought that the most beautiful living woman, and she a queen, was in love with him.
But whatever satisfaction of that sort Gilbert may
have felt was traversed in an opposite direction by

the cool sense of his own indifference. And besides, that was a simple age in which sins were
called by their own names and were regarded with a
sort of semi-religious, respectful abhorrence by most
honest gentlemen; and what was only the general
expression of a narrow but high morality had been
branded upon Gilbert's soul during the past months
in letters that were wounds by the ever-present
memory of his own mother's shame.

The confusion of his reflections was simplified by
the appearance of Queen Eleanor. At the window
of the lower story, which opened to the ground, she
stepped out, looked up and down the deserted yard,
and then came towards him. Gilbert had been long
enough in Paris to understand that Queen Eleanor
had not the slightest regard for the set rules, formal
prejudices, and staid traditions of her husband's
court; and when King Louis gravely protested
against her dressing herself in man's mail, bestrid-
ing his own favourite charger, and tilting at the
Saracen quintain in the yard, she hinted with more
or less good or ill nature, according to her mood,
that her possessions were considerably more exten-
sive than the kingdom of France, and that what she
had been taught to do by William of Aquitaine was
necessarily right, and beyond the criticism of Louis
Capet, who was descended from a Paris butcher.
Nevertheless, the Englishman had some reasonable doubts and misgivings at finding himself,
a humble squire, alone in that quiet corner with
the most beautiful and most powerful of reigning
queens. But she, whose quick intuition was a gift

"PERHAPS THAT IS ONE REASON WHY I LIKE YOU"

almost beyond nature, knew what he felt before she had reached his side. She spoke quite naturally and as if such a meeting were an everyday occurrence.

"You did not know that the window was mine?" she said quietly. "I saw how surprised you were when I looked out. It is a window of a little hall behind my room. There is a staircase leading down. I often come that way, but I hardly ever look out. To-day as I was passing I heard that silly child's angry voice, and when I saw his face and heard what he said, I could not help laughing."

"The young Count is in earnest," said Gilbert, quietly, for it would have seemed disloyal to him to join in the Queen's laughter.

"In earnest! Children are always in earnest!"

"They deserve the more respect," retorted the Englishman.

"I never heard of respecting children," laughed the Queen.

"You never read Juvenal," answered Gilbert.

"You often say things which I never heard before," answered the Queen. "Perhaps that is one reason why I like you."

She stopped and leaned against the penthouse, for they had reached the corner of the court, and she thoughtfully bit a sprig of rosemary which she had picked from her window in passing. Gilbert could not help watching the small white teeth that severed the little curling grey leaves like ivory knives, but the Queen's eyes were turned from him and were very thoughtful.

Gilbert deemed it necessary to say something.

"Your Grace is very kind." He bowed respectfully.

"What makes you so sad?" she asked suddenly, after a short pause, and turning her eyes full upon him. "Is Paris so dull? Is our court so grave? Is my Gascony wine sour, that you will not be merry like the rest, or"— she laughed a little —"or are you not treated with the respect and consideration due to your rank?"

Gilbert drew himself up a little as if not pleased by the jest.

"You know well that I have no rank, Madam," he said ; "and though it should please you to command of me some worthy deed, and I should, by the grace of God, deserve knighthood, yet I would not have it save of my lawful sovereign."

"Such as teaching me to play tennis?" she asked, seeming not to hear the end of his speech. "You should as well be knighted for that as for any other thing hard to do."

"Your Grace is never in earnest."

"Sometimes I am." Her eyelids drooped a little as she looked at him. "Not often enough, you think? And you — too often. Always, indeed."

"If I were Queen of France, I could be light-hearted, too," said Gilbert. "But if your Grace were Gilbert Warde, you should be perhaps a sadder man than I."

And he also laughed a little, but bitterly. Eleanor raised her smooth brows and spoke with a touch of irony.

"Are you so young, and have you already such desperate sorrows?"

But as she looked, his face changed, with that look of real and cruel suffering which none can counterfeit. He leaned back against the penthouse, looking straight before him. Then she, seeing that she had touched the nerve in an unhealed wound, glanced sidelong at him, bit upon her sprig of rosemary again, turned, and with half-bent head walked slowly along to the next buttress; she turned again there, and coming back stood close before him, laying one hand upon his folded arm and looking up to his eyes, that gazed persistently over her head.

"I would not hurt you for the world," she said very gravely. "I mean to be your friend, your best friend — do you understand?"

Gilbert looked down and saw her upturned face. It should have moved him even then, he thought, and perhaps he did not himself know that between her and him there was the freezing shadow of a faint likeness to his mother.

"You are kind, Madam," he said, somewhat formally. "A poor squire without home or fortune can hardly be the friend of the Queen of France."

She drew back from him half a step, but her outstretched hand still rested on his arm.

"What have lands and fortune to do with friendship — or with love?" she asked. "Friendship's home is in the hearts of men and women; friendship's fortune is friendship's faith."

"Ay, Madam, so it should be," answered Gilbert, his voice warming in a fuller tone.

"Then be my friend," she said, and her hand turned itself palm upward, asking for his.

He took it and raised it to his lips in the act of bending one knee. But she hindered him; her fingers closed on his with a strength greater than he had supposed that any woman could possess, and she held him and made him stand upright again, so that he would have had to use force to kneel before her.

"Leave that for the court," she said; "when we are alone let us enjoy our freedom and be simply human beings, man and woman, friend and friend."

Gilbert still held her hand, and saw nothing but truth in the mask of open-hearted friendship in which she disguised her growing love. He was young and thought himself almost friendless; a generous warmth was suddenly at his heart, with something compounded of real present gratitude and of the most chivalrous and unselfish devotion for the future.

She felt that she had gained a point, and she forthwith claimed the privilege of friendship.

"And being friends," she said, still holding his hand as he stood beside her, "will you not trust me and tell me what it is that seems to break your heart? It may be that I can help you."

Gilbert hesitated, and she saw the uncertainty in his face, and pressed his hand softly as if persuading him to speak.

"Tell me!" she said. "Tell me about yourself!"

Gilbert looked at her doubtfully, looked away, and then turned to her again. Her voice had a persuasion of its own that appealed to him as her beauty could not. Almost before he knew what he was doing he was walking slowly by her left side, in the shade of the church, telling her his story; and she listened, silently interested, always turning her face a little toward his, and sometimes meeting his eyes with eyes of sympathy. He could not have told his tale to a man; he would not have told it to a woman he loved; but Eleanor represented to him a new and untried relation, and the sweet, impersonal light of friendship waked the dark places of his heart to undreamt confidence.

He told her what had befallen him, from first to last, but the sound of his own words was strange to him; for he found himself telling her what he had seen two and three years ago, in the light of what he had known but a few months, yet almost as if he had known it from the first. More than once he hesitated in his speech, being suddenly struck by the horror of what he was telling, and almost doubting the witness of his own soul to the truth. One thing only he did not tell — he never spoke of Beatrix, nor hinted that there had been any love in his life.

They turned, and turned again many times, and he was hardly aware that at the end the Queen had linked one hand in his right arm and gently pressed it from time to time in sign of sympathy. And when he had finished, with a quaver in his deep voice as he told how he had come out into the world to seek his fortune, she stopped him, and they both stood still.

"Poor boy!" she exclaimed softly. "Poor Gilbert!"—and her tone lingered on the name, — "the world owes you a desperate debt — but the world shall pay it!"

She smiled as she spoke the last words, pressing his arm more suddenly and quickly than before; and he smiled, too, but incredulously. Then she looked down at her own hand upon his sleeve.

"But that is not all," she continued thoughtfully; "was there no woman — no love — no one that was dearer than all you lost?"

A faint and almost boyish blush rose in Gilbert's cheek, and disappeared again instantly.

"They took her from me, too," he said in a low, hard voice. "She was Arnold de Curboil's daughter — when he married my mother he made his child my sister. You know the Church's law!"

Eleanor was on the point of saying something impulsively, but her eyelids suddenly drooped and she checked herself. If Gilbert Warde did not know that the Church granted dispensations in such cases, she saw no good reason for telling him.

"Besides," he added, "I could not have her now, unless I could take her from her father by force."

"No," said the Queen, thoughtfully. "Is she fair?"

"Very dark," said Gilbert.

"I meant, is she beautiful?"

"To me, yes: the most beautiful in the world. But how should I know? I have never heard others speak of her; she is not beautiful as your Grace is, — not radiantly, supremely, magnificently perfect, — yet to my eyes she is very lovely."

"I should like to see her," said the Queen.

In the silence that followed they began to walk up and down again side by side, but Eleanor's hand no longer rested on Gilbert's arm. She could see that his eyes were fixed upon a face that was far

away, and that his hand longed for a touch not hers;
and a painful little thrill of disappointment ran
through her, for she was not used to any sort of
opposition, in great things or small. The handsome
Englishman attracted her strangely, and not by his
outward personality only. From the first a sort of
mystery had hung over him, and she had felt, when
she was with him, the inexplicable fascination of a
curiosity which she should be sure to satisfy sooner
or later. And now, having learned something of
his life, and liking him the more for what she knew,
she was suddenly filled with an irresistible longing
to see the girl who had made the first mark on Gilbert's life. She tried to conjure up the young face,
and the dark hue he had spoken of brought the vision
of a fateful shadow. Her mind dwelt upon the girl,
and she started visibly when Gilbert spoke to her.

"And has your Grace no deed for me to do?" he
asked. "Is there nothing whereby I may prove my
thanks?"

"Nothing, save that you be indeed my friend —
a friend I can trust, a friend to whom I may speak
safely as to my own soul, a friend whom I may tell
how heartily I hate this life I lead!"

She uttered the last words with a sudden rising
accent of unruly discontent, as genuine as every
other outward showing of her vital nature.

"How can your life be hateful?" asked Gilbert,
in profound astonishment, for he did not know her
half as well as she already knew him.

"How can it be anything else?" she asked.
"How should life not be hateful, when every natural

thing that makes life worth living is choked as soon as it is awake? Oh, I often wish I were a man!"

"Men do not wish you were," answered Gilbert, with a smile.

Suddenly, while they were speaking, a sound of voices filled the air with loud chanting of Latin words. Instinctively the Queen laid her hand on Gilbert's sleeve and drew him into the shadow of a buttress, and he yielded, scarcely knowing what he did. The chanting swelled on the air, and a moment later the procession began to appear beyond the corner of the church. Two and two, led by one who bore a cross, the song-boys in scarlet and white came first, then Benedictine monks in black, then priests of the cathedral in violet cloth with fine white linen surplices and bearing wax candles. And they all chanted as they walked, loudly, fervently, as if a life and a soul depended on every note. Then, as the Queen and Gilbert looked on from the shade where they stood, they saw the canopy of cloth of gold borne on its six gilded staves by slim young men in white, and beneath it walked the venerable bishop, half hidden under the vast embroidered cope from which the golden monstrance emerged, grasped by his closely wrapped hands; and his colourless eyes were fixed devoutly upon the Sacred Host, while his lips moved in silent prayer.

Just as the canopy was in sight the procession halted for some time. In the shadow of the buttress Eleanor knelt upon the turf, looking towards the

Sacred Host, and Gilbert dropped upon one knee at her side, very reverently bending his head.

Eleanor looked straight before her with more curiosity than religious fervour, but in her ear she heard Gilbert's deep voice softly chanting with the monks the psalms he had so often sung at Sheering Abbey. The Queen turned her head at the sound, in surprise, and watched the young man's grave face for a moment without attracting his attention. Apparently she was not pleased, for her brows were very slightly drawn together, the corners of her eyes drooped, and the deep bright blue was darkened. At that moment the canopy swayed a little, the ancient bishop moved his shoulders under the heavy cope in the effort of starting again, and the procession began to move onward.

Next after the bishop, from behind the end of the church, the King came into sight, walking, monk-like, with folded hands, moving lips and downcast eyes, the long embroidered bliaut reaching almost to his feet, while the scarlet mantle, lined with blue and bordered with ermine, fell straight from his shoulders and touched the turf as he walked. He was bareheaded, and as Eleanor noticed what was evidently intended for another act of humility, the serene curve of her closed lips was sharpened in scorn. And suddenly, as she gazed at her husband's cold, white features in contempt, she heard Gilbert's voice at her elbow again, chanting the Latin words musically and distinctly, and she turned almost with a movement of anger to see the bold young face saddened and softened by the essence of a profound belief.

"Was I born to love monks!" she sighed half
audibly; but as she looked back at the procession
she started and uttered a low exclamation.

Beside her husband, but a little after him as the
pageant turned, a straight, thin figure came into sight,
clad in a monk's frock scarcely less dazzling white
than the marvellous upturned face. At Eleanor's
exclamation Gilbert also had raised his eyes from the
ground, and they fixed themselves on the wonderful
features of the greatest man of the age, while his
voice forgot to chant and his lips remained parted
in wonder. Upon the bright green grass against
the background of hewn stone walls, in the glorious
autumn sunshine, Bernard of Clairvaux moved like
the supernal vision of a heavenly dream. His head
thrown back, the delicate silver-fair beard scarcely
shadowing the spiritual outlines of an almost divine
face, his soft blue eyes looked upward, filled with a
light not earthly. The transparent brow and the
almost emaciated cheeks were luminously pale, and
seemed to shed a radiance of their own.

But it would have been impossible to say what it
was in the man's form or face that made him so
utterly different and distinct from other men. It
was not alone the Christlike brow, nor the noble
features inherited from a line of heroes; it was not
the ascetic air, the look of bodily suffering, nor
the fine-drawn lines of pain which, as it were,
etched a shadowy background of sorrow upon which
the spiritual supremacy blazed like a rising star:
it was something beyond all these, above name
and out of definition, the halo of saintship, the

glory of genius, the crown of heroism. Of such a man, one's eyes might be filled, and one might say, 'Let him not speak, lest some harsh tone or imperfect speech should pierce the vision with sharp discord, as a rude and sudden sound ends a soft dream.' Yet he was a man who, when he raised his hand to lead, led millions like children; who, when he opened his lips to speak, spoke with the tongue of men and of angels such words as none had spoken before him — words which were the truth made light; one who, when he took pen in hand to write to the world's masters, wrote without fear or fault, as being the scribe of God, but who could pen messages of tenderest love and gentlest counsel to the broken-hearted and the heavy-laden.

Gilbert's eyes followed the still, white glory of the monk's face, till the procession turned in a wide sweep behind the wing of the palace, and even then the tension of his look did not relax. He was still kneeling with fixed gaze when the Queen was standing beside him. The scorn was gone from her lips and had given place to a sort of tender pity. She touched the young man's shoulder twice before he started, looked up, and then sprang to his feet.

"Who is that man?" he asked earnestly.

"Bernard, Abbot of Clairvaux," answered the Queen, looking far away. "I almost worshipped him once, when I was a child, — it is the will of Heaven that I should lose my heart to monks!"

She laughed, as she had laughed from the window.

"Monks?" Gilbert repeated the word with curiosity.

"Are you one of those persons for whom it is necessary to explain everything?" asked Eleanor, still smiling and looking at him intently. "I think you must be half a monk yourself, for I heard you singing the psalms as sweetly as any convent scholar."

"Even if I were not half a monk, but one altogether, I should not wholly understand your Grace's speech;" Gilbert smiled, too, for he was immeasurably far from guessing what was in her mind.

"So I have thought, in all these weeks and days while we have been together."

Her eyes darkened as she looked at him, but his were clear and calm.

"Do you understand this?" she asked, and she laid her two hands upon his shoulders.

"What?" he asked in surprise.

"This," she said, very softly, drawing herself near to him by her hands.

Then he knew, and he would have straightened himself, but her hands sprang to meet each other round his neck, and her face was close to his. But the vision of his own sinful mother rose in her eyes to meet him.

She held him fast, and three times she kissed him before she would let him go.

CHAPTER VIII

GILBERT had reached Paris in the train of Duke
Geoffrey in September; the Christmas bells were ringing when he first caught sight of the walls and towers
of Rome. As he drew rein on the crest of a low hill,
the desolate brown waste of the Campagna stretched
behind him mile upon mile to northward, toward
the impenetrable forests of Viterbo, and Rome was
at last before him. Before him rose the huge half-
ruined walls of Aurelian, battered by Goth and
Saracen and imperial Greek; before him towered the
fortress of Hadrian's tomb, vast, impregnable, fero-
cious. Here and there above the broken crenellation
of the city's battlements rose dark and slender towers,
square and round, marking the places where strong
robbers had fortified themselves within the city.
But from the point where Gilbert halted, Rome
seemed but a long brown ruin, with portions standing whole, as brown as the rest under the bright
depths of vaulted blue, unflecked by the least fleece
of cloud, in the matchless clearness of the winter's
morning. Profound disappointment came upon him
as he looked. With little knowledge and hardly any
information from others who had journeyed by the
same road, he had built himself an imaginary city
of unspeakable beauty, wherein graceful churches
rose out of sunlit streets and fair open places planted

with lordly avenues of trees.   There, in his thoughts,
walked companies of men with faces like the face of
the great Bernard, splendid with innocence, radiant
with the hope of life.   Thither, in his fancy, came the
true knights of the earth, purified of sin by vigils in
the holy places of the East, to renew unbroken vows
of chastity and charity and faith.   There, in his
dream, dwelt the venerable Father of Bishops, the
Vicar of Christ, the successor of Peter, the Servant
of the servants of God, the spotless head of the Holy
Roman Catholic and Apostolic Church.   There, in
his heart, he had made the dwelling of whatsoever
things are upright and just and perfect in heaven,
and pure and beautiful on earth.   That was the city
of God, of which his soul was the architect, and in
which he was to be a dweller, in peace that should
pass understanding.

He had left behind him in Paris another vision
and one that might well have dazzled him — such
favour as falls to few; such hopes as few can plant
in their lives and still fewer can rear to maturity;
such love as few indeed could hope for — the love
of supreme and royal beauty.

When he had ridden out of the castle on the island,
older by some months, richer by such gifts as it was
no shame for him to take of Duke Geoffrey and young
Henry Plantagenet, he had believed himself wiser,
too, by half a lifetime.

He was confident in his own strength, in his own
wisdom, in his own endurance; he fancied that he
had fought against a great temptation, where he had
in truth been chilled and terrified by the haunting

vision of another's evil; he imagined that the little
sharp regret, which stung his heart with longing for the sweetness of a sin that might have
been, was the evil remnant of a passion not wholly
quenched, whereas it was but the craving of a
natural vanity that had not been strong enough to
overcome a repugnance which he himself only half
understood.

He seemed in his own eyes to have made the sacrifice of his worldly future for the sake of his knightly
ideal; but in truth, to a man without ambition, the
renunciation had been easy and had been made in
acquiescence with his real desires, rather than in
opposition to them.

And now he looked upon the city of his hope, and
it crumbled to a dusty ruin under his very hand; he
stood on ground made reverent by the march of history and sanctified by the blood of Christians, and it
was but one great wilderness, of which he himself
was the centre. His heart sank suddenly within him,
and his fingers clutched at the breast of his tunic
under his surcoat, as though the pain were bodily
and real. Long he sat in silence, bending a little
in the saddle, as if worn out with fatigue, though
he had ridden only three hours since daybreak.

"Sir," said his man Dunstan, interrupting his
master's meditations, "here is an inn, and we may
find water for our horses."

Gilbert looked up indifferently, and then, as there
was no near building in sight, he turned inquiringly
to his man. A sardonic smile played on Dunstan's
lean dark face as he pointed to what Gilbert had

taken for three haystacks. They were, indeed, nothing but conical straw huts standing a few steps aside from the road, thirty yards down the hill. The entrance to each was low and dark, and from the one issued wreaths of blue smoke, slowly rising in the still, cold air. At the same entrance a withered bough proclaimed that wine was to be had. A ditch beyond the furthest hut was full of water, and at some distance from it a rude shed of boughs had been set up to afford the horses of travellers some shelter from winter rain or summer sun. As Gilbert looked, a man came out, bowing himself almost double to pass under the low aperture. He wore long goatskin breeches and a brown homespun tunic, like a monk's frock, cut short above the knees, and girdled with a twisted thong. Shaggy black hair thatched his square head, and a thin black beard framed the yellow face, which had the fever-stricken look of the dwellers in the Campagna.

Though this was the first halting-place of the kind to which Gilbert had come in the Roman plain, he was no longer easily surprised by anything, and he did not even smile as he rode forward and dismounted.

Besides his own men he had with him the muleteer who acted as guide and interpreter, and without whom it was impossible for a foreigner to travel in Italy. The peasant bowed to the ground, and led Gilbert to the entrance of the hut where he usually served his customers with food and drink, and in the gloom within Gilbert saw a rough-hewn table and two benches standing upon the well-swept floor of

beaten earth. But the Englishman made signs that
he would sit outside, and the scanty furniture was
brought out into the open air. The third hut was a
refuge and a sleeping-place for travellers overtaken
at nightfall on their way to the city.

"The monk is asleep," said the peasant host, lifting his finger to his lips because Gilbert's men were
talking loud near the entrance.

Gilbert understood as much as that without his
interpreter; for in those days the Provençal tongue
was an accomplishment of all well-born persons, and
it was not unlike certain dialects of Italy.

"A monk?" repeated Gilbert, indifferently.

"He calls himself one, and he wears a grey
frock," answered the other. "But we are glad when
he comes, for he brings us good fortune. And you
may see that I speak the truth, since he came late in
the night, and your lordship is the first guest at the
huts this morning."

"Then you know him well?"

"Every one knows him," answered the man.

He turned, and Gilbert saw him lift up a hurdle
of branches and disappear underground. His cellar
was deep and cool, one of the many caverns which
communicate with the catacombs and riddle the
Campagna from Rome to the hills. Gilbert seated
himself upon the smaller of the two benches at the
end of the table; his three men took the other, and
laid aside their caps out of respect for their master.
The horses were tethered under the shed of boughs
till they should be cool enough to be watered. The
southern side of the hut was sunny and warm, and

the place smelled of dry grass, of clean straw, and, faintly, of smouldering fire.

Gilbert was hardly conscious that he was thinking of anything as he stared out at the rolling waste, folding his hands together upon the hilt of his long sword. Just then a man emerged from the third hut, drew himself up facing the sun, and rubbed his eyes before he looked toward the party at the other table. When he saw them, he hesitated for a moment, and then came up to Gilbert with the apparent intention of addressing him.

Above the height of average men, the figure looked unnaturally tall by its gauntness, and the heavy folds of the grey woollen frock fell together below the breast as if they covered a shadow. Long, bony hands, that seemed woven of sinews and leather, but which were not without a certain nervous refinement, hung from loose-jointed brown wrists left bare by sleeves that were too short. The head was so roughly angular that even the thick masses of dark brown hair which fell to the shoulders could not make the angles seem like curves, and the face displayed the fervent features of a fanatic — dark, hollow cheeks, deep-sunk, blazing eyes, the vast lines of an ascetic mouth, a great jaw scarcely fringed by the scant black beard. Gilbert saw before him a face and figure that might have belonged to a hermit of Egypt, an ascetic of the Syrian desert, a John the Baptist, an Anthony of Thebes. The man wore a broad leathern girdle; a blackened rosary, with beads as large as walnuts, hung from his side and ended in a rough cross of wrought iron.

Gilbert half rose from his seat, moved to one end of the short bench, and invited the stranger to sit beside him. The monk bent his head slightly, but not a feature moved as he took the proffered place in silence. He folded his great hands on the edge of the rough-hewn board and stared at the ruinous brown city to southward.

"You are a stranger," he said in Provençal, after a long pause and in a singularly musical voice, but without turning his eyes to Gilbert.

"I have never seen Rome before," answered Gilbert.

"Rome!" There was a sort of almost heartbroken pity in the tone of the single syllable that fell from the lips of the wandering monk.

"You have never seen Rome before? There it lies, all that is left of it — the naked bones of the most splendid, the most beautiful, the most powerful city in the world, murdered by power, done to death by popes and emperors, by prefects and barons, sapped of life by the evil canker of empire, and left there like a dead dog in the Campagna, to be a prey to carrion beasts and a horror to living men."

The gaunt stranger set his elbows upon the table and bit his nails savagely, while his burning eyes fixed themselves on the distant towers of Rome. Then Gilbert saw that this man was no common wandering friar, begging a meal for his frock's sake, but one who had thoughts of his own, and with whom to think was to suffer.

"It is true," said Gilbert, "that Rome is less fair to see than I had supposed."

"And you are deceived of your hopes before you
have entered her gate," returned the other. "Are
you the first? Are you the last? Has Rome made
an end of deceiving, and found the termination of
disappointment? Rome has deceived and disappointed the world. Rome has robbed the world of
its wealth, and devoured it, and grown gaunt to the
bone. Rome has robbed men of their bodies and of
their lives, and has torn them limb from limb wantonly, as a spoiled hawk tears a pheasant and scatters
the bright feathers on the ground. Rome has robbed
men of their souls and has fed hell with them to its
surfeit. And now, in her turn, her grasping hands
have withered at the wrists, her insatiable lips are
cracking upon her loosening teeth, and the mistress
of the world is the sport of Jews and usurers."

"You speak bitterly," said Gilbert, looking curiously at his new acquaintance.

The monk sighed, and his eyes softened wonderfully as he turned to the young man. He had been
speaking in a tone that slowly rose to shrillness, like
a cry of bodily pain. When he spoke again his voice
was low and sweet.

"Bitterly, but for her sake, not for mine," he said.
"If I have given my life for her, she will not give
me hers. Though I have laid at her feet all that I
had, she shall put nothing into my hand nor give me
anything but a ditch and a handful of earth for my
bones, unless some emperor or pope shall leave them
upon a gallows. But I have asked of her, for herself and her own sake, that she should do by herself
honourably, and draw her neck from the yoke and

shake off the burdens under which she has stumbled
and fallen. I have asked of her to stand upright
again, to refuse to eat from the hand that has
wounded her, and not to hearken to the voice of
violence and cursing. I have asked that Rome
should cast out the Stranger Emperor, and cast down
the churchman from the king's throne, and take
from him the king's mask. I have asked Rome
to face her high robbers whom she calls barons,
her corruption, her secret weakness, as a brave man
faces his sins and confesses them and steadfastly
purposes to offend God no more. All this I have
asked, and in part she has heard; and I have paid
the price of my asking, for I am an outcast of many
kingdoms and a man excommunicated under the
Major Interdiction."

A gentle smile, that might have been half indifference, half pity, wreathed the ascetic lips as he spoke
the last words. They were not empty words in those
days, and unawares Gilbert shrank a little from his
companion.

"I see that you are a devout person," said the friar,
quietly. "Let my presence not offend you at your
meal. I go my way."

But as he began to rise, Gilbert's hand went out,
and his fingers met round the skeleton arm in the
loose grey sleeve.

"Stay, sir," he said, "and break your fast with
us. I am not such a one as you think."

"You shrank from me," said the stranger, hesitating to resume his seat.

"I meant no discourtesy," answered Gilbert. "Be

seated, sir. You call yourself an outcast. I am but
little better than a wanderer, disinherited of his own."

"And come you hither for the Pope's justice?"
asked the friar, scornfully. "There is no Pope in
Rome. Our last was killed at the head of a band of
fighting men, on the slope of the Capitol, last year,
and he who is Pope now is as much a wanderer as
you and I. And in Rome we have a Republic and
a Senate, and justice of a kind, but only for Romans,
and claiming no dominion over mankind ; for to be
free means to set free, to live means to let live."

"I shall see what this freedom of yours is like,"
said Gilbert, thoughtfully. "For my part I am not
used to such thoughts, and though I have read some
history of Rome, I could never understand the Roman
Republic. With us the strongest is master by natural
law. Why should the strong man share with the
weak what he may keep for himself? Or if he must,
in your ideal, then why should not the strong nation
share her strength and wealth with her weak neighbour? Is it not enough that the strong should not
wantonly bruise the weak nor deal unfairly by him?
The Normans can see no more harm or injustice in
holding than we see in taking what we can ; and
so we shall never understand your republics and
your senates."

"Are you a Norman, sir?" asked the friar. "Are
you a kinsman of Guiscard and of them that last
burnt Rome? I do not wonder that the civilization
of a republic should seem strange to you!"

Gilbert was listening, but his eyes had wandered
from the friar's face in the direction of the dusty road

that led to Rome, and between his companion's words
his quick ear had caught the sound of hoofs, although
no horses were yet in sight but his own. Just as
the friar ceased speaking, however, a troop of seven
riders appeared at the turn of the road. They were
rough-looking men in long brown cloaks that were
in tatters at the edge; they wore round caps of mail
on their heads, with a broad leathern strap under the
chin; their faces were dark, their beards black and
unkempt, and they rode small, ragged horses, as ill
cared for as themselves.

Gilbert sprang up almost as soon as he saw them,
for he knew that, not being travellers, they could
hardly be anything but highwaymen. His own men
were on their feet as soon as he, while the muleteer
guide disappeared round the hut quietly and swiftly,
like a mouse when a cat is in sight. Gilbert made
straight for his horses, followed by Dunstan and the
groom; but before he could reach them, two of the
riders had jumped the ditch from the road and inter-
cepted him, while the others rode on toward the shed
to carry off his horses. His sword was out in a flash,
his men were beside him, their weapons in their
hands, and the grimy riders drew theirs also; it was
like a little storm of steel in the bright air. The
Englishman's long blade whirled half a circle above
his head; the blow would beat down the horseman's
guard and draw blood, too.

But in mid-air his wrist was seized in the sudden
grasp of sinewy fingers, and the friar was already
between him and his adversary, warning the other
off with his outstretched hand. The loose sleeve had

slipped back from his wrist, baring a brown, emaciated arm and elbow upon which the swollen veins seemed to twist and climb like leafless vines upon a withered tree. His lips were white, his eyes blazed, and his voice was suddenly harsh and commanding.

"Back!" he cried, almost savagely.

To Gilbert's very great astonishment, the single word produced an instantaneous and wonderful effect. The riders lowered their weapons, looked at one another, and then sheathed them; the others, who were loosing Gilbert's horses and mules, suddenly desisted at the sound of the friar's voice. Then the one nearest to Gilbert, who was a shade less grimy than the rest, and who wore in his cap a feather from a pheasant's tail, slipped to the ground, and bending low under his tattered brown cloak, took the hem of the monk's frock in his right hand and kissed it fervently. Gilbert stood aside, leaning upon his unsheathed sword, and his wonder grew as he looked on.

"We ask your pardon, Fra Arnoldo," cried the chief, still kneeling. "How could we guess that you were breakfasting out here this morning? We thought you far in the north."

"And therefore thought yourselves free to rob strangers and steal cattle, and cut one anothers' throats?"

"This is probably a part of the civilization of a republic," observed Gilbert, with a smile.

But the highwaymen, all dismounted now, came crowding to the feet of Arnold of Brescia in profound, if not lasting, contrition, and they begged a blessing of the excommunicated monk.

CHAPTER IX

GILBERT lodged at the sign of the Lion, over against the tower of Nona, by the bridge of Sant' Angelo. The inn was as old as the times of Charlemagne, when it had been named in honour of Pope Leo, who had crowned him emperor. But the quarter was at that time in the hands of the great Jewish race of Pierleoni, whose first antipope, Anacletus, had not been dead many years, and who, though they still held the castle and many towers and fortresses in Rome, had not succeeded in imposing the antipope Victor upon the Roman people, against the will of Bernard of Clairvaux.

Rome lay along the river, in those days, like wreckage and scum thrown up on the shore of a wintry sea. Some twenty thousand human beings were huddled together in smoky huts, most of which were built against the outer walls and towers of the nobles' strongholds — a miserable population, living squalidly in terrible times, starving while the nobles fought with one another, rising now and then like a vision of famine and sword to take back by force the right of life which force had almost taken from them. Gilbert wandered through the crooked, unpaved streets, in and out of gloomy courts and over desolate wastes and open places, the haunts of ravenous dogs and homeless cats that kept themselves alive on the choice pickings of the city's garbage. He went armed and followed by his men, as he saw that other gentlemen of his condition did, and when he knelt in a church to hear mass or to say a prayer, he was careful to kneel with his back to the wall or to a pillar, lest some light-handed worshipper should set a razor to his wallet strings or his sword-belt.

At his inn, too, he lived in a state of armed defence against every one, including the host and the other guests; and the weekly settlement was a weekly battle between Dunstan, who paid his master's scores, the little Tuscan interpreter, and Ser Clemente, the innkeeper, in which the Tuscan had the most uncomfortable position, finding himself placed buffer-like between the honest man and the thief, and exposed to equally hard hitting from both. Rome was poor and dirty and a den of thieves, murderers, and all malefactors, dominated alternately by a family of half-converted Jews, who terrorized the city from strong points of vantage, and then, on other days, by the mob that followed Arnold of Brescia when he appeared in the city, and who would have torn down stone walls with their bare hands at his merest words, as they would have faced the barons' steel with naked breast. At such times men left their tasks — the shoemaker his last, the smith his anvil, the crooked tailor his bench — to follow the northern monk to the Capitol, or to some church where he was to speak to them; and after the men came the women, and after the women the children, all drawn along by the mysterious attraction which they could neither understand nor resist. The tramping of many feet made a dull bass to the sound of many

human voices, high and low, crying out lustily for
'Arnold, a Senate, and the Roman Republic'; and
then taking up the song of the day, which was a
ballad of liberty, in a long minor chant that broke
into a jubilant major in the burden — the sort of
song the Romans have always made in time of change,
the kind of ballad that goes before the end of a kingdom, like a warning voice of fate.

On such days, when the mob went howling and
singing after its idol, southwards to the Capitol
or even to the far Lateran where Marcus Aurelius
sat upon his bronze horse watching the ages go by,
then Gilbert loved to wander in the opposite direction, across the castle bridge and under the haunted
battlements of Sant' Angelo, where evil Theodora's
ghost walked on autumn nights when the south wind
blew, and through the long wreck of the fair portico
that had once extended from the bridge to the basilica,
till he came to the broad flight of steps leading to the
walled garden-court of old Saint Peter's. There he
loved to sit musing among the cypresses, wondering
at the vast bronze pine-cone and the great brass peacocks which Symmachus had brought thither from
the ruins of Agrippa's baths, wherein the terrible
Crescenzi had fortified themselves during more than
a hundred years. Sitting there alone, while Dunstan puzzled his uncertain learning over deep-cut
inscriptions of long ago, and Alric, the groom, threw
his dagger at a mark on one of the cypress trees, hundreds of times in succession, and rarely missing his
aim, Gilbert felt, in the silence he loved, that the soul
of Rome had taken hold of his soul, and that in Rome

it was good to live for the sake of dreaming, and that
dreaming itself was life. The past, with his mother's
sins, his own sorrows, the friendship of the boy
Henry, the love of Queen Eleanor, were all infinitely
far removed and dim. The future, once the magic
mirror in which he had seen displayed the glory of
knightly deeds which he was to do, was taken up
like a departing vision into the blue Roman sky.
Only the present remained, the idle, thoughtful,
half-narcotic present, with a mazy charm no man
could explain, since so far as any bodily good was
concerned there was less comfort to be got for
money, more fever to be taken for nothing, and a
larger element of danger in everyday life in Rome
than in any city Gilbert had traversed in his wander-
ings. Yet he lingered and loved it rather for what
it denied him than for what it gave him, for the
thoughts it called up rather than for the sights it
offered, for that in it which was unknown, and therefore dear to dwell upon, rather than for the sadness
and the darkness and the evil that all men might
feel.

But through all he felt, and in all he saw, welding
and joining the whole together, there was the still
fervour of that something which he had at first known
in Sheering Abbey — something to which every fibre
of his nature responded, and which, indeed, was
the mainspring of the world in that age. For devotion was then more needful than bread, and it profited
a man more to fight against unbelievers for his
soul's sake than to wear hollows in altar-steps with
his knees, or to forget his own name and put off

his own proper character and being, as a nameless
unit in a great religious order.

At first the enormous disappointment of Rome had
saddened and hurt him. He had fancied that where
there was no head there could be no house, that
where the leader was gone the army must scatter
and be hewn in pieces. But as he stayed on, from
week to week and from month to month, he learned
to understand that the Church had never been more
alive, more growing, and more militant than at that
very time when the true and rightful pontiffs were
made outcasts one after the other, while their places,
earthly and spiritual, were given to instruments of
feud and party. For the Church was the world,
while Rome meant seven or eight thousand half-
starved and turbulent ruffians, with their wives and
children, eager always for change, because it seemed
that no change could be for the worse.

But in the ancient basilica of Saint Peter there was
peace; there the white-haired priests solemnly offici-
ated in the morning and at noon, and toward evening
more than a hundred rich voices of boys and men
sang the vesper psalms in the Gregorian tones;
there slim youths in violet and white swung silver
censers before the high altar, and the incense floated
in rich clouds upon the sunbeams that fell slanting
to the ancient floor ; there, as in many a minster
and cloister of the world, the Church was still herself, as she was, and is, and always will be; there
words were spoken and solemn prayers intoned which
had been familiar to the lips of the Apostles, which
are familiar to our lips and ears to-day, and of

which we are sure that lips unborn will repeat
them to centuries of generations. Gilbert, type of
Christian layman, kneeled in the old cathedral, and
chanted softly after the choir, and breathed the
incense-laden air that seemed as natural to him as
ever the hay-scented breeze of summer had been, and
he was infinitely refreshed in soul and body. But
then again, alone in his room at the Lion Inn, late
in the night, when he had been poring over the
beautifully written copy of Boëthius, given him by
the Abbot of Sheering, he often opened wide the
wooden shutters of his window and looked out at
the castle and at the flowing river that eddied and
gleamed in the moonlight. Then life rose before
him in a mystery for him to solve by deeds, and he
knew that he was not to dream out his years in the
shadowy city, and the strong old instinct of his race
bade him go forth and cut his fortune out of the
world's flank alive. Then his blood rose in his
throat, and his hands hardened one upon the other,
as he leaned over the stone sill and drew the night
air sharply between his closed teeth; and he resolved
then to leave Rome and to go on in search of strange
lands and masterful deeds. On such nights, when
the wind blew down the river in the spring, it brought
to him all the hosts of fancy, spirit armies, ghostly
knights, and fairy maidens, and the forecast shadows
of things to come. There was a tragic note, also;
for on his right, as he looked, there rose the
dark tower of Nona, and from the highest turret he
could clearly see in the moonlight how the long
rain-bleached rope hung down and swayed in the

breeze, and the noose at the end of it softly knocked
upon the tower wall; more than once, also, when he
had looked out in the morning, he had seen a corpse
hanging there by the neck, stiff and staring and wet
with dew.

But when the spring day dawned and the birds
sang at his window, and when, looking out, he felt
the breath of the sweet south and saw that Rome
smiled again, then his resolutions failed, and instead
of bidding Dunstan pack his armour and his fine
clothes for a journey, he made his men mount and
ride with him to the far regions of the city. Often
he loitered away the afternoon in the desolate regions
of the Aventine, riding slowly from one lonely
church to another, and sometimes spending an hour
in conversation with a solitary priest who, by living
much alone and among inscriptions and old carvings,
had gathered a little more learning than was common
among the unlettered Romans.

He met with no adventures; for though the high-
ways in the country swarmed with robbers always
on the watch for a merchant's train or for a rich
traveller, yet within the city's limits, small as was
the authority of the Senate and of the Prefect, thieves
dared not band together in numbers, and no two or
three of them would have cared to come to blows
with Gilbert and his men.

Nor did he make friends in Rome. His first intention had been to present himself to the principal
baron in the city, as a traveller of good birth, and
to request the advantages of friendship and protection; and so he would have done in any other

European city. But he had soon learned that Rome
was far behind the rest of the world in the social
practices of chivalry, and that in placing himself
under a Roman baron's protection he would, to all
intents and purposes, be taking service instead of
accepting hospitality. Even so, he might have been
willing to take such a position for the sake of adven-
ture; yet he could by no means make up his mind
to a choice between the half-Jewish Pierleoni and
the rough-mannered Frangipani. To the red-handed
Crescenzi he would not go; the Colonna of that time
were established on the heights of Tusculum, and the
Orsini, friends to the Pope, had withdrawn to distant
Galera, in the fever-haunted marsh northwest of Rome.

But here and there he made the acquaintance of
a priest or a monk whose learned conversation har-
monized with his thoughts and helped the grave
illusion in which — perhaps out of sheer idleness —
he loved to think himself back in the abbey in England. And so he led a life unlike the lives around
him, and many of the people in the quarter learned
to know him by sight, and called him and his
men 'the English'; and as most of the people of
Rome were very much occupied with their own
affairs, chiefly evil, Gilbert was allowed to live as
he pleased. But for the fact that even his well-filled
purse must in the course of time be exhausted, he
might have spent the remainder of his life in the
Lion Inn, by the bridge, carelessly meditative and
simply happy. But other forces were at work to
guide his life into other channels, and he had reckoned ill when he had fancied, being himself unmoved,

that the love of such a woman as Queen Eleanor was
a mere incident without consequence, forgotten like
a flower of last year's blossoming.

Several times during the winter and in the spring
that followed, the friar Arnold came to see him in
his lodgings and talked of the great things that were
coming, of the redemption of man from man by the
tearing down of all sovereign power, whether of pope
or 'emperor, or king or prince, to make way for the
millennium of a universal republic. Then the fanatic's burning eyes flashed like beacons, his long arms
made sudden and wild gestures, his soft brown hair
stood from his head as though lifted by a passing
breeze, and his whole being was transfigured in the
flash of his own eloquence. When he spoke to
the Romans with that voice and with that look,
they rose quickly to a tumult, as the sea under a
gale, and he could guide them in their storming to
ends of destruction and terror. But there was no
drop of southern blood in Gilbert's veins nor anything to which the passionate Italian's eloquence
appealed. Instead of catching fire, he argued; instead of joining Arnold in his attempt to turn the
world into a republic, he was more and more persuaded of the excellence of all he had left behind him
in the north. He incarnated that aristocratic temper
which has in all times, since Duke William crossed
the water, leavened the strong mass of the Anglo-
Saxon character, balancing its rude democratic
strength with the keenness of a higher physical
organization and the nobility of a more disinterested
daring, and again and again rousing the English-

speaking races to life and conquest, when they were
sunk deep in the sordid interests of trade and money-
making. So when Arnold talked of laws and insti-
tutions which should again make Rome the mistress
of the world, Gilbert answered him by talking of
men who had the strength to take the world and to
be its masters and make it obey whatsoever laws
they saw fit to impose. Between the two there was
the everlasting difference between theory and action;
and though it chanced that just then Arnold, the
dreamer, was in the lead of change and revolution,
while Gilbert, the fighter, was idling away weeks
and months in a dream, yet the fact was the same,
and in manly strength and inward simplicity of
thought Gilbert Warde, the Norman, was far nearer
to the man who made Rome imperial than was the
eloquent Italian who built the mistress city of his
thoughts out of ideas and theories, carved and
hewn into shapes of beauty by the tremendous tools
of his wit and his words. At the root of the great
difference between the two there was on the one side
the Norman's centralization of the world in himself,
as being for himself, and on the other the Latin's
power and readiness to forget himself in the imagi-
nations of an ideal state.

"Men are talking of a second Crusade," said
Arnold, one day, when he and Gilbert had chanced
to meet in the garden court of Saint Peter's.

Gilbert was standing with his back against one of
the cypress trees, watching the fiery monk with
thoughtful eyes.

"They talk of Crusades," said Arnold, stopping

"THE WORD ON THEIR LIPS IS CHRIST"

to face the young man. "They talk of sending hundreds of thousands of Christian men to die every death under God's sun in Palestine — for what? To save men? To lift up a race? To plant good, that good may grow? They go for none of those things. The sign on their breasts is the cross; the word on their lips is Christ; the thought in their hearts is the thought of all your ruthless race — to take from others and add to your own stores; to take land, wealth, humanity, life, everything that can be taken from conquered man before he is left naked to die."

Gilbert did not smile, for he was wondering whether there were not some truth in the monk's accusation.

"Do you say this because Norman men hold half of your Italy?" he asked gravely. "Have they held it well or ill?"

"Ill," answered Arnold, fixing his eyes sharply on Gilbert's face. "But that is not the matter; some of them have helped me, too. There are good men and bad among Normans, as among Saracens."

"I thank you," said Gilbert, smiling now, in spite of himself.

"The devils also believe and tremble," retorted Arnold, grimly quoting. "The taking of the South proves my words; it is not half my meaning. Men take the cross and give their lives for a name, a tradition, the sacred memories of a holy place. They will not give a week of their lives, a drop of their blood, for their fellow-men, nor for the beliefs that alone can save the world."

"And what are those beliefs?" asked Gilbert.

Arnold paused before he replied, and then as he lifted his face, it was full of light.

"Faith, Hope, Charity," he answered, and then, as his head drooped with a sudden look of hopelessness, he turned away with slow steps toward the great gate.

Gilbert did not change his position as he looked after him rather sadly. The man's perfect simplicity, his eagerness for the most lofty ideals, the spotless purity of his life, commanded Gilbert's most true admiration. And yet to the Norman, Arnold of Brescia was but a dreamer, a visionary, and a madman. Gilbert could listen to him for a while, but then the terrible tension of the friar's thought and speech wearied him. Just now he was almost glad that his companion should depart so suddenly; but as he watched him he saw him stop, as if he had forgotten something, and then turn back, searching for some object in the bosom of his frock.

"I had forgotten what brought me here," said the friar, producing a small roll of parchment tied and bound together with thin leathern laces, and tied again with a string of scarlet silk to which was fastened a heavy leaden seal. "I have here a letter for you."

"A letter!" Gilbert showed a not unnatural surprise. He had never received a letter in his life, and in those days persons of ordinary importance rarely sent or received messages except by word of mouth.

"I went to your lodging," replied the monk, handing Gilbert the parchment. "I guessed that I might find you here, where we have met before."

"I thank you," said Gilbert, turning the roll over in his hands as if hardly knowing what to do. "How came you by this?"

"Last night there arrived messengers from France," answered Arnold, "bringing letters for the Senate and for me, and with them was this, which the messenger said had been delivered into his hand by the Queen of France, who had commanded him to find out the person to whom it was addressed, and had promised him a reward if he should succeed. I therefore told him that I would give it to you."

Gilbert was looking at the seal. The heavy disk of lead through which the silken strings had been drawn was as large as the bottom of a drinking-cup and was stamped with the device of Aquitaine; doubtless the very one used by Duke William, for it bore the figures of Saint George and the Dragon. which Eleanor was afterwards to hand down to English kings to this day. Gilbert tried to pull the silk cord through the lead, but the blow that had struck the die had crushed and jammed them firmly.

"Cut it," suggested the friar, and his ascetic face relaxed in a smile.

Gilbert drew his dagger, which was a serviceable blade, half an ell long, and as broad as a man's three fingers under the straight cross-hilt, and as sharp as a razor on both edges, for Dunstan was a master at whetting. Gilbert cut the string and then the laces, and slipped the seal into his wallet, unrolling the stiff sheet till he found a short writing, some six or eight lines, not covering half the page, and signed, 'Eleanora R.'

But when he had opened the letter he saw that it was not to be read easily. Nevertheless, his eye lighted almost at once upon the name which of all others he should not have expected to find there, 'Beatrix.' There was no mistaking the letters, and presently he found them once again, and soon after that the sense was clear to him.

'If this reach you,' it said, in moderately fair Latin, 'greeting. I will that you make haste and come again to our castle in Paris, both because you shall at all times be welcome, and more especially now, and quickly, because the noble maiden Beatrix de Curboil is now at this court among my ladies, and is in great hope of seeing you, since she has left her father to be under my protection. Moreover, Bernard, the abbot, is preaching the Cross in Chartres and other places, and is coming here before long, and to Vézelay. Beatrix greets you.'

"Can you tell me where I can find the messenger who brought you this?" asked Gilbert, looking up when he had at last deciphered every word.

But Arnold was gone. The idea that an acquaintance whom he had been endeavouring to convert to republican doctrines should be in correspondence with one of those sovereigns against whom he so bitterly inveighed had finally disgusted him, and he had gone his way, if not in wrath, at least in displeasure. Seeing himself alone, Gilbert shrugged his shoulders indifferently, and began to walk up and down, reading the letter over and over. It was very short, but yet it contained so much information that he found some difficulty in adjusting his thoughts to

what was an entirely new situation, and one which
no amount of thinking could fully explain. He was
far too simple to suppose that Eleanor had called
Beatrix to her court solely for the sake of bringing
him back to Paris. He therefore imagined the most
complicated and absurd reasons for Queen Eleanor's
letter.

He told himself that he must have been mistaken
from beginning to end; that the Queen had never felt
anything except friendship for him, but a friendship
far deeper and more sincere than he had realized;
and he was suddenly immensely grateful to her for
her wish to build up happiness in his life. But
then, again, she knew as well as he — or as well as
he thought he knew — that the Church would not
easily consent to his union with Beatrix, and as he
closed his eyes and recalled scenes of which the
memories were still vivid and clear, the shadow that
had chilled his heart in Paris rose again between
him and Eleanor's face, and he distrusted her, and
her kiss and her letter, and her motives. Then, too,
it seemed very strange to him that Beatrix should
have left her father's house; for Arnold de Curboil
had always loved her, and it did not occur to Gilbert that his own mother had made the girl's life
intolerable. He was to learn that later, and when
he knew it, he tasted the last and bitterest dregs of
all. Nevertheless, he could not reasonably doubt
the Queen's word; he was positively certain that
he should find Beatrix at the French court, and from
the first he had not really hesitated about leaving at once. It seemed to be the only possible

course, though it was diametrically opposed to all the good resolutions which had of late flitted through his dreams like summer moths.

On the next day but one, early in the spring morning, Gilbert and his men rode slowly down the desolate Via Lata, and under Aurelian's arch, past the gloomy tomb of Augustus on the left, held by the Count of Tusculum, and out at last upon the rolling Campagna, northward, by the old Flaminian Way.

CHAPTER X

JUNE was upon Italy, as a gossamer veil and a garland on the brow of a girl bride. The first sweet hay was drying in Tuscan valleys; the fig leaves were spreading, and shadowing the watery fruit that begins to grow upon the crooked twigs before the leaves themselves, and which the people call "fig-blossoms," because the real figs come later; the fresh and silvery olive shoots had shed a snow-flurry of small white stars; the yellow holy thorn still blossomed in the rough places of the hills, and the blending of many wild flowers was like a maiden blush on the earth's soft bosom.

At early morning Gilbert rode along the crest of a low and grassy hill that was still sheltered from the sun by the high mountains to eastward, and he drank in the cool and scented air as if it had been water of paradise, and he a man saved out of death to life by the draught. There was much peace in his heart, and a still security that he had not felt yet since he had seen his father lying dead before him. He knew not how it was, but he was suddenly sure that Beatrix loved him and had escaped to the court of France in the hope of finding him, and was waiting for him day by day. And he was also sure that the Church would not cut him off from her in the end, let the

123

churchmen say what they would. Was not the Queen of France his friend? She would plead his case, and the Pope would understand and take away the bar. He thought of these things, and he felt his hopes rising bright, like the steady sun.

He reached the end of the crest and drew rein before descending, and he looked down into the broad valley and the river winding in and out among trees, gleaming like silver out there in the sun beyond the narrowing shadow, then dark blue, and then, in places, as black as ink. The white road, broad and dusty, winding on to Florence, followed the changing river. Gilbert took his cap from his head and felt the coolness of the morning on his forehead and the gentle breath of the early summer in his fair hair; and then, sitting there in the deep silence, bareheaded, it seemed to him that he was in the very holy place of God's cathedral.

"The peace of God, which passeth all understanding," he repeated softly and almost involuntarily.

"Now the God of peace be with you all, amen," answered Dunstan.

But there was a tone in his voice that made Gilbert look at him, and he saw in the man's face a quiet smile, as if something amused him, while the black eyes were fixed on a sight far away. Dunstan was pointing to what he saw; so Gilbert looked, too, and he perceived a gleaming, very far off, that moved slowly on the white road beside the shining river.

"They are expecting a fight to-day," said Gilbert, "for they are in mail and their mule-train is behind them."

"Shall we turn aside and ride up the mountain, to let them pass?" asked Dunstan, who could fight like a wildcat, but had also the cat's instinctive caution.

"It would be a pity not to see the fight," answered Gilbert, and he began to ride forward down the descent.

The track was worn down to the depth of a man's height by the hoofs of the beasts that had trodden it for ages; and in places it was very narrow, so that two laden mules could hardly pass each other. Young chestnut shoots of three or four years' growth sprang up in thick green masses from the top of the bank on each side, and now and then the branches of nut trees almost joined their broad leaves across the way, making a deep shade that was cool and smelt of fresh mould and green things. A little way down the hill a spring of water trickled into a little pool hollowed out by travellers, and the water overflowed and made thick black mud of the earth churned up with last year's dead leaves.

Gilbert let his horse stop to drink, and his men waited in single file to take their turn.

"Psst!" The peculiar hiss which Italians make to attract attention came sharp and distinct from the low growth of the chestnut shoots.

Gilbert turned his head quickly in the direction of the sound. A swarthy face appeared, framed in a close leathern cap on which small rings of rusty iron were sewn strongly, but not very regularly. Then a long left arm, clad in the same sort of mail, pushed the lower boughs aside and made a gesture in the direction whence Gilbert had come, which was meant to warn him back — a gesture of the flat hand, held across the breast with thumb hidden, just moving a little up and down.

"Why should I go back?" asked Gilbert, in his natural voice.

"Because yes," answered the dark man, in the common Italian idiom, and in a low tone. "Because we are waiting for the Florentines, certain of us of Pistoja, and we want no travellers in the way. And then — because, if you will not — "

The right arm suddenly appeared, and in the hand was a spear, and the act was a threat to run Gilbert through, unmailed as he was, and just below his adversary. But as Gilbert laid his hand upon his sword, looking straight at the man's eye, he very suddenly saw a strange sight; for there was a long arrow sticking through the head, the point out on one side and the feather on the other; and for a moment the man still looked at him with eyes wide open. Then, standing as he was, his body slowly bent forward upon itself as if curling up, and with a crash of steel it rolled down the bank into the pool of water, where the lance snapped under it.

For little Alric, the Saxon groom, had quietly slipped to the ground and had strung his bow, suspecting trouble, and had laid an arrow to the string, waiting; and little Alric's aim was very sure; it was also the first time that he had shot a man, and he came of men who had been bowmen since Alfred's day, and before that, and had killed many, for generations, so that it was an instinct with them to slay with the bow.

"Well done, boy!" cried Gilbert.

But his horse reared back, as the dead body fell splashing into the pool, and Alric quietly unstrung his bow again and remounted to be ready. Then, Gilbert would have ridden on, but Dunstan hindered him.

"This fellow was but a sentinel," he said. "A little further on you will find these woods filled with armed men waiting to surprise the riders we saw from above. Surely, I will die with you, sir; but we need not die like rats in a corn-bin. Let us ride up a little way again, and then skirt the woods and take the road where it joins the river, down in the valley."

"And warn those men of Florence that they are riding into an ambush," added Gilbert, turning his horse.

So they rode up the hill; and scarcely were they out of sight of the spring when a very old woman and a ragged little boy crept out of the bushes, with knives, and began to rob the dead man of his rusty mail and his poor clothes.

Gilbert reached the road a long stone's-throw beyond the last chestnut shoots, and galloped forward to meet the advancing knights and men-at-arms. He drew rein suddenly, a dozen lengths before them, and threw up his open right hand. They were riding leisurely, but all in mail, some having surcoats with devices embroidered thereon, and most of them with their heads uncovered, their steel caps and hoods of mail hanging at their saddle-bows.

"Sirs," cried Gilbert, in a loud, clear voice, "you

ride to an ambush! The chestnut woods are full of
the men of Pistoja."

A knight who rode in front, and was the leader,
came close to Gilbert. He was a man not young,
with a dark, smooth face, as finely cut as a relief
carved upon a shell, and his hair was short and iron-
grey.

Gilbert told him what had happened in the woods,
and the elderly knight listened quietly and thoughtfully, while examining Gilbert's face with half-
unconscious keenness.

"If you please," said the young man, "I will
lead you by the way I have ridden, and you may
enter the bushes from above, and fight at better
advantage."

But the Florentine smiled at such simple tactics.
To feel the breeze, he held up his right hand, which
issued from a slit in the wrist of his mail, so that
the iron mitten hung loose; and the wind was blowing toward the woods. He called to his squire.

"Take ten men, light torches, and set fire to
those young trees."

The men got a cook's earthenware pot of coals,
fed all day long with charcoal on the march, lest
there should be no fire for the camp at night; and
they lit torches of pitched hemp-rope, and presently
there was a great smoke and a crackling of green
branches. But the leader of the Florentines put on
his steel cap and drew the mail hood down over his
shoulders, while all the others who were bareheaded
did the same.

"Sir," said the knight to Gilbert, "you should

withdraw behind us, now that you have done us this great service. For presently there will be fighting here, and you are unmailed."

"The weather is overwarm for an iron coat," answered Gilbert, with a laugh. "But if I shall not trespass upon the courtesies of your country by thrusting my company upon you, I will ride at your left hand, that you may the more safely slay with your right."

"Sir," answered the other, "you are a very courteous man. Of what country may you be?"

"An Englishman, sir, and of Norman blood." He also told his name.

"Gino Buondelmonte, at your service," replied the knight, naming himself.

"Nay, sir," laughed Gilbert, "a knight cannot serve a simple squire!"

"It is never shame for gentle-born to serve gentle-born," answered the other.

But now the smoke was driving the men of Pistoja out of the wood, and the hillside down which Gilbert had ridden was covered with men in mail, on horseback, and with footmen in leather and such poor armour as had been worn by the dead sentinel. Buondelmonte thrust his feet home in his wide stirrups, settled himself in the saddle, shortened his reins, and drew his sword, while watching all the time the movements of the enemy. Gilbert sat quietly watching them, too. As yet he had never ridden at a foe, though he had fought on foot, and he unconsciously smiled with pleasure at the prospect, trying to pick out the man likely to fall by his sword. In England, or in France, he would certainly have put on the good mail which was packed on the sumpter mule's back; but here in the sweet Italian spring, in the morning breeze full of the scent of wild flowers, and the humming of bees and the twittering of little birds, even fighting had a look of harmless play, and he felt as secure in his cloth tunic as if it had been of woven steel.

The position of the Florentines was the better, for they had the broad homeward road behind them, in case of defeat; but the men of Pistoja, driven from the woods by the thick smoke and the burning of the undergrowth, were obliged to scramble down a descent so steep that many of them were forced to dismount, and they then found themselves huddled together in a narrow strip of irregular meadow between the road and the foot of the stony hill. Buondelmonte saw his advantage. His sword shot up at arm's length over his head, and his high, clear voice rang out in a single word of command.

In a moment the peace of nature was rent by the scream of war. Hoofs thundered, swords flashed, men yelled, and arrows shot through the great cloud of dust that rose suddenly as from an explosion. In the front of the charge the Italian and the Norman rode side by side, the inscrutable black eyes and the calm olive features beside the Norman's terrible young figure, with its white glowing face and fair hair streaming on the wind, and wide, deep eyes like blue steel, and the quivering nostrils of the man born for fight.

Short was the strife and sharp, as the Florentines

spread to right and left of their leader and pressed the foe back against the steep hill in the narrow meadow. Then Buondelmonte thrust out straight and sure, in the Italian fashion, and once the mortal wound was in the face, and once in the throat, and many times men felt it in their breasts through mail and gambison and bone. But Gilbert's great strokes flashed like lightnings from his pliant wrist, and behind the wrist was the Norman arm, and behind the arm the relentless pale face and the even lips, that just tightened upon each other as the death-blows went out, one by one, each to its place in a life. The Italian destroyed men skilfully and quickly, yet as if it were distasteful to him. The Norman slew like a bright destroying angel, breathing the swift and silent wrath of God upon mankind.

Blow upon blow, with clash of steel, thrust after thrust as the darting of serpents, till the dead lay in heaps, and the horses' hoofs churned blood and grass to a green-red foam, till the sword-arm waited high and then sank slowly, because there was none for the sword to strike, and the point rested among the close-sewn rings of mail on Buondelmonte's foot, and the thin streams of blood trickled quietly down the dimmed blade.

"Sir," said Buondelmonte, courteously, "you are a marvellous fine swordsman, though you fence not in our manner, with the point. I am your debtor for the safety of my left side. Are you hurt, sir?"

"Not I!" laughed Gilbert, wiping his broad blade slowly on his horse's mane for lack of anything better.

Then Buondelmonte looked at him again and smiled.

"You have won yourself a fair crest," he laughed, as he glanced at Gilbert's cap.

"A crest?" Gilbert put up his hand, and uttered an exclamation as it struck against a sharp steel point.

A half-spent arrow had pierced the top of his red cloth cap and was sticking there, like a woman's long hairpin. He thought that if it had struck two inches lower, with a little more force, he should have looked as the man in the woods did, whom Alric had killed. He plucked the shaft from the stiff cloth with some difficulty, and, barely glancing at it, tossed it away. But little Alric, who had left the guide to take care of the mules and had followed the charge on foot, picked up the arrow, marked it with his knife and put it carefully into his leathern quiver, which he filled with arrows he picked up on the grass till it would hold no more. Dunstan, who had ridden in the press with the rest, was looking among the dead for a good sword to take, his own being broken.

"Florence owes you a debt, sir," said Buondelmonte, an hour later, when they were riding back from the pursuit. "But for your warning, many of us would be lying dead in that wood. I pray you, take from the spoil, such as it is, whatsoever you desire. And if it please you to stay with us, the archbishop shall make a knight of you, for you have won knighthood to-day."

But Gilbert shook his head, smiling gravely.

"Praised be God, I need nothing, sir," he answered. "I thank you for your courteous hospitality, but I cannot stay, seeing that I ride upon a lady's bidding. And as for a debt, sir, Florence has paid hers largely in giving me your acquaintance."

"My friendship, sir," replied Buondelmonte, not yielding in compliment to the knightly youth.

So they broke bread together and drank a draught, and parted. But Buondelmonte gave Dunstan a small purse of gold and a handful of silver to little Alric and the muleteer, and Gilbert rode away with his men, and all were well pleased.

Yet when he was alone in the evening, a sadness and a horror of what he had done came over him; for he had taken life that day as a man mows down grass, in swaths, and he could not tell why he had slain, for he knew not the men who fought on the two sides, nor their difference. He had charged because he saw men charging, he had struck for the love of strife, and had killed because it was of his nature to kill. But now that the blood was shed, and the sun which had risen on life was going down on death, Gilbert Warde was sorry for what he had done, and his brave charge seemed but a senseless deed of slaughter, for which he should rather have done penance than received knighthood.

"I am no better than a wild beast," he said, when he had told Dunstan what he felt. "Go and find out a priest to pray for those I have killed to-day."

He covered his brow with his hand as he sat at the supper table.

"I go," answered the young man. "Yet it is a

pleasant sight to see the lion weeping for pity over the calf he has killed."

"The lion kills that he may eat and himself live," answered Gilbert. "And the men who fought to-day fought for a cause. But I smote for the wanton love of smiting that is in all our blood, and I am ashamed. Bid the priest pray for me also."

CHAPTER XI

THE court of France was at Vézelay — the King, the Queen, the great vassals of the kingdom at the King's command, and those of Aquitaine and Guienne and Poitou in the train of Eleanor, whose state outshone and dwarfed her husband's. And there was Bernard, the holy man of Clairvaux, to preach the Cross, where old men remembered the voice of Peter the Hermit and the shout of men now long dead in far Palestine, crying, "God's will! God's will!"

Because the church of Saint Mary Magdalen was too small to hold the multitude, they were gathered together in a wide grassy hollow without the little town, and there a raised floor of wood had been built for the King and Queen and the great nobles; but the rest of the knights and Eleanor's three hundred ladies stood upon the grass-grown slope, and were crowded together by the vast concourse of the people.

The sun was already behind the hill, and the hot July air had cooled a little; but it was still hot, and the breathing of the multitude could be heard in the silence. Gilbert had come but just in time; he had left his men to find him a lodging if they could, and now he pressed forward as well as he might, to see and hear, but most of all to find out, if he could, the face of Beatrix among the three hundred.

There sat the Queen, in scarlet and gold, wearing the crown upon her russet hair, and the King in gold and blue beside her, square, grave, and pale as ever; and when Gilbert had searched the three hundred fair young faces in vain, his eyes came back to the most beautiful woman in the world. He saw that she was fairer than even his memory of her, and he felt pride that she should call herself his friend.

Then suddenly there was a stir among the knights behind the throne, and though they were standing closely, shoulder to shoulder, and pressed one against another, yet they divided to let the preacher go through. He came alone, with quiet eyes, thanking the knights to right and left because they made way for him, and he passed between them quickly like a white shadow. So thought pierces matter and the spiritual being penetrates the terrestrial being and is unchanged.

But when Bernard had ascended the white wooden stage and stood near the King and Queen, then the hushed stillness became a dead silence, and the eyes of all that multitude were fastened upon his face and form, as each could see him. For a moment every man held his breath as if an angel had come down from heaven, bringing on his lips the word of God and in his look the evidence of eternal light. He was the holy man of the world even while he lived, and neither before him nor after him, since the days of the Apostles, has any one person so stood in the eyes of all mankind.

The gentle voice began to speak, without effort
to be heard, yet as distinct and clear as if it spoke
to each several ear, pleading for the cause of the
Cross of Christ, and for the suffering men who
held the holy places in the East with ever-weaken-
ing hands, but still with undaunted, desperate
courage.

"Is there any man among you who has loved his
mother, and has received her dying breath with her
last blessing, and has laid her to rest in peace, in a
place holy to him for her sake, and who would
suffer that her grave should be defiled and defaced
by her enemies, so long as he, her son, has in his body
blood of hers to shed? Is there any among you who
would not fight, while he had breath, to save his
father's dead bones from dishonour? Do you not
daily boast that you will lay down your lives in a
quarrel for the good name of your ladies, as you
would for your own daughters' fair fame and your
own wives' faithfulness?

"And now, I say, is not the Church of God your
mother, and are not her temples your most holy
places? You boast that you are ready to die for an
honourable cause: yet Christ gave His life for us,
not because of our honour, but because of our dishonour, and our sins which are many and grievous;
and having atoned for us in His Holy Passion, He was
laid at rest after the manner of men. And the place
where He rested is sacred, for the Lord from Heaven
lay therein when He had washed away our iniquity
with His holy blood, when He had healed us by His
stripes, when He had given His life that we might

live, when He had endured the bondage of this dying
flesh that we might be raised undying in the spirit,
by Him, and through Him, and in Him.

"Shall the earth that drank that blood be as other
earth? Shall the place that echoed the seven words
of agony be as other places? Is the tomb where God
rested Him of His crucified manhood to be given up
to forgetfulness and defilement? Or are we sinless,
that we need not even the memory of the sacrifice,
and so pure that we need no purification? I
would that we were. The world is evil, the hour
is late, the Judge is at hand, and we are lacking
of good and eaten of evil, so that there is no whole
part in us.

"And yet we move not to save ourselves, though
Christ gave His life to save us if we would stir
ever so little, if we would but stretch out our hands
to the hand that waits for ours. He bids us not be
crucified, as He was for us. He bids us only take up
our cross and follow Him, as He took it up Himself,
and bore it to the place of death."

Thus Bernard began to speak, gently at first, as
one who rouses a friend from sleep to warn him of
danger, and fears to be rough, yet cannot be silent;
but by and by, in the breathing stillness, the sweet
voice was strengthened and rang like the first clarion
at dawn on the day of battle, far off and clear, heart-
stirring and true. And with the rising tone came
also the stronger word, and at last the spirit that
moves more than word or voice.

"Lay the Cross to your hearts as you wear it on
your breasts. Bear it with you on the long day

marches, and in the watches of night bow before it inwardly, and pray that you may have grace to bear it to the end. So shall your footsteps profit you, and your way shall be the way of the Cross, till you stand in the holy place. But if so be that God ask blood of you, blessed shall they be among you who shall give life freely, to die for the Cross of our Lord Christ; and they shall stand in the place that is holy indeed, before the Throne of God.

"Yet beware of one thing. I would not that you should go out to fight for the Sepulchre as some of our fathers did, boasting in the Cross, yet in heart each for his own soul and none for the glory of Christ, counting the weariness, and the hurts, and the drops of blood as a sure reckoning to be repaid to you in heaven, as if you had lent God a piece of money which He must pay again. The Lord Jesus gave not His life at an account, nor His blood at usury; He counted not the pain, nor was His suffering set down in a book; but He gave all freely, of His love for men. Shall men therefore ask of God a return, saying: 'We have given Thee so much, as it were a wound, or it may be a life, or else a prayer, and a day of fasting, see that Thou pay us what is just'? That were not giving to God what is a man's own; it were rather lending or selling to God what is His. See that you do not thus, but if you have anything to give, let it be given freely; or else give not at all, for it is written that from him that hath not faith shall be taken even such things as he hath.

"But if you take the Cross, and arm yourselves to fight for it, and go your way to Palestine to help your brethren in their sore need, go not for yourselves, suffer not for yourselves, fight not for yourselves. For as God is greater than man, so is the glory of God greater than the glory of self and more worthy that you should die for it. Think not therefore of earning a reward, but of honouring the Lord Christ in the holy place where He died for you.

"March not as it were to do penance for your old sins, hoping for forgiveness, as a trader that brings merchandise looks for a profit! Strike not as slaves, who fight lest they be beaten with rods, neither as men in fear of everlasting fire and the torments of hell! Neither go out as thieves, seeking to steal the earth for yourselves, and striving not with the unbeliever, but with the rich man for his riches, and with the great man for his possessions! I say, go forth and do battle for God's sake and His glory! March ye for Christ and to bring the people to Him out of darkness! Take with you the Cross to set it in the hearts of men, and the seed of the tree of life to plant among desolate nations!

"Ye kings, that are anointed leaders, lead ye the armies of Heaven! Ye knights, that are sworn to honour, draw your unsullied swords for the honour of God! Men and youths, that bear arms by allegiance, be ye soldiers of Christ and allegiant to the Cross! Be ye all first for honour, first for France, first for God Most High!"

"CROSSES! GIVE US CROSSES!"

With those words the white-sleeved arm was high above his head, holding up the plain white wooden cross, and there was silence for a moment. But when the people saw that he had finished speaking, they drew deep breath, and the air thundered with the great cry that came.

"Crosses! Give us crosses!"

And they pressed upon one another to get nearer. The King had risen, and the Queen with him, and he came forward and knelt at Bernard's feet, with bent head and folded hands. The great abbot took pieces of scarlet cloth from a page who held them ready in a basket, and he fastened them upon the King's left shoulder and then raised his right hand in blessing. The people were silent again and looked on, and many thought that the King, in his great mantle and high crown, was like a bishop wearing a cope, for he had a churchman's face. He rose to his feet and stepped back; but he was scarcely risen when the Queen stood in his place, radiant, the evening light in her hair.

"I also will go," she said in a clear, imperious voice. "Give me the Cross!"

She knelt and placed her hands together, as in prayer, and there was a fair light in her eyes as she looked up to Bernard's face. He hesitated a moment, then took a cross and laid it upon her mantle, and she smiled.

A great cry went up from all the knights, and then from the people, strong and triumphant, echoing, falling, and rising again.

"God save the Queen! — the Queen that wears the Cross!"

And suddenly every man held up his sword by the sheath, and the great cross-hilts made forests of crosses in the glowing air. But the Queen's three hundred ladies pressed upon her.

"We will not leave you!" they cried. "We will take the Cross with you!"

And they thronged upon Bernard like a flight of doves, holding out white hands for crosses, and more crosses, while he gave as best he could. Also the people and the knights began to tear pieces from their own garments to make the sign, and one great lord took his white mantle and made strips of the fine cloth for his liege vassals and his squires and men; but another took Bernard's white cape from his shoulders and with a sharp dagger made many little crosses of it for the people, who kissed them as holy things when they received them.

In the throng, Gilbert pressed forward to the edge of the platform where the Queen was standing, for he was strong and tall. He touched her mantle softly, and she looked down, and he saw how her face turned white and gentle when she knew him. Being too far below her to take her hand, he took the rich border of her cloak and kissed it, whereat she smiled; but she made a sign to him that he should not try to talk with her in the confusion. Then looking down again, she saw that he had yet no cross. She took one from one of her ladies, and, bending low, tried to fasten it upon his shoulder.

"I thank your Grace," said Gilbert, very gratefully. "Is Beatrix here?" he asked in a low
tone.

But, to his wonder, the Queen's brow darkened,
and her eyes were suddenly hard; she almost
dropped the cross in her hurry to stand upright,
nor would she again turn her eyes to look at
him.

CHAPTER XII

IN the late dusk of summer Bernard went his way
from the place where he had preached, to the presbytery of Saint Mary Magdalen, where he was to lodge
that night. The King and Queen walked beside
him, their horses led after them by grooms in the
royal liveries of white and gold; and all the long
procession of knights and nobles, priests and laymen,
gentlefolk and churls, men, women, and children,
streamed in a motley procession up the road to the
village. As they went, the King talked gravely with
the holy man, interlarding and lining his sententious
speeches with copious though not always correct
quotations from the Vulgate. On Bernard's other
side Eleanor walked with head erect, one hand upon
her belt, one hanging down, her brows slightly drawn
together, her face clear white, her burning eyes fixed
angrily upon the bright vision cast by her thoughts
into the empty air before her.

She had used the only means, and the strongest
means, of bringing Gilbert back to France; she had
foredreamt his coming, she had foreknown that
from the first he would ask for Beatrix; but she had
neither known nor dreamt of what she should feel
when he, standing at her feet below the platform,
looked up to her offering eyes with a hunger in his
face which she could not satisfy, and a desire which

she could not fulfil. His very asking for the other
had been a refusal of herself, and to be refused is a
shame which no loving woman will accept while love
is living, and an insult which no strong woman for-
gives when love is dead.

But neither the King nor the abbot heeded her as
they walked along, talking in Latin mixed with Norman French. The monk, not tall, slender, spiritualized
even in the remnant of his flesh, the incarnation of
believing thought and word, the exposition of matter's servitude to mind, was the master; the King,
heavy, strong, pale, obedient, was the pupil, proving
the existence of the greater force by his blind submission to its laws. Beside them the Queen imaged the
independence of youthful life, believing without realizing, strong with blood, rich with colour, fearing regret
more than remorse, thoughtlessly cruel and cruelly
thoughtless, yet able to be very generous and brave.

The bell of Saint Mary's tolled three strokes, then
four, then five, then one, thirteen in all, and then
rang backward for the ending day. The sun had
set a full half-hour and the dusk had almost drunk
the dregs of the red west. Bernard stood still, bareheaded in the way, with folded hands, and began
the Angelus Domini; the King from habit raised
his hand to take his cap from his head, and touched
the golden crown instead. Instantly a little colour
of embarrassment rose in his pale cheeks, and he
stumbled over the familiar response as he clasped
his hands with downcast eyes, for in some ways he
was a timid man. The Queen stood still and spoke
the words also, but neither the attitude of her head

nor the look in her eyes was changed, nor did she take her hand from her belt to clasp it upon the other. The air was very soft and warm, there was the musical, low sound of many voices speaking in the monotone of prayer, and now and then, on whirring wings, a droning beetle hummed his way from one field to another, just above the heads of the great multitude.

The prayer said, they all moved onward, past the first houses of the village and past the open smithy with its shelter of twisted chestnut boughs, beneath which the horses were protected from the sun while they were being shod. But the smith had not been to the preaching, because Alric, the Saxon groom, had brought him Gilbert's horse to shoe just when he was going, and had forced him to stay and do the work with the threat of an evil spell learned in Italy. And now, peering through the twilight, he stood watching the long procession as it came up to his door. He was a dark man, with red eyes and hairy hands, and his shirt was open on his chest almost to his belt. He stood quite still at first, gazing on Bernard's face, that was luminous in the dusk; but as he looked, something moved him that he could not understand, and he came forward in his leathern apron and his blackened hose, and knelt at the abbot's feet.

"Give me also the Cross," he cried.

"I give thee the sign, my son," answered Bernard, raising his hand to bless the hairy man. "The crosses we had are all given. But thou shalt have one to-morrow."

But as the smith looked up to the inspired face
the light came into his own eyes, and something he
could not see took hold of him suddenly and hard.

"Nay, my lord," he answered, "I will have it
to-day and of my own."

Then he sprang up and ran to his smithy, and
came back holding in his hand a bar of iron that
had been heating in the coals to make a shoe. The
end of it was glowing red.

"In the name of the Father, and of the Son, and
of the Holy Ghost!" he cried in a loud voice.

And as he spoke the words, he had laid the red-hot
point to his breast and had drawn it down and crosswise; and a little line of thin, white smoke followed
the hissing iron along the seared flesh. He threw
the bar down upon the threshold of his door and
came to join the throng, the strange smile on his
rough face and the light of another world in his fire-
reddened eyes. But though the multitude sent up
a great cry of praise and wonder, yet Bernard shook
his head gravely and walked on, for he loved not any
madness, not even a madness for good deeds, and
the light by which he saw was as steady and clear
and true as a life-long day.

Moreover, even while he had been speaking he had
felt that fanatic deeds were not far off, and a deep
sadness had fallen upon him, because he knew that
true belief is the fulness of true wisdom and by no
means akin to any folly.

Therefore, when he was alone that night, he was
very heavy-hearted, and sat a long time by his square
oak table in the light of the three-cornered brazen

lamp which stood at his elbow. The principal
chamber of the presbytery was cross-vaulted and
divided into two by a low round arch supported on
slender double columns with capitals fantastically
carved. The smaller portion of the room beyond
the arch made an alcove for sleeping, which could
be completely shut off by a heavy curtain; the
larger part was paved with stone, and in one corner
a low wooden platform, on which stood a heavy table
before a carved bench fastened to the wall, was set
apart for writing and study. On the table, besides
the lamp, there stood a reading-desk, and above the
bench a strong shelf carried a number of objects,
including several large bottles of ink, a pot of glue
for fastening leaves of parchment, and two or three
jars of blue and white earthenware. On nails
there hung a brush of half dried broom, a broad-
brimmed rush hat, and a blackened rosary. On the
other side of the table, and by the window, there was
a small holy-water basin with a little besom. On
the walls were hung pieces of coarse linen roughly
embroidered with small crosses flory, worked in dark
red silk. The vault was blank and white, and
rushes were strewn on the stone pavement. In the
deep embrasures of the windows there were dark
window-seats worn black with age.

The abbot had begun a letter, but the pen lay
beside the unfinished writing, his elbow rested on
the parchment, and he shaded his eyes from the
light. The brilliancy was gone from his face and
was succeeded by an almost earthy pallor, while
his attitude expressed both lassitude and dejection.

He had done what had been required of him, he had
fired the passion of the hour, and one hour had shown
him how completely it was to be beyond his control.
He remembered how Peter the Hermit had led the vast
advance-guard of the First Crusade to sudden and
miserable destruction before the main force could be
organized ; he had seen enough on that afternoon
to prove to him that the air was laden with such
disaster, of which the responsibility would surely
be heaped upon himself. He regretted not the
thoughts he had preached, but the fact of having
yielded to preach at all to such men and at such a
time. He had begun to set forth all this and much
more in a letter to Pope Eugenius, but before he had
written a dozen lines the pen had fallen from his hand,
and he had begun to reflect upon the impossibility
of stemming the tide since it had turned to flood.

A soft step sounded in the outer hall beyond the
curtained doorway, but Bernard, absorbed in his
meditations, heard nothing. A jewelled hand
pushed aside the thick folds of the hanging, and
the most beautiful eyes in the world gazed curiously
upon the unheeding abbot.

" Are you alone ? " asked the Queen's voice.

Without waiting for an answer she came forward
into the room and paused beside the low platform,
laying one hand upon the table in a gesture half
friendly, half deprecating, as if she still feared
that she had disturbed the holy man. His transparent fingers fell from his eyes, and he looked up
to her, hardly realizing who she was, and quite
unable to guess why she had come. A dark brown

mantle completely covered her gown, and only a little of her scarlet sleeve showed as her hand lay on the table.   Her russet-golden hair hung in broad waves and lightened in the rays of the oil lamp.   Her eyes, that looked at Bernard intently and inquiringly, were the eyes of old Duke William, whom the Abbot of Clairvaux had brought to confession and penance long ago, and who had gone from the altar of his grand-daughter's marriage straight to solitary hermitage and lonely death in the Spanish hills ; they were eyes in which all thoughts were fearless and in which tenderness was beautiful, but in which kindness was often out of sight behind the blaze of vitality and the burning love of life that proceeded from her and surrounded her as an atmosphere of her own.

"You do not welcome me," she said, looking into his face.   "Are you too deeply occupied to talk with me awhile ?   It is long since we have met."

Bernard passed his hand over his eyes as if to brush away some material veil.

"I am at your Grace's service," he said gently, and he rose from his seat as he spoke.

"I ask no service for myself," she answered, setting her foot upon the platform and coming to his side. "Yet I ask something which you may do for others."

Bernard hesitated, and then looked down.

"Silver and gold have I none," he said, quoting, "but such as I have I give unto thee."

"I have both gold and silver, and lands, and a crown," answered the Queen, smiling carelessly, and yet in earnest. "I lack faith. And so, though my people have swords and armour, and have taken upon them the Cross to succour their brethren in the Holy Land, yet they have no leader."

"They have the King, your husband," answered Bernard, gravely.

Eleanor laughed, not very cruelly, nor altogether scornfully, but as a man might laugh who was misunderstood, and to whom, asking for his sword, a servant should bring his pen.

"The King!" she cried, still smiling. "The King! Are you so great in mind and so poor in sense as to think that he could lead men and win? The King is no leader. He is your acolyte — I like to see him swinging a censer in time to your prayers and flattening his flat face upon the altar-steps beatified by your footsteps!"

The Queen laughed, for she had moods in which she feared neither God, nor saint, nor man. But Bernard looked grave at first, then hurt, and then there was pity in his eyes. He pointed to the window-seat beside the table, and he himself sat down upon his carved bench. Eleanor, being seated, rested her elbows on the table, clasped her beautiful hands together, and slowly rubbed her cheek against them, meditating what she should say next. She had had no fixed purpose in coming to the abbot's lodging, but she had always liked to talk with him when he was at leisure and to see the look of puzzled and pained surprise that came into his face when she said anything more than usually shocking to his delicate sensibilities. With impulses of tremendous

force, there was at the root of her character a youthful and almost childlike indifference to consequences.

"You misjudge your husband," said the abbot, at
last, drumming on the table nervously and absently
with the tips of his white fingers. "They who do
their own will only are quick to condemn those who
hope to accomplish the will of Heaven."

"If you regard the King as the instrument of
Divine Providence," answered Eleanor, with curling
lip, "there is nothing to be said. Providence, for
instance, was angered with the people of Vitry.
Providence selected the King of France to be the
representative of its wrath. The King, obedient as
ever, set fire to the church, and burned several priests
and two thousand more or less innocent persons at
their prayers. Nothing could be better. Providence
was appeased —"

"Hush, Madam!" exclaimed Bernard, lifting a
thin hand in deprecation. "That was the devil's
work."

"You told me that I was condemning one who is
accomplishing the will of Heaven."

"In leading the Crusade, yes —"

"Then my husband works for both parties. To-
day he serves God; to-morrow he serves Mammon."
Eleanor raised her finely pencilled eyebrows. "I believe there is a parable that teaches us what is to
become of those that serve two masters."

"It applies to those who try to serve them at the
same time," answered the abbot, meeting her contemptuous look with the quiet boldness of a man
sure of power. "You know as well as I that the

King took oath to lead a Crusade out of repentance for what he did at Vitry."

"A bargain, then, of the very kind against which you preached to-day." The Queen still smiled, but less scornfully, for she fancied herself as good as Bernard in an argument.

"It is a very easy thing to fence with words," Bernard said. "It is one thing to argue, it is quite another to convince your hearers."

"I do not desire to convince you of anything," answered Eleanor, with a little laugh. "I would rather be convinced."

She looked at him a moment and then turned away with a weary little sigh of discontent.

"Was it without conviction that you took the Cross from my hands to-day?" asked Bernard, sadly.

"It was in the hope of conviction."

Bernard understood. Before him, within reach of his hand, that great problem was present which, of all others, Paganism most easily and clearly solved, but with which Christianity grapples at a disadvantage, finding its foothold narrow, and its danger constant and great. It is the problem of the conversion of great and vital natures, brave, gifted and sure of self, to the condition of the humble and poor in spirit. It is easy to convince the cripple that peace is among the virtues ; the sick man and the weak are soon persuaded that the world is a sensuous illusion of Satan, in which the pure and perfect have no part nor share ; it is another, a greater and a harder matter, to prove the strong man a sinner by his strength, and to make woman's passion ridiculous in comparison of heaven. The clear flame of the spirit burns ill under the breath of this dying body, and for the fleeting touch of a loving hand the majesty of God is darkened in a man's heart.

Bernard saw before him the incarnate strength and youth and beauty of her from whom a line of kings was to descend, and in whom were all the greatest and least qualities, virtues and failings of her unborn children — the Lion Heart of Richard, the heartless selfishness of John, the second Edward's grasping hold, Henry the Third's broad justice and wisdom; the doubt of one, the decision of another, the passions of them all in one, coursing in the blood of a young and kingly race.

"You wish not to convince others, but to be convinced," Bernard said, "and yet it is not in your nature to yield yourself to any conviction. What would you of me? I can preach to them that will hear me, not to those that come to watch me and to smile at my sayings as if I were a player in a booth at a fair. Why do you come here to-night? Can I give you faith as a salve, wherewith to anoint your blind eyes? Can I furnish you the girdle of honesty for the virtue you have not? Shall I promise re- pentance for you to God, while you smile on your next lover? Why have you sought me out?"

"If I had known that you had no leisure, and the Church no room for any but the altogether perfect, I would not have come."

She leaned back in the window-seat and folded her arms, drawing the thin dark stuff of her cloak into severe straight lines and shadows, in vivid contrast with the radiant beauty of her face. Her straight and clear-cut brows lowered over her deep eyes, and her lips were as hard as polished coral.

Bernard looked at her again long and earnestly, understanding in part, and in part guessing, that she had suffered a secret disappointment on that day and had come to him rather in the hope of some kind of mental excitement than with any idea of obtaining consolation. To him, filled as he was with the lofty thoughts inspired by the mission thrust upon him, there was something horrible in the woman's frivolity — or cynicism. To him the Cross meant the Passion of Christ, the shedding of God's blood, the Redemption of mankind. To her it was a badge, an ornament, the excuse for a luxurious pilgrimage of fair women living delicately in silken tents, and clothed in fine garments of a fanciful fashion. The contrast was too strong, too painful. Eleanor and her girl knights would be too wholly out of place, with their fancies and their whims, in an army of devoted men fighting for a faith, for a faith's high principle as between race and race, and for all which that faith had made sacred in its most holy places. It was too much. In profoundest disappointment and sadness Bernard's head sank upon his breast, and he raised his hands a little, to let them fall again upon his knees, as if he were almost ready to give up the struggle.

Eleanor felt the wicked little thrill of triumph in his apparent despair which compensates schoolboys for unimaginable labour in mischief, when they at last succeed in hurting the feelings of a long-suffering teacher. There had been nothing but an almost childish desire to tease at the root of all that she had said; for before all things she was young and gay, and her surroundings tended in every way to repress both gayety and youth.

"You must not take everything I say in earnest," she said suddenly, with a laugh that jarred on the delicate nerves of the overwrought man.

He turned his head from her as if the sight of her face would have been disagreeable just then.

"Jest with life if you can," he said. "Jest with death if you are brave enough; yet at least be earnest in this great matter. If you are fixed in purpose to go with the King, you and your ladies, then go with the purpose to do good, to bind up men's wounds, to tend the sick, to cheer the weak, and by your presence to make the coward ashamed."

"And why not to fight?" asked the Queen, the light of an untried emotion brightening in her eyes. "Do you think I cannot bear the weight of mail, or sit a horse, or handle a sword as well as many a boy of twenty who will be there in the thick of battle? And if I and my court ladies can bear the weariness as well as even the weakest man in the King's army, and risk a life as bravely, and perhaps strike a clean blow or drive a straight thrust for the Holy Sepulchre, shall our souls have no good of it, because we are women?"

As she spoke, her arm lay across the table, and her small strong hand moved energetically with her speech, touching the monk's sleeve. The fighting blood of the old Duke was in her veins, and there was battle in her voice. Bernard looked up.

" If you were always what you are at this moment," he said, " and if you had a thousand such women as yourself to ride with you, the King would need no other army, for you could face the Seljuks alone.

" But you think that by the time I have to face them my courage will have cooled to woman's tears, like hot vapour on a glass."

She smiled, but gently now, for she was pleased by what he had said.

" You need not fear," she continued, before he had time to answer her. " We shall not bear ourselves worse than men, and there will be grown men there who shall be afraid before we are. But if there were with us a leader of men, I should have no fear. Men will fight for the King, they will shed their blood for Eleanor of Guienne, but they would die ten deaths at the bidding of — "

She paused, and fixed her eyes on Bernard's face.

" Of whom ? " he asked, unsuspecting.

" Of Bernard of Clairvaux."

There was a short silence. Then in a clear far-off voice, as if in a dream, the abbot repeated his own name.

" Bernard of Clairvaux — a leader of men ? A soldier ? A general ? " He paused as if consulting himself. " Madam," he said at last, " I am neither general, nor leader, nor soldier. I am a monk, and a churchman as the Hermit was, but not like him in this — I know the limitation of my strength. I can urge men to fight for a good cause, but I will not lead them to death and ruin, as Peter did, while there are men living who have been trained to the sword as I to the pen."

"I do not ask that you should plan battles, lead for-lorn charges, nor sit down in your tent to study the destruction of walled towns. You can be our leader without all that, for he who leads men's souls com-mands men's bodies and lives in men's hearts. Therefore, I bid you to come with us and help us, for although a sword is better at need than a hun-dred words, yet there are men at whose single word a thousand swords are drawn like one."

"No, Madam," said the abbot, his even lips closing after the words, with a look of final decision, "I will not go with you. First, because I am unfit to be a leader of armies, and secondly, because such life as there is left in me can be better used at home than in following a camp. Lastly, I would that this good fight might be fought soberly and in earnest, neither in the fever of a fanatical fury nor, on the other hand, lightly, as an amusement and a play, nor selfishly and meanly in the hope of gain. My words are neither deep, nor learned, nor well chosen, for I speak as my thoughts rise and overflow. But thanks be to Heaven, what I say rouses men to act rather than moves them to think. Yet it is not well that they be over-roused or stirred when a long war is before them, lest their heat be consumed in a flash of fire, and their strength in a single blow. You need not a preacher, but a captain; not words but deeds. You go to make history, not to hear a prophecy."

"Nevertheless," said the Queen, "you must go

with us, for if the spirit you have called up sinks from men's memories, our actions will be worse than spiritless. You must go."

"I cannot."

"Cannot? But I say you must."

"No, Madam — I say no."

For a long time the two sat in silence facing each other, the Queen confident, vital, fully roused to the expression of her will; Bernard, on the other hand, as fully determined to oppose her with all the fervent conviction which he brought to every question of judgment or policy.

"If we fall out among ourselves," said Eleanor, at last, "who shall unite us? If men lose faith in the cause before them and grow greedy of the things that lie in their way, who shall set them right?"

The abbot shook his head sorrowfully and would not meet her eyes, for in this he knew that she was right.

"When an army has lost faith," he said, "it is already beaten. When Atalanta stooped to pick up the golden apples, her race was lost."

"As when love dies, contempt and hatred take its place," said Eleanor, as if in comment.

"Such love is of hell," said Bernard, looking suddenly into her face, so that she faintly blushed.

"Yes," she retorted scornfully, "for it is the love of man and wife."

The holy man watched her sadly and yet keenly, for he knew what she meant, and he foresaw the end.

"Lucifer rebelled against law," he said.

"I do not wonder," said the Queen, with a sharp

laugh. "He would have rebelled against marriage. Love is the true faith — marriage is the dogma." She laughed again.

Bernard shrank a little as if he felt actual pain. He had known her since she had been a little child, yet he had never become used to her cruelties of expression. He was a man more easily disgusted in his æsthetic sensibilities than shocked by the wickedness of a world he knew. To him, God was not only great, but beautiful; Nature, as some theologians maintain, was cruel, evil, hurtful, but she was never coarse, nor foul in his conception, and her beauty appealed to him against his will. So also in his eyes a woman could be sinful, and her sins might seem terrible to him, and yet she herself was to him a woman still, a being delicate, refined, tender even in her wickedness; but a woman who could speak at once keenly and brutally of her marriage reacted upon him as a very ugly or painful sight, or as a very harsh and discordant sound that jars every nerve in the body.

"Madam," he said in a low voice, but very quietly and coldly, "I think not that you are in such state of grace as to bear the Cross to your good."

Eleanor raised her head and looked at him haughtily, with lids half drooped as her eyes grew hard and keen.

"You are not my confessor, sir," she retorted. "For all you know, he may have enjoined upon me a pilgrimage to the Holy Land. It is a common penance." For the third time she laughed.

"A common penance!" cried the abbot, in a tone of despair. "That is what it has come to in these days. A man kills his neighbour in a quarrel and goes to Jerusalem to purge him of blood, as he would take a physician's draught to cure him of the least of little aches. A pilgrimage is a remedy, as a prayer is a medicine. To repeat the act of contrition so and so often, or to run through a dozen rosaries of an afternoon, is a potion for the sick soul."

" Well, what then ? " asked the Queen.

" What then ? " repeated the abbot. " Then there is no faith left in the true meaning of the Crusade — "

" That is what I fear," answered Eleanor. " That is why I am begging you to come with us. That is why the King will be unable to command men without you. And yet you will not go."

" No," he replied, " I will not."

" You have always disappointed me," said the Queen, rising, and employing a weapon to which women usually resort last. " You stand in the front and will not lead, you rouse men to deeds you will not do, you give men ideals in which you do not believe, and then you go back to the peace of your abbey of Clairvaux, and leave men to shift for themselves in danger and need. And if, perhaps, some trusting woman comes to you with overladen heart, you tell her that she is not in a state of grace. It must be easy to be a great man in that way."

She turned as she spoke the last words and stepped from the platform to the stone pavement. At the enormous injustice of her judgment, Bernard's face grew cold and stern ; but he would not answer what she said, for he knew how useless it would be, In

her, and perhaps in her only, of all men and women
he had known, there was the something to which he
could not speak, the element that was out of harmony with his own being, and when he had talked
with her it was as if he had eaten sand. He could
understand that she, too, was in contradiction with
her natural feelings in her marriage with such a man
as the King; he could be sorry for her, he could pity
her, he could forgive her, he could pray for her —
but he could not speak to her as he could to others.

A dozen times before she reached the door he
wished to call her back, and he sought in the archive
of his brain and in the treasury of his heart the
words that might touch her. But he sought in vain.
So long as she was before his eyes, a chilled air, dull
and unresonant, divided his soul from hers. Her
hand was on the curtain to go out when she turned
and looked at him again.

"You will not go with us," she said. "If we fail,
we shall count the fault yours; if we quarrel and
turn our swords upon one another, the sin is yours; if
our armies lose heart, and are scattered and hewn in
pieces, their blood will be on your head. But if we
win," she said at the last, drawing herself to her
height, "the honour of our deeds shall be ours alone,
not yours."

She had raised the curtain, and it fell behind her
as she spoke the last word, leaving the abbot no
possibility of a retort. But she had missed her
intention, for he was not a man to be threatened
from the right he had planned. When she was gone,
his face grew sad, and calm, and weary again, and

presently, musing, he took up the pen that lay beside the half-written page.

But she went on through the outer hall to the vestibule, drawing her thin dark mantle about her, her lips set and her eyes cruel, for she had been disappointed. Beneath the idle wish to hear Bernard speak, behind the strong conviction that he must follow the army to the East if it was to be victorious, there had been the unconscious longing for a return of that brave emotion under which, in the afternoon, she had taken the Cross with her ladies. And a woman disappointed of strong feeling, hoped for and desired, is less kind than a strong man defeated of expectation.

She was alone. Of all women, she hated most to be followed by attendants and watched by inferiors when she chose solitude. Reliant on herself and unaffectedly courageous, she often wondered whether it were not a more pleasant thing to be a man than to be even the fairest of womankind, as she was. She stood still a moment in the vestibule, drawing the hood of her cloak over her head and half across her face. The outer door was half open; the single lamp, filled with olive-oil and hanging from the middle of the vault, cast its ray out into the night. As Eleanor stood arranging her headdress and almost unconsciously looking toward the darkness, a gleam of colour and steel flashed softly in the gloom. It disappeared and flashed again, for a man was waiting without and slowly walking up and down before the door. The Queen had chosen to come alone, but had no reason for con-

cealing herself; she made two steps to the threshold and looked out, opening wide one half of the
door.

The man stood still and turned his head without
haste as the fuller light fell upon him. It was
Gilbert, and as his eyes turned to the Queen's face,
dark against the brightness within, she started a
little, as if she would have drawn back, and she
spoke nervously, in a low voice, hardly knowing
what she said.

"What is it?" she asked. "Why did you come
here?"

"Because I knew your Grace was here," he answered quietly.

"You knew that I was here? How?"

"I saw you — I followed."

Under her hood, the Queen felt the warm blood
in her cheeks. Gilbert was very good to see as he
stood just outside the door, in the bright lamplight.
He was pale, but not wan like Bernard; he was
thin with the leanness of vigorous youth, not with
fasting and vigils; he was grave, not sad; ener-
getic, not inspired; and his face was handsome rather
than beautiful. Eleanor looked at him for a few
moments before she spoke again.

"You followed me. Why?"

"To beg a word of your Grace's favour."

"The question you asked today?"

"Yes."

"Is it so urgent?" The Queen laughed a little,
and Gilbert started in surprise.

"Your Grace wrote urgently," he said.

"Then you are zealous only to obey me? I like that. You shall be rewarded! But I have changed my mind. If the letter were to be written again, I would not write it."

"It was the letter of a friend. Would you take it back?"

Gilbert's face showed the coming disappointment. In his anxiety he pressed nearer to her, resting his hand on the doorpost. The Queen drew back and smiled.

"Was it so very friendly?" she asked. "I do not remember — but I did not mean it so."

"Madam, what did you mean?" His voice was steady and rather cold.

"Oh — I have quite forgotten!" She almost laughed again, shaking her hooded head.

"If your Grace had need of me, I might understand. Beatrix is not here. I looked at each of your ladies to-day, through all their ranks — she was not among them. I asked where she was, but you would not answer and were angry —"

"I? Angry? You are dreaming!"

"I thought you were angry, because you changed colour and would not speak again —"

"You were wrong. Only a fool can be angry with ignorance."

"Why do you call me ignorant? These are all riddles."

"And you are not good at guessing. Come! To show you that I was not angry, I will have you walk with me down through the village. It is growing late."

"Your Grace is alone?"

"Since you followed me, you know it.   Come."

She almost pushed him aside to pass out, and a
moment later they were crossing the dark open space
before the church.   Gilbert was not easily surprised,
but when he reflected that he was walking late at
night through a small French village with one of the
most powerful sovereigns in Europe, who was at the
same time the most beautiful of living women, he
realized that his destiny was not leading him by
common paths.   He remembered his own surprise
when, an hour earlier, he had seen the Queen's unmis-
takable figure pass the open window of his lodging
And yet should any one see her now, abroad at such
an hour, in the company of a young Englishman,
there would be much more matter for astonishment.
Half boyishly he wished that he were not himself, or
else that the Queen were Beatrix.   As for his actual
position in the Queen's good graces, he had not the
slightest understanding of it, a fact which just then
amused Eleanor almost as much as it irritated her.
The road was uneven and steep beyond the little
square.   For some moments they walked side by
side in silence.   From far away came the sound of
many rough voices singing a drinking-chorus.

"Give me your arm," said Eleanor, suddenly.

As she spoke, she put out her hand, as if she feared
to stumble.   Doing as she begged him, Gilbert
suited his steps to hers, and they were very close
together as they went on.   He had never walked
arm in arm in that way before, nor perhaps had he
ever been so close to any other woman.   An inde-

scribable sensation took possession of him; he felt that his step was less steady, and that his head was growing hot and his hands cold ; and somehow he knew that whereas the idea of love was altogether beyond and out of the question, yet he was spell-bound in the charm of a new and mysterious attraction. With it there was the instantaneous certainty that it was evil, with the equally sure knowledge that if it grew upon him but a few moments longer he should not be able to resist it.

Eleanor would not have been a woman had she not understood.

" What is the matter?" she asked gently, and under her hood she was smiling.

" The matter?" Gilbert spoke nervously. "There is nothing the matter ; why do you ask? "

" Your arm trembled," answered the Queen.

" I suppose I was afraid that you were going to fall.'

At this the Queen laughed aloud.

" Are you so anxious for my safety as that?" she inquired.

Gilbert did not answer at once.

" It seems so strange," he said at last, "that your Grace should choose to be abroad alone so late at night."

" I am not alone," she answered.

At that moment her foot seemed to slip, and her hand tightened suddenly upon Gilbert's arm. But as he thought her in danger of falling, he caught her round the waist and held her up; and, as he almost clasped her to him, the mysterious influence strength-ened his hold in a most unnecessary manner.

"I never slip," said Eleanor, by way of explaining the fact that she had just stumbled.

"No," answered Gilbert. "Of course not."

And he continued to hold her fast. She made a little movement vaguely indicating that she wished him to let her go, and her free right hand pretended to loosen his from her waist. He felt infinitesimal lines of fire running from his head to his feet, and he saw lights where there were none.

"Let me go," she said, almost under her breath; and accentuating her words with little efforts of hand and body, it accidentally happened that her head was against his breast for a moment.

The fire grew hotter, the lights brighter, and, with the consciousness of doing something at once terrible yet surpassingly sweet to do, he allowed his lips to touch the dark stuff that hid her russet hair. But she was quite unaware of this desperate deed. A moment later she seemed to hear something, for she turned her head quickly, as if listening, and spoke in an anxious half-whisper.

"Take care! There is somebody — "

Instantly Gilbert's hand dropped to his side and he assumed the attitude of a respectful protector. The Queen continued to stare into the darkness a moment longer, and then began to walk on.

"It was nothing," she said carelessly.

"I hear men singing," said Gilbert.

"I dare say," answered Eleanor, with perfect indifference. "I have heard them for some time."

One voice rose higher and louder than the rest as the singers approached, and the other voices joined in the rough chorus of a Burgundy drinking-song. Near the outskirts of the village, lights were flashing and moving unsteadily in the road as those who carried them staggered along. To reach the monastery which was the headquarters of the court, the Queen and Gilbert would have to walk a hundred yards down the street before turning to the right. Gilbert saw at a glance that it would be impossible for them to reach the turning before meeting the drunken crowd.

"It would be better to go back by another way," he said, slackening his pace.

But the Queen walked quietly on without answering him. It was clear that she intended to make the people stand aside to let her pass, for she continued to walk in the middle of the street. But Gilbert gently drew her aside, and she suffered him to lead her to a doorway, raised two steps above the street, and darkened by an overhanging balcony. There they stood and waited. A dense throng of grooms, archers and men-at-arms came roaring up the steep way toward them. A huge man in a dirty scarlet tunic and dusty russet hose, with soft boots that were slipping down in folds about his ankles, staggered along in front of the rest. His face was on fire with wine, his little red eyes glared dully from under swollen lids, and as he bawled his song with mouth wide open, one might have tossed an apple between his wolfish teeth. In his right hand he held an earthen jug in which there was still a little wine; with his left he brandished a banner that had been made by sewing a broad red

cross upon a towel tied to one of those long wands
with which farmers' boys drive geese to feed. Half
dancing, half marching, and reeling at every step, he
came along, followed closely by a dozen companions
one degree less burly than himself, but at least quite
as drunk ; and each had upon his breast or shoulder
the cross he had received that day. Behind them
more and more, closer and closer, the others came
stumbling, rolling, jostling each other, howling the
chorus of the song. And every now and then the
leader, swinging his banner and his wine jug, sent a
shower of red drops into the faces of his followers,
some of whom laughed, and some swore loudly in
curses that made themselves felt through the roaring
din. But loudest, highest, clearest of all, from within
the heart of the drunken crowd, came one of those
voices that are made to be heard in storm and battle.
In a tune of its own, regardless of the singing of all
the rest, it was chanting the Magnificat anima mea
Dominum. Long-drawn, sustained, and of brazen
quality, it calmly defied all other din, and as the crowd
drew nearer Gilbert saw through the torchlight the
thin white face of a very tall man in the midst, with
half-closed eyes and lips that wore a look of pain
as he sang — the face, the look, the voice of a man
who in the madness of liquor was still a fanatic.

The hot close breath of the ribald crew went before it in the warm summer night, the torches threw
a moving yellow glare upon faces red as flame, or
ghastly white, and here and there the small crosses
of scarlet cloth fastened to the men's tunics caught
the light like splashes of fresh blood.

Eleanor drew back as far as she could under the doorway, offended in her sovereign pride and disgusted as gentlewomen are at the sight of drunkenness. By her side, Gilbert drew himself up as if protesting against a sacrilege and against the desecration of his holiest thoughts. He knew that such men would often be as riotous again before they reached Jerusalem, and that it would be absurd to expect anything else. But meanwhile he realized what a little more of disgust would be enough to make him hate what was before him. For a moment he forgot the Queen's presence at his side, and he closed his eyes so as not to see what was passing before them.

A little angry sound, that was neither of pain nor of fear, roused him to the present. A man with a bad face and a shock head of red hair had fallen out of the march and stood unsteadily before the Queen, plucking at her mantle in the hope of seeing all her face. He seemed not to see Gilbert, and there was a wicked light in his winy eyes. The Queen drew back, and used her hands to keep her mantle and hood close about her; but the riot pressed onward and forced the man from his feet, so that he almost fell against her. Gilbert caught him by the neck with his hand; and when he had torn the cross from his shoulder, he struck him one blow that flattened his face for life. Then he threw him down into the drunken crowd, a bruised and senseless thing, as island men throw a dead horse from the cliff into the sea.

In a moment the confusion and din were ten times

greater than before. While some marched on, still yelling the tipsy chorus, others stumbled across the body of their unconscious fellow as it lay in the way; two had been struck by it as it fell, and were half stunned; others turned back to see the cause of the trouble; many were forced to the ground, impotently furious with drink, and not a few were trampled upon, and hurt, and burnt by their own torches.

Eleanor looked down upon a writhing mass of miserable human beings who were blind with wine and stupid with rage against the unknown thing that had made them fall. She shrank to Gilbert's side, almost clinging to him.

"We cannot stay here," she said. "You must not let me be recognized by these brutes."

"Keep between me and the wall, then," he answered authoritatively.

His sword was in his hand as he descended the two steps to the level of the street and began to force his way along between the houses and the crowd. It was not easy at first. One sprang at him blindly to stop him, but he thrust him aside; another drew his dagger, but Gilbert struck him on temple and jaw with his flat blade so that he fell in a heap; and presently the man who was sober was feared by the drunken men, and they made little resistance. But many saw by the torchlight that the hooded figure of a woman was gliding along beside him, and foul jests were screamed out, with howls and catcalls, so that the clean Norman blood longed to turn and face the whole throng together with edge and thrust, to be avenged of insult. Yet Gilbert remembered that if he did that, he might be slain, leaving Eleanor to the mercy of ruffians who would not believe that she was the Queen. So he resigned himself and went steadily on along the wall, forcing his opponents out of his way, striking them, stunning them, knocking them down mercilessly, but killing none.

The time had been short from the beginning of the trouble till Gilbert reached the turning for which he was making. And all the while the high, brazen voice was chanting the words of the Canticle, above the roaring confusion. When Eleanor, safe at last, slipped into the shadows beyond the corner, the voice was singing, " He hath visited and redeemed his people," and far up the street the red-cross banner was waving furiously in the glare of the torchlight.

As Gilbert sheathed his sword, Eleanor laid her hand on his.

" You please me," she said; and though there was no light, he knew by her tone that she was smiling. " Thank you," she added softly. " Ask what you will, it is yours."

In the dark he bent down and kissed the hand that held him.

" Madam," he said, " I thank Heaven that I have been allowed to serve a woman in need."

" And you ask nothing of me ? " There was an odd little chill in her voice as she spoke.

Gilbert did not answer at once, for he was uncertain whether to press her with a question about Beatrix, or to ask nothing.

"If I asked anything," he said at last, "I should ask that I might understand your Grace, and why you bade me come in haste to one who is not even with you."

They were within a few steps of the abbey, and the Queen separated a little from him and walked nearer to the wall. Then she stopped short.

"Good-night," she said abruptly.

Gilbert came close to her and stood still in silence.

"Well?" She uttered the single word with a somewhat cold interrogation.

"Madam," said Gilbert, suddenly determined to know the truth, "is Beatrix here with you or not? I have a right to know."

"A right?" There was no mistaking the tone now, but Gilbert was not awed by it.

"Yes," he answered; "you know I have."

Without a word Eleanor left him and walked along the wall in the deep shadow. A moment later Gilbert saw two forms of women beside the taller figure of the Queen. He made a step forward, but instantly stopped again, realizing that he could not press the question in the presence of her ladies. She had doubtless placed them there when she had come out, to wait until she should return.

When he could no longer see her in the gloom, he turned and retraced his steps. The drunken soldiers were gone on their way to join others in some tavern beyond the church, and the street was deserted. The moon, long past the full, was just rising above the hills to eastward, and shed a melancholy light upon the straggling village. Resentful of the

Queen's mysterious silence, and profoundly sad from the impression made upon him by the drunken throng through which he had forced his way, Gilbert slowly climbed the hill and went back to his lodging near the church.

He spent a restless night, and the early summer dawn brought him to his open window with that desire which every man feels, after a troubled day and broken rest, to see the world fresh and clean again, as if nothing had happened — as the writing is smoothed from the wax of the tablet before a new message can be written. Gilbert listened to the morning sounds, — the crowing of the cocks, the barking of the dogs, the calls of peasants greeting one another, — and he breathed the cool dawn air gratefully, without trying to understand what the Queen wanted of him.

CHAPTER XIII

THE Crusade became a fact on that day when the sovereigns of France and Guienne together took the scarlet cross from Bernard's hand. But all was not ready yet. Men were roused, and the times were ripe, but not until the Abbot of Clairvaux had given Europe the final impulse could the armies of the King and of the Queen, and of Conrad, who was never to be crowned Emperor in Rome, begin the march of desperate toil and weariness that lay between their homes and their death. From Vézelay the master preacher and inspirer of mankind went straight to Conrad's court, doing the will of others in faith and without misgiving of conscience, to the greater glory of God, yet haunted in sleep and waking by the dim ghosts of ruin and defeat. He prophesied not, and he saw no visions, but he who was almost the world's physician in his day felt fever in its pulse and heard distraction in the piercing note of its rallying-cry.

There were multitudes without order, there were kings without authority, there were leaders more fit to follow than to head the van. And always, when he had preached and breathed fire through the dry stubble of men's parched hopes, till the flame was broad and high and resistless, there came to him, in the solitude wherein he found no rest, the deadly memory of the Hermit's blasted host, overtaken, overcome, crushed to a heap of bones in one wild battle with the Seljuk horde.

Many a time he told himself that Peter had been no soldier, that stronger and wiser men had won what he had failed even to see, and that the memories of Godfrey's fearful wrath, of Raymond's brave wisdom, and of Tancred's knightly deeds were more than half another victory gained. Yet always, too, in his deep intuition of men's limits, he felt that the soldiers of his day were not those great knights who had humbled the Emperor of the East and taught a lesson of fear to Kilidj Arslan, and who had grasped the flowers of Syria and Palestine with iron hands. It was indeed God's will that a great host should go forth again, but neither Bernard nor any other man could surely tell that in the will of Heaven there was victory too. The first to win or die must always and ever be the first alone; those who come after them imitate them, profit by them, or find ruin sown in the ravaged track of conquest; do what they may, believe as they can, be their faith ever so high and pure, they can never feel the splendid exultation of the soul that has found out some godlike and untried deed to do.

The times had changed in forty years. The modern world is turned by the interests of the many, but the world of old revolved about the ambitions of the few, and the transition began in Bernard's day after the furnace of the eleventh century had poured its molten material out upon the world to settle and cool again in the castings of nations, separate and individual. There was less impulse, more rigidity; here and there, there was more strength, but everywhere there was

N

less fire; and as interests grew in opposite directions and solidified apart, the chances of any universal rising or joint battle for belief grew less. Mankind moves westward with the sun; men's thoughts turn back to the bright East, the source of every faith that moves humanity; at first, for faith's sake, men may retrace their migration to its source and give their own blood for their holy places; and after them a generation will give its money for the honour of its God; but at the last, and surely, comes the time of memory's fading, the winter of belief, the night of faith's day, wherein a delicately nurtured and greedy race will give neither gold nor blood, but only a prayer or a smile for the hope of a life to come.

Gilbert Warde began the great march, as some others did, in earnest trust and belief. He had struck blows in self-defence, and for vengeance; he had fought once in Italy for sheer love of fighting and the animal joy of the strong northerner in cut and thrust, and lately, at Vézelay, he had fought a herd of drunken brutes for a woman's safety; but he had not known the false and fierce delight of killing men to please God. That was still before him, and he looked forward to it with that half-deadly, half-voluptuous longing for bloodshed sanctioned and sanctified by justice or religion, which is at the main root of every soldier's nature, let men say what they will.

When the Crusade began its pilgrimage of arms, Gilbert had not yet seen Beatrix, nor had he any distinct proof, even by the Queen's word, that she was really in France. Eleanor herself had kept him at a distance during the months that elapsed between Bernard's preaching at Vézelay and the departure of the host; and he had been much alone, being more knight than squire, and yet not having knighthood, because he would not ask it of the Queen, since that would have seemed like begging for a reward, and she did not offer it freely, while the King, of course, knew nothing of what had taken place. One night, as he sat alone in his chamber, a man entered, cloaked and hooded, and laid before him something heavy wrapped in a silk kerchief that might have been a woman's; and the man went out quickly before Gilbert had thought of asking a question. In the kerchief there was a purse of gold, which indeed he sorely needed, and yet after the man was gone he sat stupidly staring at the contents for a long time. At first it seemed to him almost certain that the money came from the Queen; but as he remembered her coldness ever since the riot at Vézelay, and recollected how many times he had of late tried to attract her attention without success, the conviction lost ground, and he began to believe it possible, if not certain, that the gift had proceeded from another source. As men did in those days, and as many would do now, he might have taken thankfully such fortune as he found in his path, not inquiring too closely whether he had deserved it or not. But yet he hesitated, and then, turning the thing over, he saw on the seal the device of the Abbot of Sheering, and he thanked Heaven for such a friend.

And again, as living much alone made him more prone to self-questioning, he asked himself whether he had ever loved Beatrix at all. He heard men

talk of love, he heard men sing the love-songs of a
passionate and earnest age, and it seemed to him that
he could nowhere find in his heart or soul the chords
that should answer directly to that music. In him
the memory was a treasure rather than a power; and
while he loved to dream himself again through the
pleasant passages of youth, calling up the kind and
girlish face that was always near him in shadow-land,
and although the image came, and he heard the voice
and could almost fancy that he touched the little
hand, yet it was all soft rather than vivid, it was
full of tenderness rather than of a cruel and insatiate
longing, it was a satisfaction rather than a desire.
And therefore, though the mere name of Beatrix
had been enough to bring him back from Rome, and
though he had asked many questions in the hope of
seeing her, he attempted nothing daring in order
to be assured of the truth.

Then came the final preparations, the testing of
armour, the providing of small things necessary on
the march, the renewal of saddle and bridle, and all
the hundred details which every knight and soldier
in those days understood and cared for himself. Then
the first march eastward through a changing country
which Gilbert had not yet seen, the encampment
upon the heights about Metz, the days spent in
roaming over the old city, long ago a fortress of
the Romans — and during all that time Gilbert
scarcely caught a glimpse of the Queen, though he
saw the King often at religious functions in the
lately built church of Saint Vincent; for as yet the
great cathedral was not even begun.   Last of all, on

the morning of the final departure the royal armies assembled before dawn at the church, the court and the greater knights within, the vast concourse of men-at-arms and footmen and followers in the open air outside. But Gilbert passed boldly in among the high nobles of France and Guienne, and knelt with them in the dim nave, where little oil-lamps hung under the high vaults, and many candles burned upon the altars in the side-chapels, shedding a soft light on dark faces and mailed breasts and rich mantles. Out of the dusky choir rang the high plain-chant of monks and singing-boys, from the altar the bishop's voice alone intoned the Preface of the Holy Cross, and presently, in the deep silence, the Sacred Host was lifted high, and then the golden chalice.

The King and Queen knelt side by side to receive the holy bread, and after them the nobles and the knights in turn went up to communicate, in long pro-cession, while the day dawned through the clerestory windows high overhead, and the King and Queen knelt all the time with folded hands till the mass was over. Then at last the standard of the cross was brought forth, with the great standards of France and of Gui-enne — the banner of Saint George and the Dragon, which Eleanor was to hand down to her sons and sons' sons, kings of England, for generations; and the choir began to sing " Vexilla regis prodeunt " (" The stand-ards of the king go forth "). So all that great and noble host went out in state, chanting the lofty hymn that rang with tones of victory, while among cypress groves on far Asian hillsides the ravens waited for

the coming feast of Christian flesh, and the circling
kite scanned the broad earth and dancing water
for the living things that were to feed him full of
death.

At last the worst of the fearful march was over,
and the Crusaders lay before Constantinople, travel-
stained, half-starved and wan, but at rest. The great
open space of undulating ground before the wall that
joined the Golden Horn with the Sea of Marmara
was their camping-ground, and countless tents were
pitched in uneven lines as far as one could see. The
King, and Queen Eleanor, and a few of the greater
nobles had entered the city and were lodged in its
palaces about the Emperor's gardens, but all the rest
remained without. For the German hosts had been
first to reach the Bosphorus, and where they had
passed they had left a broad track of dust and ashes
and a great terror upon all living things. Even in
Constantinople itself, where the Emperor had received them as guests, they had robbed and ravaged
and burned as if they had been in an enemy's country;
and when at last he had persuaded them to cross over
to Asia, they had left the great city half sacked behind them, so that the Emperor's heart was resentfully hardened against every man who bore the
cross.

And indeed he had been long-suffering, for many in
his place would have borne less; and if he persuaded
the Crusaders on false pretences to leave his capital
and push on into Asia, he did so as the only
means of saving his own people from robbery and
violence.

Though the King and the court only were lodged within the walls, while the main force of fighting men was encamped without, yet the guard at the gates was not over-strictly kept, and many knights went in with their squires to see the great sights and, if possible, to get a glimpse of the Emperor himself. Gilbert did like the rest and gave the captain of the Second Military Gate a piece of silver to go in.

At the first glance he saw that there was little safety for any stranger who should chance to wander from the chief streets. Safe-conduct and security had been proclaimed for every soldier who wore a cross, and the fear of a cruel death was enough to enforce the imperial edict wherever watchmen or soldiers were present to remind men of it; but there was no rigorous counter-rule on the Crusaders' side, and if the rough Burgundian men-at-arms and the wild riders of Gascony who were in Eleanor's train had been admitted in numbers, they would hardly have withheld their hands from such desirable things as they chanced to find in their way. The Greeks stood watching in their doorways and their women sat huddled together in the small low balconies above, or at narrow windows whence they could see the street. Whenever a party of knights appeared, the men withdrew within their houses, the women were out of sight in a moment, and within the windows the curtains were closely drawn. Looking to right and left for the sign of a friendly tavern or the more desirable attraction of henna-dyed hair and painted cheeks and

darkened eyes, the strangers saw nothing on each
side of the street but blank houses and closed doors.
But when they had passed, the curtains were parted,
the doors were ajar again, and curious eyes looked
after the big mailed figures, the gaudy cloaks, and
the enormous cross-hilted swords of the Frenchmen.
Of the poorer people in the streets and those whose
business kept them abroad on that day, the men
scowled resentfully at the intruders and the women
drew their veils closely across their faces. For
although the French were gentler and less uncouth
to see than the rough Germans who had wrecked the
city a few weeks earlier, the Greeks were past trusting any one, and looked upon all strangers with like
fear and ever-increasing distrust.

When he was within the gate, Gilbert saw three
broad roads before him, stretching downward from
the higher land on which the city wall was built.
Vast and magnificent, Constantinople lay at his feet,
a rich disorder of palaces and churches and towers.
On the left, the quiet waters of the Golden Horn
made a broad, blue path to meet the Bosphorus in
the hazy distance before him; on the right, the Sea
of Marmara was dazzling white under the morning
sun, where its mirror-like reflections could be seen
between the towers of the sea-wall. The air was
full of light and colour, and the smell of late roses
and autumn fruits and the enchantment of sights
altogether new took hold of the young man's senses.
Far before him and, as it seemed, near the end
of the central street, a dome rose above the
level of the surrounding city, raising its golden

cross to the deep sky. Without hesitation Gilbert chose that road and followed it nearly a full hour before he stood at the gate of Saint Sophia's church.

He stood still and looked up, he had heard much of the great cathedral and had wished to see it and the treasures it contained; but now, by an impulse which he followed without attempting to understand it, instead of going in he turned on his heel and went away. He said to himself that there would be plenty of time for visiting the church, and possibly the idea of leaving the beautiful daylight for the dark aisles and chapels of an ancient cathedral was distasteful. In his change of intention there seemed not to be that little element of chance that makes a man turn to the right rather than to the left when there is no choice of ways. He went on skirting the buttresses and outbuildings and following the steep descent by the northwest side of the cathedral. Here, to his surprise, he found the life of the city going on as usual, and as yet none of the Crusaders had found their way thither. The tide of business at that hour set toward the great markets and warehouses, to the north of which one of the Emperor's smaller palaces was built amid shady gardens that ran down to the water's edge. Gilbert was carried along by the stream of hurrying men, who, seeing that he was a stranger and alone, jostled him with little ceremony. He had too much wit and perhaps too much self-respect, to rouse a street brawl on his own behalf, and when any one ran against him with unnecessary roughness he contented himself with stiffening his

back and holding his own in passive resistance. He
had reached his full strength and was a match for
many little Greeks, yet the annoyance was distasteful
to him, and he was glad to find himself pushed into
a narrow lane between high walls and crossed by a
low covered bridge; and at the end, under overhanging branches, he saw the blue light of the sea.
He followed the byway down to the water, supposing that there must be some beach or open
space there, where he might be alone. But, to
his surprise, both walls were built out on little
piers into the sea, shutting off the view on each side.
Looking straight before him, he saw the trees and
white houses of distant Chalcedon, within the Sea of
Marmara, but Chrysopolis was hidden on the left.
The lane ended in a little beach, some six feet wide,
and a skiff lay there with a pair of oars, half out of
water, and made fast by a chain to a ring in the
masonry. A cool breeze drew in through the narrow entrance, and the clear salt water lapped the
clean sand softly, and splashed under the stern and
along the wales of the half-beached boat.

Gilbert rested one hand against the wall and looked
out, breathing the bright sea air with a sort of
voluptuous enjoyment, and letting his thoughts
wander as they would. The march had been long
and full of hardships, mingled often with real bodily
suffering, and those who had escaped without disease
were reckoned fortunate. The war was still before
them, but no imaginable combat with men could
be compared with the long struggle for existence
through which the Crusaders had won their way

to Constantinople. It seemed as if the worst
were altogether past and as if rest-time had come
already.

In the cool and shady retreat from the crowd to
which Gilbert's footsteps had led him, an Italian
might have lain dreaming half the day, and an
Oriental would have sat down to withdraw himself
from the material tedium of life in the superior
atmosphere of *kêf*. But Gilbert was chilled to a
different temper by the colder and harder life of the
North, and the springs of his nature could not be so
easily and wholly relaxed. In a few moments he
grew restless, stood upright and began to look
about him, letting his hand fall by his side from its
hold on the wall. The walls were solid from end to
end of the narrow lane, and not less than three times
a man's height. The stones of the masonry were
damp for six or seven feet above the ground, showing
that the earth was at a higher level behind them
than in the lane, and the trees of which the branches
overhung the way were of the sort found in Eastern
gardens, a cedar of Lebanon on the one side, a syca-
more on the other; and with the light breeze there
came to Gilbert's nostrils the aromatic scent of young
oranges still green on the trees. It flashed upon him
that the lane divided the imperial gardens and that the
walls were built out into the water in order to prevent
intrusion. One end of the boat's chain was shackled
to a ring-bolt in the bows, and the other was made fast
to the ring in the wall by one of those rude iron pad-
locks which had been used in Asia since the times of
Alexander. Gilbert had heard wonderful tales of the

gardens at Constantinople, and he resented the idea of
being so near them and yet so effectually excluded.
He tried to wrench the boat's chain from the bows,
and, failing, he tried to force the lock, but the iron was
solid and the lock was good; moreover, the chain was
too short to allow the skiff to float to the end of the
wall, if he had launched it.   The idea of seeing into
the garden became a determination as soon as he
found that there were serious obstacles in the way,
and by the time he had persuaded himself that the
boat could not help him he would have readily risked
life and limb for his fancy.   A few moments' reflection showed him, however, that there need be no great
danger in the undertaking, for the defence had a weak
point.   The foundations on which the walls stood
were above water by several inches and were wide
enough to give him a foothold if he could only keep
himself upright against the flat surface.   The latter
difficulty could easily be overcome by using one of
the oars from the boat, and he began to attempt the
passage at once, cautiously putting one foot before
the other and steadying himself with the oar against
the opposite wall.   It did not occur to him that to
get into the Emperor's gardens by stealth might be
looked upon as a serious matter.   In a few moments
he had reached the end and was getting back to the
land on the other side.

From the water's edge three little terraces led up
like steps to the level of the garden, where the trees
grew thick and dark; and, although it was early
autumn, each terrace was covered with flowers of a
different hue —pink and soft yellow and pale blue.

Gilbert had never seen anything made to grow in such orderly profusion, and when he reached the top by narrow steps built against the wall, he found himself treading on a fine white gravel surface on which not even a single dead leaf had been allowed to lie, and which extended some thirty yards inwards under the trees to a straight bank of moss that had a sheen like green velvet where the sun fell upon it through the parted leaves overhead. Very far away between the trunks of the trees there was the gleam of white marble walls.

Gilbert hesitated a little, and then walked slowly forward toward the bank. As yet he had seen no trace of any living thing in the garden, but as he advanced and changed his position he noticed a small dash of colour, like the corner of a dark blue cloak, beside the trunk of one of the larger trees. Some one was sitting on the other side, and he moved cautiously and almost noiselessly till he saw that the person was a lady, seated on the ground and absorbed in a book. He did not remember to have seen more than two or three women reading in all his life, and one of them was Queen Eleanor; another was Beatrix, who, as a lonely child in the solitude of her father's castle, had acquired some learning from the chaplain, and delighted in spelling out the few manuscripts in her father's possession.

Gilbert Warde was as much a born sportsman as he was a fighter, and he had stalked the fallow-deer in Stortford woods since he had been old enough to draw an arrow's head to his finger.

Step by step, from tree to tree, with cat-like tread,

he came nearer, amused by an almost boyish pleasure
in his own skill. Once the lady moved, but she
looked in the opposite direction, and then at last,
when he was within a dozen yards of her, half-
sheltered by a slender stem, she looked straight across
toward him, and the light fell upon her face. He
knew that she saw him, but he could not have moved
from the spot if it had been to save his life, for the
lady was Beatrix herself. In spite of a separation
that had lasted two years, in spite of her final growth
out of early girlhood, he knew that he was not mistaken, and her dark eyes were looking straight into
his, telling him that she knew him, too. There was
no fear in them, and she showed no surprise, but as
she looked, a very lovely smile came into her sad face.
He was so glad to see her that he thought little or
not at all of her looks. But she was not beautiful
in any common sense, and, saving the expression in
her face, she could hardly have passed for pretty in
the presence of Queen Eleanor and of most of her
three hundred ladies. Her forehead was round and
full rather than classic, and the thick dark eyebrows
were somewhat rough and irregular, turning slightly
upwards as they approached each other, a peculi-
arity which gave an almost pathetic expression to the
eyes themselves; the small and by no means perfectly
shaped nose was sensitively drawn at the nostrils,
but had also an odd look of independence and inquiry; and the wide and shapely lips were more apt
to smile with a half-humorous sadness than to part
with laughter. Small and well-modelled ears were
half covered by dark brown hair that had been almost

black in childhood, and which fell to her shoulders
in broad waves, in the fashion used by the Queen.
While Gilbert looked and remained motionless, the
girl rose lightly to her feet, and he saw that she was
shorter than he had expected, but slight and delicately
made.   With one hand he could have lifted her from
the ground, with two he could have held her in the
air like a child.   She was not the Beatrix he remembered, though he had known her instantly; she was
not the solemn, black-eyed maiden of whom he sometimes dreamed; she was a being full of individual
life and thought, quick, sensitive, perhaps capricious, and charming, if she could charm at all, by a
spell that was quite her own.

Half-frightened at last by his motionless attitude
and his silence, she called him by name.

"Gilbert !   What is the matter?"

He shook his broad shoulders as if waking to consciousness, and the smile in her face was reflected
in his own.

The voice, at least, had not changed, and the first
tones called up the long-cherished record of childish
years; for scent and sound can span the wastes of
years and the deserts of separation, when sight is
dull and even touch is unresponsive.

Gilbert came forward, holding out both hands;
and Beatrix took them when he was close to her,
and held them in hers.   The little tears had started
in her eyes, that were glad as flowers at dewfall, and
in her very clear, pale cheeks the colour lightened
like the dawn.

The man's face was quiet, and his heart was in no

haste, though he was so glad. He drew her toward
him, as he had often done, and she seemed light and
little in his hands. But when he would have kissed
her cheek as in other times, she turned in his hold
like a bow that is bent but not strung, and straightened herself again quickly; and something tingled
in him suddenly, and he tried hard to kiss her; yet
when he saw that he must hurt her, he let her go,
and laughed oddly. Her blush deepened to red and
then faded all at once, and she turned her face
away.

"How is it that I have never found you before
now?" Gilbert asked softly. "Were you with the
Queen at Vézelay? Have you been with her on all
the march?"

"Yes."

"And did you not know that I was with the
army?"

"Yes ; but I could not send you any word. She
would not let me." The girl looked round quickly
in sudden apprehension. "If she should find you
here, it would be ill for you," she added, with a
gesture of pushing him away.

But he showed that he would not go away.

"The Queen has always been kind to me," he
said. "I am not afraid."

Beatrix would not turn to him, and was silent.
He was not timid, but words did not come easily
just then; therefore, manlike, he tried to draw her
to him again. But she put away his hand somewhat
impatiently and shook her head, whereat he felt the
tingling warmth in his blood again. Then he remem-

bered how he had felt the same thing on that night in Vézelay, when the Queen had pressed his arm unexpectedly, and once before, when she had kissed him in the tennis-court, and he was angry with himself.

"Come," she said, "let us sit down and talk. There are two years between us."

She led the way back in the direction whence he had come, and when they had reached the bank of moss she seated herself and looked out under the trees, at the blue water. He stood still a moment as though hesitating, and then sat down beside her, but not quite close to her, as he would have done in earlier years.

"Yes," he said thoughtfully, "there are two years between us. We must bridge them."

"And between what we were and what we are there is something more than time," she answered, still looking far away.

"Yes."

He was silent, and he thought of his mother, and he knew that Beatrix was thinking of her too, and of her own father. It had not occurred to him that Beatrix could resent the marriage as bitterly as he, nor that she could in any way be as great a loser by it as he was.

"Tell me why you left England," he said at last.

"And you? Why did you leave your home?"

She turned to him, and the little melancholy smile that was characteristic of her was in her face.

"I had no home left," he answered gravely.

"And had I? How could I live with them? No

— how could I have lived with them, knowing what
I did, even had they been ever so kind?"

"Were they unkind to you?"

Gilbert's deep eyes grew suddenly pale as they
turned to hers, and his words came slowly and
distinctly, like the first drops of a thunder shower.

"Not at first. They came to the castle where I
had been left all alone after they were married, and
my father told me that I must call the Lady Goda
my mother. She kissed me as if she were fond of
me for his sake."

Gilbert started a little, and his teeth set together,
while he clasped his hands over one knee and waited
to hear more. Beatrix understood his look, and knew
that she had unintentionally hurt him. She laid her
hand softly upon his arm.

"Forgive me," she said. "I should not talk about
it."

"No," he said harshly, "go on! I feel nothing ;
I am past feeling there. They were kind to you at
first, you said."

"Yes," she continued, looking at him sideways.
"They were kind when they remembered to be, but
they often forgot. And then, it was hard to treat
her with respect when I came to know how she had
got your inheritance for my father, and how she
had let you leave England to wander about the
world. And then, last year, it seemed to me all at
once that I was a woman and could not bear it any
longer, for I saw that she hated me. And when a
son was born to them, my father turned against me
and threatened that he would send me to a nunnery.

So I fled, one day when my father had ridden to
Stoke and the Lady Goda was sleeping in her chamber. A groom and my handmaid helped me and
went with me, for my father would have hanged
them if they had stayed behind; so I took refuge with
the Empress Maud at Oxford, and soon there came
a letter from the Queen of France to the Empress,
asking that I might be sent to the French court if I
would. And something of the reason for the Queen's
wish I can guess. But not all."

She ceased, and for some moments Gilbert sat silent
beside her, but not as if he had nothing to say. He
seemed rather to be checking himself lest he should
say too much.

"So you were at Vézelay," he said at last; "yet I
sought your face everywhere, and I could not see you."

"How did you know?" asked Beatrix.

"The Queen had written to me," he answered;
"so I came back from Rome."

"I understand," said the young girl, quietly.

"What is it that you understand?"

"I understand why she has prevented me from
seeing you, when you have been near me for almost
a year."

She checked a little sigh, and then looked out at
the water again.

"I wish I did," Gilbert answered, with a short
laugh.

Beatrix laughed too, but in a different tone.

"How dull you are!" she cried. Gilbert looked
at her quickly, for no man likes to be told that he is
dull, by any woman, old or young.

"Am I? It seems to me that you do not put things very clearly."

Beatrix was evidently not persuaded that he was in earnest, for she looked at him long and gravely.

"We have not met for so long," she said, "that I am not quite sure of you."

She threw her head back and scrutinized his face with half-closed lids; and about her lips there was an attempt to smile, that came and went fitfully.

"Besides," she added, as she turned away at last, "you could not possibly be so simple as that."

"By 'simple,' do you mean foolish, or do you mean plain?"

"Neither," she answered without looking at him. "I mean innocent."

"Oh!"

Gilbert uttered the ejaculation in a tone expressive rather of bewilderment than of surprise. He did not in the least understand what she meant. Seeing that she did not enlighten him, and feeling uncomfortable, it was quite natural that he should attack her on different ground.

"You have changed," he said coldly. "I suppose you have grown up, as you call it."

For a moment Beatrix said nothing, but her lips trembled as if she were trying not to smile at what he said; and suddenly she could resist no longer, and laughed at him outright.

"I cannot say the same for you," she retorted presently; "you are certainly not grown up yet!"

This pleased Gilbert even less than what she had said before, for he was still young enough to wish himself older. He therefore answered her laughter with a look of grave contempt. She was woman enough to see that the time had come to take him by surprise, with a view of ascertaining the truth.

" How long has the Queen loved you ? " she asked suddenly; and while she seemed not to be looking at him, she was watching every line in his face, and would have noticed the movement of an eyelash if there had been nothing else to note. But Gilbert was really surprised.

" The Queen! The Queen love me! Are you beside yourself ? "

" Not at all," answered the young girl, quietly; " it is the talk of the court. They say that the King is jealous of you."

She laughed — gayly, this time, for she saw that he really had had no idea of the truth. Then she grew grave all at once, for it occurred to her that she had perhaps made a mistake in putting the idea into his head.

" At least," she said, as if correcting herself, " that is what they used to say last year."

" You are quite mad," he said, without a smile. " I cannot imagine how such an absurd idea could have suggested itself to you. In the first place, the Queen would never look at a poor Englishman like me — "

" I defy any woman not to look at you," said Beatrix.

"Why?" he asked, with curiosity.

"Is this more simplicity, or is it more dulness?"

"Both, I suppose," answered Gilbert, in a hurt tone. "You are very witty."

"Oh, no!" she exclaimed. "Wit is quite another thing."

Then her tone changed and her face softened wonderfully as she took his hand.

"I am glad that you do not believe it," she said; "and I am glad that you do not care to be thought handsome. But I think it is true that the Queen loves you, and if she sent to England for me, that was merely in order to bring you back to France. Of course she could not know —"

She checked herself, and he, of course, asked what she had meant to say, and insisted upon knowing.

"The Queen could not know," she said at last, "that we should seem so strange to each other when we met."

"Do I seem so strange to you?" he asked, in a sorrowful tone.

"No," she answered, "it is the other way. I can see that you expected me to be very different."

"Indeed, I did not," answered Gilbert, with some indignation. "At least," he added hastily, "if I thought anything about it, I did not expect that you would be half so pretty, or half —"

"If you thought anything about it," laughed Beatrix, interrupting him.

"You know what I mean," he said, justly annoyed by his own lack of tact.

"Oh, yes; of course I do — that is the trouble."

"If we are going to do nothing but quarrel," he said, "I am almost sorry that I came here."

Again her tone changed, but this time she did not touch his hand. Hearing her voice, he expected that she would, and he was oddly disappointed that she did not.

"Nothing could make me sorry that you found me," she answered. "You do not know how hard I have tried to see you all through this last year!"

Her tone was tender and earnest, and though they had been long parted, she was nearer to him than he knew. His hand closed upon hers, and in the little thrill that he felt he forgot his disappointment.

"Could you not send me any word?" he asked.

"I am a prisoner," she answered, more than half in earnest. "It would be ill for you if the Queen found you here; but there is no danger, for they are all gone to the high mass in the cathedral."

"And why are you left behind?" he asked.

"They always say that I am not strong," she replied, "especially when there might be a possibility of your seeing me. She has never allowed me to be with all the others when the court is together, since I was brought over from England."

"That is why I did not see you at Vézelay," he said, suddenly understanding.

And with him to understand was to act. He might have had some difficulty in persuading himself at leisure that he was seriously in love with Beatrix, but being taken suddenly and unawares, he had not the slightest doubt as to what he ought to do. Before she could answer his last words, he had risen to his feet and was drawing her by the hand.

"Come," he cried. "I can easily take you by the way I came. It is only a step, and in five minutes you shall be as free as I am!"

But, to his great surprise, Beatrix seemed inclined to laugh at him.

"Where should we go?" she asked, refusing to leave her seat. "We should be caught before we reached the city gates, and it would be the worse for us."

"And who should dare touch us?" asked Gilbert, indignantly. "Who should dare to lay a hand on you?"

"You are strong and brave," answered Beatrix, "but you are not an army, and the Queen — but you will not believe what I say."

"If the Queen even cared to see my face, she could send for me. It is three weeks since I caught a glimpse of her, five hundred yards away."

"She is angry with you," answered the young girl, "and she thinks that you will wish to be with her, and will find some way of seeing her."

"But," argued Gilbert, "if she only meant to use your name in order to bring me from Rome, it would have been quite enough to have written that letter without having brought you at all."

"And how could she tell that I did not know where you were, or that I could not send you a message which might contradict hers?"

"That is true," Gilbert admitted. "But what does it matter, after all, since we have met at last?"

"Yes; what does it matter?"

They asked the answerless question of each other almost unconsciously, for they were finding each other again. There are plants which may be plucked up half-grown, before their roots have spread in the earth or their buds ripened to blossoming, and they may lie long in dry places till they seem withered and dead; but there is life in their fibres still, and the power to grow is in the shrivelled stem and in the dusty leaf, so that if they be planted again and tended they come at last to their due maturity. Gilbert and Beatrix might have lived out their lives apart, and in the course of years they would have been the merest memories to each other; but having met in the slow weaving of fate's threads, they became destined to win or lose together.

Their conversation needed but the slightest direction to take them back to the recollections of other times, and one of the first elements of lasting love is a common past, though that past may have covered but a few days. To that memory lovers go back as to the starting-point of life's journey, and though they may not speak of it often, yet its existence is the narrow ledge on which they have reared their stronghold in the perilous pass. And the English boy and girl had really lived a joint life, in their sympathies and surroundings, for years before a joint misfortune had overtaken them. In their meeting after a long separation they felt at the same time the rare delight of friendship renewed, and the still rarer charm of finding new acquaintances in old friends; but besides the well-remembered bond of

habit, and the strong attraction of newly awakened
interest, there was the masterful, nameless something upon which man's world has spun for all ages,
as the material earth turns on its poles toward the
sun — always to hope beyond failure, always to life
beyond death, always and forever to love beyond
life. It is the spark from heaven, the stolen fire,
the mask of divinity with which the poorest of mankind may play himself a god. It has all powers, and
it brings all gifts — the gift of tongues, for it is
above words; the gift of prophecy, for it has foreknowledge of its own sadness; the gift of life, for
it is itself that elixir in which mankind boasts of
eternal youth.

The two sat side by side and talked, and were
silent, and talked again, understanding each other
and happy in finding more to understand. The sun
rose high and fell through the rustling leaves in
fanciful warm tracery of light; down from the Bosphorus the sweet northerly breeze came over the
rippling water, laden with the scent of orange-blossoms from the Asian shore and with the perfume
of late roses from far Therapia. Between the
trees they could see the white sails of little vessels
beating to windward up the narrow channel, and now
and then the dyed canvas of a fisherman's craft set
a strangely disquieting note of colour upon the sea.
There seemed to be no time, for all life was theirs,
and it was all before them; an hour had passed, and
they had not told each other half; another came and
went, and what there was to tell still gained upon
them.

BEATRIX AND GILBERT

They talked of the Crusade, and of how the Queen had given her ladies no choice, commanding them to follow her, as a noble would order his vassals to rise with him to the king's war. Three hundred ladies were to wear mail and lead the van of battle, the fairest ladies of France and Aquitaine, of Gascony, of Burgundy, and of Provence. So far, a few had ridden, and many had been carried in closed litters slung between mules or borne on the broad shoulders of Swiss porters; and each lady had her serving-maid, and her servants and mules heavy laden with the furniture of beauty, with laces and silks and velvets, jewellery and scented waters, and salves for the face, of great virtue against cold and heat. It was a little army in itself, recruited of the women, and in which beauty was rank, and rank was power; and in order that the three hundred might ride with Queen Eleanor in the most marvellous masquerade of all time, a host of some two thousand servants and porters crossed Europe on foot and on horseback from the Rhine to the Bosphorus. The mere idea was so vastly absurd that Gilbert had laughed at it many a time by himself; and yet there was at the root of it an impulse which was rather sublime than ridiculous. Between its conception and its execution the time was too long, and the hot blood of daring romance already felt the fatal chill of coming failure.

Gilbert looked at the delicate features and the slight figure beside him, and he resented the mere thought that Beatrix should ever be exposed to weariness and hardship. But she laughed.

"I am always left behind on great occasions," she said. "You need not fear for me, for I shall certainly not be seen on the Queen's left hand when she overcomes the Seljuks without your help. I shall be told to wait quietly in my tent until it is all over. What can I do?"

"You can at least let me know where you are," answered Gilbert.

"What satisfaction shall you get from that? You cannot see me ; you cannot come to me in the ladies' camp."

"Indeed I can, and will," answered Gilbert, without the least hesitation.

"At the risk of the Queen's displeasure?"

"At any risk."

"How strange it is!" exclaimed Beatrix, raising her eyebrows a little, but smiling happily. "This morning you would not have risked anything especial for the sake of finding me, but now that we have met by chance you are ready to do anything and everything to see me again."

"Of some things," answered her companion, "one does not know how much one wants them till they are within reach."

"And there are others which one longs for till one has them, and which one despises as soon as they are one's own."

"What things may those be?" asked Gilbert.

"I have heard Queen Eleanor say that a husband is one of them," answered Beatrix, demurely, "but I dare say that she is not always right."

Side by side the two sat in the autumn noonday,

each forgetful of all but the other, in the perfect unconsciousness of the difference their meeting was to make in their lives from that day onward. Yet after the first few words they did not speak again of Beatrix's father nor of Gilbert's mother. By a common instinct they tried to lose both, in the happiness of again finding one another.

Then, at last, a cloud passed over the sun, and Beatrix felt a little chill that was like the breath of a coming evil while Gilbert became suddenly very grave and thoughtful.

Beatrix looked round, more in fear than in suspicion, as a child does at night, when it has been frightened by a tale of goblins; and, turning, she caught sight of something and turned farther, and then started with a scared cry and half rose, with her hand on Gilbert's arm. Anxious for her, he sprang up to his height at the sound of her voice, and at the same moment he saw what she saw, and uttered an exclamation of surprise. It was not a cloud that had passed between them and the sun.

The Queen stood there, as she had come from the Office in the church, a veil embroidered with gold pinned upon her head in a fashion altogether her own. Her clear eyes were very bright and hard, and her beautiful lips had a frozen look.

" It is very long since I have seen you," she said to Gilbert, " and I had not thought to see you here — of all places — unbidden."

" Nor I to be here, Madam," answered the Englishman.

"Did you come here in your sleep?" asked the Queen, coldly.

"For aught that I can tell how I got here, it may be as your Grace says. I came by such a way as I may not find again."

"I care not how soon you find another, sir, so that it be a way out."

Gilbert had never seen the Queen gravely displeased, and as yet she had been very kind to him when he had been in her presence. Against her anger he drew himself up, for he neither loved her nor feared her, and as he looked at her now he saw in her eyes that haunting memory of his own mother which had disturbed him more than once.

"I ask your Grace's pardon," he said slowly, "for having entered uninvited. Yet I am glad that I did, since I have found what was kept from me so long."

"I fancied your idol so changed that you might not care to find it after all!"

Beatrix hardly understood what the words meant, but she knew that they were intended to hurt both her and Gilbert, and she saw by his face what he felt. Knowing as she did that the Queen was very strongly attracted by him, she would not have been human if she had not felt in her throat the pulse of triumph, as she stood beside the most beautiful woman in the world, pale, slight, sad-eyed, but preferred before the other's supreme beauty by the one man whose preference meant anything at all. But a moment later she forgot herself and feared for him.

"Madam," he said very slowly and distinctly, "I trust that I may not fail in courtesy, either toward your Grace, or toward any other woman, high or low ; and none but the blind man would deny that, of all women, you are fairest, wherefore you may cast it in the face of other ladies of your court that you are fairer than they. But since your Grace would wear a man's armour and draw a knight's sword, and ride for the Cross, shoulder to shoulder with the gentlemen of Normandy and Gascony and France, I shall tell you without fear of discourtesy, as one man would tell another, that your words and your deeds are less gentle than your royal blood.''

He finished speaking and looked her quietly in the face, his arms folded, his brow calm, his eyes still and clear. Beatrix fell back a step and drew anxious breath, for it was no small thing to cross words boldly with the sovereign next in power to the Emperor himself. And at the first, the seething blood hissed in the Queen's ears, and her lovely face grew ashy pale, and her wrath rose in her eyes with the red shadow of coming revenge. But no manlike impulse moved her hand nor her foot, and she stood motionless, with half her mantle gathered round her. In the fierce silence, the two faced each other, while Beatrix looked on, half sick with fear. Neither moved an eyelash, nor did the glance of either flinch, till it seemed as if a spell had bound them there for-ever, motionless, under the changing shadows of the leaves, only their hair stirring in the cool wind. Eleanor knew that no man had ever thus faced her before. For a few moments she felt the absolute confidence in herself which had never failed her yet; the certainty of strength which drove the King to

take refuge from her behind a barrier of devotion
and prayer; the insolence of wit and force against
which the holy man of Clairvaux had never found a
weapon of thought or speech. And still the hard
Norman eyes were colder and angrier than her own,
and still the man's head was high, and his face like
a mask. At last she felt her lids tremble, and
her lips quiver; his face moved strangely in her
sight, his cold resistance hurt her as if she were
thrusting herself uselessly against a rock; she knew
that he was stronger than she, and that she loved
him. The struggle was over; her face softened, and
her eyes looked down. Beatrix could not understand, for she had expected that the Queen would
command Gilbert to leave them, and that before long
her vengeance would most certainly overtake him.
But instead, it was the young soldier without fame
or fortune, the boy with whom she had many a time
played children's games, before whom Eleanor,
Duchess of Guienne and Queen of France, lost
courage and confidence.

A moment later she looked up again, and not a
trace of her anger was left to see. Simply and
quietly she came to Gilbert's side and laid her hand
upon his sleeve.

"You make me say things I do not mean," she said.

If she had actually asked his forgiveness in words,
she could not have expressed a real regret more
plainly, nor perhaps could she have done anything
so sure to produce a strong impression upon the
two who heard her. Gilbert's face relaxed instantly,
and Beatrix forgot to be afraid.

" I crave your Grace's pardon," said the young
man. " If I spoke rudely let my excuse be that it
was not for myself. We were children together," he
added, looking at Beatrix, " we grew up together,
and after long parting we have met by chance.
There is much left of what there was. I pray that
without concealment I may see the Lady Beatrix
again."

The Queen turned slowly from them and stood
for a few moments looking toward the sea. Then
she turned again and smiled at Gilbert, not unkindly;
but she said no word, and presently, as they stood
there, she left them, and walked slowly away with
bent head, toward the palace.

P

CHAPTER XIV

THREE weeks the French armies lay encamped
without the walls of Constantinople, while the
Emperor of the Greeks used every art and every
means to rid himself of the unwelcome host, without giving overmuch offence to his royal guests.
The army of Conrad, he said, had gained a great
victory in Asia Minor. Travel-stained messengers
arrived in Chrysopolis, and were brought across the
Bosphorus to appear before the King and Queen
of France, with tales of great and marvellous deeds
of arms against the infidels. Fifty thousand Seljuks
had been drowned in their own blood; three times
that number had fled from the field, and were
scattered fainting and wounded in the Eastern
hills; vast spoils of gold and silver had fallen to
the Christians, and if the Frenchmen craved a share
in the victories of the Cross, or hoped for some part
or parcel of the splendid booty, it was high time
that they should be marching to join the Germans in
the field.

Yet Louis would have tarried longer to complete
the full month of devotions and thanksgiving for
the march accomplished, and many of his followers
would cheerfully have spent the remainder of their
days on the pleasant shores of the Bosphorus and the
Golden Horn; but the Queen was weary of the long

preface to her unwritten history of arms, and grew impatient, and took the Greek Emperor's side, believing all the messages which he provided for her imagination. And so at last the great multitude was brought over to Asia by boat, and marched by quick stages to the plain of Nicæa. There they pitched their camp by the Lake of Ascanius, and waited for news of the Germans ; for the messengers had brought information that the German Emperor desired to make Nicæa the trysting-place. But the messengers had all been Greeks, and the French waited many days in vain, spoiling the country of all they could take, though it was in the dominion of Christians, and no man dared raise a hand to defend his own against the Crusaders.

Among the French, there were many, both of the great lords and of the simple knights, and of poor men-at-arms, who would have counted it mortal sin to take anything from a stranger without payment, who had come for faith's sake, to fight for faith, and who looked for faith's reward. Yet as there can be in logic nothing good excepting by its own comparison with things evil, so in that great pilgrimage of arms the worst followed the best in a greedy throng, as the jackal and the raven cross the desert in the lion's track. And the roads by which they had marched, and the lands wherein they had camped, lay waste as lie the wheat-fields of Palestine in June, when the plague of locusts has eaten its way from east to west.

When they came to a resting-place after many days' march, mud-stained or white with dust, weary

and footsore, their horses lame, their mules overladen with the burdens of those that had died by the
way, beards half grown, hair unkempt, faces grimy,
clothes worn shapeless, they were more like a multitude of barbarians wandering upon the plains of
Asia than like nobles of France and high-born Crusaders. At first, when they reached the halting-place
by stream or river or lake, there was a struggle for
drinking and a strife for the watering of horses and
beasts of burden, so that sometimes men and mules
were trampled down and hurt, and some were killed;
but it mattered little in so great a host, and a spade's
depth of earth was ample burial for a man, and if a
priest could be found to bless his body on the spot where
he lay it was enough, since he had died on the road
to Jerusalem; but the jackals and wild dogs followed
the march and lay in wait for dead beasts. Then
when the first confusion was over, when hunger and
thirst were satisfied, the tents were unpacked with
their poles, and the sound of the great wooden mallets striking upon the tent-pegs was like the irregular pounding stroke of the fullers' hammers as the
water-wheel makes them rise and fall; and though
the army had crossed Europe and had encamped in
many places, the colours of the tents were bright still,
and the pennants floated in streaks of vivid colour
against the sky. Soon, when the first work was over
and the little villages of red and green and purple
and white canvas were built up in their long irregular lines, the smoke of camp-fires rose in curling
wreaths, and bag and baggage, pack and parcel, were
opened and the contents spread out. As if for some

great festival, men and women chose their gayest
clothes and richest ornaments, so that when they
met again before the open tents which were set
up for chapels, one for each little band of fellow-
townsmen and neighbours at home, and afterwards
when they ate and drank together according to their
rank, under wide awnings at noontide, or beneath
the clear sky in the cool of the evening, it was a
goodly sight, and every man's heart was lightened
and his courage returned as he felt that he himself
had his share and part of the glorious whole.   For
it was as it always is and always must be, where
power and wealth are masters of the scene, and there
is no acting room for misery or sorrow or such poor
strolling players as sickness and death.   The things
which please not the eye are quick to offend souls
nursed in a faultless taste, and the charnel-house of
failure receives whatsoever things have not the power
of pleasing.

Now when they came to Nicæa, hope was high,
and the light of victory to come seemed to be
shining in every man's eyes.   There for the first
time Queen Eleanor led out her three hundred
ladies in battle array, clad in bright mail, with skirts
of silk and cloth of gold, and long white mantles,
each with the scarlet cross upon the shoulder ; and
on their heads they wore light caps of steel orna-
mented with chiselled gold and silver, and here and
there with a metal crest or a bird's wing, beaten
out of thin silver plate.

It was at noonday under the fair autumn sun.   A
broad meadow, green still in patches, where the grass

had not been burned brown by the early summer heat,
stretched toward the Lake of Ascanius, where the
ground rose in hillocks, to end abruptly in a sheer
fall of thirty or forty feet to the water's edge.
There were places where there was no grass at all,
and where the dry gravel lay bare and dusty, yet on
the whole it was a fair field for a great assembly of
men on horseback and on foot. To southward the
meadow rose, rolling away to the distant hills,
whither the German host was already gone. The
great lords, with their men-at-arms and squires,
riding each in the midst of his vassal knights, went
out thither to see such a sight as none had seen
before, and ranged themselves by ranks around the
field, so that there was room for all. And thither
Gilbert went also with his man Dunstan, in the
King's train, for he owed no service nor allegiance
to any man there. But they waited long for the
Queen.

She came at last, leading her company and mounted
on a beautiful white Arab mare, the gift of the
Greek Emperor, as gentle a creature as ever obeyed
voice and hand, and as swift as the swiftest of the
breed of Nejd. She rode alone, ten lengths before
the rest, tall and straight in the saddle as any man,
a lance in her right hand, while her left held the
bridle low and lightly; and at the very first glance
every soldier in that great field knew that there
was none like her in the troop. Yet her fair ladies
made a good showing and rode not badly as they
cantered by, brilliant and changing as a shower
of blossoms, with black eyes, and blue, and brown,

fair cheeks and dark, and laughing lips not made to talk of rough deeds save to praise them in husband or lover.

Next to the Queen and before the following ranks rode one who bore the standard of Eleanor's ancient house, Saint George and the Dragon, displayed on a white ground and now for the first time quartered in a cross. The Lady Anne of Auch was very dark, and her black hair streamed like a shadow in the air behind her, while her dark eyes looked upward and onward. Splendidly handsome she was, and doubtless Eleanor had chosen her for her beauty to be standard bearer of the troop, well knowing that no living face could be compared with her own, and willing to outshine a rival whose features and form were the honour and boast of the South.

They rode in a sort of order, in squadrons of fifty each, but not in serried ranks, for they had not the skill to keep in line, though they rode well and boldly. And before each squadron rode a lady who for her beauty or her rank, or for both, was captain, and wore upon her steel cap a gilded crest. Each squadron had a colour of its own, scarlet and green and violet, and the tender shade of anemones in spring, and their mantles had been dyed with each hue in the dyeing-vats of Venice, and were lined with delicately tinted silks from the East, brought to the harbours of France by Italian traders. For the merchants of Amalfi filled the Mediterranean with their busy commerce and had quarters of their own in every Eastern city, and had then but lately founded the saintly order of the Knights Hospi-

tallers of Saint John of Jerusalem, whence grew the
noble community of the Knights of Malta, which
was to live through many centuries even to our
day.

Nor could the Queen's ladies have worn mail and
steel and wielded sword and lance, so that at a long
stone's throw they might almost have passed for
men, but that cunning jewellers and artificers of
Italy, and Moorish smiths from Spain, had been
brought at great pains and cost to France to make
such armour and weapons as had never been wrought
before. The mail was of finest rings of steel sewn
upon soft doeskin, fitted so closely that there was
no room for gambison or jerkin; and though it might
have stopped a broad arrow or turned the edge of a
blade, a sharp dagger could have made a wound
beneath it, and against a blow it afforded less protection than a woollen cloak. Many had little rings
of gold sewn regularly in the rows of steel ones,
that caught the light with a warmer sparkle, and
the clasps of their mantles were of chiselled gold and
silver. The trappings of each horse were matched
in colour with the ladies' mantles, and the captains of
the squadrons wore golden spurs.

They dropped the points of their lances as they
passed the King where he sat on his horse, a stone's
throw from the high shore of the lake, in the
midst of his chief barons, his pale face expressing
neither interest nor pleasure in what he saw, and
his eyes distrustful, as always, of his Queen and her
many caprices. She, when she had saluted him with
a smile that was almost a laugh, rode on a little way,

and then, with a sharply uttered word of command, she wheeled by the left, crossed half the broad field, and led her ladies back straight toward the King. Within five lengths of him she halted suddenly, almost bringing her horse's haunches to the ground, and keeping her seat in a way that would have done credit to a man brought up in the saddle. To tell the truth, very few of her ladies were able to perform such a feat with any ease or assurance, and in the sudden halt there was more than a little disorder, accompanied by all sorts of exclamations of annoyance and ejaculations of surprise; yet, in spite of difficulty, the whole troop came to a standstill; moreover, a hundred thousand or more of knights and soldiers on horseback and on foot were so much more interested in the looks of the riders than in their horsemanship, and the whole effect of the gay confusion, with its many colours, its gleams of gold and glint of silver, was so pretty and altogether novel, that a great cry of enthusiasm and delight rang in the sunny air. A faint flush of pleasure rose in the Queen's cheeks, and her eyes sparkled with triumph at the long applause which was on her side against the King's disapproval. She dropped the point of her lance until it almost touched the ground, and spoke to her husband in a high clear voice that was heard by many.

"I present to your Grace this troop of brave knights," she said. "In strength the advantage is yours, in numbers, you far outdo us, in age you are older, in experience there are those with you who have lived a lifetime in arms. Yet we have some skill also, and those who are old in battles know that the victory belongs to the spirit and the heart, before it is the work of the hand; and in these my knights are not behind yours."

The men who heard her words and saw the lovely light in her wondrous face threw up their right hands and shouted great cheers for her and her three hundred riders, but the King spoke no word of praise, and his face was still and sour. Again the Queen's cheek flushed.

"Your Grace leads the army of France," she said, "an army of brave men. My knights are many, and brave too, the troops of Guienne and of Poitou and of Gascony and of more than half of all the duchies that speak our tongue and owe me allegiance. But of them all, and before them all, to ride in van of this Holy War, I choose these three hundred ladies. My Lord King, and you, lords, barons, knights, and men, who have taken upon you the sign of the Cross, you, the flower of French chivalry and manhood, your comrades in arms are these, the flowers of France! Long live the King!"

She threw up her lance and caught it easily in her right hand as she uttered the cry, laughing in the King's face, and well knowing her power compared with his; and as the high young voices behind her took up the shout, the great multitude that bordered the meadow took it up also; but one word was changed, and a hundred thousand throats shouted, "Long live the Queen!"

When there was silence at last, the King looked awkwardly to his right and left as if seeking advice;

but the nobles about him were watching the fair ladies, and had perhaps no counsel to offer. In the great stillness the Queen waited, still smiling triumphantly, and still he could find nothing to say, so that a soft titter ran through the ladies' ranks, whereat the King looked more sour than ever.

" Madam," he began at last. And after that he seemed to be speaking, but no one heard what he said.

Apparently with the intention of showing that he had nothing more to say, — and indeed it was of very little importance whether he had or not, — he waved his hand with a rather awkward gesture and slightly bowed his head.

" Long live the monk ! " said Eleanor, audibly, as she wheeled to the right to lead her troop away.

Gilbert Warde sat on his horse in the front line of the spectators, some fifty yards from the King, and near the edge of the lake. As the Queen cantered along the line, gathering her harvest of admiration in men's faces, her eyes met the young Englishman's and recognized him. On his great Norman horse he sat half a head taller than the men on each side of him, motionless as a statue. Yet his look expressed something which she had never seen in his face till then; for, being freed from her immediate influence and at liberty to look on her merely as the loveliest sight in the world, more strangely beautiful than ever in her gleaming armour, he had not thought of concealing the pleasure he felt in watching her.

Not all the cheering of the great army, not all the light in the thousands of eyes that followed her, could have done more than bring a faint colour to her face, nor could any man in all that host have found a word to make her heart beat faster. But when she saw Gilbert the blood sank suddenly and her eyes grew darker. They lingered on him as she rode by, and turned back to him a little with drooping lids, and a slight bend of the head that had in it a grace beyond her own knowledge or intention. He, like those beside him, threw up his hand and cheered again, and she did not see that almost before she had passed him he was looking along the ranks for another face.

The three hundred cantered slowly round half the meadow, and the cheer followed them as they went, like the moving cry of birds on the wing; and first they rode along the line of the King's men, but presently they came to the knights and soldiers of Eleanor's great vassalage, and all at once there were flowers in the air, wild flowers from the fields and autumn roses from the gardens of Nicæa, plucked early by young squires and boys, and tied into nose-gays and carefully shielded from the sun, that they might be still fresh when the time came to throw them. The light blossoms scattered in the air, and the leaves were blown into the faces of the fair women as they passed. Moreover, some of the knights had silken scarfs of red and white, and waved them above their heads while they cheered and shouted. And so the troop rode round three sides of the great meadow.

But at the last side there was a change that fell like a chill upon the whole multitude of men and women, and a cry came ringing down the air that struck a discord through the triumphant notes, long, harsh, bad to hear as the howl of wild beasts when the fire licks up the grass of the wilderness behind them. At the sound, men turned their heads and looked in the direction whence it came, and many, by old instinct, slipped their left hands to the hilts of sword and dagger, and felt that each blade was loose in its sheath. As she galloped along, Queen Eleanor's white mare threw up her head sideways with a snort and swerved, almost wrenching the bridle from the Queen's hold, and at the same moment the lusty cheering broke high in the air and died fitfully away. The instinct of fear and the foreknowledge of great evil were present, unseen and terrible, and of the three hundred ladies who reined in their horses as the Queen halted, nine out of ten felt that they changed colour, scarcely knowing why. With one common impulse all turned their eyes towards the rising ground to southward.

There were strange figures upon the low hillocks, riding out of the woods at furious speed towards the meadow, and already the deep lines began to open and part to make way for the rush. There were men bareheaded, with rags of mantles streaming on the wind, spurring lame and jaded horses to the speed of a charge, and crying out strange words in tones of terror. But only one word was understood by some of those who heard.

" The Seljuks ! The Seljuks ! "

Down the gentle slope they came spurring like madmen. As they drew nearer, one could see that there was blood on their armour, blood on the rags of their cloaks, blood on their faces and on their

hands; some were wounded in the head, and the
clotted gore made streaks upon their necks; some
had bandages upon them made of strips of torn-up
clothes — and one man who rode in the front, when
his horse sprang a ditch at the foot of the hill, threw
up an arm that was without a hand.

No man of all the throng who had ever seen war
doubted the truth for one moment after the first of
the wild riders was in sight, and the older and more
experienced men instinctively looked into each other's
faces and came forward together.   But even had they
been warned in time, they could have done nothing
against the fright that seized the younger men and
the women at the throat like a bodily enemy, choking out hope and strength and youth in the dreadful
premonition of untimely death.   The squires pressed
upon the knights, the boys and young men-at-arms
and the followers of the camp forced their weight
inward next, and the inner circle yielded and allowed
itself to be crushed in upon the troop of ladies, whose
horses began to plunge and rear with their riders'
fright; and still, on one side, the crowd tried to part
before the coming fugitives.   The first came tearing
down, his horse's nostrils streaming with blood, himself wild-eyed, with foam-flecked lips that howled the
words of terror.   "The Seljuks!   The Seljuks!"

A dozen lengths before the terror-stricken wall of
human beings that could not make way to let him in,
without warning, without a death-gasp, the horse
doubled his head under himself as he galloped his
last stride, and falling in a round heap rolled over
and over forwards with frightful violence, till he

suddenly lay stiff and stark with twisted neck and outstretched heels, within a yard of the shrinking crowd, his rider crushed to death on the grass behind him. And still the others came tearing down the hill, more and more, faster and faster, as if no earthly power could stop their rush. First a score and then a hundred, and then the torn remnants of a vanquished host, blown, as it were like fallen leaves by the whirlwind of the death they had but just escaped. Many of them, not knowing and not caring what they did, and remembering only the wrath from which they fled, did not even try to rein in their horses, and the beasts themselves, mad with fright and pain, charged right at the ranks of people on foot and reared their full height at the last bound rather than override a living man ; and many were crushed in the press, and many fell from their jaded mounts, too weary to rise and too much exhausted to utter any words save a cry for water.

Nevertheless, two or three who had more life in them than the rest were able to stand, and were presently led round the close-packed crowd to the edge of the lake, where the King was quietly waiting with his courtiers until the confusion should end itself, saying a prayer or two for the welfare of every one concerned, but making not the slightest attempt to restrain the panic nor to restore order. But the Queen and her ladies were in danger of being crushed to death in the very midst of the seething, bruising, stifling mass of humanity.

Gilbert was near the King, and sitting high on his great horse he saw farther than most men above the

wild confusion.   It was as if some frightful, unseen
monster were gathering a hundred thousand men in
iron coils, always inward, as great snakes crush their
prey, thousands upon thousands, the bodies of horses
and men upon men and horses, with resistless force,
till the human beings could struggle no longer, and
the beasts themselves could neither kick nor plunge,
but only trample all that was near them, while
they moved slowly towards the centre.   In thousands and thousands again, on an almost even level,
the small round caps of many colours were pressed
together, till it seemed impossible that there could be
room for the bodies that belonged to them.   As when,
in vintage time, the gathered fruit is brought home to
the vats in the sweating panniers of wood, pressed
down and level to the brim, and the red and white and
blue and green grapes lie closely touching each other
almost floating in the juice, rocking and bobbing all
at once with every step of the laden mule — so, as
Gilbert looked out before him, the bright-hued,
close-fitting caps moved restlessly and without ceasing all round a central turmoil of splendid colour,
shaded by tender tones of violet and olive, and shot
by the glare of sunlit gold, and the sheen of silver,
and the cold light of polished steel.

But there in the heart of the press there was
danger, and from far away Gilbert saw clearly
enough, through the cloud of light and colour, the
lifeless tones that are like nothing else of nature, the deadly unreflecting paleness of frightened
faces, and the cries of women hurt and in terror
came rising over the heads of the multitude.   He

sat still and looked before him as if his sight could distinguish the features of one or another at that distance, and he felt icy cold when he thought of what might happen, and that all those fair young girls and women, in their beauty and in their youth, in their fanciful dresses, might be crushed and trampled and kicked to death before thousands who would have died to save them. His first instinct was to charge the crowd before him, to force the way, even by the sword, and to bring the Queen and her ladies safely back; but a moment's thought showed him how utterly futile any such attempt must be, and that even if the whole throng had felt as he felt himself, and had wished to make way for any one, it would have had no power to do so. There was but one chance of saving the women, and that evidently lay in leading off the crowd by some excitement counter to its present fear.

The instant the difficulty and the danger flashed upon him Gilbert began to look about him for some means of safety for those in peril, and in his distress of mind every lost minute was monstrously lengthened as it passed. Beside him, his man Dunstan stood in silence, apparently indifferent to all that was taking place, his quiet dark face a trifle more drawn and keen than usual; and though a very slight contraction of the curved nostrils expressed some inward excitement, it was scarcely perceptible. Gilbert knew that his own face showed his extreme anxiety, and as he in vain attempted to find some expedient, the man's excessive coolness began to irritate him.

"You stand there," said Gilbert, rather coldly, "as

Q

if you did not care that three hundred ladies of
France are being crushed to death and that we Englishmen can do nothing to help them."

Dunstan raised his lids and looked up at his
master without lifting his head.

"I am not so indifferent as the King, sir," he answered, barely raising a finger in the direction of the
knot of courtiers, in the midst of whom, some fifty
yards away, the cold, pale face of the King was just
then distinctly visible. "France might be burned
before his eyes, yet he would pray for his own soul
rather than lift a hand for the lives of others."

"We are as bad as he," retorted Gilbert, almost
angrily, and moving uneasily in his saddle as he felt
himself powerless.

Dunstan did not answer at once, and he bit one side
of his lower lip nervously with his pointed teeth.
Suddenly he stooped down and picked up something
against which his foot had struck as he moved.
Gilbert paid no attention to what he did.

"Do you wish to draw away the crowd so as to
make room for the Queen?" he asked.

"Of course I do!" Gilbert looked at his man
inquiringly, though his tone was harsh and almost
angry. "We cannot cut a way for them through the
crowd," he added, looking before him again.

Dunstan laughed quietly.

"I will lay my life against a new tunic that I can
make this multitude spin on itself like a whipped
top," he said. "But I admit that you could not,
sir."

"Why not?" asked Gilbert, instantly bending

down in order to hear better. "What can you do that I cannot?"

"What gentle blood could never do," replied the man, with a shade of bitterness. "Shall I have the new tunic if I save the Lady Beatrix — and the Queen of France?"

"Twenty! Anything you ask for! But be quick —"

Dunstan stooped again, and again picked up something from under his foot.

"I am only a churl," he said as he stood upright again, "but I can risk my life like you for a lady, and if I win, I would rather win a sword than a bit of finery."

"You shall win more than that," Gilbert answered, his tone changing. "But if you know of anything to do, in the name of God do it quickly, for it is time."

"Good-by, sir."

Gilbert heard the two words, and while they were still in his ears, half understood, Dunstan had slipped away among the squires and knights around them, and was lost to sight.

One minute had not passed when a wild yell rent the air, with fierce words, high and clear, which thousands must have heard at the very first, even had they not been repeated again and again.

"The King has betrayed us! The King is a traitor to the Cross!"

At the very instant a stone flew straight from Dunstan's unerring hand, and struck the King's horse fairly between the eyes, upon the rich frontlet, heavy with gold embroidery. The charger reared

up violently to his height, and before he had got his
head down to plunge, Dunstan's furious scream split
the air again, and the second stone struck the King
himself full on the breast, and rolled to the saddle
and then to the ground.

" The King has betrayed us all! Traitor! Traitor!
Traitor! "

There never yet was a feverish, terror-struck
throng of men, suddenly disheartened by the un-
answerable evidence of a great defeat by which they
themselves might be lost, that would not take up the
cry of " Traitor ! " against their leaders. Before he
raised his voice, Dunstan had got among men who
knew him neither by sight nor by name, and the second
stone had not sped home before he was gone again in
a new direction, silent now, with compressed lips, his
inscrutable dark eyes looking sharply about him.
He had done his work, and he knew what might
happen to him if he were afterwards recognized.
But none heeded him. The uproar went surging
towards the King with a rising fury, like the turn of
the tide in a winter storm, roaring up to the breaking pitch, and many would have stoned him and
torn him to pieces ; but there were many also, older
and cooler men, who pressed round him, shoulder
to shoulder, with swords drawn and flashing in the
sunlight, and faces set to defend their liege lord and
sovereign. In an instant the flying Germans were
forgotten ; and the Emperor and his army, and the
meaning of the Holy War and of the Cross itself,
were gone from men's minds in the fury of riot on
the one side, in the stern determination of defence

on the other. The vast weight of men rolled forward, pushed by those behind, forcing the King and
those who stood by him to higher ground. In dire
distress, and almost hopeless of extricating her gentle
troop from destruction, the Queen heard the new
tumult far away, and felt the close press yielding on
one side. The word 'traitor' ran along like a quick
echo from mouth to mouth, repeated again and again,
sometimes angrily, sometimes in tones of unbelief,
but always repeated, until there was scarcely one man
in a hundred thousand whose lips had not formed the
syllables. Eleanor saw her husband and his companions with their drawn swords moving in the air,
on the knoll; she heard the stinging word, and a hard
and scornful look lingered in her face a moment.
She knew that the accusation was false, that it was
too utterly empty to have meaning for honest men ;
yet she despised her husband merely because a madman could cast such a word at him; and in the
security of power and dominions far greater than
his, as well as of a popularity to which he could
never attain, she looked upon him in her heart as a
contemptible kinglet, to marry whom had been her
most foolish mistake. And it had become the object
of her life to put him away if she could.

For a few moments she looked on across the sea
of heads that had already begun to move away. Her
mare was quieter now in the larger space, being a
docile creature, but many of the other ladies' horses
were still plunging and kicking, though so crowded
that they could do each other little hurt. She saw
how the knights were forcing their way to the King's

side, and how the great herd of footmen resisted them,
while the word of shame rose louder in their yells;
and though she despised the King, the fierce instinct
of the great noble against the rabble ran through her
like a painful shock, and her face turned pale as she
felt her anger in her throat.

There was room now, for the great throng was
rushing from her, spreading like a river, and dividing
at the hillock where it met the knights' swords, and
flowing to right and left along the edge of the lake.
The Queen looked behind her, to see what ladies were
nearest to her, and she saw her standard bearer,
Anne of Auch, fighting her rearing charger; and
next to her, quiet and pale, on a vicious Hungarian
gelding a great deal too big for her, but which she
seemed to manage with extraordinary ease, sat Beatrix de Curboil, a small, slim figure in a delicate
mail that looked no stronger than a silver fishing-net,
her shape half hidden by her flowing mantle of soft
olive-green with its scarlet cross on the shoulder, and
wearing a silver dove's wing on her light steel cap.

Her eyes met Eleanor's and lightened in sympathy
of thought, so that the other understood in a flash.
The Queen's right hand went up, lifting the lance
high in air; half wheeling to the left, and turning
her head still farther, she called out to those behind
her: —

"Ladies of France! The rabble is at the King —
Forward!"

An instant later, the fleet Arab mare was galloping
straight for the crowd, and Eleanor did not look behind her again, but held her lance before her and a

little raised, so that it was just ready to fall into rest. Directly behind her rode the Lady Anne, the shaft of the standard in the socket of her stirrup, her arm run through the thong, so that she had both hands free; she sat erect in the saddle, her horse already at a racing gallop, neck out, eyes up, red nostrils wide, delighting in being free from restraint; and Beatrix was there, too, like a feather on her big brown Hungarian, that thundered along like a storm, his wicked ears laid straight back, and his yellowish young teeth showing under his quivering lip. But of all the three hundred ladies none followed them. The others had not understood the Queen's command, or had not heard, or could not manage their horses, or were afraid. And the three women rode at the mob, that was now four hundred yards away.

Straight they rode, heedless and unaware that they were alone, nor counting how little three women could do against thousands. But the people heard the hammering hoofs of the two big horses, and the Arab's light footfall resounded quickly and steadily, as the fingers of a dancer striking the tambourine. Hundreds glanced back to see who rode so fast, and thousands turned their heads to know why the others looked; and all, seeing the Queen, pressed back to right and left, making way, partly in respect for her and much in fear for themselves. Far up the rising ground, the riot ceased as suddenly as it had begun; the men-at-arms drew back in shame, and many tried to hide their faces, lest they should be known again. The tide of human beings divided before the swiftly riding women, as the cloud-bank splits before the

northwest wind in winter, and the white mare sped
like a ray of light between long wavering lines of
rough faces and gleaming arms.

The Queen glanced scornfully to each side as she
passed in a gale, and the dear sense of power soothed
her stirred pride.   Still the line opened, and still she
rode on, scarcely rising and sinking with the mare's
wonderful stride.   But the way that was made for her
was not straight to the King now; the throng was
more dense there, and the people parted as they
could, so that the three ladies had to follow the only
open passage.   Suddenly, before them, there was
an end, where the rolling ground broke away
sharply in a fall of forty feet to the edge of the
lake below.   The heads of the last of the crowd
who stood at the brink were clear and distinct
against the pale sky.   The Queen could not see the
water, but she felt that there was death in the leap.
Her two companions looked beyond her and saw
also.

Eleanor dropped her lance quietly to the right, so
that it should not make her followers fall, and
with hands low and weight thrown back in the
deep saddle she pulled with all her might.   Her
favourite black horse, broken to her own hand, would
have obeyed her ; she might have been able to stop
Beatrix's great Hungarian, for her white hands were
as strong as a man's ; but the Arab mare was trained
only to the touch of an Arab halter and the deep
caress of an Arab voice, and at the first strain of the
cruel French bit she threw up her head, swerved,
caught the steel in her teeth, and shot forward again

at twice her speed. Eleanor tried in vain to wrench the mare's head to one side, into the shrinking crowd.

The Queen's face turned grey, but her lips were set and her eyes steady, as she looked death in the face. Behind her, Beatrix's little gloved hands were like white moths on her steadily jerking bridle, the Hungarian's terrific stride threw up the sods behind her, and there was a hopeless, far-away look in her face, almost like a death-smile. Only the strong dark woman of the South seemed still to have control over her horse, and he slowly slackened his speed, and fell a little behind the other two.

In the fearful danger the crowd was silent and breathless, and many men turned pale as they saw. But none moved.

One second, two seconds, three seconds, and to every second two strides ; the end of three women's lives was counted by the wild hoof-strokes. The race might last while one could count ten more.

Gilbert Warde had at first tried to press nearer to the King, but he saw that it was useless, because the latter was already shoulder to shoulder with the nobles and knights. So he had turned back to face the crowd with those about him, and with the flat of his blade he had beaten down some few swords which men had dared to draw; but he had wounded no one, for he knew that it was a madness which must pass and must be forgiven.

Then he found himself with his horse on the very edge of the open track made by the dividing people, and he looked and saw the Queen, and Beatrix three or four lengths behind her, as the matchless Arab gained ground in the race. He had been above the deep fall and understood. Instantly he was on his feet on the turf, a step out in the perilous way; and he wished that he had the strength of Lancelot in his hands, with the leap of a wild beast in his feet, but his heart did not fail him.

In one second he lived an hour. His life was nothing, but he could only give it once, to save one woman, and she must be Beatrix, let such chance befall Eleanor as might. Yet Eleanor was the Queen, and she had been kind to him, and in the fateful instant of doom his eyes were on her face; he would try to save the other, but unconsciously he made one step forward again and stood waiting in midway. One second for a lifetime's thought, one for the step he made, and the next was the last. He could hear the rush of the wind, and Eleanor was looking at him.

In that supreme moment her face changed, and the desperate calm in her eyes became desperate fear for him she loved even better than she knew.

"Back!" she cried, and the cry was a woman's agonized scream, not for herself.

With all her might, but utterly in vain, she wrenched sideways at the mare's mouth and she closed her eyes lest she should see the man die. He had meant to let her pass to her death, for the girl was dearer to him, and he had gathered his strength like a bent spring to serve him. But he saw her eyes and heard her cry, and in the flash of instinct he knew she loved him, and that she wished him to save himself rather than her; and thereby is real love proved on the touchstone of fear.

"HE . . . HELD, WHILE EARTH AND SKY WHIRLED WITH HIM"

As he sprang, he knew that he had no choice, though he did not love her. The fall of her mare, if his grip held, might stop the rest. He sprang; he saw only the Arab's bony head and the gold on the bridle, as both his hands grasped it. Then he saw nothing, but yet he held, and, dead, he would have held still, as the steel jaws of the hunter's trap hold upon the wolf's leg-bone. He knew that he was thrown down, dragged, pounded, bruised, twisted like a rope till his joints cracked. But he held, and felt no pain, while earth and sky whirled with him. It was not a second; it was an hour, a year, a lifetime; yet he could not have loosed his hands, had he wished to let go, for there were in him the blood and the soul of the race that never yielded its grip on whatsoever it held.

It lasted a breathing-space, while the mare plunged wildly and staggered, and her head almost touched the ground and dragged the man's hands on the turf; then as his weight wrenched her neck back, her violent speed threw her hind quarters round, as a vane is blown from the gale. At the same instant the great Hungarian horse was upon her, tried to leap her in his stride, struck her empty saddle with his brown chest, and fell against her and upon her with all his enormous weight, and the two rolled over each other, frantically kicking. The standard bearer's horse, less mad than the others and some lengths behind, checked himself cleverly, and after two or three short, violent strides, that almost unseated his rider, planted his fore feet in the turf and stood stock-still, heaving and trembling. The race was over.

With the strength and instinct of the born rider, Eleanor had slipped her feet from the stirrups and had let herself be thrown, lifting herself with her hands on the high pommel and vaulting clear away. She fell, but was on her feet before any man of the dazed throng could help her. She saw Gilbert lying his full length on his side, his body passive, but his arms stretched beyond his head, while his gloved hands still clenched upon the bridle and were pulled from side to side by the mare's faintly struggling head. His eyes were half open toward the Queen, but they were pale and saw nothing. The Hungarian had rolled half upon his back, little hurt, and the pommels of the saddle under him kept him from turning completely over.

Beatrix lay like one dead. She had been thrown over the Arab's back, striking her head on the turf, and the mare in her final struggle had rolled upon her feet. The light steel cap had been forced down over her forehead in spite of its cushioned lining, and the chiselled rim had cut into the flesh so that a little line of dark blood was slowly running across the white skin; and her white gloved hands were lying palm upward, half open and motionless. The Queen scarcely glanced at her.

Many men sprang forward when the danger was past, and they dragged Beatrix out and began to get her horse upon his feet. Eleanor knelt by Gilbert and tried to take his fingers from the bridle, but could not, so that she had to loose the buckle from the long bars of the bit. Her hands chafed his temples softly, and she bent lower and blew upon his face, that her cool breath might wake him. There were drops of blood on his forehead and on his chin, his cloth tunic was torn in many places, and the white linen showed at the rents; but Eleanor saw only the look in his face, serene and strong even in his unconsciousness, while in the dream of his swoon he saved her life again.

In that moment, knowing that he could not see her, she thought not of her own face as she gazed upon his, nor of hiding what she felt; and the thing she felt was evil, and it was sweet. But suddenly there was life in his look, with a gentle smile, and the strained fingers were loosed with a sigh, and a long-unused word came from his lips.

"Mother!"

Eleanor shook her beautiful head slowly. Then Gilbert's face darkened with understanding and the old pain clutched at his heart sharply, even before the keen bodily hurt awoke in his wrung limbs. All at once thought came, and he knew how, in a quick fall of his heart, he had forgotten Beatrix and had almost given his life to save the Queen. As if he had been stung, he started and raised himself on one hand, though it was as if he forced his body among hot knives.

"She is dead!" he cried, with twisting lips.

"No — you saved us both."

The words came soft and clear, as Eleanor laid her hand upon his shoulder to quiet him, and watched the change as the agony in his eyes faded to relief and brightened to peace.

"Thank God!"

He sank upon her arm, for he was much bruised.
But her face changed, too, and she suffered new
things, because in her there was good as well as evil;
for as she loved him more than before he had saved
her, so she would give him more, if she might, even
to forgetting herself.

And so, for a few moments, she knelt and watched
him, heedless of the people about her, and scarcely
seeing a dark man whom she had never noticed before,
and who bent so low that she could not see his face,
quietly loosening his master's collar and then feeling along his arms and legs for any bone hurt there
might be.

"Who are you?" asked the Queen, at last, gently,
as to one who was helping him she loved.

"His man," answered Dunstan, laconically, without looking up.

"Take care of him and bring me word of him,"
she answered, and from a wallet she gave him gold,
which he took, silently bending his head still lower
in thanks.

He, too, had saved her that day, and knew it,
though she did not.

She stood up at last, gathering her mantle round
her. Less than ten minutes had passed since she
had thrown up her hand and called to her ladies to
follow her. Since then the world had been in herself and on fire, leaving no room for other thoughts;
but now the crowd had parted wide, and the King
was coming towards her, slow and late, to know
whether she were hurt, for he had seen her ride.

"Madam," he said, when he had dismounted, "I

thank the mercy of Heaven, which deigned to hear the prayers I was continually offering up for your safety while your life was threatened by that dangerous animal. We will render thanks in divine services during ten days before proceeding farther, or during a fortnight if you prefer it."

"Your Grace," said Eleanor, coldly, "is at liberty to praise Heaven by the month if it seems good to you. But for that poor Englishman, who lies there in a swoon, and who caught my horse's bridle at the risk of his life, you might have been ordering masses for my soul instead of for my bodily preservation. They would have been much needed had I been killed just then."

The King crossed himself devoutly, half closed his eyes, bent himself a little, and whispered a short prayer.

"It would be better," observed the Queen, "to move on at once and support the Emperor."

"It has pleased God that the army of the Emperor should be totally destroyed," answered the King, calmly. "The Emperor himself will be here in a few hours, unless he has perished with the rest of his knights, slain by the Seljuk horsemen who are pursuing the fugitives."

"The more reason why we should save those who are still alive. My army shall march to-morrow at daybreak — your Grace may stay behind and pray for us."

She turned from him scornfully. Dunstan and some foot-soldiers had made stretchers with lances and pikes and were just beginning to carry Beatrix and Gilbert away, northward, in the direction of the camp.

CHAPTER XV

WHEN Gilbert learned from his man that Beatrix was badly hurt and suffering great pain, he turned his face away and bit hard on the saddle-bag that served him for a pillow. It was late in the afternoon, and Dunstan had just come back from making inquiries in the ladies' lines, half a mile away.

Nothing could have been simpler than his round tent, which had a single pole and covered a circle four or five paces in diameter. The dry ground had been sprinkled with water and beaten with mallets so as to harden it as much as possible. Gilbert and his two men slept on smoke-cured hides over which heavy woollen blankets were spread, almost as thick as carpets, hand-woven in rough designs of vivid blue and red, the coarse work of shepherds of Auvergne, but highly valued.

Against the pole the saddles were piled one upon another, Gilbert's own on top, with its curved pommels; Dunstan's, covered with plaited lines for binding on rolled blankets and all sorts of light packages and saddle-bags before and behind the rider's seat; and the mule's pack-saddle, on which little Alric rode, perched upon the close-bound bundles, when the road was fair. During most of the journey the sturdy Saxon had trudged along on foot, as Dunstan did also, but it was not seemly that a man of gentle blood should be seen walking on the march, except of great necessity.

Above the saddles Gilbert's mail hung by the neck, with a stout staff run through both arms to stretch it out, lest dampness should rust it; also his other armour and his sword were fastened up like an ancient trophy, with bridles and leathern bottles and other gear. Beside the saddles, on the ground, the shining copper kettle held three bright brass bowls, well-scoured wooden trenchers, a long wooden ladle, an iron skewer, and three brass spoons, the simple necessities for cooking and eating. Forks had not been thought of in those days.

Gilbert lay on his back and turned his face away from his man. He was bruised and scratched, and his head ached from being struck on the ground when the mare had dragged him; but he was whole and sound in limb, and Dunstan had stretched his joints and pressed his bruises with a wise touch that had in it something of Oriental skill. He lay wrapped in a long robe of coarse white linen, as thick as wool — a sensible Greek garment which he had got in Constantinople. The afternoon was warm, and though the flap of the tent was raised and stretched out like an awning, there was little air, and the place smelt of the leathern trappings and of hot canvas; and through the side to which he turned his face Gilbert could see little dazzling sparks of rays where the sun was beating full upon the out-side.

He wished that in the mad rush of the Arab the life might have been pounded out of him, and that

R

he might never have waked to know what he had done; for although in his sober senses he did not love the Queen, it seemed to him that he had loved her in the moment when he sprang to save her life, and that he could never again forget the look of fear for him in her eyes and her cry of terror for his sake. All that Beatrix had said to him in the garden at Constantinople came back to him now; until now, he had disbelieved it all, as a wild and foolish impossibility, for he was over-modest and diffident of himself in such matters.

Beatrix would certainly have been killed but for the chance which had thrown the mare across the narrow way, and he had risked his life to save another woman. It mattered not that the other was the Queen; that was not the reason why he had leapt upon the bridle. He had done it for a glance of her eyes, for the tone of her voice, as it were in an instant of temptation, when he had stepped out of the rank to face destruction for a dearer sake. It seemed like a crime, and it proved against his own belief that he loved what he loved not. Had he let the Queen pass, and had he stopped Beatrix's horse instead, she might have been unhurt, and one other brave man might have saved Eleanor at the brink. Indeed, he thought of the sad face with its pathetic little smile, drawn with pain and hot upon the pillow, by his fault; and he thought with greater fear of the danger that some deep hurt might leave the slender frame bent and crippled for life.

But meanwhile the news had spread quickly that it was the silent Englishman, neither knight nor

squire, who had saved the Queen, and outside the
tent men stopped and talked of the deed, and asked
questions of Alric, who had picked up enough
Norman-French to give tolerably intelligible an-
swers. At first came soldiers, passing as they went
to fetch water from the lake, and again as they came
back with copper vessels filled to the brim and drip-
ping upon their shoulders, they set down their burdens and talked together. Presently came a great
knight, the Count of Montferrat, brother to the
Count of Savoy, who had been at Vézelay, where
Gilbert had talked with him. He walked with
slow strides, his bright eyes seeming to cut a
way for him, his long mantle trailing, his soft red
leather boots pushed down in close creases about
his ankles, his gloved hand pressing down the cross-
hilt of his sword, so that the sheath lifted his mantle behind him. On each side of him walked his
favourite knights, and their squires with them, all
on their way to the King's quarters, where a council
of war was to be held, since it was known how the
great German host had been routed, and that the
Emperor himself might follow Duke Frederick of
Suabia. This Duke had already reached the camp,
after beating off the Seljuk skirmishers who had
harassed his retreat and driven in the first fright-
struck Germans.

The soldiers and grooms made way for the noble,
but he asked which might be the tent of Gilbert
Warde, the Englishman; so they pointed to the
raised flap, where Alric stood with his sturdy legs
apart, under the shadow of Gilbert's long shield,

which was hanging from a lance stuck in the ground.
The shield was blank, though many gentlemen
already painted devices on theirs, and sovereign
lords displayed the heraldic emblems of their houses
long before their vassals began to use their coats-
of-arms on their shields in war. But Gilbert would
bear neither emblem nor device till some great deed
should make him famous.

The Count of Montferrat glanced at the blank shield
thoughtfully, and asked little Alric of what family
his master was; and when he heard that his forefathers had been with Robert the Devil when he
died, and with William at Hastings, and with Godfrey at Jerusalem, and that his father had died
fighting for Maud against the usurper, but that
Gilbert had not knighthood for all that, he wondered
gravely. Yet knowing that he was hurt and ill at
ease, the Count would not go in, but gave Alric a
piece of gold and bade him greet the young Lord
of Stoke and tell him that the Count of Montferrat
craved better acquaintance with him when he should
be recovered.

He went on his way, and was not gone far when
the Count of Savoy and the lord of fated Coucy
came strolling side by side, with their trains of
knights and squires, on their way to the council.
And having seen Montferrat stop at the tent, they did
likewise, and asked the same questions, giving Alric
money out of respect for his master's brave deed
and good name, according to custom. Many others
came after them, great and small, and the great gave
the groom money, and the poor men-at-arms asked

him to drink with them after supper; so that his flat leathern wallet, which was cracking in its creases from having been long empty, was puffed out and hard, and weighed heavily at his belt, and as for the wine promised him, he might have floated a boat in it.

There was one of the Greek guides who stood near the tent, playing with a string of thick beads, and keeping behind Alric; and when there was a crowd around him this Greek slipped nearer, with his razor in the palm of his hand, and stealthily tried to cut the thongs by which the wallet was fastened. So the Saxon turned quickly and smote him between the eyes with his fist, and it was an hour before the Greek came to himself and crawled away, for nobody would lift him. But Alric laughed often as he sucked the trickling blood from his knuckles, and though he was a little man and young, the soldiers looked at him with respect, and many more of them asked him to drink.

So on that afternoon Gilbert's reputation grew suddenly, as a bright lily that has been long in bud under a wet sky breaks out like a flame in the first sunshine; and the days were over when he must trudge along unnoticed in the vast throng of nobles, with his two men and his modest baggage.

Meanwhile the council was held in the King's tent of state, within which three hundred nobles sat at ease after the King himself had taken his place on the throne, with the Queen on his right hand. There the red-bearded Frederick of Suabia, nephew to Conrad and famous afterward as the Emperor Bar-

barossa, stood up and told his tale: how the wild German knights had truly forced their leaders to take the mountain road and fight the Seljuks at a disadvantage; how the Seljuks appeared and disappeared again from hour to hour, falling upon their prey at every turn, reddening every pass with blood, and leaving half-killed men among the slain to wonder whence the swift smiters had come and whither they were gone. He himself had wounds not healed, and he told how, day by day, the mad bravery of the Germans, and the fury of his Black Forest men-at-arms, had risen again and again to very desperation, to sink before evening in a new defeat; until, at last, as the Seljuk swords still killed and killed, a terror had fallen upon the host in the passes, and men had thrown away their armour and fled like rats from a burning granary, so that their leaders could not hold them. He, with a few strong helpers, had covered his flying troops, and the brave Emperor Conrad, giant in strength, the greatest swordsman of the world, was even now fighting at the hindmost rear of the army to save whom he could.

It had been madness, he told them all, to try the mountain ways. To Palestine there were two roads, and they might choose between them, either following the long coast round Asia Minor to the Gulf of Cyprus, or else, going down to the Propontis, they might get ships from Constantinople and sail to the ports of Syria. The short way was death, and though death were nothing, it meant failure and destruction to the Christian power in Jerusalem and Antioch.

Thus he spoke, and the King and Queen and all the great nobles heard him in silence. There were the great Counts of Flanders and Toulouse, of Savoy, of Montferrat and Dreux and Blois, and the lords of Lusignan, of Coucy, of Courtenay, and of Bourbon, and the Bishops of Toul and Metz, and all the great knights of Gascony and Poitou, with many others of high name and good blood, who heard the red-bearded Duke speak. But when he had finished, none answered him, and the French King sat on his throne, repeating the prayers for the dead in a low voice. But Eleanor's eyes flashed fire and her gloved hand strained impatiently upon the carved arm of the chair of state.

"Requiem eternam dona eis," muttered the King.

"Amen!" responded Eleanor, in a clear, contemptuous voice. "And now that prayers are over, let us do deeds. Let us mount and ride forth at dawn to meet the Emperor, and help him in his need at the last. Let us ride in even order, sending out scouts and skirmishers before us, and keeping good watch, armed and ready at all moments. Then, when all are safe who are alive, we will return here, that the Germans may rest themselves by this good lake; and afterward we will set forth again by the safest road, cautiously, not wasting upon skirmishes the strength we shall need hereafter for a great victory."

"The Emperor will surely be here to-morrow, without our help," said the King, in manifest discontent. "It is of no use to go and meet him."

"If he is so near, let us mount to-night, this

very hour, rather than have on us the shame of lying idly here while men who wear the cross are in need of us."

The King said nothing, but at Eleanor's words a low murmur of assent ran through the assembly of brave men, from those at her feet to those farthest from her; and the impatient touch of each hand on sword or dagger, at the thought of fight, made a sound of softly moving steel and leather and buckle, which one may only hear among soldiers.

Eleanor stood up, untired by her terrible ride, unshaken by her fall, her eyes full of the brightness of pride. It was her daily food and her perpetual necessity to have the better of the King in the eyes of men, whether the matter were great or small. She stood up to her height, as if to show all her beauty and strength to the world, and the low sun streamed through the wide entrance to the tent and fell full upon her face and her unblinking eyes.

"My lords and barons, gentlemen of Guienne and France, our journey is over to-day, our battles begin to-morrow! Our brothers are in danger, the enemy is in sight! Men of the Cross, to arms!"

"To arms!" rang the reply in many voices, both high and deep, like a major chord sounding from the heart.

As she rose, the nobles had risen, too, and only the King kept his seat, his pale face bent, his hands folded upon the hilt of the sword that stood between his knees. The Queen said no more, and, without glancing at her husband, as if she alone were sovereign, she descended the two steps from the throne to the floor of the tent. Three knights, one of Gascony, one of Poitou, and one of her own Guienne, who were her guard of honour, followed her as she passed out, smiling to the great nobles on her right and left. And many showed that they desired to speak with her — first among them the Count of Montferrat.

"Madam," he said, when he had bowed low before her, "I praise God and the Holy Trinity that your Grace is alive to-day. I pray that you will deign to accept the homage and felicitations of Montferrat!"

"Of Bourbon, Madam!" cried a voice beside her.

"Of Savoy, your Grace!" said another.

"Of Coucy, of Courtenay, of Metz — " the voices all rang at once, as the lords pressed round her, for she had not been seen since she had left the field after her fall.

"I thank you," she answered, with a careless smile. "But you should thank also the man who saved my life, if you love me."

"Madam, we have," replied Montferrat. "And if your Grace will but let me have the man, I will do him much honour for your Highness's sake."

"He is no vassal of mine," Eleanor said. "He is a poor English gentleman, cheated of his lands, a friend of young Henry Plantagenet."

"The friend of a boy!" The Count laughed lightly.

But Eleanor grew thoughtful on a sudden, for beyond her rare beauty and her splendid youth, and

within her world of impatient passion, there were
wisdom and knowledge of men.

"A boy? Yes, he may be fourteen years old,
not more. But there are boys who are not children,
even in their cradles, and there are men who are
nothing else — their swaddling-clothes outgrown,
and their milk teeth cast, but not their whimpering
and fretting."

The nobles were silent, for she spoke over-boldly
and meant the King, as they knew.

"As for this Englishman," she continued after
an instant's pause, "he is not mine to give you, my
lord Count. And as for doing him honour for his
brave deed, though I would gladly please you, I
should be loth to let you do my duty for your
pleasure."

She smiled again very graciously, for she was
glad that men should praise Gilbert Warde to her;
and it was strangely pleasant to think that no one
guessed half of what she would give him if he
would take it. For among the nobles there were
great lords, goodly men and young, who dreamed of
her fair face, but would not have dared to lift up
their eyes to her.

So she passed out, with her knights behind her,
and most of the lords and barons followed her at
a distance, leaving the King within.

When she was gone he rose slowly, and giving
his sword to the chamberlain who stood waiting, he
went to his chapel tent, with downcast eyes and
clasped hands, as if walking in a solemn procession.
A little bell rang, the sun was low, and it was the

hour of the Benediction. The King knelt down before the rich altar, and when he had prayed earnestly for strength and courage, and for wisdom to win the war of the Cross, he prayed from the bottom of his unhappy heart that, if it were the will of Heaven, he might by some means be delivered from the woman of Belial who marred his life and burdened his soul.

CHAPTER XVI

To the south side of the camp the Germans came
by thousands, all that day and far into the night,
weary, half starved, on jaded beasts that could hardly
set one foot before the other, or on foot themselves,
reeling like men drunk, and almost blind with ex-
haustion. But the panic had not lasted long, for
the few score of Seljuk riders who had fallen upon
the van of the retreating column for the last time had
been finally scattered by the Duke of Suabia, so that
the remainder of the army came in with a show of
order, bringing the greater part of the baggage.
The Seljuks had not attempted to carry away plunder, which would have hampered them in their
dashing charges and instant retreats.

Last of all, before daybreak, came the Emperor
himself, covering the rear of his army with chosen
men, untired, though his great horse was staggering
under him, alert and strong as if he had not been
in the saddle the better part of four days and nights.
He seemed a man of iron; and few could ride with
him, or watch with him, or fight with him.

When the sun rose, the great standard of the Holy
Roman Empire waved before the imperial tent, and
though he had not rested, Conrad knelt beside King
Louis at early mass. Far to southward the German
tents rose in long lines by the shore of the lake,

where Eleanor had displayed her troop on the
previous day, and countless little squads of men
with mules came and went between the camp and
the distant walled city of Nicæa. In the French
lines, where the first preparations had been made for
marching, men were again unpacking their belongings; for word had gone round at midnight that the
Emperor was safe, and needed no help, and would
be in the camp in the morning.

Then there was secret rejoicing among the ladies,
and those who had no bruise nor scratch from
yesterday's accidents called their tirewomen and
spent happy hours, holding up their little silver
mirrors to their hair, and holding them down to see
the clasp at the throat, and trying some of the silks
and embroideries which they had received as gifts
from the Greek Emperor. It was almost a miracle
that none but Beatrix should have been gravely
hurt, but many were a little bruised and much tired,
and altogether inclined to ask sympathy of the
rest, receiving visits in their tents and discussing
the chances of the war and the beauty of Constantinople, until they began to discuss one another, after
which the war was not spoken of again on that day.

Then came the Queen with her attendants, from
her tent in the midst of the ladies' lines, pitched as
far as possible from the King's; and leaving outside
those who were with her, she went in and sat
down by Beatrix's bedside.

The girl was very pale and lay propped up by
pillows, her eyelids half shut against the light,
though there was little enough under the thick

double canvas and a brazier of glowing woodcoals made
the tent almost too warm. A great Norman woman
with yellow hair crouched beside her, slowly fanning
her face with a Greek fan of feathers. The Queen
stood still a moment, for she had entered softly, and
Beatrix had not opened her eyes, nor had the woman
known her in the dimness. But when she recognized the Queen, the maid's jaw dropped and her
hand ceased to move. Eleanor took the fan from
her, and with a gesture bade her make way, and then
sat down in her place to do her duty.

Hearing the rustle of skirts and feeling that
another hand fanned her, the sick girl moved a
little, but did not open her eyes, for her head hurt
her, so that she feared the light.

"Who is it?" she asked in the voice of pain.

"Eleanor," answered the Queen, softly.

Still fanning, she took the beautiful little white
hand that lay nearest to her on the edge of the bed.
Beatrix opened her eyes in wonder, for though the
Queen was kind, she was not familiar with her ladies.
The girl started, as if she would have tried to rise.

"No," said Eleanor, quieting her like a child,
"no, no! You must not move, my dear. I have
come to see how you are — there, there! I did not
mean to startle you!"

She smoothed the soft brown hair, and then, with
a sudden impulse, kissed the pale forehead, and
fanned it, and kissed it again, as if Beatrix had
been one of her own little daughters instead of being
a grown woman not very far from her own age.

"I thank your Grace," said Beatrix, faintly.

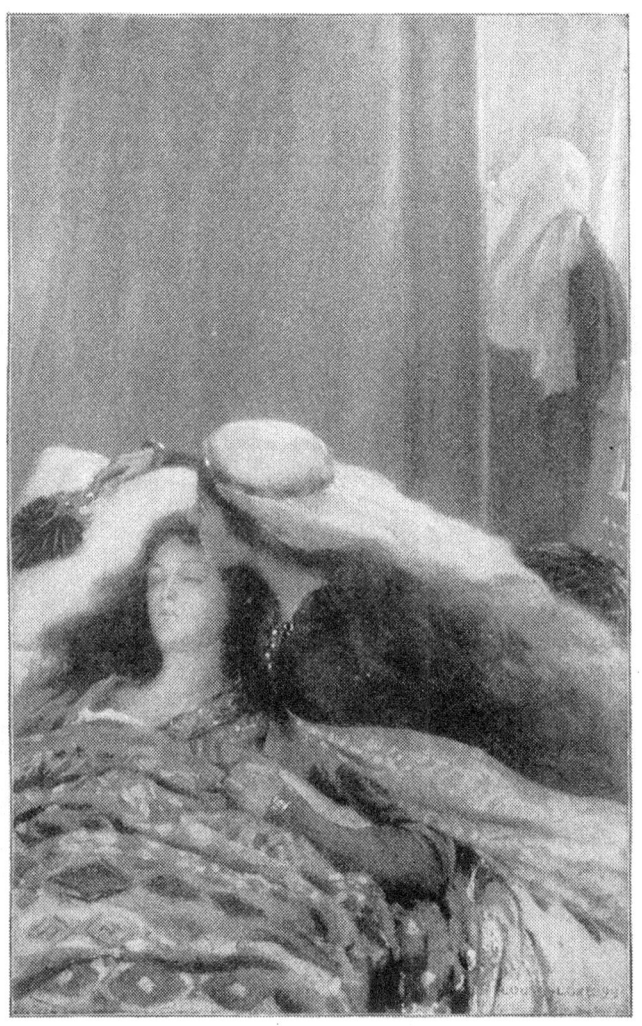

"KISSED THE PALE FOREHEAD"

" We are nearer than thanks since yesterday. Or if there were to be thanking, it should be from me to you who followed me with one other, when three hundred stayed behind. And we are closer than that, for one man saved us both."

She stopped and looked round. The Norman woman was standing respectfully near the door of the tent, with eyes cast down and hands hidden under the folds of her skirt, which were drawn through her girdle in the servants' fashion.

"Go," said Eleanor, quietly. "I will take care of your mistress for a while. And do not stay at the door of the tent, but go away."

The woman bent her head low and disappeared.

"Yes," Beatrix said, when they were alone, "I saw Gilbert Warde stop your horse, and yours stopped mine. He saved us both."

There was silence, and the fan moved softly in the Queen's hand.

"You have loved him long," she said presently, in a tone that questioned.

Beatrix did not answer at once, and on her smooth young forehead two straight lines made straight shadows that ended between her half-closed eyes. At last she spoke, with an effort.

"Madam, as you have a soul, do not take him from me!"

She sighed and withdrew her hand from Eleanor's, as if by instinct. The Queen did not start, but for an instant her eyes gathered light into themselves and her mouth hardened. She glanced at the weak girl, broken and suffering, and looking so small

beside her, and she was angry that Gilbert should
have chosen anything so pitiful against her own
lofty beauty. But presently her anger ceased, not
because it was unopposed, but because she was too
large-hearted for any meanness.

"Forget that I am the Queen," she said at last.
"Only remember that I am a woman and that we
two love one man."

Beatrix shivered and moved uneasily on her pillow, pressing her hand to her throat as if something
choked her.

"You are cruel!" Her voice would not serve her
for more just then, and she stared at the roof of the
tent.

"Love is cruel," answered Eleanor, in a low voice,
and suddenly the hand that held the fan dropped upon
her knee, and her eyes looked at it thoughtfully.

But Beatrix roused herself. There was more
courage and latent energy in the slight girl than
any one dreamed. Her words came clearly.

"Yours is — not mine! For his sake you call
yourself a woman like me, but for his sake only.
Is your face nothing, is your power nothing, is it
nothing that you can hide me from him at your
pleasure, or let me see him as you will? What is
any one to you, who can toss a king aside like a
broken toy when he thwarts you, who can make
war upon empires with no man's help, if you choose?
Is Gilbert a god that he should not yield to you?
Is he above men that he should not forget me, and
go to you, the most beautiful woman in the world,
and the most daring, and the most powerful — to you,

Eleanor of Guienne, Queen of France? You have all; you want that one thing more which is all I have! You are right — love is cruel!"

The Queen listened in silence, too generous still to smile at the girl, too much in earnest to be hurt.

"A man has a right to choose for himself," she answered when Beatrix paused at last.

"Yes, but you take that right from him. You thrust a choice upon him — that is your cruelty."

"How?"

"Look at me and look at yourself. Would any man think twice in choosing? And yet — " a faint smile flickered in the mask of pain — "in Constantinople — in the garden — "

She stopped, happy for a moment in the memory of his defence of her. The Queen was silent and faintly blushed for her cruel speech on that day. She could have done worse deeds and been less ashamed before herself. But Beatrix went on.

"Besides," she said, turning her suffering eyes to Eleanor's face, "your love is sinful, mine is not."

The Queen's look darkened suddenly. This was different ground.

"Leave priests' talk to priests," she answered curtly.

"It will soon be the talk of other men besides priests," reproved Beatrix.

"For that matter, are you better?" retorted the Queen. "Have you not told me that your father has married his mother? You are far within the forbidden degrees of affinity. You cannot marry Gilbert Warde any more than I can. Where is the difference?"

s

"You know it as well as I." The young girl
turned her face away. "You know as well as I
that the Church can pass over what is a mere legal
regulation to hinder marriages made only for fortune's sake. I am not so ignorant as you think.
And you know what your love for Gilbert Warde
is, before God and man ! "

The blood rose in her white face as she spoke.
After that there was silence for some time; but
presently the Queen began to fan Beatrix again,
and mechanically smoothed the coverlet. There
are certain things which a womanly woman would
do for her worst enemy almost unconsciously, and
Eleanor was far from hating her rival. Strong and
unthwarted from her childhood, and disappointed
in her marriage, she had grown to look upon herself as a being above laws of heaven or earth, and
answerable to no one for her deeds. Feminine in
heart and passion, she was manlike in mind and in
her indifference to opinion. Save for Gilbert, she
liked Beatrix; yet, as matters stood, she both looked
upon her as an obstacle and was sorry for her at
the same time. Not being in any way confident
of Gilbert's love herself, the girl she pitied and half
liked was as much her rival as the most beautiful
woman in Europe could have been. She was made
up of strong contrasts — generous yet often unfor-
giving; strong as a man yet capricious as a child ;
tender as à woman, and then in turn sudden, fierce,
and dangerous as a tigress.

Beatrix made a feeble gesture as if she would not be
fanned by the hand that was against her, but the Queen

paid no attention to the refusal. The silence lasted long, and then she spoke quietly and thoughtfully.

"You have a right to say what you will," she began, "for I sat down beside you, as one woman by another, and you have taken me at my word. Love is the very blood of equality. You blame me, and I do not blame you, though I brought up the Church's rule against your love. You are right in all you say, and I am sinful. I grant you that freely, and I will grant also that if I had my due I should be doing penance on my knees instead of defending my sins to you if indeed I am defending them. But do you think that our bad deeds are weighed only against the unattainable perfection of saints' and martyrs' lives, and never at all against the splendid temptations that are the royal garments of sin? God is just, and justice weaves a fair judgment. It is not an unchangeable standard. A learned Greek in Constantinople was telling me the other day a story of one Procrustes, a terrible highway robber. He had a bed which he offered to those he took captive, on condition that they should exactly fit its length ; and if a man was too long, the robber hewed off his feet by so much, but if he was too short, he stretched him on a rack until he was tall enough. If God were to judge me as He judges you, by a ruled length of virtue, alike for all and without allowance for our moral height, God would not be God, but Procrustes, a robber of souls and a murderer of them."

"You speak very blasphemously," said Beatrix, in a low voice.

"No; I speak justly. You and I both love one man. In you, love is virtue, in me it is sin. You blame me with right, but you blame me too much. You tell me that I am beautiful, powerful, the Queen of France, and it is true. But even you do not tell me that I am happy, for you know that I am not."

"And therefore you would rob me of all I have, to make your happiness, when you have so much that I have not! Is that your justice?"

"No," answered Eleanor, almost sadly, "it is not justice. It is my excuse to God and man, before whom you say I am condemned."

The girl roused herself again, and though it was sharp pain to move, she raised her weight upon her elbow and looked straight into the Queen's eyes.

"You argue and you make excuses," she said boldly. "I ask for none. I ask only that you should not take the one happiness I have out of my life. You say that we are speaking as woman to woman. What right have you to the man I love? No, do not answer me with another dissertation on the soul. Woman to woman, tell me what right you have?"

"If he loves me, is that no right?"

"If he loves you? Oh, no! He does not love you yet!"

"He saved me yesterday — not you," answered the Queen, cruelly, and she remembered his eyes. "Does a man risk his life desperately, as he did, for the woman he loves, or for another, when both are in like danger?"

"It was not you, it was the Queen he saved. It

is right that a loyal man should save his sovereign first. I do not blame him. I should not have blamed him had I been more hurt than I am."

"I am not his sovereign, and he is no vassal of mine." Eleanor smiled coldly. "He is an Englishman."

"You play with words," answered Beatrix, as she would have spoken to an equal.

"Take care!"

They faced each other, and on the instant the fierce pride of royalty sprang up, as at an insult. But Beatrix was brave — a sick girl against the Queen of France.

"If you are not his sovereign, you are not mine," she said. "And were you ten times my Queen, there can be no fence of royalty between you and me from this hour, or if there is, you are doubly playing with the meaning of what your lips say. Are you to be a woman to me, a woman, at one moment, and a sovereign to me, a subject, at the next? Which is it to be?"

"A woman, then, if nothing more. And as a woman, I tell you that I will have Gilbert Warde for myself, body and soul."

The girl's eyes lightened suddenly. Men said that in her mother's veins there had run some of the Conqueror's blood, and his great oath sprang to her lips as she answered : —

"And by the splendour of God, I tell you that you shall not!"

"Then it is a duel between us," the Queen said, and she turned to go.

"To death," answered the girl, as her head sank back upon the pillows, pitifully weak and tired in her aching body, but dauntless in spirit.

Eleanor crossed the carpeted floor of the tent slowly toward the door. She had not made four steps when she stood still, looking before her. A great shame of herself came upon her for what she had said — the loyal, generous shame of the strong who in anger has been overbearing with the weak. She stood still, and she felt as an honest man does who has struck a fallen enemy in unreasoning rage. It was the second time that she had fallen so low in her own eyes, and her own scorn of herself was more than she could bear.

Quickly she came back to Beatrix's side. The girl lay quite still, with parted lips and closed eyes that had great black shadows under them. Her small white hands twitched now and then spasmodically, but she seemed hardly to breathe. Eleanor knelt beside her and propped her up higher, thrusting one arm under the pillow while she fanned her with the other hand.

"Beatrix!" she called softly.

She thought that the girl's eyelids quivered, and she called her again; but there was no answer, nor any movement of the hand this time, and the face was so white and deathly that any one might have believed life gone, but for the faintly perceptible breath that stirred the feathers of the Greek fan when the Queen held it close to the lips. She grew anxious and thought of calling the Norman serving-woman and of sending for her own physician. But, in the first place, she thought that Beatrix might have only fainted, to revive at any moment, in which case she had things to say which were not for other ears; and as for her physician, it suddenly occurred to her that, although he had been in her train five years, she had never under any circumstances had occasion to consult him, and that he was probably what he looked, a solemn fool and an ignorant drencher, whereas there were younger men with wise heads who had followed the army and made a fat living by concocting draughts for those who overcloyed themselves with Greek sweetmeats, physicians who could make salves for bruises, who knew the cunning Italian trick of opening a vein in the instep instead of in the arm, and who, on occasion, could cast a judicial figure of the heavens and interpret the horoscope of the day and hour.

But while she hesitated, Eleanor brought water from a bright brass ewer and dashed drops upon the girl's face; she found also a cup with Greek wine in it, that smelt of fine resin, and she set it to the pale lips and held it there. Presently Beatrix opened her eyes a little, and suddenly she shuddered when she saw Eleanor and heard her voice in the deep stillness.

" As one woman to another — I ask your forgive-ness."

CHAPTER XVII

GILBERT sat in the door of his tent at noon, the sun shining down upon him and warming him pleasantly, for the day was chilly, and he was still aching. As he idly watched the soldiers going and coming, and cooking their midday meal at the camp-fires, while Dunstan and Alric were preparing his own, he was thinking that this was the third day since he had saved the Queen's life, and that although many courtiers had asked of his condition, and had talked with him as if he had done a great deed, yet he had received not so much as a message of thanks from Eleanor nor from the King, and it seemed as if he had been forgotten altogether. But of Beatrix, Dunstan told him that she was in a fever and wandering, and the Norman woman had said that she talked of her home. Gilbert hated himself because he could do nothing for her, but most bitterly because he had yielded to the Queen's eyes and to her voice in the instant of balanced life and death.

The great nobles passed on their way to their tents from the King's quarters, where the council met daily to trace the march. And still Gilbert's shield hung blank and white on his lance, and he sat alone, without so much as a new mantle upon him, nor a sword-belt, nor any gift to show that the royal favour had descended upon him as had been expected. So some of the nobles only saluted him with a grave gesture in which there was neither friendship nor familiarity, and some took no notice of him, turning their faces away, for they thought that they had made a mistake, and that the Englishman had given some grave offence for which even his brave action was not a sufficient atonement. But he cared little, for his nature was not a courtier's, and even then the English Normans were colder and graver men than those of France, and more overbearing in arms, but less self-seeking, one against another, in court.

Dunstan came from behind the tent, where the fire was, bringing food in two polished brass bowls, and Gilbert went in to eat his dinner. Coarse fare enough it was, a soup of vegetables and bread, with pieces of meat in it, and little crumbs of cheese, scraped off with a sharp knife, and floating on the thick liquid; and then, in the other bowl, small gobbets of roasted beef run by sixes on wooden skewers that were blackened at the ends by the fire. And it all tasted of smoke, for the wood was yet green on the hillsides. But Gilbert ate and said nothing, neither praising nor blaming, for very often on the long march he had eaten the dried bread of the German peasants and the unleavened wheat-cakes of the wild Hungarians, with a draught of water, and had been glad even of that. Also on Fridays and Saturdays, and on the vigils of feast days, and on most days in Lent, he had eaten only bread and boiled vegetables, such as could be found, and the fasting reminded him of the old days in Sheering Abbey.

For in his nature there was the belief of that age

in something far above common desires and passions,
dwelling in a temple of the soul that must be reached
by steps of pain; there was the spirit of men who
starved and scourged their bodies almost to death
that their souls might live unspotted; and the terribly primitive conception of every passional sin as
equal in importance to murder, and only less deadly
than an infamous crime in the semi-worldly view of
knightly honour, which admitted private vengeance
as a sort of necessity of human nature.

The mere thought that he could love the Queen, or
could have believed that he loved her for one instant,
seemed ten thousand times worse than his boyish
love of Beatrix had once seemed, when he had supposed that there was no means of setting aside the
bar of affinity; and it was right that he should think
so. But though temptation is not sin, he made it
that, and accused himself; for it was manifest that
the merest passing thrill of the blood, such as he had
felt on that night in Vézelay, and now again, must
be an evil thing, since it had brought about such a
great result in a dangerous moment.

These were small things, and nice distinctions, that
a strong man should dwell on them and bruise his
heart for its wickedness. But they were not small if to
neglect them meant the eternity of torture that awaited
him who looked upon his neighbour's wife to covet
her. There were among the nobles who had taken
the Cross not a few to whom the law seemed less
rigid and perdition less sure, and Eleanor herself
gave her sins gentle names; but the Englishman was
old-fashioned, and even the good Abbot of Sheering

had been struck by his literal way of accepting all beliefs, in the manner of a past time when the world had trembled at the near certainty of the Last Judgment, expiating its misdeeds by barefooted pilgrimages to Jerusalem, and its venial faults by cruel macerations of the flesh.

Gilbert, therefore, looked upon all bodily weariness and suffering and privation which he chanced to encounter on the march as so much penance to be borne cheerfully because it should profit his soul; and while the young blood coursed in his veins, and youth's bright lights danced in his eyes, the cold spirit of the ascetic fought against the warm life toward an end which the man felt rather than saw, and of which the profound melancholy would have appalled him, could he have realized it.

As month followed month, though his strength increased upon him under much labour, and though his cheeks were tanned by sunshine and weather, the broad forehead grew whiter under his cap, and more thoughtful, and his eyes were saddened and his features more spiritual; also, while he longed daily to draw his sword and strike great blows at unbelievers for faith's sake and to the honouring of the Holy Cross, the rough fighting instinct of his people, that craved to see blood for its redness and to take the world for love of holding it, no longer awoke suddenly in him, like hunger or thirst, at the wayward call of opportunity. He could not now have plucked out steel to hew down men, as he had done on that spring morning among the flowers of the Tuscan valley, only because it was good to see the dazzling red line follow the long quick sword-stroke, and to ride weight at weight to overthrow it, swinging the death-scythe through the field of life. He wanted the cause and the end now, where once he had desired only the deed, and he had risen another step above the self that had been.

He knew it, and nevertheless, as he sat still after he had eaten his midday meal, he saw that his years had been very sad since his first great sorrow; and each time when he thought he had gone forward some strong thing had driven him back, or some great grief had fallen upon him, and he himself had almost been forced down. He had been proud of his arms and his boyish skill at Faringdon, and before his eyes his father had been foully slain; he had faced the murderer in the cause of right, and he himself had been half killed; he had believed in his mother as in heaven, and she had defiled his father's memory and robbed her son of his inheritance; he had sought peace in Rome, and had found madness and strife; he had desired to do knightly deeds and had killed men for nothing; he loved a maiden with a maiden heart, and at the touch of a faithless woman his blood rose in his throat, and for a look of hers and a tone of her voice he had put forth his hands to grapple with sudden death, forgetting the other, the better, the dearer.

So he was thinking, and the door of his tent was darkened for a moment, so that he looked up. There stood one of Queen Eleanor's attendant knights, in tunic and hose, one hand on his sword-hilt, the other holding his round cap in the act of salutation. He was a Gascon, of middle height, spare and elastic as a steel blade, dark as a Moor, with fiery eyes and thin black mustaches that stuck up like a cat's whiskers. His manner was exaggerated, and he made great gestures, but he was a true man and brave. Gilbert rose to meet him, and saw behind him a soldier carrying something small and heavy on one shoulder, steadying it with his hand.

" The Lord of Stoke? " the knight began in a tone of inquiry.

" If I had my own, sir," answered the Englishman, " but I have not. My name is Gilbert Warde."

" Sir Gilbert — " began the Gascon, bowing again and waving the hand that held his cap in a tremendous gesture, which ended on his heart as if to express thanks for the information.

" No, sir," interrupted the other. " Of those who would have given me knighthood I would not have it, and they of whom I would take it have not offered it."

" Sir," answered the knight, courteously, " those of whom you speak cannot have known you. I come from her Grace the Duchess of Gascony."

" The Duchess of Gascony? " asked Gilbert, unaccustomed to the title.

The knight drew himself up till he seemed to be standing on his toes, and his hand left his sword-hilt to give his mustache a fierce upward twist.

" The Duchess of Gascony, sir," he repeated. " There are a few persons who call her Highness the Queen of France, doubtless without meaning to give offence."

Gilbert smiled in spite of himself, but the knight's eyes took fire instantly.

"Do you laugh at me, sir?" he asked, his hand going back to his sword, and his right foot advancing a little as if he meant to draw.

"No, sir. I crave your pardon if I smiled, admiring your Gascon loyalty."

The other was instantly pacified, smiled too, and waved his long arm several times.

"I come, then, from her Grace the Duchess," he said, insisting on the title, "to express to you her sovereign thanks for the service you did her the other day. Her Grace has been much busied by the councils, else she would have sent me sooner."

"I am most respectfully grateful for the message," answered Gilbert, rather coldly, "and I beg you, sir, to accept my appreciation of the pains you have taken to bring it to me."

"Sir, I am most wholly at your service," replied the knight, again laying his hand upon his heart. "But besides words the Duchess sends you, by my hand, a more substantial evidence of her gratitude."

He turned and took the heavy leather bag from his attendant soldier, and offered it to Gilbert, holding it out in his two hands, and coming nearer. Gilbert stepped back when he saw what it was. The money was for a deed which might have cost Beatrix her life. He felt sick at the sight of it, as if it had been as the price of blood which Judas took. His face turned very pale under his tan, and he clasped his hands together nervously.

" No," he said quickly, "no, I pray you! Not money — thanks are enough ! "

The knight looked at him in surprise at first, and then incredulously, supposing that it was only a first refusal, for the sake of ceremony.

" Indeed," he answered, " it is the Duchess's command that I should present you with this gift in most grateful acknowledgment of your service."

" And I beg you, by your knighthood, to thank her Grace with all possible respect for what I cannot receive." Gilbert's voice grew hard. " She is not my sovereign, sir, that I should look to her for my support in this war. It pleased God that I should save a lady's life, but I shall not take a lady's gold. I mean no discourtesy to her Grace, nor to you, sir."

Seeing that he was in earnest, the Gascon's expression changed, and a bright smile came into his sallow face, for he had found a man after his own heart. He threw the heavy bag toward the soldier, and it fell chinking to the floor before the man could reach it; and turning to Gilbert again, he held out his hand with less ceremony and more cordiality than he had hitherto shown.

" With a little accent," he said, " you might pass for a Gascon."

Gilbert smiled as he shook hands, for it was clear that the knight meant to bestow upon him the highest compliment he could put into words.

" Sir," answered the Englishman, " I see that we think alike in this matter. I pray you, let not the Queen be offended by the answer you shall give her from me ; but I shall leave it to your courtesy

and skill to choose such words as you think best, for
I am a poor speaker of compliments."

"The Duchess of Gascony shall think only the
better of you when she has heard me, sir."

Thereupon, with a great gesture and a bow to
which Gilbert gravely responded, the knight took
his leave and went to the door; but then, suddenly
forgetting all his manner, and with a genuine impulse, he turned, came back and seized Gilbert's
hand once more.

"A little accent, my friend! If you only had a
little accent!"

His wiry figure disappeared through the door a
moment later, and Gilbert was alone. He asked
himself whether the Queen had meant to insult him,
and he could not believe it. But presently, as he
remembered all that had happened, it occurred to
him that she might be ashamed of having shown him
her heart in a moment of great danger, and now, as
if to cover herself, she meant him to understand that
he was nothing to her but a brave man who ought to
be substantially and richly rewarded for having risked
his life on her behalf.

Strangely enough, the thought pleased him now,
as much as the brutal offer of the gold had outraged
his honourable feeling. It was far better, he reflected,
that the Queen should act thus and help him to look
upon her as a being altogether beyond his sphere, as
she really was. After this, he thought, it would be
impossible and out of the question that any look or
touch of hers could send a thrill through him, like
little rivers of fire, from his head to his heels. The

hand that had been held out to pay him money for its own life, must be as cold as a stone and as unfeeling. She was helping him to be true.

He shook himself and stretched his long arms as if awaking from sleep and dreaming. The motion hurt him, and he felt all his bruises at once, but there was a sort of pleasure in the pain, that accorded with his strange state of heart, and he did it a second time in order to feel the pain once more.

T

CHAPTER XVIII

THE knight, whose name·was Gaston de Castignac, faithfully fulfilled Gilbert's wishes, using certain ornate flourishes of language which the Englishman could certainly not have invented, and altogether expressing an absolute refusal in the most complimentary manner imaginable. The Queen bade him return the gold to her seneschal without breaking the leaden seal that pinched the ends of the knotted strings together. When she was alone, her women being together in the outer part of the tent, she hid her face in her white hands, as she sat, and bending forward, she remained in that attitude a long time, without moving.

It was as Gilbert had thought. In the generous impulse that had prompted her to ask Beatrix's forgiveness she had done what was hardest for her to do, in a sort of wild hope that, by insulting the man who had such strong attraction for her, she might send him away out of her sight forever. Had he accepted the money, she would assuredly have despised him, and contempt must kill all thoughts of love; but since he refused it, he must be angry with her, and he would either leave her army, and join himself to the Germans during the rest of the campaign, or, at the very least, he would avoid her.

But now that it was done and he had sent back the

274

money in scorn, as she clearly understood in spite of
her knight's flowery speeches, she felt the shame of
having treated a poor gentleman like a poor servant,
and then the certainty that he must believe her ungrateful began to torment her, so that she thought of
his face, and longed to see him with all her heart.
For Beatrix's sake and her own honour she would
not send for him; but she called one of her women
and sent for the Lady Anne of Auch, who bore
the standard of the ladies' troop, the same who had
stopped her horse without a fall. In her the Queen
had great faith for her wisdom, for she had a man's
thoughts with a woman's heart.

She came presently, tall and grave as a stately
cypress among silver birches and shimmering white
poplar trees.

"I have sent for you to ask you a question," the
Queen began, "or, perhaps, to ask your advice."

The Lady Anne bowed her head, and when
Eleanor pointed to a folding-stool beside her, she sat
down and waited, fixing her black eyes on a distant
part of the tent.

"You saw that young Englishman who stopped my
horse," the Queen began. "I wish to reward him.
I have sent him five hundred pieces of gold, and he
has refused to receive the gift."

The black eyes turned steadily to the Queen's face,
gazed at her for a moment, and then looked away
again, while not a feature moved. There was silence,
for Anne of Auch said nothing while Eleanor waited.

"What shall I do now?" Eleanor asked after a
long pause.

"Madam," answered the dark lady, smiling thoughtfully, "I think that, since you have offered him gold
first, he would refuse a kingdom if you should press
it upon him now, for he is a brave man."

"Do you know him?" asked Eleanor, almost
sharply, and her eyes hardened.

"I have seen him many times, but I have never
spoken with him. We talk of him now and then,
because he is unlike the other knights, mixing little
with them in the camp and riding often alone on
the march. They say he is very poor, and he is
surely brave."

"What does Beatrix de Curboil say of him?" The
Queen's voice was still sharp.

"Beatrix? She is my friend, poor girl. I never
heard her speak of this gentleman."

"She is very silent, is she not?"

"Oh, no! She is sometimes sad, and she has told me
how her father took a second wife who was unkind
to her, and she speaks of her own childhood as if she
were the daughter of a great house. But that is all."

"And she never told you her stepmother's name,
and never mentioned this Englishman?"

"Never, Madam, I am quite sure. But she is
often very gay and quick of wit, and makes us laugh,
even when we are tired and hot after a day's march
and are waiting for our women; and sometimes she
sings strange old Norman songs of Duke William's
day, very sweetly, and little Saxon slave songs which
we cannot understand."

"I have never heard her laugh nor sing, I think,"
said Eleanor, thoughtfully.

"She is very grave before your Grace. I have noticed it. That may be the English manner."

"I think it is." The Queen thought of Gilbert, and wondered whether he were ever gay. "But the question," she continued, "is what am I to do for the man?"

She spoke coldly and indifferently, but her eyes were watching the Lady Anne's face.

"What should you do yourself?" she asked, as the noble woman made no answer.

"I should not have sent him gold first," replied Anne of Auch. "But since that cannot be undone, your Grace can only offer him some high honour, which may be an honour only, and not wealth."

"He is not even a knight!"

"Then give him knighthood and honour too. Your Grace has made knights,—there is Gaston de Castignac,—and the fashion of receiving knighthood from the Church only, is past."

"I have heard him say that he would have it from his own liege sovereign, or not at all. He will not even set a device in his shield, as many are beginning to do, to show in the field that they are of good stock."

"Give him one, then—a device that shall be a perpetual honour to his house and a memory of a brave deed well done for a Queen's sake."

"And then? Shall that be all?"

"And then, if he be the man he seems, single him out for some great thing, and bid him risk his life again in doing it for the Holy Cross, and for your Grace's sake."

"That is good. Your counsel was always good. What thing shall I give him to attempt?"

"Madam, the Germans have been betrayed by the Greek Emperor's Greek guides, and we ourselves have no others, so that we in turn shall be led to slaughter if we follow them. If it please your Grace, let this Englishman choose such men as he trusts, and go ever before our march, till we reach Syria, sending tidings back to us, and receiving them, and bearing the brunt of danger for us."

"That would be indeed an honourable part," said the Queen, thoughtfully, and she turned slowly pale, careless of her lady's straight gaze. "He can never live to the end of it," she added, in a low voice.

"It is better to die for the Cross than to die or live for any woman's love," said Anne of Auch, and there was the music of faith in her soft tones.

The Queen glanced at her, wondering how much she guessed, and suddenly conscious that she herself had changed colour.

"And what device shall I set in this man's shield?" she asked, going back to the beginning, in order to avoid what touched her too closely.

"A cross," answered Anne. "Let me see — why not your Grace's own? The Cross of Aquitaine?"

But the Queen did not hear, for she was dreaming, and she saw Gilbert, in her thoughts, riding to sure death with a handful of brave men, riding into an ambush of the terrible Seljuks, pierced by their arrows — one in his white throat as he reeled back in the saddle, his eyes breaking in death. She shuddered, and then started as if waking.

"What did you say?" she asked. "I was think-ing of something else."

"I said that your Grace might give him the Cross of Aquitaine for a device," answered the Lady of Auch.

Her quiet black eyes watched the Queen, not in suspicion, but with a sort of deep and womanly sympathy; for she herself had loved well, and on the eighth day after she had wedded her husband, he had gone out with others against the Moors in the southern mountains; and they had brought him home on his shield, wrapped in salted hides, and she had seen his face. Therefore she had taken the Cross, not as many ladies had taken it, in light-ness of heart, but earnestly, seeking a fair death on the field of honour for the hope of the life to come.

"Yes," said the Queen, "he shall have the Cross of Aquitaine. Fetch me some gentleman or squire skilled with colours, and send for the Englishman's shield."

"Madam," said Anne of Auch, "I myself can use a brush, and by your leave I will paint the device under your eyes."

It was no uncommon thing in that day for a lady of France to understand such arts better than men, and Eleanor was glad, and ordered that the shield should be brought quickly, by two of the elder pages who were soon to be squires.

But Alric, the groom, who lay in the shade out-side Gilbert's tent, chewing blades of grass and wish-ing himself in England, would not let the messengers take the shield from the lance without authority, and he called Dunstan, who went and asked Gilbert what he should do. So Gilbert came and stood in the door of his tent, and spoke to the young men.

"We know nothing, sir, save that we are bidden to bring your shield to the Queen."

"Take it. And you shall tell her Grace from me that I crave excuse if the shield be of an old fashion, with rounded shoulders, for it was my father's; and you shall say also that she has power to take it, but that I will not sell it, nor take anything in return for it."

The two young men looked at him strangely, as if doubting whether he were in his right mind. But as they went away together, the one who bore the shield said to the other that they should not give the message, for it was discourteous and might do harm to themselves. But the other was for telling the truth, since they could call Gilbert's men to witness of the words.

"And if we are caught in a lie," he said, "we shall be well beaten."

For they were young and were pages, not yet squires, and still under education.

"Also we shall be beaten if we say things uncourtly to the Queen," retorted the first.

"This air smells of sticks," said the other, as he sniffed, and laughed at his jest, but somewhat nervously.

"You shall speak for us," concluded his companion, "for you are the truth-teller."

So they came to the Queen, and laid the blank shield at her feet, and neither would say anything.

"Saw you the gentleman to whom it belongs?" she asked.

" Yes, Madam ! " they answered in one breath.

" And said he anything ?   Have you no message ? "

" He said, Madam — " said one, and stopped short.

" Yes, Madam, he said that we should tell your Grace — "

But the page's courage failed him, and he stopped also.

" What said he ? " asked Eleanor, bending her brows.   " Speak out ! "

" May it please your Grace, the gentleman said that it was his father's shield."

" And that he craved excuse if it were of an old fashion," added the other.

" And that he would not sell it," concluded the one who was the bolder of the two.

Then he shrank back, and his companion too, and they seemed trying to get behind each other ; for the Queen's eyes flashed wrath, and her beautiful lips parted a little over her gleaming teeth, that were tightly closed.   But in an instant she was calm again, and she took money from her wallet and gave each page a piece of gold, and spoke quietly.

" You are brave boys to give me such a message," she said.   " But if I chance to find out that you have changed it on the way, you shall each have as many blows as there are French deniers in a Greek bezant — and I doubt whether any one knows how many there may be."

" We speak truth, Madam," said the two, in a breath, " and we humbly thank your Grace."

She sent them away, and sat looking at the shield at her feet, while Anne of Auch waited in silence.

Eleanor's eyes burned in her head, and her hands were cold, and would have shaken a little if she had not held them tightly clasped together.

"It was unknightly of him to say that," she cried at last, as if it hurt her.

But her lady was still silent, and the Queen turned her hot eyes to her.

"You say nothing. Was it not unknightly of him?"

"Madam," answered Anne of Auch, "since you wished to pay him for your life, it is little wonder if he thinks you may offer to buy his arms."

They said no more for a long time, and from the outer tent the sweet subdued voices of many women, talking and laughing softly together, floated into the silence like the song of birds at dawn. At last the Queen spoke, but it was to herself.

"He had the right," she said bitterly, and bent her head a little, and sighed. "Paint me the shield, Lady Anne," she added, a moment later, looking up calmly once more. "On a field azure, for the faith he keeps, gild him the cross flory of Aquitaine —for me!"

She rose and began to walk slowly up and down the tent, glancing at Anne from time to time. The lady had sent for her colours, ground on a piece of white marble, and a small chafing-dish with burning coals, in which a little copper pot of melted wax mixed with resin stood on an iron tripod. She warmed her brush in the wax, and took up the costly blue on it, and spread it very dexterously over all the long shield. When it was cool, the resin made it very hard, and with rule and dividers she measured out the cross with its equal arms, all flowered, and drew it skilfully, while the Queen watched her deft fingers. And last of all she moistened the cross with Arabian gum, a little at a time, and laid strong gold-leaf upon it with a sharp steel instrument, blowing hard upon each leaf as soon as it was laid, to press it down, and smoothing it with a hare's-foot. When it was all covered and dry, she took a piece of soft leather wrapped about her forefinger, and carefully went round the outline, taking off the superfluous leaf that spread beyond the gummed part. She had learned these things from an Italian who had come to Auch to adorn the chapel of her father's house.

The Queen had sat down long before it was finished, but her eyes followed the Lady Anne's brush and her fingers, while neither of the women spoke.

"It is a fair shield," said Eleanor, when it was done. "Lady Anne, shall I send it to him, or shall he come here? Were you in my place, which should you do?"

"Madam, I would send for the Englishman. From your Grace's hands he cannot refuse honour."

Eleanor did not answer, but after a moment she rose and turned away.

"Nor death," she said in a low voice, as to herself, and stood still, and pressed her hand to her forehead. "Send for him, and leave me alone till he comes, but stay when he is here," she added, in clear tones; and still not looking at the Lady Anne, she bent her head and went out.

The tall, old-fashioned shield stood on its point,

leaning against the table. Eleanor looked at it, and her features were moved, now that she was alone, and her eyes were veiled. She lifted it in both her hands, wondering at its weight, and she pushed aside an inner curtain and set the shield upon an altar that was there, hidden from the rest of the tent for a little oratory, as in many royal chambers. Then she knelt down at the kneeling-stool and folded her hands.

She was not ungenerous, she was not at heart unjust; she deserved some gentleness of judgment, for she was doing her best to fight her love, for her royal honour's sake and for the sick girl who seemed so poor a rival, but who loved Gilbert Warde as well as she and less selfishly. As she knelt there, she believed that she was in the great struggle of her life, and that at once and forever she could make the sacrifice, though it had grown to be a great one.

She meant to send him before the army, and the wager for his death was as a hundred to one. Let him die — that was the consecration of the sacrifice. Dead in glory, dead for Christ's sake, dead in the spotless purity of his young knighthood, she could love him fearlessly thereafter, and speak very gentle words upon his grave. It was not cruel to send him to die thus, if his days were numbered, and he himself would gratefully thank her for preferring him before others to lead the van of peril; for the way of the Cross leads heavenwards. But if he should come alive through the storm of swords, he must win great honour for all his life.

Thereupon she prayed for him alone, and she

dedicated his great shield on her own altar, in her own words, with all her passionate heart, wherein beat the blood of her grandsire, dead in a hermit's cell after much love and war, and the blood of the son she was to bear long after, whom men were to call the Lion-Hearted.

And she prayed thus, with a pale face : —

" Almighty God, most just, who art the truth, and who orderest good against evil, with pain, that men may be saved by overcoming, help me to give up what is most dear in my life. Hear me, O God, a sinful woman, and have mercy upon me ! Hear me, O God, and though I perish, let this man's soul be saved !

" Lord Jesus Christ, most pitiful and kind, to Thee I bring my sin, and I steadfastly purpose to be faithful, and to renounce and abhor my evil desires and thoughts. Hear me, O Christ, a sinful woman ! To Thy service and to the honour of Thy most sacred Cross, I dedicate this true man. Bless Thou this shield of his, that it may be between him and his enemies, and his arms, also, that he may go before our host, and save many, and lead us to Thy holy place in Jerusalem ! Endue him with grace, fill him with strength, enlighten his heart. Hear me and help me, O Christ, a sinful, loving woman !

" Holy Spirit of God, Most High, Creator, Comforter, let Thy pure gifts descend upon this clean-hearted man, that his courage fail not in life, nor in the hour of death. Hear me, a sinful woman, Thou who, with the Father and the Son, livest and reignest in glory forever ! "

When she had prayed, she knelt a little while longer, with bowed head pressing against her clasped hands on the praying-stool till they hurt her. And that was the hardest, for it had been her meaning to make a solemn promise, and she saw between her and her love the barrier of her faith to be kept to God, and of her respect of her own plighted honour.

Rising at last, she took the shield again, and kissed it once between the arms of the cross ; and her lips made a small mark on the fresh gold-leaf.

" He will never know what it is," she said to herself, as she looked at the place, " but I think that no arrow shall strike through it there, nor any lance."

Suddenly she longed to kiss the shield again, and many times, to thousands, as if her lips could give it tenfold virtue to defend. But she thought of her prayer and would not, and she brought the shield back into the tent, out of the oratory, and set it upright against the table.

Then, after a time, Anne of Auch lifted the curtain to let Gilbert in, standing by the entrance when he had passed her.

He bent his head courteously but not humbly, and then stood upright, pale from what he had suffered, his eyes fixed as if he were making an inward effort. The Queen spoke, coldly and clearly.

" Gilbert Warde, you saved my life, and you have sent back a gift from me. I have called you to

THE KNIGHTING OF GILBERT

give you two things. You may scorn the one, but the other you cannot refuse."

He looked at her, and within her outward cold-ness he saw something he had never seen before — something divinely womanly, unguessed in his life, which touched him more than her own touch had ever done. He felt that she drew him to her, though it were now against her better will. There-fore he was afraid, and angry with himself.

"Madam," he said, with a sort of fierce coldness, "I need no gifts to poison your good thanks."

"Sir," answered Eleanor, "there is no venom in the honour I mean for you. I borrowed your shield, — your father's honourable shield, — and I give it back to you with a device that was never shamed, that you and yours may bear my cross of Aquitaine in memory of what you did."

She took the shield and held it out to him with a look almost stern, and as her eyes fell upon it they dwelt on the spot she had kissed. Gilbert's face changed, for he was moved. He knelt on one knee to receive the shield, and his voice shook.

"Madam, I will bear this device ever for your Grace's sake and memory, and I pray that I may bear it honourably, and my sons' sons after me."

Eleanor waited a breathing-space before she spoke again.

"You may not bear it long, sir," she said, and her voice was less hard and clear, "for I desire of you a great service, which is also an honour before other men."

"What I may do, I will do."

"Take, then, at your choice two or three score lances, gentlemen and men-at-arms who are well mounted, and ride ever a day's march before the army, spying out the enemy and sending messengers constantly to us, as we shall send to you; for I trust not the Greek guides we have. So you shall save us all from the destruction that overtook the German Emperor in the mountains. Will you do this?"

Again Gilbert's face lightened, for he knew the danger and the honour.

"I will do it faithfully, so help me God."

Then he would have risen, but the Queen spoke again.

"Lady Anne," she said, "give me the sword of Aquitaine."

Anne of Auch brought the great blade, in its velvet scabbard, with its cross-hilt bound with twisted wire of gold for the old Duke's grip. The Queen drew it slowly and gave back the sheath.

"Sir," she said, "I will give you knighthood, that you may have authority among men."

Gilbert was taken unawares. He bowed his head in silence, and knelt upon both knees instead of on one only, placing his open hands together. The Queen stood with her left hand on the hilt of the great sword, and she made the sign of the cross with her right. Gilbert also crossed himself, and so did the Lady Anne, and she knelt at the Queen's left, for it was a very solemn rite. Then Eleanor spoke.

"Gilbert Warde, inasmuch as you are about to receive the holy order of knighthood at my hands without preparation, consider first whether you are in any mortal sin, lest that be an impediment."

" On the honour of my word, I have no mortal sin upon my soul," answered Gilbert.

" Make, then, the promises of knighthood. Promise before Almighty God that you will lead an honest and a clean life."

" I will so live, God helping me."

" Promise that to the best of your strength you will defend the Christian faith against unbelievers, and that you will suffer death, and a cruel death, but not deny the Lord Jesus Christ."

" I will be faithful to death, so God help me."

" Promise that you will honour women, and protect them, and shield the weak, and at all times be merciful to the poor, preferring before yourself all those who are in trouble and need."

" I will, by God's grace."

" Promise that you will be true and allegiant to your liege sovereign."

" I promise that I will be true and allegiant to my liege Queen and Lady, Maud of England, and to her son and Prince, Henry Plantagenet, and thereof your Grace is witness."

" And between my hands, as your liege sovereign's proxy, lay your hands."

Gilbert held out his joined hands to the Queen, and she took them between her palms, while Anne of Auch held the great sword, still kneeling.

" I put my hands between the hands of my Lady, Queen Maud of England, and I am her man," said Gilbert Warde.

U

But Eleanor's touch was like ice, and she trembled a little.

Then she took the sword of Aquitaine and held it up in her right hand, though it was heavy, and she spoke holy words.

"Gilbert Warde, be a true knight in life and death! 'Whatsoever things are true, whatsoever things are honest, whatsoever things are just, whatsoever things are pure, whatsoever things are lovely, whatsoever things are of good report; if there be any virtue, and if there be any praise, think on these things' — and do them, and for them live and die."

When she had spoken, she laid the sword flat upon his left shoulder, and let it linger a moment, and then lifted it and touched him twice again, and sheathed the long blade.

"Sir Gilbert, rise!"

He stood before her, and he knew what remained to be done, according to the rite, and it was not fire that ran through him, but a chill of fear. The Queen's face was marble pale and as beautiful as death. One step toward him she made with outstretched arms, her right above his left, her left under his right as he met her. Then she coldly kissed the man she loved on the cheek, once only, in the royal fashion, and he kissed her.

She drew back, and their eyes met. Remembering many things, he thought that he should see in her face the evil shadow of his mother, as he had seen it before; but he saw a face he did not know, for it was that of a suffering woman, coldly brave to the best of her strength.

" Go, Sir Gilbert! " she said. " Go out and fight, and die if need be, that others may live to win battles for the Cross of Christ."

He was gone, and Anne of Auch stood beside her.

" Lady Anne," said the Queen, " I thank you. I would be alone."

She turned and went into the little oratory, and knelt down before the altar, looking at the place where the shield had stood.

CHAPTER XIX

So Gilbert Warde was made a knight, and to this day the Wards bear the cross flory in their shield, which was given to their forefathers by Eleanor of Aquitaine before she was English Queen. And so, also, Sir Gilbert promised to ride a day's march before the rest, with a handful of men whom he chose among his acquaintance; and many envied him his honour, but there were more who warmed themselves by the camp-fire at night most comfortably, and were glad that they had not been chosen to live hardly, half starving on their half-starved horses, with a cloak and a blanket on the ground for a bed, watching in turns by night, and waking each morning to wonder whether they should live till sunset.

In truth there was less of danger than of hardship at first, and more trouble than either; for though Gilbert was sent on with the best of the Greek guides to choose the way, and had full power of life and death over them, so that they feared him more than Satan and dared not hide the truth from him, yet when he had chosen the line of the march and had sent word by a messenger to the army, the answer often came back that the King and the Emperor were of another mind, because they had listened to some lying Greek; and since the Emperor and the King and Queen had agreed that any one of them must always yield to the opinion of the other two, Eleanor's advice, which was Gilbert's and founded on real knowledge, was often over-ridden by the others, and she was forced to give way or make an open breach. Then Gilbert ground his teeth silently and did the best he could, retracing his steps over many miles, exploring a new road, and choking down the humiliation bravely, because he had given his word.

But little by little that humiliation turned to honour, even among the men who were with him; for most of them were taken from the Queen's army, and besides, they saw every day that Gilbert was right, so that they trusted him and would have followed him through storm and fire. Also in the Queen's army it began to be known, and it spread to the other French, and to the Germans, and to the Poles and the Bohemians, that when the troops followed the march chosen by Gilbert, all went well, and they found water and forage for their horses, and food and a good camping-ground; but often, when the King and the Emperor had their way, there was hunger and cold and lack of water.

The men began to say to each other, when they knew, " This is Sir Gilbert's road, and to-day is a feast-day ; " and then, " This is the King's road, and to-day is Friday." And on Gilbert's days they sang as they marched, and trudged along cheerfully, and his name ran like a sound of gladness along the endless lines. He grew, therefore, to be beloved by many who had never seen him in the great host, and at last even by the most of the soldiers.

So they came to Ephesus at last, very weary, and
with some sick persons among them. Conrad the
Emperor was in ill case, though he was of the
strongest, and at Ephesus messengers met him who
had come by sea from the Emperor of the Greeks,
begging that he and all his men would sail back to
Constantinople and spend the rest of the winter
there, and afterwards go by sea again to Syria.
And they did so, for the brave Germans were much
broken and worn because of their marches and
defeats before they had gone back to Nicæa, and the
armies of the King and Queen went on without them,
to a great meadow by the Mæander, where they
encamped to keep the Christmas feast with great
thanksgiving for their preservation thus far.

On Christmas eve Gilbert came into camp with his
companions, and when they were seen, a great cry
arose throughout the army, and men left their fires
and their mending of arms and clothes, and ran out
to meet him, a gaunt man in rusty armour, on a gaunt
horse, followed by others in no better plight. His
mantle was all stained with rain and mud, and was
rent in many places, and his mail was brown, save
where it had been chafed bright by his moving; his
great Norman horse was rough with his winter coat
and seemed all joints and bones, and Dunstan and
Alric rode in rags with the men-at-arms. His face
was haggard with weariness and lack of food, but
stern and high, and the first who saw him ceased
shouting and looked up at him with awe; but then
he smiled so gently and kindly that the cheer broke
out again and rang across the camp, far and wide.

Presently those who cheered began to follow the little train of horsemen, first by twos and tens and twenties, till thousands were drawn into the stream and pressed round him, so that he was obliged to move slowly. For many weeks they had heard his name, knowing that it meant safety for them, and wonderful tales had been told over the camp-fires of his endurance and courage. So his coming back was his first triumph, and the day was memorable in his life. While the army rested there was no work for him, and he had returned in order to rest himself; but he had nothing of immediate importance to report to the leaders, and he bade his men find out his baggage among the heaps of packs that had been unloaded from the general train of mules, and to pitch his tent near those of his old comrades on the march.

While Dunstan and Alric were obeying his orders, he sat on his saddle on the ground, with his weary horse standing beside him, his nose plunged into a canvas bag half full of oats. Gilbert looked on in a sort of mournfully indifferent silence. Everything he saw was familiar, and yet it all seemed very far away and divided from him by weeks of danger and hard riding. The vast crowd that had followed him had begun to disperse as soon as it was known that he was not going before the King, and only three or four hundred of the more curious stood and moved in groups around the open space where the tent was being pitched. Many of his acquaintance came and spoke to him, and he rose and shook their hands and spoke a few words to each; but none of the greater nobles who had sought him out after he had saved the Queen took any pains to find him now, though they and their followers owed him much. The praise of the multitude and their ringing cheers had been pleasant enough to hear, but he had expected something else, and a cold disappointment took possession of his heart as he sat in his tent some hours later, considering, with Dunstan, the miserable condition and poor appearance of his arms and the impossibility of procuring anything better. He was as lonely and unnoticed as if he had not been devoting every energy he possessed to the safe guidance of a great army during the past two months.

"There is nothing to complain of, sir," said Dunstan, in answer to a disconsolate ejaculation of Gilbert's. "Your body is whole, you have received back your belongings with nothing stolen, which is more than I expected of the Greek muleteers, you have a new tunic and hose to wear, and bean soup for supper. The world is not so bad as it looks."

"On the other hand," answered Gilbert, with a sour smile, "my bones ache, my armour is rusty, and my purse is empty. Make what good cheer you can of that."

He rose, and leaving Dunstan to set to work upon the injured coat of mail, he took his cap and strolled out alone to breathe the afternoon air. It was Christmas-time, and the day had been bright and clear; but he wore no mantle, for the overwhelmingly good reason that he possessed only one, which was in rags; and, indeed, he had been

so much exposed to bad weather of late that he was
hardened to every sort of discomfort — a little more
or less was not worth counting.

Dunstan was quite right of course, and Gilbert
had no reasonable cause for complaint. The Queen
would doubtless send for him on the morrow, and
had he chosen to present himself before her at once
he would have been received with honour. But
he was in an ill humour with himself and the
world, and being still very young, it seemed quite
natural to yield to it rather than to reason himself into a better temper. He got out of the camp
as soon as he could, and walked by the green
banks of the still Mæander. It was winter, but
the grass was as fresh as it might have been in
spring, and a salt breeze floated up from the not
distant sea. He knew the country, for he himself
had chosen the spot as a camping-place for the army,
and had advanced still farther when messengers had
brought him word to come back. To northward
rolled away the gentle hills beyond Ephesus, while
to the south and east the mountains of the Cadmus
and Taurus rose rugged and sharp against the pale
sky — the range through which the army must next
make its way to Attalia. The time lacked an hour
of sunset, and the clear air had taken the first tinge
of evening. Here and there in the plain the evergreen ilex trees grew in little clumps, black against
the sunlight, but dark green, with glistening points
among their shadows, where the afternoon sun struck
full upon them.

Gilbert had hoped to be alone, but there were

parties of idlers along the river-bank as far as he could see, and among them were many who bore evergreen boughs and young cypress shoots of three and four years' growth, which they were carrying back to the camp for the Christmas festival. For there were many Normans in the army, and Franks from Lorraine, and Northern men from Poland and Bohemia, and all the men of the North would have their Yule trees before their tents, as their heathen forefathers had done before them in the days of the old faith.

There were ladies of Eleanor's troop also, riding for pleasure, in rich gowns and flowing mantles, and knights with them, all unarmed save for a sword or dagger; and there were many dark-eyed Greeks, too, both men and women, who had come out from Ephesus in holiday clothes to see the great camp. It was all calm, and bright, and good to see, but out of harmony with Gilbert's gloomy thoughts. At the bend of the stream the ground rose a little, somewhat away from the bank, and the rocks stuck up rough and jagged out of the green grass, a sort of little wilderness in the midst of the fertile plain. Almost instinctively, Gilbert turned aside and climbed in and out among the stones until he reached the highest ledge, on which he seated himself in profound satisfaction at having got away from his fellow-creatures. The place where he had perched was about sixty feet above the river-bank, and though he could not distinctly hear the conversation of the passing groups he could see the expression of every face clearly, and

"GILBERT . . . REACHED THE HIGHEST LEDGE"

he found himself wondering how often the look of each matched the words and the unspoken thoughts.

The sun sank lower, and he had no idea how long he had sat still, when he became conscious that he was intently watching a party of riders who were coming toward him. They were still half a mile away, but he saw a white horse in the front rank, and even at that distance something in the easy pace of the creature made him feel sure that it was the Queen's Arab mare. They came on at a canter, and in two or three minutes he could make out the figures of those best known to him — Eleanor herself, Anne of Auch, Castignac, and the other two attendant knights who were always in the Queen's train, and a score of others riding behind by twos and threes. Gilbert sat motionless and watched them, nor did it occur to him that he himself, sitting on the highest boulder and dressed in a tunic of dark red, was a striking object in the glow of the setting sun. But before she was near enough to recognize him, Eleanor had seen him, and her curiosity was roused; a few minutes more, and she knew his face. Then their eyes met.

She drew rein and walked her horse, still looking up, and wondering why he gazed at her so fixedly, without so much as lifting his cap from his head; and then, to her infinite surprise, she saw him spring to his feet and disappear from view among the rocks. She was so much astonished that she stopped her horse altogether and sat several seconds staring at the ledge on which he had sat, while all

her attendants looked in the same direction, expecting Gilbert to appear again; for several of them had
recognized him, and supposed that he would hasten
down to salute the Queen.

But when he did not come, she moved on, and
though her face did not change, she did not speak
again till the camp was reached, nor did any of her
party dare to break the silence.

Had she looked back, she might have caught sight
of Gilbert's figure walking steadily with bent head
across the plain, away from the river and from the
camp, out to the broad solitude beyond. He had
acted under an impulse, foolishly, almost unconsciously, being guided by something he did not
attempt to understand.

Two months had passed, and more, since he had
seen her, and in his life of excitement and anxiety
her face had disappeared from his dreams. While
he had been away from her, she had not existed for
him, save as the only leader of the three to whom
he looked for approbation and support; the woman
had been lost in the person of the sovereign, and
had ceased to torment him by the perpetual opposition of that which all men coveted to that which he
truly loved. But now, at the very first sight of her
face, it seemed as if the Queen were gone again,
leaving only the woman to his sight, and at the instant in which he realized it he had turned and fled,
hardly knowing what he did.

He walked steadily on, more than two miles, and
all at once he cast no shadow, for the sun had gone
down, and the pale east before him turned to a cool

purple in the reflection. The air was very chilly, for the night wind came down suddenly from the mountains as the sea breeze died away, and the solitary man felt cold; for he had no cloak, and exposure and fighting had used his blood, while within him there was nothing to cheer his heart.

It had seemed to him for two years that he was always just about to do the high deed, to make the great decision of life, to find out his destiny, and he had done bravely and well all that he had found in his way. The chance came, he seized it, he did his best, and the cheers of the soldiers had told him a few hours ago that he was no longer the obscure English wanderer who had met Geoffrey Plantagenet on the road to Paris. Thousands repeated his name in honour and looked to him for their safety on the march, cursing those who led them astray against his warning. In his place on that day, most men would have gone to the Queen, expecting a great reward, if not claiming it outright. But he was wandering alone at nightfall in the great plain, discontented with all things, and most of all with himself. Everything he had done rose up against him and accused him, instead of praising him and flattering his vanity; every good deed had a base motive in his eyes, or was poisoned by the thought that it had not been done for itself, but for an uncertain something which came over him when the Queen spoke to him or touched his hand. It is not only inactive men who grow morbid and fault-finding with themselves; for the wide breach between the ideal good and the poor accomplishment holds as much that can disappoint the heart as the mean little ditch between thought and deed, wherein so many weak good men lie stuck in the mud of self-examination. He who stands at the edge of the limit, with a lifetime of good struggles behind him, may be as sad and hopeless as he who sits down and weeps before the mountain of untried beginnings. The joy of the earthly future is for the very great and the very little. For as charity leads mankind by faith to the hope of the life to come, so, on the mind's side, by faith in its own strength, the work of genius in the past is its own surety for like work to come.

Gilbert Warde was not of that great mould, but more human and less sure of himself; and suddenly, as the sun went down, a strong desire of death came upon him, and he wished that he were dead and buried under the grass whereon he stood, for very discontent with himself. It would be so simple, and none would mourn him much, except his men, perhaps, and they would part his few possessions and serve another. He was a burden to the earth, since he could do nothing well; he was a coward, because he was afraid of a woman's eyes and had fled from their gaze like a boy; he was a sinner deserving eternal fire since a touch of a fair woman's hand could make him unfaithful for an instant to the one woman he loved best. He had meant to tread the way of the Cross in true faith, with unswerving feet, and his heart was the toy of women; he had sworn the promises of knighthood, and he was already breaking them in his thoughts; he was his evil mother's son, and he had not the strength to be unlike her.

It was folly and madness, and Castignac, the Gascon knight, would have laughed at him, or else would have believed that he was demented. But to the Englishman it was real, for he was under that strange melancholy which only Northmen know, and which is the most real suffering in all the world. It is a dim sadness that gathers like a cloud about strong men's souls, and they fear it, and sometimes kill themselves to escape from it into the outer darkness beyond; but sometimes it drives them to bad deeds and the shedding of innocent blood, and now and then the better sort of such men turn from the world and hide themselves in the abodes of sorrow and pain and prayer. The signs of it are that when it has no cause it seizes upon trifles to make them its reasons, and more often it torments young men than the old; and no woman nor southern person has ever known it, nor can even understand it. But it follows the northern blood from generation to generation, like retribution for an evil without a name done long ago by the northern race.

It was dark night when Gilbert found his way back to his tent, more by the instinct of one used to living in camps among soldiers than by any precise recollection of the way, and he sat down to warm himself before the brazier of red coals which Alric shovelled out of the camp-fire that burned outside. His men gave him a pottage of beans, with bread and wine, as it was Christmas Eve and a fast-day, and there was nothing else, for all the fish brought up from the sea had been bought early in the day for the great nobles, long before Gilbert had come into the lines. But he neither knew nor cared, and he ate mechanically what they gave him, being in a black humour. Then he sat a long time by the light of the earthenware lamp which Dunstan occasionally tended with an iron pin, lest the charring wick should slip into the half-melted fat and go out altogether. When he was not watching the wick, the man's eyes fixed themselves upon his master's grave face.

"Sir," he said at last, "you are sad. This is the Holy Eve, and all the army will watch till midnight, when the first masses begin. If it please you, let us walk through the camp and see what we may. The tents of the great lords are all lighted up by this time and the soldiers are singing the Christmas hymns."

Gilbert shook his head indifferently, but said nothing.

"Sir," insisted the man, "I pray you, let us go, for you shall be cheered, and there are good sights. Before midnight the King and Queen and all the court go in procession to the great chapel tent, and it is meet that you should be there with them."

Dunstan brought a garment and gently urged him to rise. Gilbert stood up, not looking.

"Why should I go?" he asked. "I am better alone, for I am in a sad humour. And, besides, it is very cold."

"Your cloak shall keep you warm, sir."

"I cannot walk among the court people in rags," answered Gilbert; "and I have nothing that is whole but this one thin tunic."

But even as he spoke, Dunstan held up the surcoat for him to put on over his head, the skirts caught up in his hands, which also held the collar open.

"What is this?" asked Gilbert, in surprise.

"It is a knight's surcoat, sir," answered the man. "It is of very good stuff, and is wadded with down. I pray you, put it on."

"This is a gift," said Gilbert, suspiciously, and drawing back. "Who sends me such presents?"

"The King of France, sir."

"You mean the Queen." He frowned and would not touch the coat.

"The things were brought by the King's men, and one of the King's knights came also with them, and delivered a very courteous message, and a purse of Greek bezants, very heavy."

Gilbert began to walk up and down, in hesitation. He was very poor, but if the gifts were from the Queen, he was resolved not to keep them.

"Sir," said Dunstan, "the knight said most expressly that the King sent you these poor presents as a token that he desires to see you to-morrow and to thank you for all you have done. I thought to please you by bringing them out suddenly."

Then Gilbert smiled kindly, for the man loved him, and he put his head and arms into the knightly garment with its wide sleeves, and Dunstan laced it up the back, so that it fitted closely to the body, while the skirt hung down below the knees. It

x

was of a rich dark silk, woven in the East, and much like the velvet of later days. Then Dunstan girded his master with a new sword-belt made of heavy silver plates, finely chased and sewn on leather, and he thrust the great old sword with its sheath through the flattened ring that hung to the belt by short silver chains. Lastly he put upon Gilbert's shoulders a mantle of very dark red cloth, lined with fine fur and clasped at the neck with silver; for it was not seemly to wear a surcoat without a cloak.

"It is very noble," said Dunstan, moving back a step or two to see the effect.

Indeed, the young English knight looked well in the dress of his station, which he wore for the first time; for he was very tall and broad of shoulder, and a lean man, well-bred; his face was clear and pale, and his fair hair fell thick and long behind his cap.

"But you, Dunstan, you cannot be seen —"

Gilbert stopped, for he noticed suddenly that both his men were clad in new clothes of good cloth and leather.

"The servants are honoured with their lord," said Dunstan. "The King sent gifts for us, too."

"That was a man's thought, not a woman's," said Gilbert, almost to himself.

He went out, and Dunstan walked by his left, but half a step behind his stride, as was proper.

The camp was lit up with fires and torches as far as one could see, and all men were out of doors, either walking up and down, arm in arm, or sitting before their tents on folding-stools, or on their saddles, or on packs of baggage. The hundreds and thousands of little Christmas trees, stuck into the earth amid circles of torches before the newly whitened tents, made a great garden of boughs and evergreens, and the yellow glare shone everywhere through lacing branches, and fell on rich colours and gleaming arms, well polished for the holiday, and lost itself suddenly in the cold starlight overhead. The air smelt of evergreen and the aromatic smoke of burning resin.

The night rang with song also, and in some places as many as a hundred had gathered in company to sing the long Christmas hymns they had learned as little children far away at home — endless canticles with endless repetitions, telling the story of the Christ-Child's birth at Bethlehem, of the adoration of the shepherds, and of the coming of the Eastern kings.

In one part of the camp the rough Burgundians were drinking the strong Asian wine in deep draughts, roaring their great choruses between, with more energy than unction. But for the most part the northern men were sober and in earnest, praying as they sang and looking upward as if the Star of the East were presently to shed its soft light in the sky; and they tended the torches and lights around the trees devoutly, not guessing that their fathers had done the same long ago, in bleak Denmark and snowy Norway, in worship of Odin and in honour of Yggdrasil, the tree of life.

The Gascons and all the men of the South, on their side, had made little altars between two trees, decked with white cloths and adorned with tinsel ornaments and little crosses and small carved images carefully brought, like household gods, from the far home, and treasured only next to their arms. The thin, dark faces of the men were fervent with southern faith, and their wild black eyes were deep and still.

There were also Alsatians and Lorrainers in lines by themselves, quiet, fair-haired men. They had little German dolls of wood, and toys brightly painted, and by their trees they set out the scene of Bethlehem, with the manger and the Christ-Child, and the oxen crouching down, and the Blessed Mary and Saint Joseph, and also the shepherds and the wise kings ; and the men sat down before these things with happy faces and sang their songs. So it was through the whole camp, the soldiers doing everywhere according to their customs.

As for the nobles and knights, Gilbert saw some of them walking about like himself, and some were sitting before their tents. Here and there, as he passed, when a tent was open, he saw knights kneeling in prayer, and could hear them reciting the litanies. But it was not always so, for some were spending the night in feasting, their tents being closed, though one could hear plainly the revelry. There was more than one great tent in the French lines, of which the curtain was raised a little, and there Gilbert saw men and women drinking together, under bright lights, and he saw that the women were Greeks and that their cheeks were painted and their eyelids blackened ; and he turned away from the sight, in disgust that such things should be done on the Holy Eve of Christmas.

Further on, some very poor soldiers, in sheepskin doublets and leathern hose, were kneeling together before a sort of rough screen, on which were hung images painted in the manner of Greek eikons. These men had lᴗng and silky beards, and their smooth brown hair hung out over their shoulders in well-combed waves, and some of them had beautiful faces. One, who was a priest of their own, stood upright and recited prayers in a low chant, and from time to time, at the refrain, the soldiers all bowed themselves till their foreheads touched the ground.

"The Lord Jesus Christ be praised," sang the priest.

"To all ages. Amen," responded the soldiers.

Though they sang in the Bohemian language, and Gilbert could not understand, he saw that they believed and were of an earnest mind.

So he walked about for more than an hour, looking and listening, and his own sad humour was lightened a little as he forgot to think of himself only. For it seemed a great thing to have been chosen to lead so many through a wilderness full of danger, and to know that more than a hundred thousand lives had been in his keeping, as it were, for two months, and were to be in his hand again, till he should lead them safely into Syria, or perish himself and leave his task to another. It was a task worth accomplishing and a trust worth his life.

Then, at midnight, he was walking in a great

procession after the King and Queen. Modestly he joined the ranks, and his man walked beside him carrying a torch, so that the light fell full upon his face. Some one knew him, and spoke to his neighbour.

"That is Sir Gilbert Warde, who is our guide," he said.

In an instant word ran along the line that he was there; and in a few minutes a messenger came breathless, asking for him, and then the herald of France, Montjoye Saint Denis, came after, bidding him to a foremost place, in the name of the King and Queen. So he followed the herald, whose runner walked before him, as had been bidden by Eleanor herself.

"Make way for the Guide of Aquitaine!" cried the squire, in a loud voice.

Knights and men-at-arms stood aside to let him pass, and the tall Englishman went between them, courteously bending his head to thank those who moved out of his way, and deprecating the high honour that was done him. He heard his name repeated, both by men whose faces he could see in the light around him, when the torches blazed and flamed, and also from the darkness beyond.

"Well done, Sir Gilbert!" cried some. "God bless the Guide of Aquitaine!" cried many others. And all the voices praised him, so that his heart warmed.

Following the herald, he came to his place in the procession, in the front rank of the great vassals of the two kingdoms, and just after the sovereign lords;

and as he was somewhat taller than other men, he could look over their heads, and he saw the King and Queen in their furs, walking together, and before them the bishops and priests. At the stir made by his coming Eleanor turned and looked back, and her eyes met Gilbert's through the smoky glare, gazing at him sadly, as if she would have made him understand something she could not say.

But he would not have spoken if he could, for his thoughts were on other things. The procession went ón toward the royal altar, set up under an open tent in a wide space, so that the multitude could kneel on the grass and both see and hear the celebration. So they all knelt down, the great barons and chief vassals having small hassocks for their knees, while the King and Queen and the sovereign lords of Savoy and Alsatia and Lorraine, and of Bohemia and of Poland, had rich praying-stools set out for them in a row, next to the King and Queen.

The torches were stuck into the ground to burn down as they might, and the great wax candles shone quietly on the white altar, for the night was now very still and clear. There all the great nobles and many thousands of other men heard the Christmas mass, just after midnight, knowing that many of them should never hear it again on earth. There they all sang together, in a mighty melody of older times, the 'Glory to God in the highest,' which was first sung on the Holy Eve; and there, when the Bishop of Metz was about to lift up the consecrated bread, the royal trumpets rang out a great call to the multitude, so that all men might bow themselves to-

gether.   Then the silence was very deep, while the
Lord passed by; nor ever again in his life did Sir
Gilbert Warde know such a stillness as that was,
save once, and it seemed to him that in the Way
of the Cross he had reached a place of refreshment
and rest.

CHAPTER XX

GILBERT rose from his knees with the rest, and then
he saw that the King and Queen placed themselves
side by side and standing, and the nobles began to
go up to them according to their rank, to kiss their
hands. As Gilbert stood still, not knowing what
to do, he watched the procession of the barons from
a distance. Suddenly he felt that his eyes were wide
open, and that he was gazing at a face which he
knew, hardly believing that he saw it in the flesh;
and his back stiffened, and his teeth ground on one
another.

Ten paces from him, waiting and looking on, like
himself, stood a graceful man of middle height, of
a clear olive complexion, with a well-clipped beard
of somewhat pointed cut, grey at the sides, as was
also the smooth, dark hair. Years had passed, and
the last time he had seen that face had been in the
changing light of the greenwood, where the sunshine
played among the leaves; and as he had seen it
last, he had felt steel in his side and had fallen
asleep, and after that his life had changed. For
Arnold de Curboil was before him, looking at him,
but not recognizing him. Still Gilbert stood rooted
to the spot, trying not to believe his senses, for
he could not understand how his stepfather could
suddenly be among the Crusaders; but the divine

peace that had descended upon him that night was shivered as a mirror by a stone, and his heart grew cold and hard.

The man also was changed since Gilbert had seen him. The face was handsome still, but it was thin and sharp, and the eyes were haggard and weary, as if they had seen a great evil long and had sickened of it at last, and were haunted by it. Gilbert looked at him who had murdered his father and had brought shame to his mother, and who had robbed him of his fair birthright, and he saw that something of the score had been paid. Gradually, too, as Sir Arnold gazed, a look of something like despair settled in his face, a sort of horror that was not fear, — for he was no coward, — but was rather a dread of himself. He made a step forward, and Gilbert waited, and heard how Dunstan, who stood behind him, loosened his dagger in its brass sheath.

At that moment came the King's herald again as before, bidding him go up to the presence of the King and Queen.

"Room for the Guide of Aquitaine!"

The cry rang loud and clear, and Gilbert saw Sir Arnold start in surprise at the high-sounding title. Then he followed the herald; but in his heart there was already a triumph that the man who had left him for dead in the English woods should find him again thus preferred before other men.

The Queen's face grew paler as he came toward her and knelt down on one knee, and through her embroidered glove of state his own hand, that was cold, felt that hers was colder. But it did not tremble, and her voice was steady and clear, so that all could hear it.

"Sir Gilbert Warde," she said, "you have done well. Guienne thanks you, and France also —" She paused and looked toward the King, who was watching her closely.

Louis bent his great pale face solemnly toward the Englishman.

"We thank you, Sir Gilbert," he said, with cold condescension.

"A hundred thousand men thank you," added Eleanor, in a ringing voice that was to make up for her husband's ungrateful indifference.

There was a moment's silence, and then the voice of Gaston de Castignac, high and full, sent up a cheer that was heard far out in the clear night.

"God bless the Guide of Aquitaine!"

The cheer was taken up in the deep shout of strong men in earnest; for it was known how Gilbert cared not for himself, nor for rewards, but only for honour; and the thirty men who had been with him had told far and wide how often he had watched that they might sleep, and how he would always give the best to others, and how gently and courteously he treated those he commanded.

But in the loud cheering, Eleanor took his hand in both hers and bent down to speak to him, unheard by the rest; and her voice was low and trembled a little.

"God bless you!" she said fervently. "God bless you and keep you, for as I am a living woman, you are dearer to me than the whole world."

Gilbert understood how she loved him, as he had not understood before. And yet her touch had no evil power to move him now, and the shadow of his mother no longer haunted him in her eyes as he looked up. There, beside the Christmas altar, in the Holy Night, she was trying to complete the sacrifice of herself and her love. Gilbert answered her earnestly.

"Madam," he said, "I shall try to do your will with all my heart, even to death."

Thereafter he kept his word. But now he rose to his feet, and after bending his knee again, he looked into the Queen's sad eyes, and passed on to make way for the others, while the cheers that were for him still rang in the air.

Then he began to walk to his tent. Dunstan had lighted a fresh torch and was waiting for him. But the great barons, who had gone up to the King and Queen before him, pressed round him and shook his hand, one after another, and bade him to their feasting on the morrow; nor was there jealousy of him, as there had been when he had saved the Queen's life at Nicæa, for now that they saw him they felt that he was no courtier, and desired only the safety of the army, with his own honour.

As they thronged about him, there came Sir Arnold de Curboil, pressing his way among them, and when he was before Gilbert he also held out his hand.

"Gilbert Warde," he asked, "do you not know me?"

"I know you, sir," answered the young knight, in a clear voice that all could hear, "but I will not take your hand."

There was silence, and the great nobles looked on, not understanding, while Dunstan held his torch so that the light fell full upon Sir Arnold's pale features.

" Then take my glove ! "

He plucked off his loose leathern gauntlet and tossed it lightly at Gilbert's face. But Dunstan's quick left hand caught it in the air, while the torch scarcely wavered in his right.

Gilbert was paler than his enemy, but he would not let his hand go to his sword, and he folded his arms under his mantle, lest they should move against his will.

" Sir," he said, " I will not fight you again at this time, though you killed my father treacherously. Though you have stolen my birthright, I will not fight you now, for I have taken the Cross, and I will keep the vow of the Cross, come what may."

" Coward ! " cried Sir Arnold, contemptuously, and he would have turned on his heel.

But Gilbert stepped forward and caught him by his arms and held him quietly, without hurting him, but so that he could not easily move and must hear.

" You have called me a coward, Sir Arnold de Curboil. How should I fear you, since I can wring you to death in my hands if I will? But I will let you go, and these good lords here shall judge whether I am a coward or not because I will not fight you until I have fulfilled my vows."

" Well said," cried the old Count of Bourbon.

" Well said, well done," cried many others.

Moreover, the Count of Savoy, of whose race

none was ever born that knew fear, even to this day, spoke to his younger brother of Montferrat.

"I have not seen a braver man than this English knight, nor a better man of his hands, nor one more gentle, and he has the face of a leader."

Then Gilbert loosed his hold and Sir Arnold looked angrily to the right and left, and passed out of the crowd, all men making way for him as if they would not touch him. Some of them turned to Gilbert again, and asked him questions about the strange knight.

"My lords," he answered, "he is Sir Arnold de Curboil, my stepfather; for when he had killed my father, he married my mother and stole my lands. I fought him when I was but a boy, and he left me for dead in the forest; and now I think that he is come from England to seek occasion against me; but if I live I shall get back my inheritance. And now, if I seem to you to have dealt justly by him, I crave my leave of you, and thank your lordships for your good will and courtesy."

So they bade him good-night, and he went away, leaving many who felt that he had done well, but that, in his place, they could not have done as much. They did not know how dear it cost him, but dimly they guessed that he was braver than they, though they were of the bravest.

He was very tired, and had not slept in a good bed under his own tent for two months; yet he was sleepless, and awoke after two hours, and could not sleep again till within an hour of the winter dawn; for he feared some evil for Beatrix if her father should claim her of the Queen and take her back from Ephesus by sea, as he must have come.

At daylight, warming themselves at a fire, Dunstan told Alric all that happened in the night. The Saxon's stolid face did not change, but he was thoughtful and silent for some time, remembering how the Lady Goda had once had him beaten, long ago, because he had not held Sir Arnold's horse in the right way when the knight was mounting.

Presently Beatrix's Norman tirewoman came to the two men, wrapped in a brown cloak with a hood that covered half her face. She told them that her lady knew of Sir Arnold's coming, and begged of Sir Gilbert that for her sake he would walk by the river at noon, when every one would be at dinner in the camp, and she would try and meet him there.

CHAPTER XXI

GILBERT waited long, for he went down early to the river, and he sat on a big stone sunning himself, for the air was keen, and there was a north wind. At last he saw two veiled women coming along the bank. The shorter one was a little lame and leaned upon the other's arm, and the wind blew their cloaks before them as they came. When he saw that Beatrix limped, knowing that she had not quite recovered from her fall, and remembering that she might have been killed, his heart sank with a sickening faintness.

He took her by the hand very gently, for she looked so slight and ill that he almost feared to touch her, and yet he did not wish to let her fingers go, nor she to take them away. The tirewoman went down to the river-bank, at some distance, and they sat upon the big stone, hand in hand like two children, and looked at each other. Suddenly the girl's face lightened, as if she had just found out that she was glad; her eyes laughed, and her voice was as happy as a bird's at sunrise.

Gilbert had not seen her for a long time. To such a man, all women, and even one chosen woman, might easily become an ideal, too far from the material to have a real hold upon his manhood, and so high above earth as to have no spiritual realization. Even in that age many a knight made a divinity of his lady and a religion of his devotion to her, so that the very meaning of love was forgotten in the ascetic impulse to seek the soul's salvation in all things, even in the contempt of all earthly longings; and those men demanded as much in return, expecting it even after their own death. There were also women, like Anne of Auch, who gave such devotion freely. Nevertheless, it was not altogether in this way between Beatrix and Gilbert, and if it might have been, so far as he was concerned, she would not have had it so, and her words proved it.

"I am so proud of you!" she cried. "And I am so very glad to see you."

"Proud of me?" he asked, smiling sadly. "I am not proud of myself. For all I have done, you might be dead at Nicæa."

"But I am alive," she answered happily, "and by your doing, though I cannot yet walk quite well."

"I ought to have let the Queen pass on. I ought to have thought only of you."

He found a satisfaction in saying aloud at last what had been so long in his heart against himself, and in saying it to Beatrix herself. But she would not hear it.

"That would have been very unknightly and disloyal," she said. "I would not have had you do it, for you would have been blamed by men. And then I should never have heard what I heard yesterday and last night, the very best words I ever heard in all my life — the cry of a great army blessing one man for a good work well done."

Y

" I have done nothing," answered Gilbert, stolidly determined to depreciate himself in her eyes.

But she smiled and laid her gloved hand quickly upon his lips.

" I would not have another laugh at you, as I do ! " she cried.

He looked at her, and the mask of grave melancholy which was fast becoming his natural expression began to soften, as if it could not last forever.

" I have often thought of you and wondered whether you would think well of my deeds," he said.

" You see ! " she laughed. " And now because I am proud of you, you pretend that you have done nothing ! That is poor praise of my good sight and judgment."

He laughed, too. Since the dawn of time, women have retorted thus upon brave men too modest of their doings ; and since the first woman found the trick, it has never failed to please man. But love needs not novelty, for he himself is always young ; the stars of night are not less fair in our eyes because men knew the 'sweet influence of the Pleiades' in Job's day, nor is the scent of new-mown hay less delicate because all men love it. The old is the best, even in love, which is young.

" Say what you will," answered Gilbert, presently, " we are together to-day."

" And nothing else matters," said Beatrix. " Not even that it is two months since I have seen you, and that I have been ill, or, at least, half crippled, by that fall. It is all forgotten."

He looked at her, not quite understanding, for as

she spoke her eyebrows were raised a little, with her own expression, half sad, half laughing at herself.

" I wish I could see you more often," answered Gilbert.

Her little birdlike laugh disconcerted him.

" Indeed, I am in earnest," he said.

" And yet when you are in earnest, you do much harder things," answered Beatrix, and at once the sadness had the better of the laughter in her face. " Oh, Gilbert, I wish we were back in England in the old days."

" So do I ! "

" Oh, no ! You do not. You say so to please me, but you cannot make it sound true. You are a great man now. You are Sir Gilbert Warde, the Guide of Aquitaine. It is you, and you only, who are leading the army, and you will have all the honour of it. Would you go back to the old times when we were boy and girl ? Would you, if you could ? "

" I would if I could."

He spoke so gravely that she understood where his thoughts were, and that they were not all for her. For a few moments she looked down in silence, pulling at the fingers of her glove, and once she sighed ; then, without looking up, she spoke, in her sweet, low voice.

" Gilbert, what are we to each other ? Brother and sister ? "

He started, again not understanding, and fancying that she was setting up the Church's canon between them, which he now knew to be no unremovable impediment.

"You are no more my sister than your tire-woman there can be," he answered, more warmly than he had spoken yet.

"I did not mean that," she said sadly.

"I do not understand, then."

"If you do not, how can I tell you what I mean?" She glanced at him and then looked away quickly, for she was blushing, and was ashamed of her boldness.

"Do you mean that I love you as I might a sister?" asked Gilbert, with the grave tactlessness of a thoroughly honest man.

The blush deepened in her cheek, and she nodded slowly, still looking away.

"Beatrix!"

"Well?" She would not turn to him.

"What have I done that you should say such a thing?"

"That is it!" she answered regretfully. "You have done great things, but they were not for me."

"Have I not told you how I have thought of you day after day, hoping that you might think well of my deeds?"

"Yes. But you might have done one thing more. That would have made all the difference."

"What?" He bent anxiously towards her for the answer.

"You might have tried to see me."

"But I was never in the camp. I was always a day's march in the lead of the army."

"But not always fighting. There were days, or nights, when you could have ridden back. I would

have met you anywhere — I would have ridden hours
to see you. But you never tried. And at last it is
I who send for you and beg you to come and talk
with me here. And you do not even seem glad to
be with me."

"I did not think that I had a right to leave my
post and come back, even for you."

"You could not have helped it — if you had cared."
She spoke very low.

Gilbert looked at her long, and the lines deepened
in his face, for he was hurt.

"Do you really believe that I do not love you?"
he asked, but his voice was cold because he tried to
control it, and succeeded too well.

"You have never told me so," Beatrix answered.
"You have done little to make me think so, since we
were children together. You have never tried to see
me when it would have cost you anything. You are
not glad to see me now."

Her voice could be cold, too; but there was a
tremor in some of the syllables. He was utterly surprised and taken unawares, and he slowly repeated
the substance of what she said.

"I never told you so? Never made you think so?
Oh, Beatrix ! "

He remembered the sleepless nights he had passed,
accusing himself of letting even one thought of the
Queen come between him and the girl who was de-
nying his love — the restless, melancholy hours of
self-accusation, the cruel self-torment — how could
she know?

She was in earnest, now, though she had begun

half playfully; for if the man's heart had not changed, he had gone away from her in his active life, and in the habit of hiding all real feeling which comes from living long alone or with strangers. It was true that outwardly he had hardly seemed glad to see her, and all the ring of happiness had died away out of her voice before they had exchanged many words. He felt her mood, and it grew clear to him that he had made some great mistake which it would be very hard to set right. And she was thinking how boldly she had striven with the Queen for his love, and that now it seemed to be no love at all.

But he, whose impulse was ever to act when there was danger, however much he might weary his soul with inward examination at other times, grew desperate, and gave up thinking of a way out of the difficulty. What he loved was slipping from him, and though he loved it in his own way, it was indeed all he loved, and he would not let it go.

Thoughtless at last, and sudden, he took her into his arms, and his face was close to hers, and his eyes were in hers, and their lips breathed the same breath. She was not frightened, but her lids drooped, and she turned quite white. Then he kissed her, not once, but many times, and as if he would never let her go, on her pale mouth, on her dark eyelids, on her waving hair.

"If I kill you, you shall know that I love you," he said, and he kissed her again, so that it hurt her, but it was good to be hurt.

After that she lay in his arms, very still, and she looked up slowly, and their eyes met; and it was as if the veil had fallen from between them. When he kissed her again, his kisses were gentle and altogether tender.

"I had almost lost you," he said, breathing the words to her ear.

The Norman tirewoman sat motionless by the river's edge, waiting till she should be called. After a time they began to talk again, and their voices were in tune, like their hearts. Then Gilbert spoke of what had happened in the night, but Beatrix already knew that her father had come.

"He has come to take me away," she said, "and we have talked together. Gilbert — a dreadful thing has happened; did he tell you?"

"He told me nothing — excepting that I was a coward!" He laughed scornfully.

"I think he is half mad with sorrow." She paused and laid her hand on Gilbert's. "His wife is dead, — your mother is dead, — with the child she bore him."

Gilbert's eyes alone changed, but under her palm Beatrix felt the sinews of his hand leap and the veins swell.

"Tell me quickly," he said.

"She was burned," continued Beatrix, in a tone of awe. "She made my father grind his people till they turned, and she made him hang the leader who spoke for them. Then all the yeomen and the bondmen rose, and they burned the castle, and your mother died with the child. But my father escaped alive. Now I am again his only child, and he wants me again."

Gilbert's head fell forward, as if he had received a

blow, but he said nothing for a time, for he saw his
mother's face ; and he saw her not as when they had
parted, but as he remembered her before that, when
he had loved her above all things, not knowing what
she was. In spite of all that had gone between, she
came back to him as she had been, and the pain and the
pity were real and great. But then he felt Beatrix's
hand pressing his in sympathy, and it brought him
again to the evil truth. He raised his head.

"She is better dead," he said bitterly. "Let us
not speak of her any more. She was my mother."

He stared long at the river, and the sadness of his
homeless and lonely state in the world began to come
upon him, as it came often. Then a soft voice broke
the spell, and the words answered his thoughts.

"We are not alone, you and I," it said, and the
two small hands crept up shyly and clasped his neck,
and the loving, pathetic face looked up to his. "Do
not let him take me away ! " she begged.

His hand pressed her head to his breast, and once
more he kissed her hair.

"He shall not take you," he said. "No one shall
take you from me; no one shall come between you
and me."

Beatrix's eyes seemed to drink out of his the meaning of the words he spoke.

"Promise me that," she said, knowing that he
would promise her the world.

"I promise it with all my heart."

"On your knightly faith?" She smiled as she
insisted.

"On my honour and faith."

"And on the faith of love, too?" She almost laughed, out of sheer happiness.

"On the very truth of true love," he answered.

"Then I am quite safe," she said, and she hid her face against his surcoat. "I am glad I came to you, I am glad that I was so bold as to send for you this day, for it is the best day of my whole life. And, Gilbert, you will not wait till I send for you another time? You will try and see me — of your own accord?"

She was altogether in anxiety again, and there was a look of fear and sadness in her eyes.

"I will try — indeed I will," he said earnestly.

"Whenever you do, you shall succeed," she answered, nestling to him. "I wish I might shut my eyes and rest here — now that I know."

"Rest, sweet, rest!"

A moment, and then, from far away, a clarion call rang on the still air. With the instinct of the soldier, Gilbert started, and listened, holding his breath, but still pressing the girl close to him.

"What is it?" she asked, half frightened.

It came again, joyous and clear.

"It is nothing," he said. "It is the Christmas banquet, and perhaps the King drinks the Queen's health — and she his."

"And perhaps, though no one knows it, she —" But Beatrix stopped and laughed. "I will not say it! Why should I care?"

She was thinking that if the Queen drank a health it might be meant, in her heart, for the Guide of Aquitaine, and she nestled closer to him in the sunshine.

CHAPTER XXII

A WEEK the army stayed in camp by the pleasant waters of the Mæander, and daily at noon Gilbert and Beatrix met at the same place. She told him that she had not seen her father again, and believed that he had left the camp. The Queen knew that the lovers met, but she would not hinder them, though it was cruel pain to think of their happiness. Many have spoken and written evil things of Eleanor, for she was a haughty woman and overbearing, and she feared neither God nor man, nor Satan either; but she had a strong and generous heart, and, having promised, she kept her word as well as she could. She would not send for Gilbert, nor see him alone, lest she should fail of resolution when her eyes looked on him too closely. Beatrix knew this and took heart, and the veil of estrangement was lifted between her and Gilbert.

On the last day but one of the year he went before the King, who bade him mount again with his men and ride before the army through the passes of the Cadmus towards Attalia, seeking out the safest way and giving timely warning of the enemy. Also, because it was known that the danger must be greater now than before, the King gave him leave to choose knights and men-at-arms to the number of a hundred, to be under him, and made him rich presents of fine armour, and caused his shield to be painted afresh by a skilled Greek.   While he talked with Gilbert he watched the Queen, who sat apart somewhat pale, reading in a Book of Hours, for he was suspicious of her; but she never looked at the Englishman until he was taking his leave.   Then she beckoned him to her, before he went out, and gave him her ungloved hand, which he kissed, and she looked into his face a moment, very sadly, not knowing whether she should see him again.   So he went out, to bid Beatrix farewell.

She met him at the accustomed place by the river, and for a while they were together; but they could not talk much, being both very sad.   She took a golden ring from her hand, and would have put it upon his finger, but it was too small.

" I had hoped that you could wear it," she said, disappointed, " for it was my mother's."

Gilbert took it in his hand.   It was of very pure gold and thin, so he cut it open with the point of his dagger and bent it back and clasped it round his fourth finger, tightly.

" It is our troth," he said.

It was hard to let him go, for she also knew the peril, as the Queen knew it.

" I shall pray for you," she said, clinging to him. " God is good — you may come back to me."

They sat a long time together, saying nothing. When it was time for him to lead his men out, as he judged by the sun, he kissed her, lifting her up to him.

" Good-by," he said.

" Not yet ! " she pleaded, between his kisses.   " Oh, Gilbert, not so very soon ! "

But she knew that he must go, and he set her
gently upon her feet, for it was the last moment.
When he was gone, she sat down upon the stone,
and the Norman woman came and put one arm
round her, holding her, for she seemed fainting.
Still her eyes followed him as he strode along the
river, till he reached the turning.   There he stopped
and looked back, and kissed the ring she had given
him, and waved his hand to her; and she pressed
both her hands to her lips and threw them out to
him, as if she would have thrown him her heart and
her soul with it.

When he was gone, the sky turned black before
her eyes and time stood still, and she knew what
death meant.   But she did not faint, and she had
no tears.   Only, when she went back after some
time, she walked unsteadily and her woman helped
her.

So Gilbert rode out to seek the way, taking well-
mounted messengers with him as before, and on the
first day of the New Year the whole army began the
march again, crossing the river the first time at a
ford.   The Queen would perforce be in the van,
with her ladies, so that the speed of their riding
became the speed of the whole army, whereby the
whole host was kept together.   The first messenger
who came back told that Sir Gilbert had reached
the hills, and led the Queen by the way he had followed, saying that so far he had met no enemies.
But on the morrow, as they drew near to the mountains and rode up the rising ground, they saw afar
off a man standing by one who lay stark on the

ground, and driving off a vulture and a score of
ravens with a long staff. The Queen's heart stood
still when she saw this sight, and she spurred her
Arab mare forward before all the army till she
stopped beside the dead body and saw that the face
was not Gilbert's. The squire who was guarding
the dead told her how, very early in the morning,
some fifty Seljuk horsemen had come down from the
hills and had shot arrows at Gilbert and his men
from a distance, wheeling quickly and galloping away
out of sight before the Christians could mount ; and
this one knight had been killed, and his squire had
stayed by him till the army should come up, while
the rest rode on, and took both the horses with them
in case they should lose any of their own.

There they buried the body deep, when the
Queen's chaplain had blessed it, and they marched
on till noon, and encamped. From that time the
Queen made her ladies ride in the centre of the
great host, protected on all sides ; but she herself,
with the Lady Anne of Auch, still kept the van, for
in this way she was nearer to Gilbert. She also
sent out parties of scouts to the right and left, to
give warning of the Seljuks ; and the King guarded
the rear, where there was also great danger.

Meanwhile Gilbert went farther up into the mountains, searching out the best way to the pass, distrust-
ing the Greek guides, who nevertheless feared him
and told him the truth, though it was the secret wish
of the Greek Emperor that the army should all be
destroyed, because he desired no increase of the
western power in Asia. But Gilbert told the guides

severally and all together that he would cut off the
head of the first one who should even seem to be
false ; and he kept them under his own eye, and his
long sword was always loose in the sheath.

He went very cautiously now, setting sentinels
at night and sleeping little himself, so that he might
often go alone from post to post and see that all was
well.   But the Seljuks never came in the darkness,
for as yet there were not many of them, and they
trusted to their bows by day, when they could see ;
but they feared to come to close quarters with the
picked swordsmen of the French army.   Since they
had first shown themselves, the Christians all rode
fully armed in mail and hood, knights and men-at-
arms and young squires alike, with the half-dozen
pack-horses and a few spare mounts in the midst ;
and good mail was proof against arrows, but Gilbert
wished that he had brought fifty archers with him,
such marksmen as little Alric, his groom.

There was some fighting every day, when he was
able to overtake the swift Seljuks in some narrow
place.   They fled when they could, but when they
were brought to bay they turned savagely and
fought like panthers, yelling their war-cry : " Hurr !
Hurr ! " which in the Tartar tongue signifies : " Kill !
Kill ! "

But more often the Christians killed them, being
stronger men and better armed, and Gilbert was ever
the first to strike ; and one day, as the fiercest of a
band of Seljuks rode at him, whirling a crooked
sword and shouting the cry, Gilbert cut off his arm
at one stroke and it fell to the ground with the fist

still grasping the scimitar; whereat Gilbert laughed fiercely and mocked the unbeliever's cry.

"Hurrah! Hurrah!" he shouted, as he rode on.

Then his followers took the cry from him, jeering at their enemies, and on that morning they let not one escape, but slew them all, saving one man only, and took the horses that were alive. But from that time, the Christians began to cry, "Hurrah!" And when men shout to-day, "Hurrah for the king," they know not that they are crying, "Kill for the king."

But Gilbert saw that the place where this happened was a very dangerous one, though the entrance to it was broad and pleasant, through a high valley where there were certain huts in which shepherds dwelt, and grass and water. Therefore he turned back quickly when the killing was over, and he took the chief of the guides by the throat, holding his head down upon the pommel of his saddle, and bade him show a better way if he would keep his head on his shoulders.

"My lord, there is no other way," cried the man, fright-struck.

"Very well," answered Gilbert, drawing his red sword again. "If there is no other way, I shall not need you any more, my man."

When the fellow heard the sheath sucking the wet steel, he screamed for terror, crying out that there was another way. So they rode back to the entrance of the valley, and the man began to lead them up a steep track among trees; and above the trees they came to a desolate, stony ridge; but still they could ride, though it was a very toilsome way.

When they had reached the top, after three hours, Gilbert saw that he was at the true pass, broad and straight, opening down to grassy slopes beyond, between crags that would not give a foothold to a goat. He rode on a little way farther, and there was a very steep path, turning back, round the highest peak, and presently he looked down into a small, high valley, below which the narrow way led down to the pleasant place through which he had first ridden, and he saw that a great army could easily be destroyed there by a small one lying in ambush. He could see quite plainly the dead Seljuks lying as they had fallen, and from far and near the great vultures and the kites were sailing down from the crags, while the ravens and crows that followed his killing day by day were flying, and settling, and hopping along the ground, and flying again to the places of death.

He rode back to his men, driving the guide before him ; and the man feared for his life continually, and reeled in the saddle as if he were drunk. But Gilbert knew that a man well frightened was a man gained for what he wanted, so when he had threatened to cut off his hands and put out his eyes and leave him to die among the rocks if he tried to misguide the army again, he let him live. Then he sent ten men back to lead the host on the following day, and he remained in the pass to keep it until the vanguard should be in sight. He bade his messengers tell the King that for his life he must not go into the broad valley, though it looked so fair and open.

Now the Seljuks whom he had met were all dead but one young man; but there were many of them, some five thousand, encamped in a great hiding-place surrounded by rocks, on the other side of the pass. And the one who had escaped went to them, and told them what had happened, and that the whole French army would surely come up that way on the next day or the day after that. Therefore the Seljuks mounted, and came and lay in ambush, and two hundred of them rode down into the valley and hid themselves among the trees where the steep way began which was the right way. For they knew the mountains, and feared lest at the last moment the White Fiend, as they called Gilbert, might find out his mistake and choose that path to the pass, and save all; whereas on the steep ridge, under cover of trees, two hundred chosen bowmen, each with a great sheaf of arrows, might turn back a host. So the night passed, and Gilbert was undisturbed; but great evil was prepared for the army, though his messengers reached the camp and repeated his words to the King before nightfall.

It lacked two hours of noon when Sir Gaston de Castignac and a dozen other knights, and Gilbert's ten men, turned the spur of the mountain where the broad green valley opened, having on their right the wooded ridge where the two hundred Seljuks were hidden. A moment later the Queen herself came up, with Anne of Auch and a hundred knights, and she supposed that they should have ridden through the valley; but Castignac stopped her and told her what the men said, and that they must all begin the ascent from that point. The valley was inviting, with its pleasant water and its broad meadow, and some of the

z

knights murmured; but when Eleanor heard that
Gilbert had chosen the steeper way, she had no doubt,
and bade them all be silent; yet as there was much
space on the grass, and as the men said that the ascent
was long, it seemed better to halt awhile before
beginning to climb. Meanwhile the whole van of
the army came up, many thousands of men-at-arms
and knights, and footmen, and after them the gorgeous
train of ladies, careless and gay, feeling themselves
safe among so many armed men, and desiring a sight
of the enemy rather than fearing it. There was
little order in the march, and hitherto there had been
little danger; for the Seljuks meant to destroy them
in the mountains, and would never have tried battle
in the open with such a great host.

Still the troop came on, filling the valley from side
to side, and pressing up by sheer numbers toward
the pass; and the King came at last, and with him
certain Greek guides to whom he listened, and who
began to make a great outcry, saying that Sir Gilbert was a madman and that no horses could climb
the ridge. Thereat Gilbert's men swore that they
had climbed it on the preceding day, and that even
a woman could ride up it. And one of the Greeks
began to laugh at them, saying that they lied; so Sir
Gaston de Castignac smote him on the mouth with
his mailed hand, breaking all his teeth, and there was
a turmoil, and the people began to take opposite sides,
for many of the King's men had come up, and he
himself was for the easy way up the valley.

Then Eleanor was very angry, and she mounted
again, calling Gilbert's men to her side, and her own

knights who rode in the van; and she told the King to his face that the Guide of Aquitaine had ever led them safely, but that whenever the army had followed the King's guides, evil had befallen. But the King would not be browbeaten before the great lords and barons, and he swore a great oath that he would go by the valley, come what might. Thereupon Eleanor turned her back on him, wheeling her horse short round; and she bade her knights ride up the hill to the trees with her, and gave orders that her army should follow her, and leave the King to take his men by any way he chose. On this the confusion became greater than ever, for in the host there were thousands of men, half pilgrims, half soldiers, who had come of their own accord, as free men, bound neither to the King nor the Queen; there were also the Poles and Bohemians, who were independent. All these began to discuss and quarrel among themselves.

Meanwhile the Queen and Anne of Auch rode slowly up the hill, straight toward the trees, with Castignac and Gilbert's men before them, and the knights of Guienne following closely after; but none of them expected evil, for the place looked peaceful in the high sunshine. Eleanor and the Lady Anne rode fearlessly in their skirts and mantles, but the men were fully armed in their mail and steel caps.

The foremost were half a dozen spears' lengths from the brushwood when the sharp twang of a bowstring broke the stillness, and an arrow that was meant for the Queen's face flew just between her and the Lady Anne. The fair woman flushed suddenly at the danger; on the dark one's forehead a vein stood out, straight from the parting of the hair, downward between the eyes. The men spurred their horses instantly, and dashed into the wood before the Queen could stop them, Castignac first by a length, with his sword out. The flight of arrows that followed the first shot struck horses and men together, and three or four horses went down with their riders; but the mail was proof, and the men were on their feet in an instant and running among the trees, whence came the sound of great blows, and the sharp twanging of many bowstrings, and the yell of the Seljuks. Now and again an arrow flew from among the trees at random, and while Eleanor sat on her horse, looking down the hill and crying to her knights to come on quickly and join in the fight, she did not know that Anne of Auch covered her with her body from the danger of a stray shaft, facing the danger with a light heart, in the hope of the blessed death for which she looked.

Of those who went in under the trees, none came back, while the din of the fight rose louder and wilder, by which Eleanor guessed that the enemy were very few and were being driven up the hill, overpowered by numbers; and lest her own men should hamper each other, she stopped them and would not allow any more to go up.

Meanwhile the King looked on from below, saying prayers; for he was in mortal dread of wishing that the Queen might be killed, since that would have been as great a sin as if he had slain her with his own hand; so that whereas when there was no present danger he constantly prayed that by some means he might be delivered from the woman of Belial, he now prayed as fervently that she might be preserved. As soon as he saw her forbidding a further advance, he took it for granted that she intended to come back and go up the valley, and he gave the signal to his own knights and men to advance in that direction, away from the place where the Seljuks were fighting. Indeed, there were always many who were ready to turn their backs on danger, especially of the poorer sort, who were ill-armed ; and immediately, with great confusion and much shouting and pressing, the main body began to move on quickly, spreading out as they went, and completely filling up the valley ; but then they were crowded again, as they went higher, where the valley narrowed to the pass, and at last they were so squeezed and jammed together that the horses could hardly move at all.

The Queen's ladies, with their great throng of attendants and servants, had drawn aside at the beginning of the valley, protected by two or three thousand men-at-arms, to wait the end of the fighting, but she herself was still on the spur of the hill before the woods. Before long came Sir Gaston de Castignac, on foot and covered with blood, his mail hacked in many places by the crooked Seljuk swords, and his three-cornered shield dinted and battered. He came to the Queen's side and made a grand bow, waving his right hand towards the trees, and he spoke in a loud voice.

" The Duchess's highway is clear," he said. "The way is open and the road is swept. But the broom —"

He turned livid and reeled.

"The broom is broken!" he cried, as he fell at full length almost under the Arab mare's feet.

He had been shot through the middle with an arrow, but had lived to tell of victory. In an instant the Queen knelt beside him, trying to raise his head; and he smiled when he knew her, and died. But there were gentle tears in her eyes as she rose to her feet and bade them bury the Gascon deep, while she herself laid his shield upon his knees, and crossed his hands upon his breast.

Many others died there, and were buried quickly; but the bodies of the Seljuks were dragged aside, out of the line of the march; and it was high noon, for all that had happened had taken place in about two hours. Yet as the way was long to the summit of the pass, those of Gilbert's men who had not been killed urged the Queen to march on at once, in order that the camp might be pitched by daylight where Gilbert was waiting. So Eleanor commanded that all her people should follow her in the best order they could keep, and she began to ride up the steep way. But in the valley the King's army was pressing on and up toward the place where Gilbert had fought yesterday, where the bones of the slain Seljuks were already white, and the gorged vultures perched sleeping in the noonday sun.

Two hours passed, and because the guides knew the way well, it being now the third time of their passing there, and because the Queen and her vanguard were on sure-footed horses, they reached the top in that time, and saw Gilbert and the eighty men he still had with him sitting on the rocks in their armour, waiting, and their horses tethered near by, but saddled and bridled. Then Gilbert stood out before the rest and waited for the Queen, who cantered forward and halted beside him. She began to speak somewhat hurriedly, and she constantly looked about her, rather than into his face, telling him how they had fought in the wood, and how the King and many of the host had gone round by the valley. Thereat Gilbert became very anxious.

"The ladies are following me," said Eleanor, gently, for she knew why he was pale.

As she spoke, a cry came on the air, wild, distinct as the scream of the hungry falcon, but it was the cry of thousands.

"Hurr! Hurr! Hurr!"

"The Seljuks are upon them," said Gilbert, "for that cry is from the pass above the valley. God have mercy on the souls of Christian men!"

Dunstan, who knew him well, brought his horse at the first alarm.

"By your Grace's leave," said Gilbert, taking the bridle to mount, "I will take my men and do what I can to help them. I have explored the way round this mountain, and every man who follows me may kill ten Seljuks at an advantage, from above, just as the Seljuks are now slaying the King's men, below them."

"Hurr! Hurr! Kill! Kill!"

Ear-piercing, wild, the cry of slaughter came up from the valley again and again, and worse sounds came now on the clear air, the howls of men

pressed together and powerless, slain in hundreds
with arrows and stones, and the unearthly shrieks
of horses wounded to death.

"They are in thousands," said Gilbert, listening.
"I must have more men."

"I give you my army," said Eleanor. "Command
all, and do your best."

For one moment Gilbert looked hard at her, scarcely
believing that she meant the words. But she raised
herself in her saddle, and called out in a loud voice to
the hundreds of nobles and knights who had already
come up.

"Sir Gilbert Warde commands the army!" she
cried. "Follow the Guide of Aquitaine!"

There was light in his face as he silently bowed
his head and mounted.

"Sirs," he said, when he was in the saddle, "the
way by which I shall lead you to rescue the King is
narrow; therefore follow me in good order, two and
two, all those who have sure-footed horses. But
beyond the defile as many as a thousand may fight
without hindering each other. The rest encamp
here and protect the Queen and her ladies. Forward!"

He saluted Eleanor and rode away, leaving her
there. She hesitated and looked longingly after
him, but Anne of Auch laid a hand upon her
bridle.

"Madam," she said, "your place is here, where
there is no one to command. And here also there
may be danger before long."

All the time, the dreadful din of fight came up

from below, louder and louder. The Seljuks had
waited until not less than five thousand men, with
the King himself, had passed through the narrow
channel from the lower valley and choked the
upper gorge, pushed on by those behind; and then,
from their hiding-places among the rocks and trees,
they had sprung up in their thousands to kill those
taken in the trap like mice. First came the thick
flight of their arrows, straight and deadly, going
down with flashes into the sea of men; and then
great stones rolled from the heights, boulders that
crushed the life out of horse and man and rolled
straight through the mass of human bodies, leaving
a track of blood behind; and then more arrows,
darting hither and thither in the sunlight like rock-
swallows; and again stones and boulders, till the
confusion and the panic were at their height, and
the wild Seljuks sprang down the sides of the
gorge, yelling for death, swinging their scimitars,
to kill more surely by hand, lest they should waste
arrows on dead men.

The blood was ankle-deep in the pass, through
which more and more of the Christians were driven
up to the slaughter by those who followed them.
The King was forcing his way through his own men,
and with them, toward the side where there were
most enemies. His sluggish blood was roused at
last, and his sword was out. Nor was it long before
he was able to fight hand to hand; but many of
those around him were slain, because their arms
were hampered in the close press. The Seljuks
made room by killing, and climbed upon the slain

towards the living. In the vast and screaming din, no one could have heard a voice of command, and the air was darkening with the steam and reek of battle.

A full hour the Seljuks slew and slew, almost unharmed, and the Christians were dead in thousands under their feet. The King, with a hundred followers, was at bay by the roots of a huge oak tree, fighting as best he might, and killing a man now and then, though wounded in the face and shoulder, and sorely spent. But he saw that it was a desperate case and that all was lost, and no more of his army were coming up to the rescue, because the narrow pass was choked with dead. So he began to sing the penitential psalms in time with the swinging of his sword.

It was towards evening, for the days were short, and the westering sun suddenly poured its light straight into the gorge and upon the rising ground above. Some of the Christians looked up out of the carnage, and the King turned his eyes that way when he could spare a glance, and suddenly the sun flashed back from the height, as from golden and silver mirrors quickly moving, and foremost was an azure shield with a golden cross flory, and the Christians knew it well. Then a feeble shout went up from the few who lived.

"The Guide of Aquitaine!" they cried.

But they were not heard, for suddenly there was a louder cry from the Seljuks, and it was not their war-yell, but something like a howl of fear.

" The Wrath of God! The White Fiend! "

For they were caught in their own trap, and death rose in their eyes. On the low heights above the gorge a thousand Christians had formed in ranks quickly, with lance lowered and sword loose in sheath. A moment later, and a steel cap went whirling through the air, glancing and gleaming in the sun, till it fell among the enemy below, and then came the sharp command, the leader's single word :

" Charge ! "

The Seljuks heard the terrible, quick clanking of armour as the great troop began to move, and the Guide of Aquitaine swept down in a storm of steel, bareheaded, his fair hair streaming on the wind, his eyes on fire in the setting sun, his great sword high in air, the smile of destruction on his even lips.

" The White Fiend! The Wrath of God! " screamed the Seljuks.

They tried to fly, but there was no way out, for the pass was choked with dead below, and they must win or die, every living soul of their host. So they turned at bay, joining their strength, and standing as they could on heaps of dead bodies.

There, where they had slain, Gilbert slew them, and a thousand blades flashed red in the red sunlight, in time with his; and there was a low, sure sound of killing as steel went through flesh and bone and was wrenched back to strike again. The Seljuks fought like madmen and like wild beasts while they could; but in Gilbert's eyes there was the awful light of victory, and his arm tired not, while rank upon rank the enemy went down, and the Christians who still lived began to smite them from behind. Then the pass was filled fuller than before, and a small red river leaped down from stone to stone, following the channel to the broad valley beyond, where nearly fifty thousand powerless men watched it flowing among them. But they listened, too, and the Seljuk yell grew fainter, because few were left, and there were few to cry out.

The shout of triumphant Christian men came ringing down the evening air instead, and fear gave way to rejoicing and gladness; for though there were many dead in the upper valley, and many strong knights and men-at-arms, young and old, great and small, lay under the dead Seljuks who had killed them, yet the great body of the army was alive, the strength of the enemy was broken, and Gilbert had saved the King. In truth, he had found him in an evil case, with his back against the oak tree, and his knights dead around him; three of the last Seljuks who lived were still hacking at him with their crooked swords, while he sang his "De profundis," for his soul's good, and used his best fence for his body's safety, hewing away like a strong man and brave, as he was, notwithstanding his faults; and he was sore spent.

"Sir," he said, taking Gilbert's hand, "ask what you will of me, and if it be no sin, you shall have it, for you have saved the army of the Cross."

But the Englishman smiled and would ask nothing, for he had honour enough that day. Yet he knew not that on the cliff whence he had descended to the valley, there sat two women who dearly loved him, watching him from first to last, — the Queen and Beatrix.

There they sat, unconsciously clasping hand in hand, and their eyes were wide with fear for him, and yet bright with pride of him as they saw the splendour of his deeds, how his fair streaming hair went ever forward through the Seljuk ranks, and how his track was deep and red for others to follow, till it seemed not possible that one man could slay so many and be unhurt, and a sort of awe came over them, as if he were a being beyond nature.

Neither spoke, nor did either hand loosen on the other; but when it was done, and they saw him dismount, and stand a little apart from other men, resting on his sword, with the glory of the sunset in his face as he looked down the valley, then Beatrix turned to the Queen, and the tears of joy sprang to her eyes as she buried her girl's face in Eleanor's bosom, and she was glad of the kind arms that held her, seeming to understand all her joy. But the Queen's eyes were dry, her face was white, and her beautiful coral lips were parched as in a fever.

CHAPTER XXIII

In this way it came about that Gilbert, of whom the historians say that nothing else is known, was placed in command of the whole army of Crusaders, to lead them through the enemy's country down into Syria; and so he did, well and bravely. After the great battle in the valley there was much fighting still to be done, day by day; for the Seljuks retreated foot by foot, filling the mountains and sweeping down like storm-clouds, to disappear as quickly, leaving blood behind them. But Gilbert led the van, and held the whole pilgrimage together, commanding where the camp should be each night, and ordering the march. Men wondered at his wisdom, and at his strength to endure hardship; for all were very tired, and provision was scarce, and the Greek hill people sold at a tenfold value the little they had to sell, so that the soldiers dined not every day, and a dish of boiled goat's flesh was a feast. So the pilgrimage went on in fighting and suffering, and as time passed the people were the more in earnest with themselves and with one another, looking forward to the promised forgiveness of sins when they should have accomplished their vows in the holy places.

They came down at last from the mountains to the sea, to a place called Attalia. Thence Gilbert would have led them still by land into Syria; but the

King was weary, and the Queen also had seen the great mistake she had made in bringing her ladies into the pilgrimage; for few had the strength of the hardy Anne of Auch, or the spirit of Beatrix, to endure without murmuring, like men, and like very brave men. The ladies' train had become a company of complainers, murmuring against everything, longing for the good things of France, and often crying out bitterly, even with tears, that they had been brought out to waste their youth and freshness, or even their lives, in a wilderness. Therefore Eleanor consented at last to the King's desire, which was to take ship from Attalia to Saint Simeon's Harbour, which is close to Antioch. In Antioch also reigned her uncle, Count Raymond, a man of her own blood, and thinking as she thought; him she now desired to see and consult with, because he knew the world, and was an honourable man, and of good counsel. Yet there was danger there, too, for the King had once believed that this Count Raymond loved her, when he had been at the court, and the King was ever very jealous and sour.

He would have brought the whole army to Antioch with him, but a great outcry arose; for, whereas all the great barons and knights were for the safer journey, the poorer sort of pilgrims feared the sea more than they feared the Seljuks, and they would not take ship. So at last the King let them go, and they, not knowing whither they went, boasted that they should reach Antioch first. He gave them money and certain guides whom he trusted.

Then Gilbert, seeing that there was a choice of two ways, sat down at night and debated what he should do. He desired to follow Beatrix with the ships, for he had not seen Sir Arnold de Curboil since Christmas Eve, and he believed that he had gone back to Ephesus to sail for Syria, so that at the present time he could not suddenly surprise his daughter and carry her away, to force her to a marriage of which heirs might be born to his great possessions in England. Gilbert knew also that his command over the whole army was ended, that the enemy's country was now passed, and that all were to join forces with Count Raymond to win back Edessa in the spring. He should therefore have more time and leisure to protect Beatrix if needful; and this was a strong thing to move him, for he had seen her many times of late, and he loved her with all his heart.

But on the other hand, when he saw how many thousands of the poorer people, who had taken the Cross in simple faith that God would provide for the journey, were about to go up into the passes again, to fight their own way through, without King or Queen or army, his charity bade him stay with them and lead them, as he only could, to live or die with them, rather than to go safely by water. So it was hard to decide which he should do, and he would not see Beatrix, lest she should persuade him; nor would he let himself think too much of the people, nor mix with them, for they knew him, and honoured him greatly, and would have carried him on their shoulders to make him their leader if he would.

Therefore his debating with himself came to nothing, and he slept ill.

In the early morning, as he was walking by the seashore, he met the Lady Anne of Auch, with two women behind her, coming back from the mass, and they stood and talked together. As he looked into her face he saw friendship there, and suddenly, though he was often slow of impulse, he began to tell her his trouble, walking beside her.

"Sir Gilbert," she said quietly, "I loved a good man, who was my husband, and he loved me; but he was killed, and they brought him home to me dead. I tell you, Sir Gilbert, that the true love of man and woman is the greatest and best thing in all the world; but when two love one another, if their love be not the greatest thing save honour, then it is not true, nor worthy to be reckoned in account. Think well whether you love this lady truly, as I mean, or not, and if you do, there can be no more doubt."

"Lady Anne," said Gilbert, when he had thought a little while, "you are a very honourable woman, and your counsel is good."

After they had talked, they parted, and Gilbert went back to his lodging, being determined to go to Antioch by sea with the King and Queen; but still he was sorry for the poor pilgrims who were to be left behind to fight a way through for themselves.

The great ships that had been hired for the voyage were heavy and unwieldy vessels to see, but yet swift through the water, whether the vast lateen sails drew

full with a fair wind or were close-reefed in a gale,
till they seemed mere jibs bent to the long yards,
or even when in a flat calm the vessels were sent
along by a hundred sweeps, fifty on each side ; and
they were partly Greek galleys and partly they
were of Amalfi, whose citizens had all the commerce
of the East, and their own quarter in every town
and harbour, from the Piræus round by Constantinople and all Asia Minor and Egypt, as far as Tunis
itself.

A clear northwest wind began to blow on the very
day fixed for departure, and the big galleys swept
out one by one, close upon each other, till they
were outside and hoisted their sails, the sea being
very smooth under the land ; and when they had
run out two or three miles, with the wind aft, they
wore ship, one after another, coming to a little, to get
their sheets in, and then holding off to jibe the great
sails for the port tack, with much creaking of yards
and flapping of canvas. Then, as they ran free
along the coast to the eastward, the wind quartering,
they got out great booms to windward, guyed fore
and aft, and down to the forward beaching-hooks at
the water's edge, at the first streak under the wales ;
and they set light sails, hauling the tacks well
out and making the sheet fast after the southern
fashion, and then swaying away at the halyards,
till the white canvas was up to the mast-head,
bellying full, and as steady as the upper half of a
half-moon.

Before many days they came to Saint Simeon's
Harbour, which was the port of Antioch, and saw

the mighty walls and towers on the heights a dozen miles inshore; and when Gilbert looked from the deck of his ship, he was glad that the army was not to besiege that great and strong fortress, since it belonged to Count Raymond, the Queen's uncle. But if he had known what things were to happen to him there, rather than have ridden up to the walled city he would have gone barefoot to Jerusalem, to fulfil his vow as he might.

Count Raymond, with his broad shoulders and bronzed face and dark hair just turning gray at the temples, came down to meet the army at the shore; and first he embraced the King, according to custom, and then he kissed the Queen, his niece, not once, but four or five times, and she kissed him, for they were very glad to see each other; but it is not true, as some have said in their chronicles, that there were thoughts of love between them. Queen Eleanor had many bitter enemies, and her sins were almost as many as her good deeds, but love for Count Raymond was not among them.

Nevertheless, King Louis was very jealous as soon as he saw the two embracing, for he had always believed that there was more than he knew. But he said nothing, for he feared his Queen. So there were great rejoicings in Antioch, when all the ladies and the barons and other nobles were installed there to keep Easter together; and though they had still some days of fasting during Holy Week, they were so glad to be in the great city, and so much lightened of trouble by having left the poorer pilgrims to shift for themselves, that it would have been easy for

them to live on bread and water, instead of eating
the dainty dishes of good fish, and the imitations
of eggs made with flour and saffron and blanched
almonds, and the delicate sweetmeats, and all the
many good things which Count Raymond's fifty
cooks knew how to prepare for Lent. For the
Count lived luxuriously, though he was a good
fighter at need.

Most of all, he was a keen man, with few scruples,
and the Queen began to ask him to help her in
getting her marriage annulled, because she could no
longer bear to be the wife of a spoon-faced monk,
as she called the King; whereat Count Raymond
laughed. Then he thought awhile and bent his
broad brows; but soon his face cleared, for he had
found a remedy. The King, he said, was surely
Eleanor's cousin and within the prohibited degrees
of consanguinity, so that the marriage was null
and void; and the Pope would be obliged against
his will to adhere to the rule of the Church and pronounce it so. They were cousins in the seventh
degree, he said, because the King was descended
from Eleanor's great-great-great-great-grandfather,
William Towhead, Duke of Guienne, whose daughter, Adelaide of Poitiers, married Hugh Capet,
King of France; and the seventh degree of consanguinity was still prohibited, and no dispensation
had been given, nor even asked for.

At first the Queen laughed, but presently she sent
for the Bishop of Metz, and asked him; and he said
that Count Raymond spoke truly, but that he would
have nothing to do with the matter, since it had never

been the intention of the Church that her rules should be misused. Yet it is said that he was afterwards of the Council which declared that there had been no marriage.

So, being sure, the Queen went to the King and told him to his face that she had meant to marry a king, and not a monk as he was, and that she had now found out that her marriage was no marriage, wherefore he was living in mortal sin; and if he would save his soul he must repudiate her as soon as they should have returned to France. At this the King was overcome with grief and wept bitterly, not because he was to be delivered from the woman of Belial, as he had prayed, but because he had unwittingly lived in such great sin so many years. She laughed and went away, leaving him weeping.

From that time she spent her days and her evenings in consultation with Count Raymond, and they were continually closeted together in her apartment, which was in one of the western towers of the palace and looked out over the city walls towards the sea. It was early spring, and the air smelt of Syrian flowers and was tender to breathe.

Although the King was now sure that Eleanor was not his wife, he continued to be very jealous of her, because he had once loved her in his dull fashion, and she was very beautiful. Therefore, when he was not praying, he was watching and spying, to see whether she were alone with Count Raymond. Certain writers have spoken of the great Saladin at this time, saying that she met him secretly, for the deliverance of her kinsman Sandebeuil de Sanzay, who had been taken prisoner, and that she loved Saladin for his generosity, and that the King was jealous of him; which things are lies, because Saladin was at that time but seven years old.

Daily, as he watched, the King grew very sure that Raymond loved Eleanor, and he swore by his hope of salvation that such things should not be. In this way the feast of Easter passed, and there were great rejoicings, and feastings, and all manner of delight. Also during this time Gilbert saw Beatrix freely, so that their love grew more and more; but he seldom spoke with the Queen, and then briefly.

Now Eleanor lived in the western tower, and only one staircase led up to the vestibule of her apartments, by which way Count Raymond came, and the great nobles when she summoned them, and the guards also. But beyond her inner chamber there was a door opening into the long wing of the palace where all her ladies were lodged, and by that door she went to them and they came to her. Often the Lady Anne came in, and Beatrix, and some of the others who were more especially her familiars, and they found the Queen and Count Raymond sitting in chairs, and talking without constraint, and sometimes playing at chess by the open window which looked out on the west balcony. They thought no evil, for they knew that he had become her counsellor in the matter of the repudiation; and Beatrix cared not, for she knew well that the Queen loved Gilbert, and she never saw him there.

On an evening in the week after Easter the King

determined that he would see the Queen himself and tell her his mind. He therefore took two nobles for an escort, with torchbearers and a few guards; and when he had descended into the main court, he walked across to the west side and went up into Eleanor's tower; for he would not go through the ladies' wing, lest his eyes should see some fair and noble maiden, or some young dame of great beauty, whereby his pious thoughts might be disturbed ever so little.

Having come to the vestibule, he demanded admittance to the Queen's chamber; and the young Lord of Sanzay, who was in waiting, begged him to wait while he himself inquired if the Queen were at leisure. Then the King was angry, and said that he waited for no one, and he went forward to go in. But Sanzay stood before the door and bade the Gascon guards form in rank and keep it till he should come back. The King saw that he had small chance of forcing a way, and he stood still, repeating some prayers the while, lest he should draw his sword and fight, out of sheer anger. Then Sanzay came back.

"My lord King," he said in a clear voice, "her Grace bids me say that she has no leisure now, and that when she has need of a monk she will send for him."

At the great insult, swords were out as soon as the words, and the broken reflections of steel flashed red under the high lamps and in the torchlight; for the King drew to strike down Sanzay where he stood, and his nobles and guards drew with him, while the Gascons were as quick as they. But Sanzay would not draw his sword, for he had once saved the King's life in battle, and he thought it not knightly. Then some blows were exchanged and blood was shed; but presently, being at a disadvantage, the King stepped back and lowered his point.

"Sirs," he said, "it is not seemly that we of the Cross should kill one another. Let us go."

When Sanzay heard this, he called his guards back, and the King went away discomfited. In the courtyard he turned aside and sat down upon a great stone seat.

"Fetch me Sir Gilbert Warde," he said, "and let him come quickly."

He waited silently till the knight came and stood before him in his surcoat and mantle, with only his dagger in his belt; and the King bade all his attendants go away to a distance, leaving a torch stuck in the ring in the wall.

He desired of Gilbert that he should take a force of trusted men who would obey him, and go up the west tower to bring the Queen out a prisoner; for he would not stay in Antioch another night, nor leave her behind, and he meant to ride down to the harbour and take ship for Ptolemais, leaving the army to follow him on the morrow. But for a space Gilbert answered nothing.

At first it seemed to him impossible to do such a deed, and but for courtesy he would have turned on his heel and left the King sitting there. But as he stood thinking, it seemed to him that he had better seem to obey, and go and warn the Queen of her danger.

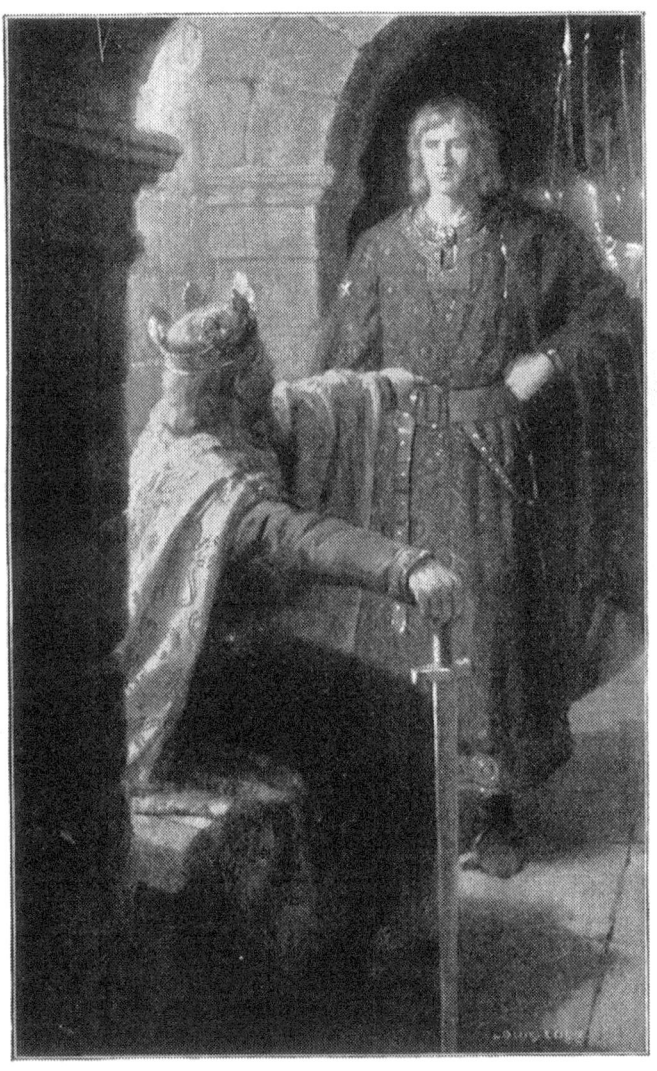

"FOR A SPACE GILBERT ANSWERED NOTHING"

"My lord," he answered at last, "I will go."

Though he said not what he would do, the King was satisfied, and rose and went toward his own apartments, to order his departure.

Then Gilbert went and sought out ten knights whom he knew, and each of them called ten of their men-at-arms, and they took their swords with them, and torches; but Gilbert had only his dagger, for those he had chosen were all of them Queen's men and would have died for her. So they went together up the broad steps of the tower, and the Gascons heard the hundred footfalls in fear and much trembling, supposing that the King had come back with a great force to slay them and go in. Then Sanzay drew his sword and stood at the head of the stairs, bidding his men keep the narrow way till they should all be dead for the Queen's sake. They were Gascons, and were ready to die, but they held their breath as they listened to the steady tramping on the stone steps below.

In the torchlight they saw Gilbert's face, and the faces of Queen's men, and that there were no swords out; nevertheless, they kept theirs drawn and stood in the doorway, and on the landing Gilbert stood still, for they did not make way for him.

"Sir Gilbert," said Sanzay, "I am here to keep the Queen's door, and though we be friends, I shall not let you pass while I live, if you mean her any violence."

"Sir," answered Gilbert, "I come unarmed, as you see, and by no means to fight with you. I pray you, sir, go in and tell the Queen that I am without, and have her men with me, and would speak with her for her safety."

Then Sanzay bade his men stand back, and the knights and men-at-arms crowded the vestibule, while he went in ; and immediately he came out again, with a clear face.

"The Queen is alone, and bids the Guide of Aquitaine pass," he said.

All stood aside, and he, taller than they, and grave and keen of face, went in ; and the door was closed behind him, and within that there was a heavy Eastern curtain, so that no voices could be heard from one side to the other.

Eleanor sat under the warm lamplight, near the open window, for the night was warm. Her head was uncovered, her russet-golden hair fell in great waves upon her shoulders and to the ground behind her chair, and she wore no mantle, but only a close-fitting gown of cream-white silk with deep embroideries of silver and pearls. She was very beautiful, but very pale, and her eyes were veiled. Gilbert came and stood before her, but she did not hold out her hand, as he had expected.

"Why have you come to me?" she asked after a time, looking out at the balcony, and not at him.

"The King, Madam, has bidden me take you a prisoner to him, in order that he may carry you away by sea to Ptolemais and to Jerusalem."

While he was speaking, she slowly turned her face to him, and stared at his coldly.

"And you are come to do as you are bidden, getting admittance to me stealthily, with men of my own who have betrayed me?"

Gilbert turned white, and then he smiled as he answered her.

"No. I am come to warn your Grace and to defend you against all violence, with my life."

Eleanor's face changed and softened, and again she looked out at the balcony.

"Why should you defend me?" she asked sadly, after a pause. "What am I to you, that you should fight for me? I sent you out to die—why should you wish me to be safe?"

"You have been the best friend to me, and the kindest, that ever woman was to man."

"A friend? No. I was never your friend. I sent you out to death, because I loved you, and trusted that I might see you never again, and that you might die honourably for the Cross and your vows. Instead, you won glory, and saved us all—all but me! You owe me no thanks for such friendship."

She looked at him long, and he was silent.

"Oh, what a man you are!" she cried suddenly. "What a man!"

He blushed like a girl at the praise, for her soul was in the words, and her great love for him, the only thing in all her life that had ever been above herself.

"What a man you are!" she said again, more softly. "Eleanor of Aquitaine, the Queen, the fairest woman in the world, would give you her soul and her body and the hope of her life to come—and you are faithful to a poor girl whom you loved when you were a boy! A hundred thousand brave men stand by to see me die, and you alone take death by the throat and strangle him off, as you would strangle a bloodhound, with those hands of yours! I send you out — oh, how selfishly! — that you may at least die bravely for your vow and leave me at sad peace with your memory, and you fight through a hell of foes and save the King and me and all, and come back to me in glory — my Guide of Aquitaine!"

She had risen and stood before him, her face dead white with passion, and her eyes deep-fired by a love that was beyond any telling. And though she would not move, her arms went out toward him.

"How can any woman help loving you!" she cried passionately.

She sank into her chair again, and covered her face with her hands. He stood still a moment, and then came and knelt on one knee beside her, resting his hand upon the carved arm of her chair.

"I cannot love you, but in so far as I may be faithful to another I give you my whole life," he said very gently.

As he spoke the last words, the curtain of the inner apartments was softly raised, and Beatrix stood there; for she had thought that the Queen was alone. But she heard not the beginning of the speech, and she grew quite cold, and could not speak nor go away.

Eleanor's hands left her face and fell together upon Gilbert's right.

"I have not mine to give," she answered in a low

voice. "It is yours already — and I would that you were not English, that I might be your sovereign and make you great among men — or that I were England's Queen — and that may come to pass, and you shall see what I will do for love of you — I would marry that boy of the Plantagenets, if it could serve you!"

"Madam," said Gilbert, "think of your own present safety — the King is very angry —"

"Did I think of your safety when I sent you out to lead us? Now if you are here, am I not safe? Gilbert —"

She let her voice caress his name, and her lips lingered with it, and she laid her hands upon his shoulders. As he knelt beside her — she bent to his face.

"Best and bravest living man" — it was a whisper now — "love of my life — heart of my heart — this last time — this only once — and then good-by."

She kissed him on the forehead, and leapt from her seat in horror, for there was another voice in the room, with a hurt cry.

"Oh, Gilbert! Gilbert!"

Beatrix was reeling on her feet, and caught the curtain, lest she fall, and her face of agony was still turned toward the two, as they stood together. Gilbert sprang forward, when he understood, and caught the girl in his arms and brought her to the light, trembling like a falling leaf. Then she started in his arms and struggled wildly to be free, and twisted her neck lest he should kiss her; but he held her fast.

"Beatrix! You do not understand — you did not hear!" He tried to make her listen to him.

"I heard!" she cried, still struggling. "I saw! I know! Let me go — oh, for God's sake, let me go!"

Gilbert's arms relaxed, and she sprang back from him two paces, and faced the Queen.

"You have won!" she cried, in a breaking voice. "You have him body and soul, as you swore you would! But do not say that I have not understood!"

"I have given him to you, soul and body," answered Eleanor, sadly. "Might I not even bid him good-by, as a friend might?"

"You are false — falser each than the other," answered Beatrix, in white anger. "You have played with me, tricked me, made me your toy —"

"Did you hear this man say that he did not love me, before I bade him good-by?" asked Eleanor, gravely, almost sternly.

"He has said it to me, but not to you, never to you — never to the woman he loves!"

"I never loved the Queen," said Gilbert. "On my soul — on the Holy Cross —"

"Never loved her? And you saved her life before mine —"

"And you said that I did well —"

"It was all a lie — a cruel lie —" The girl's voice almost broke, but she choked down the terrible tears, and got words again. "It would have been braver to have told me long ago — I should not have died then, for I loved you less."

Eleanor came a step nearer and spoke very quietly and kindly.

"You are wrong," she said. "Sir Gilbert is sent by the King to take me as a prisoner, that I may be carried away to Jerusalem this very night. Come, you shall hear the voices of the soldiers who are waiting for me."

She led Beatrix to the door and lifted the curtain, so that through the wooden panels the girl could hear the talking of many voices, and the clank of steel. Then Eleanor brought her back.

"But he would not take me," she said, "and he warned me of my danger."

"No wonder — he loves you!"

"He does not love me, though I love him, and he has said so to-night. And I know that he loves you and is faithful to you — "

Beatrix laughed wildly.

"Faithful! He? There is no faith in his greatest oath, nor in his smallest word!"

"You are mad, child; he never lied in all his life to me or you — he could not lie."

"Then he has deceived you, too — Queen, Duchess; you are only a woman, after all, and he has made sport of you, as he has of me!" Again she laughed, half furiously.

"If he has deceived me he has indeed deceived you," answered Eleanor, "for he has told me very plainly that he loves you. And now I will not stand between you and him, even in the mistake you made. I love him, yes. I have loved him enough to give him up, because he loves you. I love him so well that I will not take his warning and save myself from the King's anger, and I know not what he and his monks will do to me. Good-by, Sir Gilbert Warde — Beatrix, good-by."

"This is some comedy," answered the girl, exasperated.

"No — by the living truth, it is no comedy," answered the Queen.

She looked once more into Gilbert's face, and then turned away, stately and sad. With one movement she drew aside the great curtain, and with the next she opened wide the door, and the loud clamour of the knights and men-at-arms came in like a wave. Then it ceased suddenly, as Eleanor spoke to them in clear tones.

"I am the King's prisoner. Take me to him!"

There was silence for a moment, and then the Gascons who had fought with the King and his men cried out fiercely.

"We will not let you go! We will not let our Duchess go!"

They feared some evil for her, and were loyal men to her, hating the King. But Eleanor raised her hand to motion them back, for their faces were fierce, and their hands were on their swords.

"Make way for me, if you will not take me to him," she said proudly.

Then Sanzay, her kinsman, stepped before the rest, and spoke.

"Madam," he said, "the Duchess of Gascony cannot be prisoner to the King of France, while there are Gascons. If your Grace will go to the King, we will go also, and we shall see who is to be a prisoner."

At this there was a great shout that rang up to the vault of the lofty vestibule, and down the stone steps and out into the courtyard. Eleanor smiled serenely, for she knew her men.

" Go with me, then," she said, " and see that no bodily harm comes to me. But in this matter I shall do the King's will."

In the room behind, the words echoed clearly, and Beatrix turned to Gilbert.

" You see," she said, " it is but a play that you have thought of between you, and nothing more."

" Can you not believe us?" he asked reproachfully.

" I shall believe you when I know that you love me," she answered, and turned away, towards the door of the inner apartments.

Gilbert followed her.

" Beatrix ! " he cried. " Beatrix ! Hear me ! "

She turned once more, with a face like stone.

" I have heard you, I have heard her, and I do not believe you," she answered.

Without another word she left him and went out. He stood looking after her for a moment, while his calm face darkened slowly ; and his anger was slow and lasting, as the heating of a furnace for the smelting. He stooped and picked up his cap, which had fallen to the floor, and then he, too, followed the Queen, through the vestibule and stairs and courtyard, to the King's presence.

2 B

CHAPTER XXIV

THAT night they left hastily and went down to the sea with torches ; but it was dawn when they were on board one of the great ships, and the hawsers were cast off, and the crew began to heave up the anchor. In his anger, Gilbert had called his men, and had gone on board also, and many hours passed before he realized what he had done. Then he began to torment himself.

His angry manhood told him that he was just and that he should not bear a girl's unbelief when he was manifestly in the right ; and his love answered that he had left Beatrix without protection and perhaps at the mercy of her father, since he might come by sea at any moment and claim her from Count Raymond, who would give her up without opposition. He wondered also why Sir Arnold had not appeared, and whether, having sailed from Ephesus, he had been shipwrecked. But his thoughts soon turned back to his work, and he sat on the low rail by the main-rigging, looking down at the blue water as the ship ran smoothly along. What was there in Beatrix to hold him, after all? It was nothing but a boyish memory, revived by a mistaken idea of faith.

But suddenly he felt within him the aching hollow and the grinding hunger of heart that the loved woman leaves behind her, and he knew well that his anger was playing a comedy with him, as Beatrix had accused him and the Queen of playing a play in the past night.

It was hard that she should not have believed him; and yet when one has seen and heard, it is harder still to believe against sight and hearing. If she had loved him, he said to himself, she could not have doubted him. He would never have doubted her, no matter what he might have seen her do. But at this he began to realize and understand; for in order to persuade himself, he pictured her sitting as the Queen had sat, and a man bending over her and kissing her and calling her the love of his life and heart, and he felt another sort of anger rising fiercely in him, because the imagined sight was vivid and bad to see. Thereupon he grew calmer, seeing that she was not wholly wrong, and he began to curse his evil fate and to wish that he had not followed the Queen, but had stayed behind at Antioch.

But it was too late now, for Antioch was gone in the purple distance, and it was towards evening.

The day dawned again, and darkened, and days after that, while he perpetually blamed himself more and more and began to find a fault in every doing of his life, and the gloom of the northern temper settled upon him and oppressed him heavily, so that his companions wondered what had happened to him.

During all that time the Queen never showed herself, but remained in her cabin with the Lady Anne, who had come with her and would not be denied.

or Eleanor hated to see the King, and she was

afraid to see Gilbert, whom she knew to be in the
ship's company, and she was very sad, also, and
cared not for the daylight nor for men's voices.   It
made it worse that she had tried to sacrifice herself
for the woman Gilbert loved, since it had been in
vain, and she had not been believed, and since he had
after all come with her, she knew not why. As for the
King, he sat all day long on the quarter-deck under
an awning, telling beads, and praying fervently that
the presence of the woman of Belial might not dis-
tract his thoughts when he should at last come to
the holy places ; for before anything else he considered his own soul as of great importance.

So they came to Ptolemais, which some called
Acre, and they rode a weary way to Jerusalem, till
the young King Baldwin of Jerusalem, the third of
that name, came out to meet them with a very rich
train.   Then Gilbert lagged behind, for he had no
heart in any rejoicing or feasting, seeing that he
should not have been there at all, and had left
Beatrix in anger.   But Eleanor had come out of the
ship to the shore, more beautiful than ever, and
serenely scornful of the King, since he had not even
dared to use the power she had put into his hands,
in order to tell her his mind, and speak out his
reproaches ; and he was more ridiculous than ever in
her eyes.   From that time she paid no more attention
to him than if he had not existed, for she despised a
man who would not use the power he had.

As for Gilbert, though he was in such melancholy
mood, when he saw the walls and towers of Jerusalem at last, a hope of peace sprang up in him,

and a certainty of satisfaction not like anything which
he had known before; and it seemed to him that if
he could but be alone in the holy places he should
find rest for his soul. Therefore he rode in the rear
of the train, though he was a man of consequence,
and many young knights and squires looked up to
him and kept him company, so that he could not
escape altogether to an outward solitude.

His eyes looked up before him, and he saw the
holiest city in the world, like a vision against the
pale sky, as the day sank; and his whole being went
out to be there, floating before him in a prayer
learnt long ago. Therein, as when he had been a
child in his English home, he heard the voice of a
guardian angel praying with him — praying for the
good against the evil, for the light against the darkness, for the clean against the unclean, for the good
self against the bad; and his heart made echoes in
heaven.

He heard not the sounds that came back from the
royal train, the high talking and glad laughter; for
that would have jarred on him and set his teeth on
edge, and he had shut the doors of the body upon
himself to be alone within. It mattered not that
young Baldwin was riding by the Queen, already
half in love, and making soft speeches within sight
of the hill whereon Christ died, nor that he took a
boy's mischievous pleasure in interrupting the King's
droning litany, recited in verse and response with
the priest at his side; nor that some of the knights
were chattering of what lodging they should find,
and the young squires, in undertones, of black-eyed

Jewish girls, and the grooms of Syrian wine. They
were as nothing, all these, as nothing but the shadows of the world cast by its own ancient evil at the
toot of the Cross, and he only was real and alive,
and the Cross only was true and high in the pure
light.

And in this he was not quite dreaming, for the
train that rode up from Acre was not all of those
true Crusaders of whom many had been with the
army, both rich and poor, but of whom the rich had
stayed behind in Antioch and the poor. had perished
miserably by the swords of the Seljuks or by the
wiles of the Greeks, when they had tried to come
on by land ; and many of them had been sold into
slavery, and not one reached Jerusalem alive, out of
so many thousands. Of the forty or fifty who were
first in sight of the City, scarcely three were in heart-
felt earnest, and they were the Lady Anne of Auch,
and Gilbert Warde, and the King himself. But with
the King all faith took a material shape, which was
his own, and the buying of his own salvation had
turned his soul into a place of spiritual usury.

The Lady Anne was calm and silent, and when
young Baldwin spoke to her she hardly heard him,
and answered in few words, little to the point. She
had trusted that she might never see Jerusalem, for
she had hoped to die of wound or sickness by the
way, and so end in heaven, with him she had lost,
the pilgrimage begun on earth. For she was a most
faithful woman, and of the most faithful there is
often least to tell, because they have but one thought,
one hope, one prayer. And seeing that she had come

through alive, she neither rejoiced nor complained, knowing that there was more to bear before the end, and trusting to bear it all bravely for the dear sake of her dead love. It may be, also, that she was the most earnest of all those who had taken the Cross, because all earthly things that had made her life happy had been taken from her.

Yet of all men, Gilbert Warde had fought best and most, and in so far as bodily peril was counted, none had lived through so much as he; for many of his companions had been killed beside him, and others had taken their place, and even his man Dunstan had been wounded twice, and little Alric once, and many horses had been killed under him, but he himself was untouched, even after the great battle in the valley; and there were honours for him whenever he was seen. In this, too, he was high-hearted and thoughtless of himself, that when he saw the Holy City before him, he forgot the many risks of life and limb, and the hunger and cold and weariness through which he had passed, and forgot that he had won reward well and fairly, thinking only that the peace he felt came as a gift from Heaven.

That evening, when there was a feast in Baldwin's palace, the Lady Anne was not there; and when the King of France called for the Guide of Aquitaine to present him to the King of Jerusalem, he was not in the hall nor within the walls; and by and by the Queen herself rose and went out, leaving the two Kings at table.

For Gilbert had gone fasting to the Holy Sepulchre, with Dunstan bearing his shield, and with a man

to lead them.   Then he went into the vast church
which the crusaders had built to enclose all the sacred
ground, and little lights broke the darkness here and
there, without dispelling it, but the poor Christian who
led Gilbert had a taper in his hand.   The knight came
first to the deep-red stone whereon Nicodemus and
Joseph of Arimathea anointed the body of the Lord
for burial, and there kneeling down, he set his shield
and sword before him and prayed that he might yet
use them well.   Then the man took him to the Gol-
gotha, and he laid down his arms before him and
stood trembling, as if he were afraid, and the drops
of sweat stood out upon his forehead, and his low
voice shook like a little child's when he prayed in the
place where God died for man.   Afterwards he knelt
and touched the stones with his face, and spread out
his arms crosswise, not knowing what he did.   But
when he had lain thus some time he rose and took
up his shield and sword, and the man led him farther
through the darkness to other places.   So at last
they brought him to the Tomb, and he sent away the
man who had guided him, and bade Dunstan go back
also ; but he would not.

"I also have fought for the Cross, though I be but
a churl," said the dark-faced man.

"You are no churl," answered Gilbert, gravely.
" Kneel beside me and watch."

"I will watch with you," said Dunstan, and he
took his own sword and laid it next to Gilbert's.

But he knelt one step behind his master, on his
left side.   More than forty burning lamps hung
above the stone of the Tomb, and around the

stone itself stood a grating of well-wrought iron having a wicket with a lock of pure gold.

Then Gilbert raised his eyes, and looking through the iron fence, he saw that on the other side some one was kneeling also, and it was the Lady Anne of Auch, robed all in black, with a black hood half thrown back; but her face was white, with dark shadows, and her two white hands clasped two of the iron stanchions, while her sad eyes looked upwards fixedly, seeing a vision, and not seeing men. Gilbert was glad that she was there.

So they knelt an hour, and another hour, and no sound broke the stillness, nor did they feel any weariness at all, for their hearts were lifted up, and for a time the world fell away from them. Then a soft sound of footsteps was in the church, ceasing at some distance from the Tomb, which was not then shut off within walls of its own. But none of the three turned to see who was there, and there was silence again.

Eleanor had come alone to the Sepulchre, and stood gazing at the three, not willing to come nearer. As she looked, her sins rose in her eyes and passed before her, many and great, and where her good deeds were hidden in her soul there was darkness, and she despaired of forgiveness, for she knew her own pride, that it could never be broken in her. She looked on that most faithful woman, and on that maiden knight whom she so dearly loved, sinning daily in her heart for him, and yet for his sake fighting her loving thoughts ; and she would not have dared to go forward and kneel beside the pure in heart, in the holy light. All alone she drew back, and when she was so far that they could not have seen her, had they looked, she knelt down by a pillar, and drew her dark veil over her face, folding her hands in the hope of forgiveness and peace, and in great loneliness.

Some comfort she found in this, that for the great love of her life, the like of which she had not known nor was to know again, though she had wished evil and dreamed of sweetest sins, she had done a little good at the last, and that the man who knelt there praying had grown stronger and greater and of higher honour by her means. Yet the comfort was not of much worth in her loneliness, since she had given him to another, and none could take his place. Then she said prayers she knew, but they had no meaning, and she gazed from beneath her veil at the place where the Lord had lain ; but she felt nothing, and her heart was as stone, believing what she saw, but finding no light of faith for her in the divine beyond.

At last she rose softly, as she had knelt, and leaning against the pillar, she looked long at the man she loved, and at the shield with the cross of Aquitaine, and, in it, at the spot she had once so fervently kissed. Her hand went to her heart, where it hurt her, and with the hurt came the great pure longing that, come what might to herself, all might be well with him; and her lips moved silently, while her eyes would have given him the world and its glory.

" God, let me perish, but keep him what he is ! "

Shall any one say that such true prayers are not heard, because they are spoken by lips that have sinned? If not, God is not good, nor did Christ die to save men.

The daughter of princes, the wife of two kings, as she was to be, and the mother of two kings, and of many more in line after them, she drew down her veil that none might see her face under the dim lights, and she went out thence, very lonely and sad, into the streets of Jerusalem.

At midnight came a priest of the church to trim the lights at the tomb; yet the three did not move, and he prayed awhile and went away. But when the watchmen cried the dawning, and their voices came faintly in by the doorway, floating through the dark church, Gilbert rose to his feet, and Dunstan with him, and they took their arms with them, and went away, leaving the Lady Anne the last of them all, her white hands still clasping the iron bars, her sad black eyes still turned to heaven.

Faint streaks were in the eastern sky, but it was still almost dark as the two men turned to the left to follow the way by which they had come. Three steps from the door, Dunstan stumbled against something neither hard nor soft, and in many fights he had learned what that thing was.

"There is a dead man here," he said, and Gilbert had stopped also.

They stooped down, trying to see, and Dunstan felt along the body, touching the mantle, till he found something sharp, which was the point of a dagger out of its sheath.

"He is a knight," said Dunstan, "for he wears his surcoat and sword-belt under his mantle."

But Gilbert was gazing into the face, trying to see, while the dust under the head grew slowly grey in the dawn, and the waxen features seemed to rise up out of the earth before him. But then he started, for, as he looked down, his own eyes were but a hand-breadth from an arrow-head that stuck straight up out of the dead forehead, and the broken shaft with its feathers darkly soiled lay half under the body. Dunstan also looked, and a low sound of gladness came from his fierce lips.

"It is Arnold de Curboil!" exclaimed Gilbert, in measureless surprise.

"And this is Alric's arrow," answered Dunstan, looking at the point, and then handling the piece of the broken shaft. "This is the arrow that was sticking in your cap on that day when we fought for sport in Tuscany, and Alric picked it up and kept it. And often in battle he had but that one left, and would not shoot, saying that it was only to be shot to save his master's life. So now it has done its work, for though the knight was shot from behind, he has his dagger in his dead hand under his cloak, and he must have followed you to the door of the church to kill you in the dark within. Well done, little Alric!"

Then Dunstan spat in the face of the dead man and cursed him; but Gilbert took his man by the collar and pulled him aside roughly.

"It is unmanly to insult the dead," he said, in disgust.

But Dunstan laughed savagely.

"Why?" he asked. "He was only my father!"

Gilbert's hand relaxed and fell to his side, then he lifted it again and laid it gently on Dunstan's shoulder.

"Poor Dunstan!" he said.

But Dunstan smiled bitterly and said nothing, for he thought himself poor indeed, since if the dead man had given him a tenth of his due, he should have had land enough for a knight.

"We cannot leave him here," said Gilbert, at last.

"Why not? There are dogs."

Dunstan took up his master's shield and without more waiting turned his back on his father's body. But Gilbert stood where he was, and gazed down into the face of the man who had done him so much harm; and he remembered Faringdon and the swift stroke that had killed his father, and Stortford woods, where he himself had lain for dead. He still saw in dreams how Curboil snatched his dagger left-handed from its sheath, and now, by strong association, he wished to see whether it were still the same one, a masterpiece of Eastern art, and he stooped down in the dawn to pull back the cloak and take the weapon. It was the same, fair and keen, with the chiselled hilt. He stuck it into his own belt, for a memory, for it had once been sheathed in his own side; then he drew the cloak over the dead face and went his way, just as the hushed city began to stir, following Dunstan to his lodging, musing on the strange chances of his life, and glad that, since his enemy was to die, it had not been his ill chance to soil the blade consecrated to the Cross with blood so vile, and to slay with his own hand the father of the woman he loved.

Now also, as he thought calmly, he guessed that Beatrix must be in Jerusalem, and that Curboil, having taken her from Antioch, and meaning to kill his enemy before he sailed back to England, had brought his daughter with him, fearing lest she should escape him again and find refuge against him.

He found little Alric sitting on the low doorstep of the house where he lodged, his stolid Saxon face pink and white in the fresh dawn, and his thick hands hanging idly over his knees, while the round blue eyes stared at the street. He got up when Gilbert came near, and pulled off his woollen cap.

"Well done, Alric," said Gilbert. "That is the second time you have saved my life."

"It was a good arrow," answered Alric, thoughtfully. "I carried it two years and made it very sharp. It is a pity the man broke the shaft with his head when he fell, and I would have cut off the steel point to use it again, but I heard footsteps and ran away, lest I should be taken for a thief."

"It was well shot," said Gilbert, and he went in.

CHAPTER XXV

IT had been early dawn when they had found Sir
Arnold dead; it was toward evening when Gilbert
and Dunstan followed a young Jew to the door of
a Syrian house in a garden of the old quarter of
the city, toward the Zion gate. All day they
had searched Jerusalem, up and down, through the
narrow streets of whitened houses, inquiring everywhere for a knight who had lately come with his one
daughter, and no one could tell them anything ; for
Sir Arnold had paid well to find a retired house,
where Beatrix might be safely guarded while he went
out to seek Gilbert and kill him, and where he himself
could hide if there were any pursuit. So they asked
in vain, till at last they saw a boy sitting by the way-
side on the hill of the Temple, weeping and lamenting
in the Eastern fashion. The guide, who was also a
Jew, asked him what had chanced, and he said that
his father was gone on a journey, leaving him, his
young son, in the house with his mother. And there
had come a Christian knight with a daughter and
her woman and certain servants, desiring to hire the
house for a time because it was in a pleasant place ;
and they had let him have it, he promising by an
interpreter to pay a great price ; but he had not yet
paid it. In the morning the young man had seen
Christians carrying away the body of this knight to

bury it; and he had been to the house, but the knight's servants would not let him in, and did not understand his speech, and threatened to beat him; and now he was afraid lest his father should come home unawares and take him and his mother to account for letting strangers use the house without even paying for it beforehand.

When Gilbert saw that he had found what he sought, he first gave money to the boy, to encourage him, and bade the interpreter tell him to lead them all to the house, saying that Gilbert himself would enter, in spite of the servants. The boy took the money, and when he had measured Gilbert with his eye, he understood, and went before them with no more weeping; and the knight's step was light and quick with hope, for he had begun to doubt whether Beatrix were really in the city after all.

The house was low and white, and stood at the end of a small garden in which there were palms, and spring flowers growing in straight lines between small hewn stones, laid so as to leave little trenches of earth between them. There was a hard path, newly swept, leading to the square door of the house, and on the doorpost were clearly written certain characters in Hebrew.

Gilbert knocked on the door, not loudly, with the hilt of his dagger, but no one answered; and again louder, but there was no sound from within. Then he shook the door, trying whether it would open of itself by a push; but it was fast, and the two windows of the house that looked out on each side of the door were barred also.

"They think that some great force is with us, and are afraid," said the Jewish boy. "Speak to them, sir, for they do not understand my tongue."

And the interpreter explained what he said. Then Gilbert spoke in English, for he supposed that Curboil's men must be Englishmen, but the Jewish boy knew that the words should sound otherwise.

"In Greek, sir! Speak to them in Greek, for they are all Greeks. That is why they are afraid. All Greeks are afraid."

The interpreter began to speak in Greek, clear and loud, but no sound came. Yet when Gilbert put his ear to the door he thought that he heard something like a child's moaning. It had a sound of pain in it, and his blood rose at the thought that some weak creature was being hurt. So he took little Alric's leathern belt, such as grooms wear, and bound it round his hand to guard the flesh, and he struck the door where the leaves joined in the middle, once and twice and three times, and it began to open inward, so that they could see the iron bolt bent half double. Then with his shoulder he forced it in, so that the bolt slipped from the socket, and the leaves flew open.

There was a little court within, around which the house was built, with a well for rain-water in the middle, after the fashion that was half Roman and half Eastern. Gilbert went in, and bade all be silent that he might hear whence the moaning came; for it was more distinct now, and it seemed to come from the well, with a little splashing of water ; so he went and looked down, and when he saw what was there he cried aloud for fear.

2 c

For there he saw an upturned face, half dead, with a white thing bound across the mouth, and hands tied together, and struggling to strike the water, but heavily weighted; and it was the face of Beatrix, two fathoms below him. There were holes opposite each other, in the two sides of the well, for a man's hands and feet, for climbing down into the cistern; and Gilbert lost nc moment, but began to descend at once; yet long before he had got the bound hands together in his own, stooping and himself in peril of falling, the face had sunk below the bubbling water.

With his feet firmly planted in the holes, and standing as it might be astride of the well, he lifted the girl up; and though she was so slight, it was one of the hardest things he ever had to do, for her clothes were full of water, and he was at a disadvantage; nor could his men help him till he had raised her so high that he could rest her weight on his right knee and against his own body. Then the others climbed down and slipped their belts under her arms, and she was taken out in safety and laid upon the pavement of the little court. And then the Jewish boy went to call his mother from the house of her sister, where they two had gone to live, for Beatrix had need of a woman.

Gilbert knelt down and laid her head upon Dunstan's coat folded together, and covered her with his own mantle, gazing into the unconscious face, small and pale and pitiful, and he remembered how he had seen it last in Antioch, full of anger and unbelief, so that he had turned and left what he loved just when evil was at hand; and his heart stood still, and then smote him in his breast, and stood still again, as the smith's hammer is poised in the air between the strokes.

Beatrix did not move and seemed not to breathe, lying as one dead, and suddenly Gilbert believed that there was no life left in her. He tried to speak to Dunstan, but he could make no sound, for his tongue and his throat were suddenly parched and paralyzed, so that he was dumb in his grief; but he took the small white hands, with the wrists all cut by the cords, and folded them upon the breast, and he took his cross-hilted dagger with its sheath, and laid it between the hands for a cross, and gently tried to close the half-opened eyes.

Then, when Dunstan saw what his master meant, he touched him on the shoulder and spoke to him.

" She is not dead," he said.

Gilbert started and looked up at him, and saw that he was in earnest; but the man's lean face was drawn with anxiety.

" Sir," said Dunstan, " will you let me touch the Lady Beatrix ? "

The knight's brow darkened, for that a churl's hands should touch a high-born lady's face seemed to him something monstrous and against nature ; but in the moment he had forgotten something.

" She is quite dead," he tried to say.

Then Dunstan spoke sadly, kneeling down beside her.

" This lady is half my sister," he said. " I have some skill with half-drowned persons. Let me save her, sir, unless we are to let her die before our eyes. A gipsy taught me what to do."

The cloud passed from Gilbert's face, but still he did not believe.

"In heaven's name, do what you can, try what you know, and quickly!" he said.

"Help me, then," said Dunstan.

So he did as all skilled persons know how to do with half-drowned people, though only the gipsies knew it then. They turned her body gently so that the clear water ran from her parted lips, and laying her down again, they took her arms and drew them over her head, stretched them out, and brought them down to her sides, again and again, so as to make her breathe, and the breath was drawn in and breathed out again with a delicate foam that clung to her lips.

Still Sir Gilbert did not believe, and though he helped his man, in the despair of the instant, and in the horror of losing the least chance of life, it all seemed to him a desecration of the most dear dead, and more than once he would have let the poor little arm rest, rather than make it limply follow the motion Dunstan gave to the other.

"She is quite, quite dead," he said again.

"She is alive," answered Dunstan; "stop not now one moment, or we shall lose her."

His dark face glowed, and his unwinking eyes watched her face for the least sign of life. Ten minutes, a quarter of an hour, passed, and time seemed facing death — the swift against the immovable and eternal. Gilbert, the strong and masterful in fight, humbly and anxiously watched his man's looks for the signs of hope, as if Dunstan had been the wisest physician of all mankind; and

indeed in that day there were few physicians who
knew how to do what the man was doing. And
at last the glow in his face began to fade, and Gilbert's heart sank, and the horror of so disturbing
the dead came upon him tenfold, so that he let the
slender arm rest on the stones, and sighed. But
Dunstan cried out fiercely to him.

"For your life, go on! She is alive! See!
See!"

And even as Gilbert sadly shook his head in the
last collapse of belief, the long lashes quivered a
little with the lids and were still, and quivered
again, and then again, and the eyes opened wide
and staring, but broad awake; and then the delicate body shook and was half convulsed by the
miracle of life restored, and the slight arms quick-
ened with nervous strength, resisting the men's
strong hands, and a choking cough brought the
bright colour to the pale cheeks.

Then Gilbert lifted her from the pavement to the
stone rim of the well, that she might breathe better,
and presently the choking ceased, so that she lay
quite still with her head against his breast, and her
weight in his arms. But still she did not speak,
and the man's heart beat furiously with joy, and
then stood still in fear, lest the worst should come
again, whereof there was no danger; but he did not
know, and Dunstan and Alric were suddenly gone,
seeking wine in the house. Just when the girl
seemed to be sinking into a swoon they brought a
short draught of Syrian wine in an earthen cup; for
little Alric was not wise, but he would have found

wine in the sandy desert, and he had gone straight to a corner where a leathern bottle with a wooden plug was hung up in a cool place.

Beatrix drank, and revived again, and looked up to Gilbert.

"I knew you would come," she said faintly, and she smiled, but Gilbert could not speak.

By this time the Jewish boy had brought his mother, and they carried the girl into a room, and the woman took care of her kindly, fearing lest a Christian should die in her husband's house, and also lest she should not be paid the value of the rent, but with womanly gentleness also, wrapping her in dry clothes of her own before she laid her to rest.

For Arnold de Curboil's servants had been all Greeks, and when they had learned that their master had been killed in the night, they had bolted and barred the house, and had bound Beatrix and her Norman tirewoman hand and foot and gagged their mouths with cloths, in order that they might carry off the rich plunder, but at first they had not meant to kill the women. Only when they were just about to slip away, one at a time, so as to escape notice, they held a council, and the most of them said that it would be better to throw the women into the well, lest either of them should help the other, and getting loose, escape from the house and cause a pursuit. So they threw the Norman woman down first, and when they saw that she sank the third time, being drowned, they threw Beatrix after her. But the well was not so deep as they had thought, and was narrow, so that Beatrix had kept her head above the water a long time, her feet just touching the body of her drowned servant. And in this way the faithful woman had saved her mistress after she was dead. When this was known, they took her from the well and bore her to burial without the city, while Beatrix was asleep.

That night Gilbert and Dunstan lay on their cloaks within the half-broken door of the house, which could not be bolted, for they were tired, having watched by the Sepulchre all the night before that; and little Alric kept watch in the courtyard, walking up and down lest he should sleep, for the Syrian wine might have made him drowsy, and he had the whole bottle to himself. But he drank slowly and thoughtfully, and when he felt that his head was not clear, he let the wine alone, and walked up and down a long time talking to himself and warning himself to keep sober. This being accomplished, he swallowed another draught, wisely sipping it by half mouthfuls, and then walked again; and so all night, and in the dawn he was as fresh and rosy and sober as ever, but the big leathern bottle lay quite flat and disconsolate on the pavement; for he came of the old English archers, who were good men at a bowl, and steady on their legs.

In the morning Gilbert awoke and sat up, on the pavement, and as Alric came near he made a sign that he should not wake Dunstan, but let him rest. He looked at the sleeper's face, and thought how much this servant of his had suffered, being quite half as gentle by birth as he himself; and he remembered how the man had fought ever bravely, and had shed his blood, and had never taken gifts of money from his master, save for great necessity, and had asked for a sword rather than for a tunic when he had raised the riot to save Beatrix and the Queen in Nicæa; and Gilbert was ashamed that such a man, who was in truth the eldest born of a great house, should be a starving servant. So when Dunstan opened his eyes and started up at seeing his master awake, Gilbert spoke to him.

"You have fought with me," he said, "you have endured with me, we have fasted together on the march, and we have drunk of the same spring in battle while the arrows fell about us, and now, God willing, we are to be brothers, when I wed the Lady Beatrix, and but for you I should be mourning by her grave to-day. It is not meet that we should be any longer master and man, for you have gentle blood in you, of a great house."

"Sir Gilbert," murmured Dunstan, flushing darkly, "you are very kind to me, but I will not have gentlehood of a father who was a murderer and a thief."

"You prove yourself gentle by that speech," answered Gilbert. "Had he no other blood to give you than his own? Then the Lady Beatrix is also the daughter of a thief and a murderer."

"And of a lady of great lineage. That is different. I am no peer of my lady sister. But if so be that I may have a name, and be called gentle, then, sir, I pray you, beg of our sovereign in England that I may be called by a new name of my own, that my ill birth may be forgotten."

"And so I will," said Gilbert, "for it is better thus."

Afterwards he kept his word, and when she had her own again, Beatrix gave him a third share of her broad lands, to hold in fief to Gilbert Warde, though he had no rightful claim; and because he had saved her life, he was called Dunstan Le Sauveur, because he had saved her and many; and he had favour of King Henry and fought bravely, and was made a knight, and raised up an honourable race.

But on that morning in Jerusalem, in the little court, Beatrix came out, still weak and weary, and sat beside Gilbert in the shade of the wall, with her hand between his, and the light in her face.

"Gilbert," she said, when she had told him what had happened to her until then, "when I was angry and unbelieving in the Queen's chamber in Antioch, why did you turn and leave me, seeing that I was in the wrong?"

"I was angry, too," he answered simply.

But womanlike, she answered him again.

"That was foolish. You should have taken me roughly in your arms and kissed me, as you did by the river long ago. Then I should have believed you, as I do now."

"But you would not believe my words, nor the Queen's," he said, "nor even when she gave herself up to the King, to prove herself true, would you believe her."

"If men only knew!" Beatrix laughed softly her little bird laugh that had the music of a spring day.

"If men knew — what?"

"If men knew —" She paused, and blushed, and

laughed again. "If men knew how women love sweet words when they are happy, and sharp deeds when they are angry! That is what I mean. I would have given my blood and the Queen's kingdom for a kiss when you left me standing there."

"I wish I had known!" exclaimed Gilbert, happy but half perplexed.

"You ought to have known," answered the girl.

Her eyebrows were raised a little with the half-pathetic look he loved, while her mouth smiled.

"I shall never understand," he said, but he began to laugh too.

"I will tell you. In the first place, I shall never be angry with you again — never! Do you believe me, Gilbert?"

"Of course I do," he answered, having nothing else to say.

"Very well. But if I ever should be — "

"But you just said that you never would be!"

"I know; but if I should — just once — then take me in your arms, and say nothing, but kiss me as you did that day by the river."

"I understand," he said. "Are you angry now?" But he was laughing.

"Almost," she answered, glancing sideways in a smile.

"Not quite?"

"Yes, quite!" And her eyes darkened under the drooping lids.

Then he held her so close to him that she was half breathless, and kissed her till it hurt, and she turned pale again, and her eyes were closed.

THE WAY OF THE CROSS

"You see," she said very faintly, "I believe you now!"

Here ends the story of Gilbert Warde's crusading; for he had reached the end of his Via Crucis in the Holy City, and had at last found peace for his soul, and light and rest for his heart, after many troubles and temptations, and after much brave fighting for the good cause of the Faith against unbelievers.

After that he fought again with the army at Damascus, and saw how the princes betrayed one another, when the Emperor Conrad had come again, so that the siege of the strong town came to naught, and the armies were scattered among the rich gardens to gather fruit and drink strong wine, while their leaders wrangled. Also at Ascalon he drew sword again, and again he saw failure hanging over all, like an evil shadow, and chilling the courage in men, so that there was murmuring, and clamouring for the homeward path. There he saw how the great armies went to ruin and fell to pieces, because, as the holy Bernard had known, there was not the faith of other days, and also because there was no great leader, as Eleanor had told the abbot himself at Vézelay; and it was a sad sight, and one to sicken the souls of good men.

But though he fought with all his might when swords were out, there was no sadness in him for all these things, for life and hope were bright before him. Little by little, too, he had heard how all the poor pilgrims left at Attalia had perished; but he knew that if he had led them, Beatrix would have

died there in the court of the little house in Jerusalem, and he held her life more dear than the lives of
many, whom his own could hardly have saved.

Moreover, and last of all, he had learned and
understood that the cause of God lies not buried
among stones in any city, not even in the most holy
city of all; for the place of Christ's suffering is in
men's sinful hearts, and the glory of his resurrec-
tion is the saving of a soul from death to everlasting life, in refreshment and light and peace.